May God Bless You!

Shalom

Keith Green

The Scrapping Sky Pilot
Rev. J. U. Robins
by

Keith W. Hudson

The epic adventures of a Methodist Student Pastor
as he faces the trials of nature and man
during his mission field experiences in British Columbia in the
late 1800's

authorHOUSE®

AuthorHouse™
1663 Liberty Drive, Suite 200
Bloomington, IN 47403
www.authorhouse.com
Phone: 1-800-839-8640

First published by AuthorHouse 12/10/2009

ISBN: 978-1-4490-4404-6 (e)
ISBN: 978-1-4490-4402-2 (sc)
ISBN: 978-1-4490-4403-9 (hc)

Printed in the United States of America
Bloomington, Indiana

This book is printed on acid-free paper.

The Scrapping Sky Pilot

"Commit to the Lord whatever you do, and your plans will succeed."(NIV)
Proverb 16:3

By Keith Hudson
May, 2009

from the tapes of the Rev. J.U. Robins

CONTENTS

FORWARD

Dear Readers:

I hope you enjoy the exploits of Rev. J. U. Robins. He, along with the Archer Family and most of the incidents recorded in this book are real. The other characters and the dialogue are made to fit the information I received from my Maternal Grandfather, Rev. J. U. Robins when he was in his late 80's. The places J.U. went to are accurate – the sequence of events might be slightly off due to the information I had available.

I attempted to write this book a couple of times but always seemed to find an excuse to stop. Last year our Church, St. Paul's Presbyterian, Ingersoll Ontario, held a study series on Richard Foster's "Celebration of Discipline". During one of the small group discussion sessions I heard myself commit to finishing this novel, and I did!

I have to give special thanks to my "soul mate" and wife of over 40 years, Fran (Gooch) Hudson, for her support and her dedication as the editor and gentle motivator of this work. I think she can nearly recite this novel in her sleep.

Thank you Fran with all my heart!

Settle in, let your mind and spirit soar back to 1885 in this great country Canada and enjoy the read!

Shalom

Keith

CHAPTER I

To Live or Die

And about the ninth hour Jesus cried with a loud voice, saying, Eli, Eli, lama sabachthani? that is to say, My God, my God, why hast thou forsaken me? (KJV)
Matthew 27:46

Step by grueling step he stumbled forward into the blinding wind and snow.

Is this what the Lord has really called me to do?

To die, trying to walk through the pass outside Trout River, British Columbia?

His snow shoes felt like they weighed a thousand pounds as he forced himself to lift them and let them flop back into the ever increasing snow. He had to take them off. The fresh snow was falling so heavily it was filling up the top of the shoes and making them impossible to lift.

He was now plowing through drifts that were four to five feet deep and still heading straight up the Mountain pass.

He knew that to stop was to die.

All he heard was the roar of the wind as it drove the flesh cutting snow against his face and the voices in his head.

His face was wrapped against this ferocious foe as much as possible, but he needed a crack in his scarf see where he was going. In this storm that might not really matter. His metal-framed glasses caused pain to shoot from the bridge of his nose to the back of his head. Snow kept collecting on the exposed lenses making vision nearly impossible. If he took his glasses off he wouldn't be able to see at all He wasn't able to see anyway in the driving snow He reached up and off came his glasses and the pain in his head seemed to ease.

Ahead there were shadows that looked like they might be a grove of trees.

Where were those glasses?

He slipped them back on and stared into the blowing snow and quickly feeling the pain come back like a stabbing needle right up through his nose and out the back of his head.

Once again, the voices in his head were at work.

"I'm not sure if my eyes are playing tricks on me or there really is something out there. All I know for sure is I'm done in and I am going to have to stop soon and rest, even if it is still daylight.

Yes, I'm sure there is something out there. Come on Joe, you can do it. You've never walked away from or lost a fight in your life. Now isn't the time to give up."

Memories flashed through his mind as he put one foot in front of the other.

He remembered his Mother, a small woman who had lived a hard life on the shores of Lake Erie, standing in the door of their home in Port Rowan, Ontario, with the warmth of the kitchen behind her and the smell of the home baking – yes he could smell it even here in the Roger's Pass - the smell of home cooked bread – one step then another. What a way to celebrate a new century!

Eighteen ninety-seven and at the rate he was tiring, he would never see 1900!

The pain in his thighs was like a knife cutting to the bone, yet he had to continue on. To stop out in the open was certain death.

He was only delaying the inevitable, considering he didn't have any food, but he wouldn't give in. Just a little farther!

There was definitely something ahead and as he squinted through his snow laden scarf, it looked like it might give a little shelter.

He stumbled into the grove of brush.

"Not your oasis in the desert, yet I can feel the wind deflecting away from me." The voices continued to talk to him.

He slumped down behind one of the bushes, undid his snowshoes and stretched out his aching legs, rubbing them with his mittened hands.

Ahh... the relief that flowed through his legs.

He would just nod off for a few moments to get his strength back.

"Wait!"

"Don't be a fool – get a fire started – boil some water – then you can sleep."

He looked around for wood to start a fire and was pleased to see that close by there were sticks that would work very nicely. He crawled over to the scattered branches, having to dig them out of the frozen snow with his non-cooperative frozen hands, and brought them back to his little shelter.

Joe stamped out the base for a fire. Each time his foot hit the frozen ground – it caused sharp pain right up to his groin.

Thank goodness he still had a few matches. He would have to use some of his sermon notes to help start the fire.

He put his pack in position to block the wind, placed a couple of hard worked on sermon note pages under the kindling and carefully lit the paper and fed the kindling to the burning paper.

It caught!

Within minutes he had a good fire burning and with it, hope.

"I wonder if this sermon ever caught a person on fire?" he muttered to himself.

"Not likely, I still have a lot to learn about preaching but unless I can make it back to the town tomorrow, I won't have to worry much about the future!

Now I have to get this pot off the leather tie attached to my pack.

My fingers aren't working. They are starting to freeze now they are out of my fur mitts. I must get closer to the fire – and warm my hands up for a few seconds and try again. It feels like needles piercing my fingers and hands. Goodness, the pain is unbearable. I'm not sure I can stand it much longer. Rub them together. Get the circulation flowing again. Are they frost bitten? I don't think so – I heard once, that you can't feel them when they're frost bitten and I sure can feel my hands. Keep rubbing – stop crying – you're a man and men don't cry! Well this one sure is – oh the pain! I must be getting used to the pain – I can actually move my fingers without the flashes of pins and needles – I better get the pot while I still have some use of my fingers – I just have to pull this string - there, the pot is free. Now get your mitts back on and get some snow into the pot – I need water and I need food!"

The voices in his head were as real as if someone was in the camp talking with him.

"What did people say about hearing voices – the first sign of insanity? In my case, the voices are keeping me sane! If I keep hearing the voices – I know I'm still alive.

I Think?

Sometime I'm going to ponder the theological implications of whether people hear voices after they die... but not right now!"

Water wasn't going to be a problem with all this snow around – but food.

"I'll have to cut a piece off the top of my Mukluks and throw it into the boiling water to make soup. It will taste terrible, but at least it will have a bit of food value. It will make my stomach feel full if nothing else."

Joe cut another couple of inches off his Mukluks.

He realized that his earlier thoughts of making it to the camp by morning were conditional on the storm letting up. Already he had spent half a day fighting his way up the mountain in this seemingly never ending storm.

The owner of the halfway house had warned him it was late in the season to try to negotiate the pass. She had said that they were expecting a major storm at any time.

She had been right!

About a mile away from the halfway house the storm had hit and he still had a good five miles to go – almost straight up. He wasn't carrying any provisions. Why should he? He was intending to get them at Trout Lake City. He was told it was only a 15 mile hike from the spot on the Columbia River where the canoe had dropped him.

In retrospect the decision to head off to his new mission field at this time of year had been a big mistake.

Joe was in a hurry to return to the work of the Lord. He had been commissioned to open new Mission fields in British Columbia. He'd already spent a year in and around Rossland, Donald, New Denver, Slocan and Revelstoke developing missions and churches for the Methodist Church and reporting to Wesley College in Winnipeg, designated the Regional Headquarters for the Methodist Church in the West.

It was 1897. He had arrived in Revelstoke in the fall of 1895 as a Probationary Student Minister for the Methodist Church of Canada.

With pride, he had left behind two new Churches established in one year and it was this same pride that had made him decide to return from his furlough late in the season of 1897 to establish more churches. What did they say? "Pride goes before a fall".

Joe carried a 60 lb. pack. To lighten his load, to allow for his books, he had decided against provisions.

He was paying for it now!

Joe couldn't remember being so hungry and although it was 20 degrees below zero, he was breaking out in a sweat.

How as this possible? How could he be sweating when he was so hungry and cold?

"I must drink some mukluk soup at once, this will stop me shaking and sweating."

Joe was right, it tasted terrible, just like last night but he had to get it down.

Joe sipped and shook, then, shook and sipped and all the time the beads of sweat on his forehead were freezing into droplets of ice.

"I have to get this into me or I'll dehydrate. Once I'm finished, then I can curl up and sleep. I'll feel better in the morning. Maybe this storm will die down overnight." Thank God for the voices – at least they were making sense.

CHAPTER 2

A Call to Mission

"And he saith unto them, follow me, and I will make you fishers of men." (KJV)
Matthew 4:19

Joseph U. Robins was a student Missionary for the Methodist Church of Canada assigned to British Columbia, completing his second year as a Student Minister – or "Sky Pilot" as the men in the lumber camps tended to call him.

Joe wasn't a big man but he considered himself in good shape.

After graduating from school in Port Rowan he had moved to Detroit and was an elementary teacher in the Inner City. To supplement his meager teacher's salary, Joe had fought as a professional boxer for a couple of years before he had accepted the "Call" of the Methodist Church on his way to becoming a Minister.

Joe could remember going before the District Meeting of the Methodist Church in Hagersville when he first indicated his desire to go into Ministry.

A dourer group of men he couldn't remember ever meeting.

They held their court at the Methodist Church in Hagersville that spring day in 1885.

They had asked him if he believed in Jesus Christ as his Savior.

"Yes" said Joe.

Had he been baptized? "Yes"

Had he been confirmed in the Methodist Church? "Yes"

Did he believe in the Trinity? "Yes" responded Joe.

Would he recognize the authority of the Methodist Courts with respect to discipline? After a short pause, Joe said, "Yes".

He reasoned that one must accept the will of the employer, or quit and if he felt that strongly about a decision of the Court – then he would have to quit!

Would he abstain from the use of tobacco? "Yes"

Would he abstain from the use of snuff? "Yes"

Would he totally abstain from the use of all alcohol? Joe didn't have any use for alcohol, so a ready "Yes" was not a problem.

Finally, they asked him if he would "fast" on a regular basis as part of his spiritual journey.

Joe didn't know how to answer. He stood and stared at the assembly.

He believed in a well-balanced diet and knew from his fighting days that he needed food to have the strength to fulfill his vision. How could he answer this question honestly and not throw away his chances of being accepted. Wasn't he already defying the authority of the Court that he had just finished saying he would respect? Was he finished before he was even started? Surely this was not what God had in mind for him? He knew he had been "Called" to be a Minster.

He remembered vividly the day he was out sailing on the bay. It was this summer's holiday and he had just completed two years of teaching inner city kids in Detroit.

He knew he had had a major influence on many of the children in his care but he also knew there was no way they were getting out of the ghetto that was their home and their lives. Did he want to spend his life in this futile existence or was there something else he should be doing? He'd spend the summer holidays exploring his options.

Here he was sailing the little craft he and his father had built when he had just become a teenager.

His Father was a well respected ship builder out of Port Rowan and the hours that he and Joe had spent building this little craft were some of Joe's fondest memories.

Joe could make the little craft dance over the water. The weather was perfect, wind offshore, water calm and the sun warm. All was right in God's world.

Joe had always gone to church as a youngster and had won awards for his ability to recite verses from memory. He enjoyed both the rewards but more importantly, the recognition of the adults and his peers – especially the girls.

Joe was tacking to head off to the far shore when he heard a voice in his head say to him, "Joe, it's time to change course".

Where was this voice coming from?

He was alone in his little craft.

Again he heard the voice, as if there was someone sitting in the bow talking with him over the sound of the wind, "Joe, I want you to become a Minster in my Church and I will be there for you."

Joe didn't know what to make of all this. He lost his concentration and almost tipped the little craft over. Quickly, righting his course, he gained control of the boat and himself.

Where had that come from? Was that God speaking to him?

Yes!

He had wondered what to do with his life, and God had told him. He would immediately head for shore and seek out how he could become a Minster of God's word.

Here he was before The District and ready to loose it all. Hadn't God said he'd be with him? Where was He now when Joe really needed Him?

The Assembly was growing uneasy with this young man. Why wasn't he answering? All he had to say was yes, and he would be approved.

The other two young men who had gone before Joe had answered all these questions, including the fasting question without a hesitation.

"I don't think I can say yes to this question." Joe responded.

Well, this threw the assembly into an uproar. Never before had anyone ever challenged this direction – should they approve him for a Probationary Appointment?

Joe then went on and the room became quiet, "I am willing to fast if my Doctor says I'm healthy enough to fast and I feel it won't affect my health."

This was not an answer the Assembly wanted to hear. Immediately there were men on their feet asking for recognition to speak and question Joe, trying to get the eye of the Chair.

The Chair, Rev. Lewis, used his gavel with the assurance of a Circuit Court Judge delivering a verdict of hanging.

Bang, Bang, Bang went the gavel and gradually the Assembly resumed a certain level of decorum that allowed Rev. Lewis to speak over the din.

"Well Mr. Robins, you've certainly stirred the pot today sir!"

"I felt I had to be honest sir." responded Joe.

"Indeed you were Mr. Robins, indeed you were."

Joe turned to be able to see both the Chair, Rev. Lewis, and the members of the Court, sitting out in the sanctuary.

He couldn't remember having seen so many frowns in one room.

Were these really the men God had called to spread His word.

Do I really want to be one of these?

Lord, what should I say, he pondered?

Then he remembered a prayer he had learned in Sunday School:

"Lord I give myself to You, let your will be done."

He had prayed it before, but usually he had put conditions on the prayer. Sometimes he had even tried to bargain with God. You know, if you give me this I'll be good forever. He wasn't sure if God had ever gone for those prayers.

This time he said the prayer and meant it – no conditions – just your will be done!

He opened his mouth to speak – when all of a sudden he had an idea.

He cleared his voice again, and with a strong voice full of confidence he certainly did not feel, asked the following question?

"Mr. Chairman, Members of the Court, all of you have taken this oath at your call to Ministry. May I be so bold to ask, how many of you faithfully fast as part of your spiritual journey?"

Hands started to be raised, then slowly came down –only two of 20 still held their hands up. Rev. Lewis wasn't one of the hands that stayed up!

Rev. Lewis looked around the Court.

"I think you've made your point Mr. Robins. By looking around this room I think we would be very hypocritical of us to ask you to do something that we don't do ourselves. I am going to rephrase the question. Mr. Robins, assuming that you are in good health and your Doctor agrees with the concept of fasting, would you consider fasting as part of your spiritual journey?"

Joe immediately replied, "Yes Sir!"

"Then it is with great humility and great pride that we recommend you to be a candidate for Ordained Ministry of the Methodist Church of Canada." and the room broke out in spontaneous applause. Joe was on his way to his Mission Field.

CHAPTER 3

Where It All Started

"I can do everything through him who gives me strength."(NIV)
Philippians 4:13

He tucked in behind the wind break he had made by sticking his snow-shoes into the snow and tying a blanket around the frames.

He knew he was fighting a fever as well as the frigid cold winds.

Joe stoked up the fire with the largest branches he could find, hoping the fire would last until dawn – he didn't really want to crawl out of his blankets before then if he could help it.

Although dead tired, sleep didn't come easily to Joe as the wind continued to howl.

His mind roamed back to his childhood days on the beaches of Port Rowan – especially those summers of his youth.

The images were vivid, like he was reliving them all over again.

His Father was a tall, well built man who was a ship builder in the village of Port Rowan, Ontario, nestled on the shores of Lake Erie. Not only did he build lake boats, but had been involved in building a number of ocean clippers out of Halifax.

It was one of these ocean clippers that caused his death, in a round about way.

Joe could still remember his Father's return from Halifax a shadow of the man who had left a few years earlier. His Father had shipped to Brazil to bring back a ship that had run into trouble. He had completed makeshift repairs in the harbor in Brazil and scraped together a skeleton crew to bring the vessel back to Halifax, where proper repairs could be made.

Within the first week out, his small crew started to come down with fever and soon there was only the First Mate, a couple of seamen and his Father physically able to work the ship. For another month they worked night and day to get the vessel back to Halifax. During this time, six of the nine men that had signed on as crew had died and it would appear that they had a ship with plague on it. A ship damned with plague wasn't allowed into any Port until the sickness had run its course.

By the time they saw Halifax harbor both the First Mate and Joe's Father were so exhausted, they weren't sure if they had the plague or were just physical wrecks. However, the two remaining crew members were rallying, and it would appear that the plague had run its course. They flew the flag of distress and were met by the Harbor Master while still offshore. Once a doctor had an opportunity to complete medicals on everyone, he gave them the all clear to dock.

Joe's Father had lost over 100 lbs, had a constant cough and looked like a stranger when he got off the train in Hamilton.

Joe's Mother, Charlotte, was a wee bit of a thing with a tongue that could cause the wallpaper to peel when she was on a roll. Joe's younger brother Will and sister, Margaret had brought the wagon in from Port Rowan to Hamilton to meet the train. All they could do was stare.

This coughing, shriveled old man couldn't be Joseph Robins, their father.

He couldn't be?

He was a giant of a man in their memories.

But sure enough, he called out to them and hugged them like their Father would.

He felt like skin and bone.

Never before had he allowed one of the boys to drive the wagon if he was in attendance, but this time he was quite content to sit beside Charlotte, his wife, and hold her hand and stare out at the passing farms.

Joe felt a chill in the air as he drove the wagon home that day and it wasn't from the weather.

It wasn't a month before his Father passed away. Consumption caused by fatigue the Doctor said. The plague hadn't got him, but indirectly it had caused his death.

Now Joe was 15 and the head of the family. He had another two years of school and then what would he do?

He knew that he wasn't going to follow in his Father's footsteps. Although, he had helped out as his Father built boats he hadn't really enjoyed it. He thought back a few years ago when he and his Father had built the little sail boat for his brother, sister and himself. Boy, could that craft fly across the water with a good wind in her sail.

No, building boats wasn't for him. He would rather work with his head than his hands. He was good at school and enjoyed reading. He would grab a book and hide out in the shed and read, hoping he wouldn't be caught when his Father came looking for help. It wasn't that he was lazy. Far from it. Once in the shop, he enjoyed working along with his Father, although he was always in fear of doing something wrong, for his Father didn't abide mistakes well. He had a couple of welts on the back of his hand for cutting a board the wrong length. Measure twice – cut once his Father would roar. No it wasn't that he didn't like the shop, but rather the places he could travel and the things he could learn out of books just amazed him.

For two years, Joe continued to attend school during the day and work in the shop at night to help his dad finishing up the orders he had contracted. It was apparent to Joe that although his Dad was in the yard everyday, he wasn't getting over whatever illness he had brought back from that emergency voyage to Brazil.

They were long frustrating days as he watched his Father's strength continue slip away from him.

Then came the day his father couldn't get up out of his bed and go down to the boat yard.

Dr Russell was called to the Robins' home and after a half hour in his Father's room with Mother, he came out, looked at the three of them and shook his head.

"It is only a matter of days," he said, "I have never seen a disease like the one your Father has. Something he caught while in Brazil, I guess. I'm surprised your Father has lasted so long. He is a man of strong will with a strong belief in his God.

I'll be back this evening – or come and get me if he gets worse." With this Dr. Russell packed his black bag and put on his stove-pipe hat and started for the door.

"Isn't there something you could do?" asked Joe, a question that was in the minds of both Margaret and Will, but left to Joe to ask.

Dr. Russell had delivered these three children and loved them like his own. Joe played with his son Bill and Margaret was best friends with his daughter Emily. Then there was little Stella who was around two.

He looked at Joe as he spoke, "Joe, you know your Father hasn't been well since he returned and against my advice he has continued to work at the yard each day as his strength continued to sap away. He had no choice. He either worked – or had no money.

Joe, children, this disease has caught up to him. I've given him everything I know of to try and beat it. It's in his lungs and has affected his heart. All we can pray for now is that he doesn't suffer long before he dies. He doesn't deserve to suffer.

I'm sorry children – support your mother and say good bye to your Father.

I've given him an opium drink that will kill the pain, but I'm afraid he will be very drowsy and at times and sound like he is confused. I think he will hear you, just don't expect him to respond.

Like I said, if he gets worse, or there is a lot of pain, come and get me and I'll come right back." With that, Dr. Russell left the house and headed for his carriage.

There was no need to call the Doctor until the morning since Joe's Father stopped breathing around 3 am slipping away quietly while holding Charlotte's hand. Margaret, Will and Joe stood at the foot of the bed.

Joe led the family in prayer and gave thanks for his Father's life and asked a blessing upon the family as they entered a new life without the guidance and support of their Father.

Charlotte quietly closed Joseph's eyes and pulled the sheet up over his face.

"Thank you Joe," Charlotte whispered, "after breakfast I'll have you go up to the Doctor's house and ask him to come down and "pronounce" your Father.

Then Margaret, you and I will prepare your Father for his eternal sleep.

We can give thanks that his suffering is over.

Now off you all go to bed for a few hours sleep – dawn will be here in a couple of hours and we will have lots to do tomorrow."

They all left the bedroom and Charlotte closed the door, picked up her bible and sat on her rocker by the fire. She closed her eyes as the tears flowed down her cheeks.

Joseph had been a good husband, given her three lovely children and always provided for them, even when the pickings were slim. She loved him so much, but she knew she had to move on for the children's sake.

She opened her bible to her favourite passage, Psalm 23, and she read it to herself in the flickering light. It was obvious that David had been where she was right now.

Psalm 23:1-6
The LORD is my shepherd; I shall not want.
He maketh me to lie down in green pastures:
He leadeth me beside the still waters.
He restoreth my soul: he leadeth me in the paths of righteousness
    for his name's sake. Yea, though I walk through the valley of the
    shadow of death, I will fear no evil: for thou art with me; thy rod
    and thy staff they comfort me.
Thou preparest a table before me in the presence of mine enemies:
Thou anointest my head with oil; my cup runneth over.
Surely goodness and mercy shall follow me all the days of my life: and
    I will dwell in the house of the LORD forever. (KJV)

Joe lay in the bed he shared with Will.

Sleep was not going to come to him this night, he just knew.

His mind couldn't stop going over the last few hours… and thinking about what was ahead.

How were they going to survive without their Father?

He would have to give up school and get a job.

Joe knew he didn't want to do this – he loved school and he was a good student – he could make something of himself if given half a chance … somewhere in this argument exhaustion and sorrow caught up with Joe and he nodded off to the protection and healing powers of sleep.

When he woke up it all came tumbling back to him. The floor felt colder then ever as he got out of bed causing his arches to scream as they raised from the floor and hurriedly got into his Sunday Clothes. He knew there was a lot to do today and he had to look the part of the head of the Family.

His Mother already had porridge made and ready for them as they sat around the table. Their Father's place had been vacant over the last few weeks, but now it screamed of always being empty.

Once Joe finished his breakfast he turned to his Mother and said, "I'll go get the Doctor and stop off at the Manse on the way back to make arrangements for the funeral, if that is agreeable to you."

Charlotte tried to smile and responded in a small frail voice, "Thank you Joe, I would appreciate that."

Joe headed off to Doctor Russell's house and knocked at the door.

Emily opened the door and Joe could see the family all gathered at the breakfast table.

"Hi Joe" said Emily, "won't you come in and join us for breakfast?"

Dr. Russell had started to get up as soon as he saw it was Joe Robins at the door and proceeded over to stand behind Emily.

"No thank you Emily, I need your Father." he said, then saw Dr. Russell.

"Good Morning Dr. Russell, Pa passed during the night and Ma has asked if you would be so kind to come up to the house and pronounce him."

"Oh Joe, I'm so sorry," Emily said, "Please come in and spend a few moments with us."

"Thank you Emily, but I have continue up to the Manse and make arrangements for the funeral."

Joe knew if he stopped he'd end up crying in front of Emily and that wasn't going to happen! Not if he could get out of there quickly.

"I'll just get my bag and go right up to see your Mother," said Dr. Russell as he patted Emily on the shoulder, "Better let Joe get on with his chores, Em."

Dr. Russell could see the tears forming up behind his eyes and knew that Joe didn't want his daughter to see him crying.

"Off you go Joe; I'll catch up with you at your house later on."

With that, Joe turned and headed off towards the Manse. Joe arrived a few minutes later and knocked on the door. Mrs. McPherson, the Pastor's wife answered the door.

She was a pleasant woman, quite tall for a lady and very thin with a beak-like nose. If you didn't know her, you would think she would have the personality of a shrew, but just the opposite, she was warm and very supportive of the work of her husband. Joe had gotten to know her well by being a leader in the Church Sunday School. She always had great ideas about how to teach the younger children the stories of the Bible.

"Why Joe, this is an early visit, but a very pleasant surprise to start the day off, come in." invited Mrs. McPherson. There was a warmth in her voice that indicated the sincerity of her comments and made Joe feel welcomed and gave him comfort for the mission he was commissioned to perform.

"Good Morning Mrs. McPherson, I've come to see Rev. McPherson, if he is available," then Joe's voice began to break much to his embarrassment, "Pa passed on last night and I need to make arrangements for a funeral."

"Oh Joe...I'm so sorry." Mrs. McPherson stepped forward and encompassed Joe in a big hug. She smelled of lilac bath salts and Joe just wanted to loose himself in this hug and breathe in the fragrance of the lilac tree.

At that moment Rev. McPherson arrived on the scene and immediately knew something was wrong. His wife was not an amorous person. To hug Joe must mean a major problem in the family – likely his father has succumbed to that disease he caught while down south.

"Well, well, what do we have here? Are you trying to steal my wife Joe?"

Joe jumped back, blushing and confused. "No sir!" Joe exclaimed, "It's just that Pa passed last night and Mrs. McPherson was giving me a hug of comfort."

"And rightly she should Joe. As you know, the Lord hasn't blessed us with children and Mrs. McPherson is fond of you and especially appreciative of what you're doing in the Sunday School."

Rev. McPherson laid a hand on Joe's shoulder and steered him towards his study, which was a big room off the entrance that had a desk, a couple of wooden straight back chairs and two walls of books. The room reeked of the personality of Rev. McPherson who was a big man, broad shoulders with a reddish beard, receding red hair and had the lingering stale smell of a pipe.

Joe loved this room. He loved to spend time looking over the books and borrowing the more interesting ones to read at home. He was usually in this office for church related issues or for his own personal edification. Now he was here seeking comfort and to make the arrangements for his father's funeral.

"Joe, words can't express how deeply sorry both Mrs. McPherson and I are to learn of your loss. Your father was a well respected member of this community and this church. He was hard working and cared for his family. Joe, let's take a moment to pray."

Joe wasn't sure what prayer would do at this point, but it seemed to be a tool Rev. McPherson used on a regular basis. It sure couldn't do any more harm than had already been done. Joe bowed his head as he sat straight on the wooden chair, hoping that this wouldn't be one of Rev. McPherson's really long prayers. There were times when this man just could not seem to come to the end and seemed to go back to the beginning and start all over again. Joe didn't have to worry; this was a prayer that Rev. McPherson had said too many times during his Ministry, yet each time it seemed to come alive to him.

"Father, please receive our brother Robins into your loving embrace. He was a good man, loved his family and supported your church.

Father, we ask your blessing upon Sister Charlotte, Margaret, Will and your faithful servant Joe. Give them your support during these trying days ahead and help them know they are not alone. These things we ask in Jesus' name. Amen"

"Rev. McPherson, thank you for praying for my family and me, but why did God take my Pa from his family?" Joe blurted out.

Rev. McPherson, leaned back in his wooden office type chair and reached into the pocket of his tweed day jacket and pulled out his hand made pipe. He leaned forward to a wooden jardinière made of cherry wood and lifted off the top. He carefully filled the bowl of his pipe, using his thumb to pack in the tobacco, firmly but not too tight or he wouldn't get a good draw. Then he scooped a wooden match out of the handmade match holder, a small glass that was covered by small stones to create what looked like a small chimney. He then flicked the match head with the fingernail of his right hand and it burst to life. Slowly he passed the flame over the moist tobacco he had just packed into the barrel of his pipe and drew in, once, twice, three times and the smoke surrounded his head like a cloud.

Satisfied he had his pipe functioning properly; Rev. McPherson was now ready to respond to Joe's lament.

"Joe", Rev. McPherson slowly started as he continued to puff on his pipe, while talking, "Mrs. McPherson tells me that you have become something of a watchmaker, that you've repaired a number of broken watches for people in the village."

"Yes, I seem to have a knack for fixing mechanical things. I always warn people that I can't guarantee to fix their watch or clock until I've had a look at it. I don't charge anything if I can't fix it." Joe responded, wondering what this had to do with his original question.

"What causes most watches to stop working Joe?"

"Why, most watches just need a good cleanout – usually some dirt has gotten past the seal and got lodged in the workings. A good wash in light oil does wonders for most watches, clocks too." Joe responded still wondering where this conversation was going.

"When you get a watch that needs more than a good clean-out, what do you do?"

"Well if I have the parts that are needed I replace them and get the watch working, if I don't, I put the watch back together again and give it back to its owner and tell them that I don't have the parts or the skill to be able to fix their watch," responded Joe.

Rev. McPherson took a couple of deep puffs on his pipe, then turned it so the stem became almost like an extension of his arm as he pointed it at Joe, "Don't you see Joe, God is like the owner of the watch. He has made man like all things on this earth. He has made us that we will die sometime. Do you understand that Joe?"

"Well I never thought about it, but I guess you are right, we all have to die sometime." Joe said.

"As long as we can be repaired, cleaned, and put back together, we continue to live. Maybe someday we will be able to use spare parts to allow a person to live longer, but every clock maker knows that at some time his beautifully made watch or clock will not work anymore – will have died. He doesn't know when. He doesn't know how the owner of the clock treated his clock. He doesn't know if it has been lost, left in the rain or run over by a wagon. He lovingly made it and then turned it over to someone else to look after. Does this make any sense Joe?"

Joe looked into the eyes of his Pastor and saw great compassion, as if he was feeling his hurt.

"Yes," Joe replied, "But why my pa now?"

"That's a good question Joe," as Rev. McPherson leaned back in to his wooden chair and stared off to a far corner of the room, then he refocused his eyes on Joe's eyes and said, "First of all, you keep saying "my", we have to remember we are all watches made by the Great Watch Maker. God has placed us on the earth and we are His. Oh yes, He has created families and has given us emotions that allow us to feel like we belong to someone or someone belongs to us. Joe, we all belong to God and it's from God we come and it's to God we go.

I don't believe, like some of my colleagues, that everything is predestined by God. I believe that God has given us life and allows us to make choices and much like the watchmaker, once the watch has left his shelf, he no longer has direct control over it. I believe that God has made man to make his own decisions and those decisions have consequences.

Your Father went to Brazil to bring back a ship that he helped build. Did he have a choice to go? He could have said he was too busy at the yard and declined to help, or he could have said, 'I helped build that ship; I have a responsibility to the owners to bring it back safely'. Your Father was never a person to shirk his responsibility – his word was his bond and everyone in the village knew this. Therefore he felt he had no choice but to go and bring the ship back. In the process he became sick and like the watches you worked on, Dr. Russell did everything he knew how to do to make your Father well. Unfortunately his skills didn't match the disease and your Father has returned to his Maker.

Does this make any sense Joe?"

Joe had settled back into his chair and looked relieved.

"Pastor, it really does make sense the way you described it. I was blaming God for taking my Father away from me, when actually I should have been thanking God for taking away the pain of the last few weeks, since he couldn't be cured."

"Joe, there's a section of scripture that I really like to help explain this, it is from Ecclesiastes 3:1

To every [thing there is] a season, and a time to every purpose under the heaven:

> *A time to be born, and a time to die; a time to plant, and a time to pluck up [that which is] planted;*
> *A time to kill, and a time to heal; a time to break down, and a time to build up;*
> *A time to weep, and a time to laugh; a time to mourn, and a time to dance;*
> *A time to cast away stones, and a time to gather stones together; a time to embrace, and a time to refrain from embracing;*
> *A time to get, and a time to lose; a time to keep, and a time to cast away;*
> *A time to rend, and a time to sew; a time to keep silence, and a time to speak;*
> *A time to love, and a time to hate; a time of war, and a time of peace.*
> *(KJV)*

Joe, I would like to use this scripture at your Father's funeral, what do you think?"

Joe felt himself moving past grief into action.

"I like this verse Pastor; it's all about what we've been talking about – a time for everything under heaven.

I know it's unusual for the family to take part in the funeral service, but I wonder if I might be allowed to read this scripture?"

"Joe, I would be privileged if you would read the word of God."

Over the next hour the two of them planned the service, which would be held tomorrow at 11:00 AM, man to man.

When Joe arrived home he found the Russell kids playing with Will and Marie on the porch.

"Not sure you should go in Joe," said Will, "Mrs. Russell and Ma are preparing Pa for viewing."

"Well Will, I think I have to update Ma about the funeral and see what she needs me to do." With that, Joe opened the screen door and proceeded in. There was no way he had found over the years to open the door and close it without it squeaking when it opened and slamming when it shut.

"Who is there?" Charlotte's voice flowed out of the bedroom.

"Just me," said Joe, "I thought I should update you about the funeral and see if you had anything you needed me to do?"

"I'll be right there Joe, just wait a minute".

Joe headed over to the table and poured himself a cup of tea, adding water to weaken it, since it had been sitting since breakfast.

As he started to sip his tea, his mother bustled out of the bedroom with Mrs. Russell right behind. Both went over to the wash stand and proceeded to wash-up.

"Joe, is that fresh tea?" asked Charlotte.

"No, it's what was left over from breakfast." Joe responded.

"Would you please put the kettle on the stove then you can update us?"

"Yes Ma!" Joe filled the kettle and carried it over to the wood burning cast iron kitchen stove that his Ma always had going. He noted that the heat was dropping and he added a new log to the stove by lifting one of the four metal covers with much clanging and crashing. Then he placed the kettle over the cover.

"Sorry for the noise. That cover always sticks and I end up burning myself almost every time I take it off. Water should be ready in about five minutes." Joe explained.

"I had a really good meeting with Rev. McPherson. He is suggesting we hold the funeral in the Church, of course, tomorrow at 11:00 am – he will arrange for the Auxiliary to host a luncheon after the Service. We picked out scripture and hymns that I know were Pa's favourite. I think it will be a really meaningful service."

"Thank you Joe, that will work well. With Mrs. Russell's help, we have your Father ready for viewing this afternoon and evening.

Now, I need you to go to Butcher Cartwright and ask if your Father may stay in his ice house over night. We will arrange to have him moved to the Church before business hours tomorrow. Also, I need you to go down to the yard and put together one of Pa's coffins and get it back up here by 11. Can you do this for me please?" asked Joe's Mother confident in his answer.

"Of course, I'll head off now to Cartwright's and I'll ask Will to go down to the Yard and gather the pieces together so I can start on the construction of the coffin as soon as I arrive. Mrs. Russell, would you mind if I ask John to accompany Will, some of those boards are fairly heavy for Will alone."

"Yes, of course John can help Will." responded Mrs. Russell with a look of pride in her eyes as Joe assumed a leadership role in the family.

As Joe left, he heard Mrs. Russell speaking to his Mother, "Charlotte, you're very lucky to have a son as mature as Joe..."

Joe had slammed the screen door and was on the porch out of earshot, but he felt a sudden glow from hearing these words of Mrs. Russell – but right now he had work to do.

"Hi guys, sorry to bother you, but I need some help. Will, would you go down to the Yard and assemble the parts for a casket – you know, they're over where Pa keeps," Joe caught himself, " used to keep the raw material. John, your Ma says you can help Will if you would. I'll be over in a few minutes. I have to stop off at Cartwright's and make some arrangements for tonight."

The boys both jumped up and started off. It was obvious they were getting bored and now having something to do brought new energy into their stride as they ran off towards the Ship Yard.

"What about us?" Emily asked with anticipation in her voice.

"I know you want to help, but right now if you could keep Margaret busy for a few hours, we would be forever grateful." Joe answered. Emily felt real disappointment, she wanted very much to be with the boys, and Joe in particular but she did her very best to sound "up" and responded, "Of course Margaret, Stacy and I will have a great time together." And she turned back to the younger ones and started to rearrange the dolls on the step.

Joe wasn't fooled by Emily's response but appreciated it more than she would ever know. To be honest, Emily used the hammer as well as, if not better than John, but Joe had to make sure the little ones were kept out of Ma's way for a couple more hours.

As Joe headed down the path towards Cartwright's Butcher Shop, he couldn't help thinking how people in small communities can play so many roles and how their establishments have many different uses.

As a butcher, Cartwright had attached two buildings to his shop, one was for slaughtering animals and the other was what was referred to as an Ice House. During the winter, Cartwright would go out into the bay and saw big squares of ice, put them on a sleigh and haul them back to his Ice House. The ice would be covered with straw to delay melting during the warmer summer months. People would come from all around to buy a block of ice to keep their "ice box" cold, and of course Cartwright kept his carcasses hung from rafters in the Ice House to keep them prior to butchering. Because Cartwright had so much product in the Ice House he made sure it was always locked with a large padlock.

Cartwright owned the Ice House and he was a big strapping man able to carry a side of beef on his shoulder as if it where a big pillow. Further, Cartwright was the Sheriff for Port Rowan. Except for a few cases of too much drinking on a Saturday night, Cartwright didn't seem to have much to do in his role as Sheriff. With respect to the drunks, he'd throw them in the "cooler" or as we knew it the Ice House and lock them in until Monday morning, when they would be transported to the Town of Simcoe to appear in court.

Of course the other use of the Ice House, was why Joe was on his way there now. It was used by the community to store the bodies of the dead prior to their funeral, otherwise, the Sanctuary of the Church had a very unpleasant smell through all the service and all the flowers and all the fragrance burning didn't quite cover it.

Ma was going to make sure there wasn't going to be any smell from Pa that was going to be remembered. Pa had always got along well with Jack Cartwright. Pa had built the sleigh that Mr. Cartwright used to haul his Ice and it had held up for over 20 years. Pa, also built a small fishing boat that Mr. Cartwright used to catch fish to supplement his meat supply. Joe didn't expect he would have any problems making the arrangements.

As Joe opened the door, a bell rang out, letting Mr. Cartwright know he had a customer in the store. Usually Mr. Cartwright was in the back, butchering meat.

The door to the slaughter house smashed open and in walked a giant of a man with an apron that was covered with blood and a long curved knife in his right hand. In another time he could certainly have been a Pirate or directly off the battlefields of the crusades.

One look at Joe and he placed his knife on the counter and came around to where Joe was standing and placed his hand on Joe's shoulder and squeezed. Joe thought he would never be able to use his arm again. Cartwright saw Joe's look of pain and quickly eased off the pressure.

"I heard Joe and I'm deeply sorry", the butcher said in a voice that showed he really did care.

"Thank you Sheriff", (all the kids loved to call him by his Town designation of Sheriff, it had a real western flair to it.), "Ma has asked if you would allow Pa to spend the night in the Ice House?"

"Of course Joe, it would be an honour. Your Pa was a close friend and a really good pal. You let me know when he's coming and I'll make sure the "cooler" is open for you.

Is there going to be viewing today?"

"Yes. I'm sorry, I should have told you that Ma will be hosting friends from 2 pm until 5 pm and then we would like to bring Pa down for the night. His funeral will be tomorrow at 11 am at the Methodist Church with Pastor McPherson conducting the service. There will be a luncheon put on by the Women's Auxiliary – Mother asked that I make sure to invite you and your family to all of these events if your schedule will allow."

"Joe, Emma and I along with the children will be proud to come. You can count on us, in fact I will be surprised if there is anyone in the Port that won't be there."

With that, Joe thanked Mr. Cartwright and made arrangements for his Father to be brought down to the Ice House around 6:00 pm.

Joe headed off to his Father's boat yard which was at the other end of the Village.

When he arrived he found that Will and John had assembled most of the pieces needed for building a casket. There were some inside corner pieces that needed to be cut and shaped and they would be ready to start the assembly. Joe went about measuring and cutting the pieces while he instructed Will and John to set-up three saw horses and lay the bottom boards on them. There was a centre board and two side boards that were cut about 2/3rds of the way down that allowed the familiar shape of the casket to take shape.

Joe set in place the cross bridging, ensuring there was room for the sides to fit snuggly to the bottom frame. Once these were marked in place with a pencil, he had Will and John hammer the nails in and made sure they were counter sunk.

"Why do we have to counter sink these nails?" inquired Will.

"We don't want Pa's clothing ripping when we place him in do we?" Joe responded in a very serious voice.

"Don't see why it matters," said Will, "He won't be using it again."

"It's Pa we're making this for and he always counter sunk the nails – if he felt that was needed for others – we have to do at least as much for him."

With that, Will shut-up and looked to Joe for the next directions.

It was a good thing that there were three of them as they soon found out as they started to assemble the sides. It took two to hold the initial piece in place and one to hammer the first couple of nails into the side.

Joe started with the foot sides and attached them with nails up through the bottom and then attached the inner corner pieces. These were 45 degree angles and easy to work with. The sides were then nailed to the corner pieces. He did the same with the head sides, which were shorter in length and went together quite quickly.

Now the tricky part had to be addressed. The next inside strap wasn't a 45 degree like the others, but rather more of a 20 degree on one side. Joe wasn't quite sure how to reach this angle, so he put the inside block into the vice and planed the piece until he felt it was close to the angle he needed. He took it out of the vice and placed it in position and put the side board into place. It was still just a bit too small, so he took it out and replaced in the vice and continued, to work on the angle with great care.

As Joe watched the plane cut furrows of wood from the piece of wood that would hold his Father's casket together, he remembered how his Father had loved his hand tools and would spend quiet time before and after work, sharpening his chisel blades, saws and the blades of his planes. He would work the blade back and forth over the whet stone to ensure that every nick had been smoothed out and that the edge was as sharp as a razor.

Now these same tools were working on his eternal resting place. He had to do a good job!

Joe tried the pieces again and with a bit of sanding on a couple of spots was satisfied he had created a snug fit.

Using this first piece as a template he created the two head pieces and the other side piece.

Having everything ready, the rest of the assembly went together smoothly and he was ready to create the lid.

This was simpler than he thought it would be. It was just a copy of the bottom. However, he spent about 30 minutes cutting out and carving a cross for the top of the lid. This wasn't standard – but it was something he felt his Father would appreciate. He quickly stained the cross with a dark walnut stain and rubbed it with a wax to help it shine. This he decided he would attach the cross before the church service, or maybe at the Ice House – the stain smelled too strong to attach it now and have it in the house.

While Joe was working on the cross, he sent Will and John to the house with two saw horses and told them to get right back. He was just finishing the cross as they arrived.

"Wow", Will exclaimed, "Where did you learn to do that? It looks great"

"Thanks, don't know as I ever have learned to do this type of work. Watched Pa do some fine wood carvings on some of the boats he built, so thought I'd give it a shot. He had to admit, it didn't turn out too bad, if I do say so myself, but I won't attach it until tonight at the Ice House – stinks right now from the stain.

"Come on you two, we need to get this casket up to the house pronto. Ma asked for it by 11 and it's already five to." Joe said.

So, the three young people started the long walk up to the Robin's house with Will and John on each side at the foot and Joe supporting their work at the head.

When they passed people they would take off or tip their hats and express their sympathy to Joe and Will and let them know they would be up to the house in the afternoon.

A fifteen minute walk ended up taking almost 30 minutes with all their stops and accepting condolences.

When they arrived at the house, Will and John stumbled up the steps and nearly dropped the coffin. Joe had them rest it on the top step while he steadied it from the ground and they could get a new grip. Once everyone was ready Joe called "lift" and they proceed into the house and into the parlour.

The saw horses the boys had brought up earlier were covered with a white sheet and had been placed in front of the windows that looked out over the porch.

Charlotte instructed the boys to position the head of the casket away from the door, so people could see their Father's face as they entered the room.

Once the casket was in place, Joe was asked to help Dr. Russell who hadn't noticed when he arrived, and Jack Cartwright, who it seems the Doctor had asked to help him, move the body from the bedroom to the casket.

Joe was asked to support his Father's head and walk backwards while Dr. Russell and Mr. Cartwright carried Joseph in the bed sheet that he was laying on, one on each side. This worked well until they reached the door and there was no way Dr. Russell, Joseph and Mr. Cartwright could get through doorway. They placed Joseph down on the floor and were about to pull him through the door when Mr. Cartwright said, "Doctor, I know this isn't as dignified as you might like, but let me have him and I'll take him right into the Parlour."

With that, the giant of a man, bent down and lifted Joseph into his arms and rose and carried him as if he were child right up to the casket. Joe and Doctor Russell rushed behind and quickly helped lift and position Joseph into the casket, which now had one of Ma's favourite cushions she had spent the winter doing needle point on which to rest Pa's head.

The viewing went well with a really good turnout, most people bringing food for the table.

People ate, talked and told stories. It was a healing experience for everyone.

Joe had asked a few of his cousins if they would help move his Father down to the Ice House after the viewing was over and around five thirty one arrived with a horse and cart.

Before the men gathered in the parlour, Joe asked his family to say their last goodbyes and then he and Will placed the lid on the casket and he nailed it in place with a few nails and a hammer he'd brought up from the Yard when they brought the casket up earlier in the day.

Having completed this job, Joe asked the men to enter and they carried the casket out to the waiting cart and followed along to the Ice House, where they unloaded the cart and placed the casket in the area designated by Mr. Cartwright.

Joe spent a minute attaching his carved cross to the top of the casket.

Once the casket was in place the Ice House was locked and all agreed to come back the next day at 9:30 am to help bring the casket to the Church for the 11 am Service.

"Thank you everyone for your help." Joe said "and a special thank you to you Sheriff, for making a secure resting place for my Father tonight."

With that they all headed off to their homes and Joe returned to his family to snack on the many gifts of food that had been provided over the afternoon, and an early turn in, since they had a big day tomorrow.

Joe was up early the day of the funeral and went out and stoked up the kitchen stove and put another log on the wood burning heater that stood over in the corner of the dining room.

Once breakfast was over, Joe and Will headed off to the Ice House to meet the others. Mr. Cartwright opened up for them and together they lifted the casket holding Joseph Robins onto the waiting cart. They had to be careful, since the cold of the Ice House had cause the wood to be frosty and very slippery. But, all went as planned and they were able to place the casket in front of the communion table without any problems.

Rev. McPherson was there to greet them and let them into the Church. He was quite taken by the hand carved cross and asked Joe where it had come from?

"I carved it myself" responded Joe a little self consciously.

"I think it's a real piece of art and so meaningful." Rev. McPherson replied, "Joe, I think it is an excellent gift to your Father and I know he would be very proud of you."

The Funeral

By 10:30 the Church was overflowing and people were standing at the back and chairs were being brought up to put into the aisles, making it almost impossible to move from the front to the back of the Church.

A pew had been kept in reserve at the front for the Robins' Family and they were lead out to it about 10:55. Everyone stood as the family arrived and the low rumble of voices came to an eerie silence. As Charlotte and the children sat, there was a sound of scuffling ringing through the Church as everyone sat down, or adjusted their position and the hum of voices once again echoed through the Church.

Charlotte leaned over to Joe and said, "I really like the cross on the casket, where did it come from?"

Once again, Joe in an embarrassed voice responded, "I made it yesterday when I was putting together the casket. I meant to mention it to you and ask your permission before I affixed it to the lid. I hope you don't mind?"

"Joe, what a thoughtful son you are, of course I don't mind. I think it is beautiful and your Father would be so proud of you." answered Charlotte.

That did it! Joe could feel the tears fill up in his eyes and he knew he couldn't cry – he had to read the Old Testament in a few minutes and he could not have tears in his eyes when he did that. Rev. McPherson was giving him a great honour and he couldn't let him and his Father down.

He took out a big white hanky and pretended to blow his noise. He buried his face in it and made sure he gave his eyes a good wipe.

That was better!

At that moment, Rev. McPherson proceeded through the side door and started towards the Pulpit.

The Congregation once again rose as one like a herd of elephants.

Once in place, Rev. McPherson directed the congregation to be seated and he waited until all the shuffling and scraping had ceased, then he proceeded with the service.

In no time they were at the reading from the Old Testament. He called Joe to come forward and read Ecclesiastes 3:1- 8.

There was a rumble of voices, surprise that Rev. McPherson was letting a lay person read the scripture who wasn't one of the chosen elders, but it quieted down as Joe entered the pulpit.

Joe took a moment to look out over the congregation. There were the Robins, the Wyatts and his Mother's family the Hardys, some from St. Williams a village about two hours away by buggy and then there were the Russells, Cartwrights, and nearly every other family in the Port.

Joe opened the Bible at Ecclesiastes and turned the pages to Chapter 3. He began to read with a strong voice that rang over the congregation and as he read he remembered the discussion Rev. McPherson and he had with respect to this passage. He was careful to read the passage slowly, as he had practiced it at home last night and placed the accents on key words to make them stand out "time", "death", "peace".

Joe felt very at home in the Pulpit and wondered to himself if God hadn't intended him to follow this calling.

As he came to the conclusion, he looked up and saw the congregation hanging on to every word and he looked down and saw his Father's casket and the reality of the moment hit him. He was thinking of himself and how he was performing and had forgotten that this wasn't about him – but about his Father, Joseph Robins, as he lay at Joe's feet.

Joe bowed, and quietly said, "Forgive me Pa, I do love you and I'll miss you."

He then returned to his seat and his Mother slipped her arm through his and gave him a squeeze on the arm and whispered, "Thank you", in his ear.

The rest of the service and the committal proceeded on while time seemed to stand still. Soon they were through the reception and back at the house with all the well-wishers gone.

A New Day

Joe was down at the Boat Yard at 6 am and he stood there and looked around in a state of numbness.

Joe thought, if only he had paid more attention to the work his Father had been doing before he died – it would have made finishing these boats a lot easier. He had three boats to finish. At least the keels and ribbing was in place on all three. It was just the side planking, chine and transom that needed to be installed. Then of course the setting of the mast, installing the tiller, caulking, painting and oars to be shaped.

Joe's Father had put in 14 hour days, from six in the morning through to eight at night. Even when he wasn't well after his return from Brazil, he had spent most of his waking hours out at the shop until that last couple of weeks.

A New Day Without Pa

Joe would get up at five each morning, eat some porridge quickly and be out to the shop by five-thirty and work until eight-thirty. Off to school for nine and home by four. Then out to the shop by four-fifteen and work through until eleven.

These boats had to be finished or the family would starve over the winter.

Except for a few cents that Will earned at the general store and the sale of preserves that his Mother made, this was the only income that was going to be available to the family now that his Father had died.

Mr. Watts had come the day after his Father had died and surveyed the progress of his three boats.

"Well Joe, sorry about your Pa", Mr. Watts said, "As you know your Ma is a cousin and I wish there were something I could do, but I'm going to have to have Jake come and move these skeletons to his boat yard and get them finished as soon as possible. Your Father was to have completed them about six months ago, but when he came back sick, I knew I'd never see them finished."

"Mr. Watt", Joe responded, " I was helping my Pa with these boats when he was sick, and know I can get them done within the next two months. If Jake comes for them, he won't get them done any earlier, he is already doing work for Higman's out of St. Williams and his yard is full. I know, I was over there just a few days ago to swap some lumber that Pa wanted me to exchange with him.

Please leave the contract with me. You'll get a "Robins" ship you'll be proud of, I promise."

Joe didn't like lying, but he need this contract to stay with him or it would be a bleak winter for all.

He had been over at Jake's boat yard last week, but not to exchange wood – but to play with his son Bill, Joe's best friend. To tell Mr. Watt that he was playing would give Mr. Watt the wrong impression. Joe's play days were over as of this minute. He was now a man of the world and this was business he needed and needed bad.

"I don't know Joe" Mr. Watt's voice echoed with skepticism, " I have to have these ships by the start of the fall fishing. I don't think you are up to building one boat, never mind three. I have to have these boats by the first of September. If Jake's too busy, I'll just have to find another ship builder to complete this order."

"Mr. Watt, as you said, you are related to my Ma, and I know that you won't let family influence a business decision, however, I can do this job and to put it to you man to man, I need to complete this job for my family. You signed a contract with Robins' Boat Building Yard, you didn't sign a personal contract with my Pa, I expect you to fulfill your end of the bargain and I'll ensure that Robins' Boat Building Yard completes your three boats by September 1st."

Joe had no idea if a contract had even been signed. His father wasn't big on paper work and Joe had no idea where he had kept his records. However, Mr. Watt needed a way out of this situation and to be able to save face. The chances are he hadn't paid anything down on these boats and the lumber likely belonged to the yard.

Joe waited, holding his breath. Mr. Watt looked around the Yard and pondered and seemed to be considering his options.

With a shake of his head he replied, "Joe, I don't think you'll get one seaworthy boat finished by September, however, I do feel a family responsibility and I'll leave the contract with you but mind, I'll only pay for the work done by September."

"Thank you Mr. Watt!" Joe exclaimed and now he decided to really push his luck, "I believe it's common practice to pay one quarter of agreed upon price once the keel is laid and ribbings fastened. Would you be agreeable to forward this amount at your earliest convenience."

"Why I never! I've never heard such a thing in my life!" exclaimed Mr. Watt, " I've just agreed to leave a project with you, that by rights I should be moving on to a qualified ship builder and you have the gall to ask for money up front for work I'm not even sure will be seaworthy."

Joe knew he was close to loosing all the ground he had just made up but he needed that money now to pay expenses and purchase material to complete these boats.

"Mr. Watt, I am my Father's son. I have been around the Yard all my life and know for a fact that it is customary to receive a "Keeling Fee" when work has reached this stage. Just because I'm young, you wouldn't try to take advantage of me, now would you?"

A "Keeling Fee" where had that phrase come from? Joe had no idea, but it seemed just and now the whole deal hung in the silence. He could see Mr. Watt struggling with the idea of advancing money for a project he didn't think was going to get completed and for boats that might he not be able to use.

Watt knew that Joe was well respected in the village. Joe was a smart lad at school and well known within the Church for his leadership role in Church Sunday School and with his fellow young people. He didn't want people talking badly about him, especially if the word got out that he wasn't supporting family. There must be away out of this.

"I'll tell you what Joe, I've never heard of this "Keeling Fee" and I know it wasn't in the contract that I signed with your Pa. However, as I said earlier, I don't think you're going to get three boats completed by September 1st – I'll agree to pay one quarter of the first boat and will pay you full amount on the completion of that boat. If you can get more than one boat built, I'll pay you the same way on each of the remaining two boats."

Joe shot out his hand.

"Done" he exclaimed and vigorously shook hands with Mr. Watt.

"I'll send the money over today" Mr. Watt said.

"I'll be glad to come and get it for you", Joe replied with a smile on his face.

"I'm sure you will", said Mr. Watt, as he ambled out of the ship yard and turned to Joe,

"It will be ready at 2 pm, don't be late", he said with a laugh and turned down the street back to the village.

As Watt walked along enjoying the sun, he thought to himself, that this young lad was something else. He just might get three ship-worthy vessels by September 1st. This young lad was worth the investment and the community would be pleased he had continued to support his cousin during their time of distress. This would look good when he ran for Mayor next year. Yes, this was a good investment. Whoever heard of a "Keeling Fee"! My goodness that boy sure could think fast on his feet. Somehow, Port Rowan wasn't going to be big enough for a young man like this. He'd be surprised if Joe took over the Ship Yards. It might be worth keeping an eye on – it could be a good investment down the way.

Joe had the deal, and most importantly, he had the much needed cash to pay the bills and to buy some of the material that would be necessary to finish the ships. He knew he didn't have enough cash to buy all the material he needed. He'd have to go down to the lumber yard and see if Big Jake would advance him planking on credit.

As he approached the lumber yard, there were teams of horses pulling three and four logs, chained together into a large yard with tree trunks piled all over the place. It was a beehive of activity and if you didn't watch where you were walking you could be run over by a team of horses or caught by a rolling log that was being positioned to be hosted up onto the cutting platform. The platform was built about 8' above the ground and had a huge blade stationed in the middle. The blade had to be as tall as a man – likely 6-7 feet in radius and driven by huge belts that were connected to a turning wheel that had a small donkey attached to the spoke type turnstile. Around and around this animal would go and with every turn the log on the platform would be pulled through the huge saw, slicing off a plank with thee completions of the circle. The smell of sawdust and sap hung in the air. Joe loved this smell.

A booming voice drew Joe out of a moment of mediation.

"Well, if it isn't Joe Robins." A thundering base voice echoed above the sound of the machines and the scraping of logs along the ground. "Sorry to hear about your father. A good man – should never have died like that. Far too young!" said Big Jake of Jake Newton's Lumber Yard. "Thank you Mr. Newton," Joe responded, "Ma and I really appreciated you coming to the service."

"Wouldn't have missed it, Joe. Like I said, I really liked your Pa. As you know we grew up together in this town and there wasn't a better friend or shipbuilder on the Lake. He will be sorrowfully missed.

But what brings you to the yard today Joe?"

"Well, Mr. Newton, I have just completed renegotiating with Mr. Watts to complete the three ships that Dad had started. As you likely know, he had the keels and the ribs laid before he died. I have negotiated with Mr. Watts to complete the three vessels by mid August and I'm going to need seasoned wood for the planking and mahogany for the decking and cabin. I'm sure Dad must have contracted with you about delivery times and prices, but I haven't been able to find any paper work on these boats yet."

This really is a lie, Joe thought, he hadn't looked for any paper work – so obviously he hadn't found any and the date of mid August wasn't the date he negotiated with Mr. Watts, but it would put pressure on Big Jake to getting his cutting done in good time. Joe knew that if he could negotiate delivery times and prices, he was going to be the low person on the totem pole for getting product. He was going to have to stay on Big Jake's tail all the time until he received all of his order. He was a kid in a man's world. Sympathy only went so far when doing business – and now that Big Jake had said all the right things, Joe knew he would do his best make as much money off this kid as he possibly could. It was only good business and Big Jake didn't get to having the biggest lumber yard in the area by being a softy.

It was time to see if he had what it took to stay in business.

"Mr. Newton, I need my planking by the end of next week, and I want to inspect each board before it's shipped out of the yard. It has to be seasoned and consistent in thickness. You know what I need and I'm sure you'll put your most trusted workers on this contract." Joe stated.

"Your Pa never approved my lumber before it left the yard – he trusted me to send a good product." Big Jake roared.

"Mr. Newton, you and dad went back a long way and dad knew how to make each board work for him. He could make any board come alive as he worked with it. I'm not questioning your honesty. For me, I have to make sure that I can see how the boards are going fit together. To be honest, I can't afford spoilage on this contract – my numbers with Mr. Watts are really close to costs."

In reality, he knew that Big Jake would off load whatever pieces of junk he had in the yard onto this kid. The last thing he needed was warped wood that wouldn't lay flat on the ribbing. He didn't have time to soak and clap boards. If he was going to get this job done, he needed prime wood from the get go.

Big Jake stared at Joe and thought to himself, this kid has got guts. He's given me a way out to save face and he seems to know what he's talking about with respect to his needs. I was going to ship over that pile of green pine I had in my second stack and charge prime prices – but I don't need the community knowing that I tried to put one over on Joseph's son. No, I think I had better be as honest as I can with this kid, maybe I can make the difference up in the pricing.

"I understand your concern Joe, and I would welcome your inspection of the wood I have scheduled to be sent to you, prior to leaving the yard. Now what about the price? If I remember, I had an agreement with your Pa for 2 cents a running foot for the planking and 5 cents for the mahogany." said Big Jake hopefully.

"Gee, do you have that in writing Mr. Newton?" asked Joe

"No, I think we just had a handshake on the deal" said Mr. Newton.

" I always thought my Dad was a pretty good businessman," said Joe, "and he would really loose a lot in this deal with Mr. Watts, if he was paying you these prices. I would have thought that Dad would have negotiated .25 cents per running foot for the planking and 2 cents for the mahogany, it would be the only way he could have made any money on this deal."

This kid isn't stupid, though Big Jake, he was just about right on with respect to the price he had negotiated with Robins. He wanted this contract and he'd have to find a way to get a little more out of it. The .25 cents was right on and he had negotiated 3 cents for the mahogany.

"Well you know Joe, I might be confusing the deal I made with your Pa with one I made with another yard. Come to think of it, your Pa did drive a hard bargain and I'm willing to offer you the same one. Now let me think, if I remember it was .75 a running foot for the planking and 4 cents for the mahogany."

"That's certainly closer to what I expect I'd find in my Pa's paper work on this contract, but I have to be honest with you Mr. Newton, I can't pay more that .25 a running foot for the planking and the absolute maximum I could go for the mahogany would be 3.5 cents. To help you with your cash flow, I'd be willing to pay you 10% up front and the rest in 60 days." Joe said with a conviction in his voice that he didn't feel in his stomach. This was it, make or break. Either Big Jake would back down, or the project was down the drain.

"Joe, your Pa would be proud of you. Best deal I can give you is .25 cents a running foot – and I'm not making any money off this, I'll accept your offer of 3.5 cents on the mahogany and again you're getting a real deal. However, I need 25% up front and the rest in 30 days." Big Jake stared right into Joe's eyes and stuck out his hand.

"I think we're close Mr. Newton," Joe replied, "but I'm real tight on cash at this point. I agree with the pricing, can we do better on the terms? How about 15% up front and another 35% in 30 days? Then the remainder in 60 days?"

"Done!" boomed Big Jake, and he grabbed Joe's hand and squeezed it 'till tears started to form in Joe's eyes, but he'd never let Big Jake know and he squeezed back just as hard as he could and shook his arm up and down. It felt like his hand would never be used again and if Big Jake didn't stop pumping his hand, his arm would be coming off at the shoulder.

Joe decided that if he could just sneeze, he might break this grip. He sucked in as much air as he could and sneezed as hard as he could.

Big Jake immediately let go of his grip and stepped back with a look of surprise and disgust on his face.

"Excuse me Mr. Newton," said Joe, "must have gotten some sawdust up my noise."

Joe had a deal that would work for him and he was well aware that Big Jake had likely upped the price somewhere – and until he found his dad's notes, he would likely never know how much Big Jake was making off him, over and above the original deal. But that was business!

After negotiating delivery dates and inspection times, Joe left the lumber yard and headed home to tell his Mother all that had transpired before lunch.

As Joe sat at the table with his brother Will, sister Margaret and Mother, he bowed his head and assumed his responsibility as head of the family

"Let us say grace. Dear Lord, we miss Dad, we thank you for being with us and supporting us and helping make things well. Now we ask your blessing upon the food Mom and Margaret have prepared and know that we believe in you. Amen".

All the heads raised upon as soon as grace was over and stared at Joe.

"What happened this morning" inquired Will.

"What do you mean?" said Joe

"In your prayer you were giving thanks for something that happened this morning. Stop holding secrets Joe! What happened?"

"Please explain yourself Joe" said his Mother

Margaret didn't say anything, but she looked at her big brother with a look of trust and knowledge that if anyone could make sense out of what had happened to their family, Joe was the person.

"I met with your cousin, Mr. Watts, today and convinced him to leave the contract to build the three boats Dad had started with us. I made a commitment we would get them done by September 1st and received an advance on the job. He's agreed to pay one quarter of the first boat and will pay the full amount on the completion of that boat and he'll pay the same on each of the remaining two boats as we start planking them."

Everyone around the table started talking at once!

Joe's mother tapped her spoon on the edge of her plate and silence fell over the table.

"Joe, this is excellent news and we sure can use the money," Charlotte stated, "however, who is going to build these boats?'

"I am… with Will's help" said Joe.

"Joe, what about your schooling? I won't allow you to drop out of school. The only way you will achieve anything in this world is with an education. Otherwise, you'll end up dying early from over work like your Father. I don't want that for any of my children, do you hear me?" snapped Charlotte in a voice the children knew was her don't argue with me voice.

"I have no intention of giving up school and I can assure you I'll make sure Will finishes school too!'

"You and who else!" Will snapped back.

"Please hear me out.

I figure that Will and I can work before school and after school for the next two months until school is out and then we'll work through the summer full time. I'm confident we can complete the boats on time.

It will mean that Will and I will have to be in the Yard by five a.m. and work through until eight-forty five – then we'll head up to school and be back in the Yard by four-thirty and work through until ten or eleven." Joe explained.

"I'll never be able to get up at that hour!" wailed Will.

"Will, we don't have a choice. Without this contract we have no income to pay the bills and I agree with Mom, we both need to complete our education. This appears to me to be the only option that will let us do it. Sure it will be hard for four months – and especially hard for two months with school and work – but I know we can do it.

Are you willing Will?"

"Joe, you know I'd never let you down, but what happens after the summer?" said Will

"Will, let's worry about today and tomorrow at this point, I'll come up with a plan for after the summer."

The table grew eerily silent and they all started to eat.

Charlotte stared at her food for a good two minutes and then she slowly lifted her head.

Joe knew that she was ready to either endorse his plan, or shoot it down once and for all.

He waited in suspense with his fork half lifted to his lips. Although the food was always great that his Mother prepared, he couldn't remember what it tasted like while he waited for the verdict.

"Joe," Charlotte said with a clear voice, "I praise God that I have three children like you, Margaret and Will. I don't know how I would have survived your Father's death if it wasn't for your support. I must admit, I am concerned that you've entered into these agreements without my input. However, you seemed to have thought through the consequences of your actions and from what you've said it sounds like you've struck a good deal with Cousin Howard or as you rightly refer to him, Mr. Watts.

I want you all to know that I'm going to be monitoring your health while you are taking on these extra responsibilities and I expect, even if it means you don't get all three ships built, that you will keep up with your school work and your marks.

Do I make myself clear!"

"Yes!" they all responded at once.

All of a sudden Joe could taste the meat loaf he was eating and it never tasted better.

Charlotte looked up with a worried look on her face and Joe felt that maybe she had reconsidered.

"Joe, you've done a great job of renegotiating the contract with Cousin Howard, but I just thought, I have no idea of how much lumber stock your Father has on hand and I'm afraid Big Jake isn't going to advance any lumber, unless we pay cash up front. We just don't have the cash to do that."

Joe, looked around the table and noted that all eyes were fixed on him.

"Mom, once I had Mr. Watts' contract in hand, I went immediately to see Big Jake.

Dad had already laid the keels for all three vessels and had installed the ribbing for them. As you know, this is the most demanding and skilled job of boat building, for if you don't have a straight keel and properly spaced ribs, then you don't have a boat that will sail straight or a proper foundation for the mast. All I needed was the planking and the mahogany for the cabin.

As can be expected, Big Jake tried to renegotiate the prices of both the planking and mahogany. He wanted two cents a running foot for the planking and five cents for the mahogany."

There was a gasp from around the table. Although, none of them were involved in the daily running of the business, they had heard their Father discuss with their Mother many times the cost of buying wood and they knew that these prices were highway robbery.

"My goodness," exclaimed Charlotte, "we'll go bankrupt if we pay these prices!"

"Of course we would," said Joe excited to tell what had transpired with Big Jake, "I told him that Dad would never have agreed to such terms. I told him that I was sure Dad would have agreed to a quarter of a cent and three cents. He countered with three quarters of a cent and four cents. I told him I wasn't moving off a quarter of a cent but would be willing to go for three and half cents. With that Big Jake agreed then he wanted 25% up front and the rest in 30 days."

At that, Charlotte gasped, "We haven't got that much cash and we sure can't meet 30 days to settle the account!"

"I know," responded Joe, "I got big Jake to agree on, 15% up front and another 35% in 30 days. The remainder will be due in 60 days. This will give us time to have at least one ship completed and I hope most of the second.

With the advance on the second, I think we'll have enough to pay off most of the account. I think Big Jake will extend the remaining amount, if there is any, until we get the second ship finished and paid for. Our profit is in the third ship. We have to get this third ship finished on time.

If we can get our full fee, there will be enough profit to keep the house going, while I finish my schooling and get a job."

"Joe, I can't believe that you were able to get Big Jake to agree to those terms," exclaimed Charlotte, "I think he is charging you too much for the Mahogany though."

"You're absolutely right," agreed Joe, "but I had to let him save a little face and I knew I had to get a low down payment and extended time to pay. The latter was imperative, or we wouldn't have anything to live on for the next four months. We're not buying that much mahogany, and I'm thinking I might be able to convince Mr. Watts to accept stained birch for some of the areas Dad would normally have used mahogany. I know I can get birch at a good price. Even if he says no, we'll still do well with these figures."

"What about the Yard?" asked Will.

"Unless you have a desire to take over the business, I suggest that we close the yard after we finish Mr. Watts's contract.

I know that I have no desire to be a ship builder."

"I guess you're right Joe," replied Will, looking down at his Mother, "I'm willing to help you build these three ships, but I don't want to spend my life building ships.

I'm not sure I know what I want to do with my future, but I do know what I don't want to do!"

"Don't you think you owe Dad something for all the work he put into the Yard?" asked Margaret.

"Margaret, I know your Father never expected the boys to take over the Yard.

In fact he wanted both boys to get as much education as they could and make something of themselves. It wasn't that he didn't take pride in his trade, he did! He loved working with his hands and building the best ship he could gave him great pride. But he also knew how much this type of work took out of a man. He wanted better for his family and I want better for my family.

I think the decision to close the Yard after the summer makes sense and has my full support.

I think we might be able to sell the Yard to one of the other ship builders in the area and those funds, along with the profits from the third boat will ensure a nice nest egg for the near future.

We own this house and property clear and Margaret, you and I will continue to work the gardens. Maybe Margaret, you will help me expand the east garden and we'll plant more vegetables this spring?"

"Of course Ma," responded Margaret eagerly, "I was feeling left out of Joe's plans, but this is something I can do and I'll see if I can get a part time job at the General Store or maybe at the fishery during the summer."

"I think we have a plan!" exclaimed Joe, "Let's give thanks to the Lord."

They held each others' hands and Joe found himself reaching across the table to Will. It was with a heavy heart that he stretched passed the place his Father had always filled.

They all bowed their heads and Joe led them in prayer.

"Lord, we miss our Father, but as a family we have put together a plan that we know you helped us form. Bless this family, and help us fulfill our dreams. Amen"

Chapter 4

Love is Sweet

"For God hath not given us the spirit of fear;
but of power, and of love, and of a sound mind."(KJV)
2 Timothy 1:7

Over he next two months Joe and Will were up before dawn and watched the sunrise as they were working down at the Yard. Margaret would arrive about 7:30 am with a bowl of hot porridge for both lads and a pot of hot sweet tea.

They would take a 15 minute break, then they were right back at it till 8:45 when they would quickly pack up their tools and run up the hill to the one room schoolhouse. Thank goodness their Mother had met with their school master, Mr. Snodgrove, and explained the plan the boys had worked out and the schedule they had made for themselves. She had pleaded with the school master not to assign homework to the boys – it just wouldn't get done and they would start falling behind in their studies. Instead she encouraged him to assign more work during school hours and let the boys work ahead at their own speed. She was sure they would accomplish the curriculum by the year end.

Mr. Snodgrove was respected by the boys because of his ability at sports and his encouragement of them to participate. He had spent extra time with Joe, showing him the techniques of boxing, a sport that Mr. Snodgrove had excelled at while attending the University of Toronto. Since

Joe was left-handed, it had been a challenge to teach him how to defend himself, keep his guard up – but not let his opponent know that the jab was going to come from that same hand that had been used as a guard.

Joe was a natural and had learned quickly and trained hard to stay in shape. He would miss their sparing sessions, but he knew that Joe's family situation came first and he was pleased that Joe had found a solution that allowed him to stay in school. So many of the boys in particular, when they lost their fathers to Lake Erie, an event that happened far to often, just quit school and started fishing or farming so the family could survive.

It would have been tragic if this had been the outcome for the Robins' boys. They were both very bright and Joe was destined for University, if he had anything to say about it. Will was a little younger, but certainly had the ability if he applied himself.

There was no way that Mr. Snodgrove would go against the wishes of Charlotte Robins. She might be a wee bit of a woman, but she certainly knew her mind and she was a woman that one didn't want to cross. It would mean more work for him to change his class teaching plan to ensure everything was going to be covered within class time, but it could be done and worth the investment.

Sundays, Joe and Will really looked forward not having to go down to the Yard. It's not that they disliked working in the Yard – but a day without pressure- a day to see their friends – a day to attend worship and just sit around and read – this surely was the Day the Lord had made!

The third Sunday after they had started their new plan, they woke to find out that a Circuit Riding Preacher was planning an afternoon and evening service under his tent in the Park. The word was, he was looking for volunteers right after Sunday worship to help raise the tent.

"What say we go and help Will?" said Joe.

"I don't know, Mom will have lunch on and a day of just loafing sure looks good to me." responded Will.

"I declare Will, you're sounding like an old man and not looking for new adventure. Come on," exhorted Joe.

"Oh, alright, but I'm not going to stay around for any services. I have had enough of that stuff today." Will shared.

"Alright, I'll tell Ma we won't be home for lunch and you'll be home after we put the tent up. Think I might stay and hear this Preacher."

With that Joe went over to his Mother on the way out of Church and explained what Will and he were going to do.

"Bring the Preacher and his family back to our place for dinner, unless they have another invitation." Invited Charlotte, "Let Will know if they are coming and he can let me know when he comes home after getting the tent up."

With that Joe and Will headed off to the Park.

Reverend Archer and his family had already unloaded the tent from their wagon and had it laid out, ready for help to arrive to raise it with the large poles that were laying on the ground in their right position.

Joe went over and introduced himself to a young man who was about his own age. "Hi, I'm Joe Robins and this is my brother Will. We've come to help if needed."

"Hi, I'm Albert Archer, thanks, we need the help."

"Archer? You must be Rev. Archer's son?" questioned Joe

"Yep, I'm a P.K."

"A P.K." said Joe, "What is that?"

"Why, it means I'm a "Preacher's Kid", laughed Albert, "Yep, my Sister Nellie and I are P.Ks, right kid?"

Joe turned to see the most beautiful young woman he felt he'd ever seen.

Nellie Archer was about two inches shorter than Joe, long hair auburn, that shone in the sunlight, blue eyes and a smile that showed the most beautiful set of white teeth he had ever seen. She was very stylish, wearing a white blouse with eyelet lace and puffed sleeves, a full length blue skirt and a white, veiled hat that she wore in a rakish style over her forehead.

Joe just stared with his mouth open.

"Hello", said Nellie as she extended her hand for the formal handshake.

Her voice was soft and melodic. Joe now believed in angels and he sure he was in the process of meeting one, if he could snap out of this foolish trance. Joe took her hand and shook and continued to hold on, far too long.

He realized he was making a fool of himself and let her hand go, reluctantly.

"Hi" Joe managed to squeak out. "Your brother was telling me about being a P.K." Joe continued.

"It's a good thing that Father moves every week or Albert wouldn't have any material to use when he meets people." Nellie said with a faint, light laugh in her voice.

Joe remembered that he was to invite the Archer Family to dinner if they didn't already have an invitation and he surely hoped they didn't!

"Miss Archer", Joe began, "My Mother has asked me to extend an invitation to dinner to you and your family after your Father's afternoon service. That is, if you don't already have an invitation?"

Nellie smiled at Joe and his heart stood still, then turning her head to Albert she asked, "Albert, are you aware whether Mother and Father have accepted an invitation for dinner at this point."

"I don't think so Sis, but you better make sure by checking with Father, you know how he dislikes making mistakes with commitments.

While she is checking with Father, Joe, maybe you and your brother, Will did you say, can give me a hand with raising these poles – it really isn't too hard if we do them in the right order and together."

In a matter of minutes, under Albert's expert direction they had raised the tent and fastened off the guy ropes.

Joe enjoyed working with Albert. He seemed like a nice enough young man. Albert was quick to laugh and willing to share a complement when things went well.

Yes, Joe and Albert became good friends in only a matter of minutes.

If this could only happen with his sister Joe wished.

At this point, Nellie arrived with Rev. Archer and his wife.

"Father, Mother, may I introduce Mr. Joseph Robins and his brother Will." Nellie's voice echoed in Joe's ears, "It is Mr. Robins who brings an invitation from his mother for us to join them for dinner at their home after the afternoon worship."

"Mr. Robins," boomed Rev. Archer's voice – almost as loud as Big Jake, but far more melodic in its presentation, almost as if he was already preaching, "My family would be honoured to accept your Mother's invitation. Might I ask if your Father will be present?"

"No sir, my Dad died a few weeks ago of an unknown illness. The Doctor couldn't seem to find a medicine to make him well." explained Joe, "There will just be my Mother, my younger sister Margaret, and my brother here, Will and myself. We hope that is acceptable to you Sir?"

"Of course Mr. Robins! We would be most honoured to accept your Mother's invitation. I believe you have met my daughter Nellie and son Albert, but I don't think you've met my eldest daughter Maie."

Joe stepped forward and shook Miss Maie Archer's hand and quickly glanced her over. A nice looking lady, but she didn't have the beauty of Nellie Archer.

"A pleasure to meet you Miss Archer" and looking back to Rev. Archer, Joe continued, "Sir, our family is honoured to have you join us for dinner tonight and I look forward to your service of worship this afternoon."

"May I on behalf of my family extend to you and your brother our sincere condolences upon the death of your Father. We will remember him in our prayers in the Services today." With this acceptance from Rev. Archer, Joe nodded to Will, who excused himself from the group and headed off home to tell Mother that they would be having company and to tell Margaret that Joe had fallen head over heels for Miss Nellie!

As the Archer Family headed into the tent to prepare for the afternoon service, Joe wandered over to a bench under an old oak tree and settled in to wait the half hour before the service started.

Joe noticed that as people started to arrive, Nellie would greet them at the tent door, and talk with the young ladies from 12 years up and then direct them over behind the tent. About 15 minutes before the service, Nellie turned her greeting responsibilities over to her sister and she went behind the tent to join, what was by now, about 12 young ladies.

As he sat there wishing he could see what Nellie was doing and more importantly, stare at Nellie without her being aware that he was staring, he heard a chant of female voices, reciting a series of words. Then he heard humming that grew louder than quieter and once again soared. He recognized the tune. It was the famous hymn "Amazing Grace".

At 2:00 pm sharp, Joe was in his seat and Nellie was at the foot pump organ playing a prelude with such skill that it made a shiver run up his spin.

Rev. Archer processed up to the Pulpit and was followed by 12 young ladies that assumed their seats in front of Nellie, all beaming at their families that they had been chosen as choir members for today's service. Nellie flashed them a smile that Joe would have died for.

Rev. Archer was an imposing figure, with white hair, white beard, black robe that was filled out to its fullest by his barrel chest.

There was a good crowd.

There wasn't much else to do on a Sunday afternoon in Port Rowan. It was always an exciting day when an evangelist came to town. The local Ministers usually cancelled their evening services – no sense competing for God's children. A night off with their family was always a blessing. This was the first time that Rev. Archer had come this far. He lived near Hamilton and usually didn't go further than Simcoe. However, Joe's Minister had attended a service conducted by Rev. Archer in Simcoe and was moved by Rev. Archer's sermon and impressed by the involvement of his wife and children in the service.

When Rev. Archer started the Call to Worship with "This is the day the Lord has made, rejoice and be glad in it.", the hum of the congregation subsided immediately and there was a resounding response of "Amen".

That baritone voice of Rev. Archer had everyone's attention. There was a smile of anticipation on their faces. This was going to be a service to remember and thank goodness it was going to be a pleasure to listen to this man's voice.

Rev. Archer turned to his daughter Nellie and introduced her to the congregation as his music director, then asked Nellie to lead the "choir" in "Amazing Grace".

Nellie started pumping the foot bellows and then pulled out all the stops, as they say and performed an introduction to the Hymn that had everyone sitting on the edge of their seats. As she held the last note, she nodded to the young ladies in front of her to stand, and then she started to play more softly and had the ladies humming the first verse, swelling their voices with the organ – then the words... The young ladies sang like an experienced choir, staying together with their voices blending like they had been practicing for weeks. This sure didn't sound like the choirs that sang in local churches every week – what was the difference? Most of these young ladies sang in the choirs on Sundays – but they sure didn't sound like this.

When they completed the hymn as a choir piece, Rev. Archer had every-one join them for the first and last verse. By the time they were finished, both the women and some of the men had tears in their eyes, tears of pride and emotion.

Rev. Archer prayed for the community and made special mention of Joe's father and then he preached on John 3:16-17

> *"For God so loved the world, that he gave his only begotten Son, that whosoever believeth in him should not perish, but have everlasting life. For God sent not his Son into the world to condemn the world; but that the world through him might be saved." (KJV)*

At the end of his sermon, Rev. Archer conducted an Altar Call for those that felt they had come to Jesus during this service. While people were considering whether they felt the call of Jesus today, Mrs. Archer, Maie and Albert sang "The Holy City" with Nellie pumping out the accompaniment. Albert had a powerful Baritone voice that captured the feeling of this emotional praise song. As good as Albert was, Joe felt that the success of this song was because of the accompaniment of Miss Nellie. She was terrific!

Four people came forth and were prayed over. One of the four was, Mrs. Newton. She was saved anew at every Alter Call and people in the village kidded that she had the shortest memory or the greatest need to be saved than anyone in the village. They all wondered what she had done that needed this much saving? Of course, this was never said to her face or in the earshot of Big Jake!

After the service, Joe stayed behind to help clean up and prepare everything for the evening service. Then Joe led the Archer Family up to the Robins' house for dinner.

Charlotte and Margaret were standing in the doorway waiting for them as they proceeded up the stone walkway.

"Mother, Margaret," said Joe, "May I present Rev. and Mrs. Archer and their daughters, Maie and Nellie and their son, Albert. These two charming ladies are your hostesses, my Mother, Charlotte Robins and my sister Margaret."

"We are most pleased to welcome you to our humble house" said Charlotte and Margaret immediately stepped aside and said, "Please come in and rest, you must be tired after conducting worship today."

Mother led the Archers into the parlour, a room that was only used during times of sorrow or when guests arrived.

When everyone was seated, Mother turned to Margaret, "Would you see what people would like to drink prior to dinner". She turned back to her guests and said, "We have hot tea, cold tea, cold apple cider and lemonade."

Margaret quickly received the orders and started off to the kitchen.

"May I help you," said Nellie and got up and followed Margaret out to the kitchen. Joe watched with envy as Nellie accompanied his sister into the kitchen and was about to offer his help – so he would have a chance to be closer to Nellie, when Albert asked Joe,

"Are you still attending school Joe?"

"Yes" answered Joe

Charlotte then continued on explaining what Will and Joe were doing to the amazement of all in the room.

In the meantime, Margaret was pouring drinks and talking with Nellie. They were close in age and Margaret quickly realized that Nellie's friendliness was not a put-on, rather she really was just the way she was. What a treat! Most of the girls in the village seemed to specialize in putting on airs, except for her cousin Margaret (known to the family as Meg) and of course her girlhood friend Cynthia, whose parents owned the General.

"I think my brother Joe is really interested in you Nellie" said Margaret with a bit of a laugh.

"He is a handsome young man." replied Nellie cautiously, "I'm sure he must have a lady he's interested in locally?"

"No, Joe has lots of friends, both male and female, but he's not 'going' with anyone and now that Dad has died, he hasn't a minute to himself." said Margaret.

"What do you mean?" Nellie asked showing more interest than she had planned.

Margaret went into how Will and Joe were running the Yard and still attending school. Nellie was quite impressed with his ambition, but she had no desire to get involved with anyone who was going to spend their lives building boats. Not that she had any interest in this young man besides being a friend and being polite.

The two young ladies carried the drinks back to the parlour.

"I was beginning to think we would have to send a search party after you." Said Charlotte to Margaret.

"I'm sorry Mother, Nellie and I were talking and I didn't realize we had taken so long." She turned to Rev. and Mrs. Archer and said, " I do apologize and hope you find the drinks quenching."

"Why Miss Margaret, you don't need to apologize, we are all aware that Nel can talk the fur off a cat."

"Father!" exclaimed Nellie, "I'm not that talkative." exclaimed Nellie as she turned a bright shade of pink.

Joe thought she looked lovelier than before. He had to get an opportunity to talk with her, chaperoned of course! Maybe he could get Albert to walk back with Nellie and himself after dinner.

Dinner was a great success and the Archers went out of their way to complement Charlotte on her cooking and for sharing her table with them.

It had been a lively table discussion about local issues and learning about the life of an Evangelist.

While clearing dishes, Joe was able to get Albert aside.

"Albert, I don't quite know how to say this, but I really like your sister."

"Golly," Albert responded, "I would never have guessed it since you haven't taken your eyes off her since I introduced you to her? She is a little young for you isn't she?"

"I don't think so, I'm seventeen – she must be 15 isn't she?"

"You're the same age I am and she is my little sister, however, you seem like a nice chap and I guess two years isn't much of difference. What can I do for you?"

Joe explained that he wanted Albert to walk back with Nellie and himself and give him a chance to talk with her.

"I think we can arrange that" said Albert with a smile on his face.

Joe felt foolish, but he would do anything for Nellie.

As the Archers prepared to leave, Charlotte indicated that her family would follow in about a half hour.

Albert turned to Charlotte and asked, "Mrs. Robins, do you think Joe might accompany us, I need a little assistance in setting up some extra chairs?" turning to his Father Albert continued, "We had an excellent afternoon turn out and I'm confident we'll have more this evening."

"Of course Joe can give you a hand," responded Charlotte, "Do you feel you need Will also?"

"No thank you Mrs. Robins, I'm sure you would like Will to escort you and Margaret. I'm sure Joe and I can get this task done in no time."

With this, the Archers and Joe proceeded down the hill towards the Park. Albert winked at Nellie and speeded up to walk with his parents and entered into a heated discussion with his Father about the songs they should sing tonight. Nellie quickly realized that Albert was giving her time with Joe and she wasn't sure whether she wanted to kiss her brother or swat him on the back of the head.

Nellie of course had boys at school and many young men who saw her in their worship services try to make time with her, but she was young and didn't really have much interest in boys and in fact was a little scared of men.

However, Joe was an "in-betweener".

He was still very young, almost her age and yet had taken on the responsibility of his Mother's home by running a boat yard with his brother. He was different form the boys she had known and as much as she hated to admit it, she was attracted to him.

"Miss Nellie" Joe broke the silence of the walk down the hill, "I noted that before the service you gathered a number of girls and young women to be in your choir and took them away for a practice. I have to tell you, I've heard most of these young women sing in our Church, School or at festivals and I have never heard them sing so well. What did you do to achieve such harmony with these young ladies?"

My gosh, thought Nellie, he knows something about music, "It sounds like you know a bit about music Joe?"

"I play a flute, poorly, and enjoy singing."

"That's great Joe; we'll have to get you to play your flute the next time we're back to Port Rowan.

I'm pleased you enjoyed the choir. I have found that if you get people to hum together, they learn quickly to stay on tune and it's hard to out-hum your neighbour. If I let them sing – then all the self impressed soloists attempted to show-up their friends. Humming is a great neutralizer. We then go over the words and I tell them which words I want stressed, held and cut short.

If we have time, I talk about the composer and the meaning of the hymn and why it was chosen.

Like this afternoon, I explained that Amazing Grace was written by John Newton. At six he had become an orphan and by 11 he was sent to sea.

When he was 11 he was press ganged into the Navy and flogged for desertion.

He later became an African slave-trader. At the age of 23 he was on board a cargo ship which got caught up in a huge storm. He was convinced he was going to die. Frozen and exhausted he called out to God for mercy and help and was saved from certain death. By the time he was 39 he renounced the slave-trading business and committed his life to Christ and he became a minister of God's word. He wrote this powerful song in remembrance of the day he beseeched God to save his life in that storm when he was 23.

Understanding the reason and background of the hymn helps the ladies to sing with conviction.

We don't always have as much time as I want. Then we'll sing the hymn through once, 'a capella'. My Mother taught me how to play the piano and organ and has trained me in leading choirs. Her health is such that she can't perform these roles as she used to and she relies on Maie and myself to take over many of the things she used to do for Father."

"Your Mother looks well." Ventured Joe.

"She has what the Doctors call a heart murmur and stress or heavy lifting causes her to have "spells" where she is unable to catch her breath and has great pain in her chest. We make sure she gets her rest and doesn't do more than the Doctors recommend. However, the Doctors told her to stop accompanying Father on these Sunday Services, and she has refused to comply. She said if it is the Lord's wish to take her when she is worshiping the Lord, then His will be done."

Joe slowed then stopped. He took Nellie's hand, much to her surprise, and she had to admit, delight and looking into her eyes said, "Miss Nellie, I have never felt this way about a woman before, I hope you'll allow me to court you."

Nellie wasn't quite sure what Joe as asking, since she lived near Hamilton and he, here in Port Rowan, but she liked the sound of his request and replied, "Joe, I'd be honoured, but of course you'll have to discuss this with Father and since we have agreed upon this, I suggest you drop the "Miss" and just call me Nellie."

Joe couldn't believe his luck.

She had said yes!

He was going to have to find a way to thank Albert for allowing them this time together. Now they must catch up to the Family. He shyly slipped his hand into hers feeling the warmth radiate through his whole body. If this was love, it was wonderful!

They kind of skipped and walked quickly to catch up to the Archers. Rev. and Mrs. Archer and Maie headed off to the wagon and Albert turned and saw his sister holding hands with Joe and beaming.

"Well, I can't leave you two alone for two minutes I see. Better not let Mom and Dad catch you holding hands or you will be in deep, you know what."

"I'm sorry Nellie, I shouldn't have put you in that embarrassing position," stammered Joe with a look of pure anguish.

"Nellie is it." teased Albert. "Next you'll be announcing your wedding date, and all this after a couple of hours and a family dinner. I don't know what you said, or what you have Joe, but you sure have stricken my sister and I say, good for you old chap."

"That's enough Albert," Nellie said, "Joe will speak to Father after the service and we'll see what happens. Now you two have benches to set up and I have a choir to select and get ready."

All of a sudden, as if a switch had been thrown, Nellie had changed from a school girl interested in her young man, to the Music Director of a Service of Worship. Joe was impressed with her ability to focus and as much as he wanted to continue to hold her hand – he knew these hands had the work of the Lord to do this evening as they played the organ and led the choir. He would watch those hands with a new feeling in his heart tonight.

Albert had been right; it was a big turn out for the evening service. All the regulars from the Methodist and Anglican Church were in attendance, and a number of the farmers from the area had driven in to witness Rev. Archer and his family lead in worship.

It was amazing how word spread through the community when something good, or unfortunately something bad, happened. In this case people were extolling the preaching and music of this dynamic Preacher and his talented children.

Joe helped packed up the benches and tent into the wagon after the service. The Archers would have a good four hour trip back home and likely wouldn't get in until the wee hours of the morning.

It was Albert's responsibility to hitch up the team and to drive. Joe helped him and took the opportunity to express his appreciation for giving Nellie and himself a few minutes together.

"You're the first lad I have met that I would feel comfortable courting my sister and I look forward to you being my friend." Albert said.

"Albert, when would be a good time to talk with your Father?"

"He's wrapping up with the elders, and he's had two good service with a good offering – I think if you wandered over now he would be in as good a mood as you're ever going to get him."

With that Joe thanked Albert and went directly over to where Rev. Archer was packing up his Bible and Alter cloth.

"Sir," stated Joe, "I'm sorry to bother you when you are so busy, but I would like your permission to court Miss Nellie?" Joe stated with a strong voice that he sure wasn't feeling – in fact his knees felt like they would give out at any time.

Rev. Archer stopped what he was doing and looked down at Joe, "Nellie is still very young Joe and we live a long way from you so courting is going to be very difficult. Listening to your Mother describe your responsibilities to your family at dinner tonight makes me believe that you won't have much free time to court. Saying all this, I would be pleased to see Nellie become involved with someone who is responsible and God fearing. I'm not sure how it's going to work for either of you, but I give you my blessing to spend time with Nellie, appropriately chaperoned of course!"

"Of course Sir!" responded Joe, "and thank you Sir!"

With that, Joe shook Rev. Archer's hand and set off to find Nellie one last time before they headed off home.

Nellie was thanking the ladies of the choir and just turning to walk back to the wagon loading area when she saw Joe coming towards her with a huge smile on his face.

"Your Father has given me permission to spend time with you, appropriately chaperoned of course"

"Of course!" Nellie laughed and once again she held his hand as they sauntered over to the wagon.

"I see Father has given his permission", laughed Albert, "But sis, you haven't asked my permission."

"The day I ask you for permission for anything, will be the day the sun doesn't rise in the morning." Nellie snapped back, yet Joe could tell this was a sister/brother response that was deep in love for each other.

These two had a special relationship. I hope I never come between them thought Joe.

CHAPTER 5

David and Goliath

"So David prevailed over the Philistine with a sling and with a stone, and smote the Philistine, and slew him;..."(KJV)
1 Samuel 17:50

Rev. Archer was prophetic in his proclamation with respect to the amount of time Joe and Nellie would have together.

With distance a factor and Joe's grueling hours at the Boat Yard to get the three boats completed by Sept. 1st, they had very little time to see each other.

They wrote daily professing their love for each other, even if it was only a few lines and Nellie was able to convince her Father to include Port Rowan far more often into their circuit than he should, because of the distance. However, Nellie pointed out that Port Rowan was always a successful service, both in numbers and financially.

The Archers were regulars to the Robins' home when they were in the village giving Joe and Nellie time to see each other – always with Albert, Maie, or Margaret and Will in their company. They tried to make it Albert since he usually found ways to give them a little time to themselves. A special blessing on this friend thought Joe.

The summer was drawing to a close and the boats were going to be completed on time.

Mr. Watts had been pleasantly pleased with the first boat that was finished and had been good as his word and paid in full and advanced on the next boat.

Joe was pleased how the boat had ended up and with the way Will had worked so hard with him to make his scheme a success.

School was going well and Mr. Snodgrass had rearranged his teaching plan to allow Will and Joe to get their work done in school.

What did the future hold for September?

Mr. Snodgrass had brought Joe an article that appeared in the Windsor Star about the need for teachers in the downtown area of Detroit. He suggested to Joe that he apply for one of these positions – he was a natural teacher and this would be like mission work if he was chosen. He could attend University during the summer and take courses at night. This would allow him to earn money for the family and continue his education at the same time.

Joe wrote Nellie about this offer and they agreed she was too young for him to marry and he didn't really know what he wanted to do with his life. He told her, that he knew he didn't want to run the Boat Yard the rest of his life, but maybe teaching was what he was supposed to do. They agreed he would apply for a position and see what the Lord had in store for him. It wouldn't really be much different than how they were getting along now. If he knew what weekends they would be in Port Rowan, he would arrange to come home those weekends and they could have some time together and they always had their letters.

Detroit, USA

For two years Joe taught kids in the inner city of Detroit.

Boy, Detroit sure was different than Port Rowan!

Joe had been to Hamilton a couple of times to visit Nellie, but even Hamilton was a small town compared to Detroit. There seemed to be people everywhere.

His school was a rundown building stuck in the midst of the worst shacks he had ever seen. It was common for kids in his class to share a room with four or five brothers and sisters, sometimes even their parents. Joe had never seen so many people of colour. Over two thirds of his class were black kids, the rest from immigrant families from Ireland and European countries. The kids wore the same clothes all year – whether it was winter or spring. Why they didn't freeze he could never figure out.

He had been met by the Superintendent the day before school and welcomed to the Detroit School Board. He was told he would be paid at the end of each week and would receive 25 cents per day. If he left during a week – he would receive nothing for that week.

He later learned that most teachers only lasted a couple of months and the turn-over of teachers was almost two or three times a year per class. It was no wonder the kids had little respect for the teacher.

Now 25 cents per day wasn't going to make Joe rich, in fact, he would have to find other employment if he was going to have enough money to go back to Port Rowan on a regular basis to meet with Nellie.

He rented a room at the YMCA. It was only 5 cents per day and he was able to work out in the gym. It was here that he saw the advertisement for "Boxers Wanted". The Ad said they would pay $50.00 for any man who could go 8 rounds or could win their fight with a knock-out. Joe thought this could be easy money.

He went down to the gym listed on the notice and signed up.

"Are you kidding boy?" said the gym owner, "these are professional fighters, they will eat you alive."

"Well sir'" said Joe, "we won't know until we try."

"Do you have gloves and shorts?" asked the owner.

"No, but if you won't supply them, maybe I can get them from the YMCA." responded Joe.

"YMCA" the owner cried, "what are you some type of Christian or something?"

"Why yes," replied Joe, "I am a Christian and proud of it! I'm also a teacher and I'm living at the YMCA while I teach at Central Public School."

Well, the owner was totally taken back and wasn't sure he should let Joe fight.

"I'm not sure you should fight young man," said the owner, "It won't look good for my gym if you were killed or maimed while fighting on one of my cards."

"I'll tell you what," said Joe, "I'll gladly sign a waiver clearing you of any responsibility."

"You would have to do that anyway," said the owner, "I'm still not sure."

"Look it," said Joe, "you could bill it as the Gladiator vs. the Christian, I'm sure they would flock out to see the Christian get slain and besides that, I can hold my own with most fighters."

"Have you ever fought before?" asked the owner.

Joe had been concerned he'd be asked this question and didn't believe in lying, yet felt he might be able to stretch the truth a little.

"I have fought many times back in Canada and have never been beaten in and around my home town."

This was all true, and if the owner didn't ask him whether these were professional fights, he would be ok.

The owner kept looking Joe over as if he were a horse in an auction. He almost expected him to grab his jaw and check his teeth.

After what seemed like an incredible length of time, which was likely only a minute or two, the owner nodded his head,

"Ok kid, you're on. Come on back to the office and sign the waivers and I'll loan you a set of shorts and a pair of gloves."

After Joe signed the papers, the owner stuck out his hand, "O'Reilly is the name, Sean O'Reilly. You be at this address," O'Reilly handed Joe a scrap of paper with the address of a Gym about four blocks away, "at 7 pm tomorrow night and I'll have a trainer ready to get you suited up for a 9:00 pm bout against Pete Mahoney. He'll have about 5 pounds on you and 2" but he's the closest fighter I've got to your size and weight. Are you still willing to fight, Joe?"

"Of course Mr. O'Reilly, will I get my $50 that night when I win?"

"Why you're sure a cocky little guy, I'll say that for you. I just hope you won't be hurt to bad." O'Reilly laughingly responded.

Joe left the Gym and headed back to the YMCA.

He climbed the three flights of stairs to his room 310.

His room was big enough for a single bed with a sagging set of springs and mattress, a small desk and a chair. There was a Bible on the desk with the words, 'Property of the Detroit YMCA' written inside the cover. On the back of his door was a wooden peg to hang his clothes. There were no drapes on the windows, but it really didn't matter, for when the window was shut it was so dirty light had trouble penetrating. There was a kerosene lamp on the desk and a box of matches.

Joe had scrounged a wooden crate that had held oranges and made a little bookcase out of it.

His clothes that weren't in use, remained in his suitcase under his bed. It was imperative that he kept his room neat or he wouldn't be able to move in this, his home away from home.

Although there was a hot water rad in his room under the window, it didn't seem to work most of the time frequently causing him to freeze , and during hot weather in spring and fall, he sweltered in this room with no breeze, even with his window open.

He didn't spend much time in the room. He stayed late at school to do his lessons, and spent his free time downstairs in the gym working out, or walking the streets. He really enjoyed going to the Art Gallery and to the Detroit Zoo.

First thing Joe had done when he arrived was find the local Methodist Church and introduced himself to the Pastor, Rev. Oswald Brown.

Rev. Brown was the one that suggested the YMCA as a possible place to stay and he encouraged Joe to take a leadership role with the Senior Boys on Sunday Morning. Joe felt comfortable working with the boys; many had actually attended Central Public but were now out working or hustling to help their families out.

After returning from O'Reilly's gym, Joe went up to his room changed into his T shirt and shorts and went down to the gym and worked for two hours on skipping and the "bag".

After going back up to his room to change he headed over to the Church to talk with Rev. Brown. On his way, he slipped into a greasy spoon and ordered cabbage soup and a piece of bread. The soup was covered with grease and the bread was stale, but if you soaked it in the soup it wasn't too bad and the price was right. He had also ordered a glass of milk, much to the chuckling of those around and it arrived cold and sweet. It tasted great!

He arrived at the Church about 7:00 pm and had a chance to talk with Rev. Brown for about 15 minutes before the evening Bible Study.

"I don't know if you will approve" Joe started to explain, " but I'm short cash and won't be paid by the school for at least a couple of weeks, so I've signed up to fight Pete Mahoney."

"You've done what?" exclaimed Rev. Brown, "Do you have any idea what you have gotten yourself in for? I've read about Mahoney. He'll beat you to a pulp.

Joe, you could really get hurt."

"I appreciate your concern Rev. Brown, but I'm confident I can go 8 rounds with him. I have had some pretty good training back home from Mr. Snodgrass."

"I don't know what to say, Joe? I'm really concerned for your safety!

I was wondering about what scripture we would study tonight, but you've solved this for me. We are going to take a really close look at 1st Samuel Chapter 17."

Joe broke out laughing, "The story of David and Goliath, how appropriate! Maybe I can learn something from this story I can use tomorrow night."

There were about 40 who attended the Bible Study group and when Rev. Brown explained why he had chosen the scripture to study that evening there was a unified gasp from those in attendance and everyone started to talk at once. Rev. Brown quickly regained control of the group and explained, "I have already tried to talk Joe out of this folly, but he assures me he has a good chance to be successful and has given his word to the promoter he will there tomorrow night. I think all we can do for Joe is pray for him and spend some time looking at another who took on huge odds and was successful. Let's read 1st Samuel and see how David defeated the Philistines."

The group really became excited about the story they had heard so often and seemed so improbable.

Rev. Lewis explained how armies would move and the concept of champions went back to the time of the Greeks.

As they explored the story in more depth they were amazed that a Shepherd, could have the nerve to speak to a King, the nerve to offer to fight a warrior that no other Israelite would accept the challenge and finally how Saul responded to David:

> *1 Samuel 17:33*
> *"And Saul said to David, Thou art not able to go against this Philistine to fight with him: for thou [art but] a youth, and he a man of war from his youth." (KJV)*

Why, the group realized, this is how they had reacted to Joe when they heard he was fighting Mahoney. They couldn't get over the similarity of the situation.

At this point Joe jumped in, "Remember what David did? He was clad in armor, which he was unfamiliar with, took it off and chose five smooth pebbles from a stream and placed them in his Shepherd pouch. Already he knew what he was going to do. He was going to allow the Giant to become too self-confident, then attack him at the one point he was not protected and with an instrument of war, that most wouldn't consider to be a true weapon. This gives me an idea of how I'm going to fight Mahoney tomorrow night. I'm not sure I'll be as lucky as David and not receive any direct hits, but, I do think I know how I can defeat him."

Again, the room was a buzz and Rev. Brown had to restore order.

"Joe" asked Rev. Brown, "will you share your idea with us?"

"On Sunday, I'll be glad to share my idea with you, if I'm still able to attend worship the day after my fight. But for now, I think I better keep it to myself and work through how it will work. In fact, I'll be spending most of tomorrow working this idea out. But I want to thank you all for your support and for sharing this great Bible Story with me. We'll see on Sunday if I learned enough to put it to the test and succeed."

With that, Rev. Brown closed the meeting with prayer, which included a special prayer asking the Lord to protect their brother Joseph.

The individuals in the group wished him well. At least the men present did, the women expressed their concern about his safety and hoped he wouldn't be too hurt.

Back in his room, Joe lit his lantern and got out his own Bible from his suitcase. It was well used and felt comfortable in his right hand as he turned the pages with his left. He knew there wasn't any difference as far as the words were concerned from the Bible on the desk that had the inscription "Property of the Detroit YMCA", yet his bible was like an old friend.

He flipped to 1st Samuel 17:49-50 and read the following:

> *"And David put his hand in his bag, and took thence a stone, and slang [it], and smote the Philistine in his forehead, that the stone sunk into his forehead; and he fell upon his face to the earth. So David prevailed over the Philistine with a sling and with a stone, and smote the Philistine, and slew him; but [there was] no sword in the hand of David."(KJV)*

He read these verses ten or twelve times.

Yes, he knew what he had to do in the morning to prepare himself for his fight that night!

Joe went over to the desk and sat down. He wrote his daily letter to Nellie. Of course he didn't mention the up-coming fight, but he did make mention about the Bible Study that night and how Rev. Brown had made the scriptures come alive for him and provided some answers to challenges he had ahead of him. Nellie could assume these challenges were about his new teaching job – but he sure wasn't going to tell her about his fighting career. 'Career', listen to him. He hadn't even competed in one fight yet and he was talking about a career. Maybe Mr. O'Reilly was right? He was just a cocky kid! No, he was sure he had the answer to this challenge and tomorrow he would know if his strategy would work.

Joe blew the lantern out and climbed into bed, said his prayers remembering his Mother, Will and Margaret and of course his Nel! Then he turned over and slept soundly.

In the morning Joe went down to the room that was used for communal eating and had a bowl of porridge and a glass of milk then headed down to the gym. He went over to the workout bag that hung suspended by a large rope from a rafter in the ceiling. The bag was full of sand.

Joe went over to the shelf that held the boxing equipment and took down a pair of well worn gloves, but they fit him comfortably, even if the rawhide was almost worn off the surface of the gloves and there were holes in the palm from sweat and usage.

Joe thought to himself, David picked up five smooth stones that fitted his sling-shot well. In fact David had only needed one and if that one hadn't been successful, David likely wouldn't have had an opportunity to load a second, he thought.

What had been the weapon that killed Goliath? Not the stone, but surprise and hitting the one vulnerable spot on the Giant, his exposed forehead.

Now Joe stationed himself before the bag. He was left handed.

When he normally worked the bag he would have his right foot forward and bounce back on his left foot for balance. He would jab with his right hand and keep his left hand back for the "big punch". Keep his chin tucked in to his left shoulder. In a matter of a few hours he had to relearn years of practice. His big secret was going to be his left hand.

He had to feel comfortable boxing as if he was a right handed boxer, which most boxers are. He had to learn to jab with his left hand hold his right hand for the "Big Blow", then quickly shift his weight and jab once with his right and hammer with his left. This must be quick and it must be smooth. If he stumbled, or lost his balance, Mahoney would knock him flatter than a pancake and the match would be over. In fact, he'll likely be picking his teeth up off the ground.

Joe spent the next four hours working out. Setting up as a right handed boxer and making the shift to left without tripping over his feet. At the end of this training session he felt pretty good about his chances of making it work.

He cooled down with skipping for 30 minutes then went up to his room after picking up a washcloth and towel he sponged himself down and changed into a clean shirt and work pants. He tied the laces of his canvass shoes together, threw them over his shoulder and packed a fresh T shirt and his shorts in a paper bag.

On his way out, he stopped at the kitchen and talked the cook out of a slice of bread with fresh strawberry jam on it. She had heard he was fighting tonight and had packed him an apple and a meat sandwich to take with him. How she heard, he never did find out.

However, the whole YMCA was abuzz about his fight and people kept coming up to him and wishing him luck. A number asked him if he had any tickets for the fight tonight. To this he answered, "Just one, mine, want to take my place?"

This usually cut off the conversation pretty quick.

Joe thanked the cook for the piece of bread, the apple and sandwich.

He headed off to a park that was only a couple of blocks from the gym that was hosting the fight.

It was a perfect day with the sun shining and a light breeze. He sat under a big maple tree and leaned his back against the trunk and watched the clouds pushed by the wind and the people walk by.

He kept saying over and over again the scripture he had read last night.

> 1st Samuel 17:49-50
> "And David put his hand in his bag, and took thence a stone, and slang [it], and smote the Philistine in his forehead, that the stone sunk into his forehead; and he fell upon his face to the earth. So David prevailed over the Philistine with a sling and with a stone, and smote the Philistine, and slew him; but [there was] no sword in the hand of David."(KJV)

After a while he asked himself, have I missed something?

And then it came to him, surprise was essential, but David had hit a spot that was not covered by armor. He knew nothing about his opponent except he was 5 lbs heavier then him and would have a reach that was 2 to 5 inches longer than his.

How was he going to find a vulnerable spot for his left fist to hit?

He also knew that Mahoney was a professional fighter with a number of fights under his belt. He could assume that Mahoney knew how to protect his chin and likely a body blow wasn't going to do much damage in the short run. If he had to go more than one round with this guy, kidney jabs could wear him down, but it would also leave Joe open for a shot to the chin. No, he had to be like David and be successful right in the first round. Once he had shown his secret weapon, then Mahoney would adjust and Joe didn't know if he could last 8 two minute rounds with someone that knew what he was doing.

Where was the fighter vulnerable?

Then it came to Joe. David had hit the forehead and the force of the sling shot had allowed the stone to penetrate the forehead and had killed Goliath. If he hit the forehead with his glove it would just sting him. However, if he could get a good left hook to the temple, he was certain that his man would go down. It had to be above the eye about 1 inch and right on the soft spot of the temple.

What were his chances of hitting this spot right with a man who is weaving and dancing?

Likely not good, but it was all he had.

With this worked out, Joe felt hungry and opened his bag and brought out his sandwich made of extra thick cut bread, covered with molasses, lettuce (they never got lettuce) and a big slice of meatloaf. This was a meal fit for a man's last supper. Was this what the cook thought?

He ate the sandwich slowly, enjoying the taste and chewing carefully. He didn't want to have cramps before he fought.

He finished with his apple, which was crisp and sweet.

He pulled out his pocket watch and noted it was 6:45 pm. Where had the afternoon gone?

He got up and started towards the gym. He rounded the corner at the gym, he was startled to see a long line of men and older boys lined up before the door of the gym. There had to be nearly 100 in the line.

As Joe started to pass the men in the line, they started to swear at him and tell him to go the back of the line.

"I'm fighting tonight" he said to the laughs of those around him. They started to push at him, when all of a sudden O'Reilly appear and pushed the crowd back and took Joe by the arm and escorted him into the gym.

"Just about lost you out there" said O'Reilly, "couldn't let that happen, don't have another fighter for Mahoney and I would have a riot on my hands if I didn't have a full bill."

"Well Mr. O'Reilly, I hope you have something to fill in the time, because my fight will be over in the first round and I would like my $50.00 when I leave the gym."

O'Reilly just about doubled over with laughter and asked Joe, "Where do you want your body sent after Mahoney is through with you?"

Joe looked around, there was a ring in the middle of the room and he couldn't see how all those outside were going to fit into the space around the ring.

Joe looked at O'Reilly and said, "Where do I change?"

"Right over here," he pointed to a door off the main room.

Joe went through the door followed by O'Reilly.

"Jack, come over here and meet the lad I was telling you about." said O'Reilly

An older black man sauntered over and held his hand out to Joe.

"KO is my name" said the black man.

"Joe Robins" Joe responded as he shook KO's hand.

"What does KO stand for?" asked Joe

"Got it when I used to fight. I was Knocked Out so many times they started to call me KO." he said with a chuckle in his voice.

"KO, you know that's not true. Joe, when KO was a young man HE knocked out so many that his nickname became KO." retorted O'Reilly.

"Well Sir," said KO, "them days are gone, now it's young chaps like you that are going to make your name. Let's get you dressed Mr. Robins."

"Just call me Joe"

"Yes Sir, Mr. Joe." replied KO, "Mr. O'Reilly has left gloves and shorts for you all."

"KO, I've brought my own T shirt, shorts, gloves and shoes. Do I have to wear this gear that's provided?"

"You can't wear a T Shirt, Mr. Joe, have to bare-chested, them's the rules. I guess you could wear your own stuff, no rule against it, but you won't look too pretty in that get-up. Not sure Mr. O'Reilly is going to be too pleased."

"Well, KO, that's just to bad for Mr. O'Reilly. I came to fight, not put on a fashion show."

"Yes sir Mr. Joe, but them gloves are in pretty bad shape, are you sure you don't want to wear these nice new ones that are here?"

"I wouldn't want to get them all bloodied up KO."

"No Sir, Mr. Joe, I can see what you mean. Why don't you get them shorts and shoes on then I'll wrap your hands."

Joe quickly changed into his shorts and shoes and sat down while KO began to wrap his hands. It was obvious that KO had done this task a thousand times.

"How do want your hands to feel in the gloves, Mr. Joe?"

"I want them snug, but not padded. I want to feel the gloves."

"I know's what you mean Mr. Joe. That's how I use to like my hands in my gloves. Wanted the gloves to feel as if they was part of me. A lot of boxers are scared they are going to hurt their hands and put on so much wrap that it must feel like they is hitting with a pillow. Don't know how they can fight like that." KO talked on. Joe was aware that KO was trying to put Joe at ease and was filling in time before he would be called in the Ring.

"It's alright KO, I'm feeling good. Just need a few minutes to get my head into the task before me."

"Yes Sir Mr. Joe, I be quiet now and sit over there." He pointed to a bench beside the door and kind of followed his finger over to the bench and sat down. He stared at the floor with folded hands, yet had Joe in his sight, just in case "his" fighter needed anything.

Joe sat and went through the first 2 minutes of the fight in his head. It was imperative he stay away from Mahoney's jab and his right hook.

Joe looked up to KO, "Tell me KO, have you seen Mahoney fight?"

"Oh sure, a number of times."

"What's his right hook like?" asked Joe

"He's got a good hook, tends to come up aiming for the chin. If he catches you – that will be the end."

Joe nodded and looked down at the floor.

Remember, a few jabs, change your footing and then aim at the sweet spot on the temple.

The time had come and a gym rat came in to tell KO to get Joe into the ring.

KO came over and helped Joe to his feet. He rubbed his shoulders and his arms, then he rubbed them

again with an oil that made his pale white skin shine.

"Come on Mr. Joe, your fans are waiting." Said KO.

Joe came out of the little room where he had changed and was amazed at the number of men who were squeezed into the gym. He could hardly see or breathe for that matter with the haze of cigar smoke that lingered in the confined quarters.

KO had his hand on his shoulder and pushed him through the crowd. The comments around him weren't very flattering. In fact the crowd was dumping on Joe something fierce. Joe was concerned he might have to fight his way out of this place, if a riot broke out. Never mind his scheduled fight in the ring.

He felt the grip on his shoulder tighten as KO pushed him on and knew he was in good hands – KO's and God's.

They at last made it to the ring.

His opponent was already in the ring dressed in a gold satin robe with his name, "Mahoney", across the back, gold boxing trunks and black laced boxing shoes that went almost to his knees

O'Reilly had said this guy was about 5 lbs heavier, try 20 to 30lbs and about 2" higher, again try 4". This man was Joe's Goliath without a doubt!

KO lifted the ropes and Joe climbed into the ring and went to the corner opposite Mahoney.

At this point the bell rang four or five times and the noise dropped to a dull roar.

O'Reilly went to the centre of the ring and introduced the fighters.

Wearing gold trunks, from Boston, Massachusetts having won 35 professional fights and his last 10 fights locally by KOs I'm pleased to welcome back "Killer Mahoney. " the crowd went wild yelling their support of their recent hero.

The bell rang again – about 10 times before O'Reilly could make his voice heard over the noise.

"In the red corner, is Joe Robins from Port Rowan, Canada. Robins known as the Professor is one of Canada's best known boxers. We're pleased to have our neighbour from across the river join us tonight." At his point O'Reilly gave up as the boos and insults drowned him out. So much for neighbourly love! Here in this gym it was what have you done for me today – and how much money did I make on you."

O'Reilly called both fighters to the centre of the ring and told them he wanted a clean fight and to stop the clinches, eye scrounging, and rabbit chops behind the neck when he told them. Once a man was down, the other must go to a neutral corner. The count would be 10. It would be a 10 round fight and to be paid a fighter must go 8 rounds for $20 and $50 for a Knock Out.

"This will be the fastest $50 I've ever made" said Mahoney as he hit Joe's gloves and went back to his corner.

Joe went backed to his corner. He didn't trust either O'Reilly or Mahoney. KO sat him down and worked

his shoulders until they felt like they were going to fall off.

Clang, Clang!

Joe stood and KO took his stool and towel and climbed out of the ring.

"Don't get hurt, Mr. Joe" KO's voice rang in Joe's ears and was the last intelligent thing he remembered hearing.

Joe quickly positioned himself into his defensive position. He had almost set himself as a left handed fighter out of years of habit. However, Joe did get himself set up with his left hand jabbing out and right tucked under his chin.

Mahoney was really trying to make his words to Joe come true. His jabs were hurting his right biceps and he already had landed a couple of kidney shots that really hurt. When Joe had ducked down from the kidney shot, Mahoney had thrown his right hook aimed right for Joe's chin. Thanks to KO's word of advice, Joe had quickly danced back and deflected that shot.

However, Mahoney was stretched out and his left guard was down.

Joe quickly changed his footing as he was bouncing back, used his right hand to deflect the right hook and in doing so, caused Mahoney to continue to pass by him on his right side in order to get his balance.

Joe knew this was it. He had one chance and he better land it right.

With all his weight behind his hook, Joe threw his left, aimed at Mahoney's temple and although Mahoney was moving the same direction as the punch, Joe connected with a hook that caused his elbow to sting like being jabbed with a knitting needle.

Joe knew this had to be the hit that ended the bout, because it would take about 15 minutes for him to get any feeling back into his left arm and Mahoney wouldn't make this mistake twice.

The room went deathly quiet and Mahoney's eyes rolled up under his eyelids, and he continued to be carried to the right by the force of the hit and collapsed down to the floor with a bang.

Mahoney didn't move or make a sound!

Joe was concerned he had killed him. Hadn't David killed Goliath? Joe didn't want to kill anyone, he just wanted to make $50.

The room went crazy cheering for Joe. Just seconds ago, this same crowd was booing him. What have you done for me lately, ran through Joe's head?

O'Reilly quickly went over to look at Mahoney and spoke in his ear. There was no response. O'Reilly stood up and walked over to Joe and raised his left hand over his head and declared him the winner.

KO was already beside Joe and had a towel around his shoulder and was pounding him on the back yelling his congratulations over the noise.

"Is he alright?" Joe cried into O'Reilly's ear as he was being lead out of the ring.

"You wrung his bell kid, but, he'll be fine when he wakes up. Likely won't know where he's been for the last few hours, but he'll be fine.

Eh, you didn't tell me you were left handed," said O'Reilly.

"You didn't ask," responded Joe.

Back in the room Joe started to feel the effects of Mahoney's shots. He was hurting. It was a good thing that he had that opportunity when he did. A few more hits like Joe had taken and he wouldn't have been able to land his left. He just wouldn't have had the strength.

KO helped Joe to get his gloves off and toweled him down. Joe changed to his street clothes and packed his boxing duds into his bag and started to look around for O'Reilly and his $50.00.

Joe was being mobbed by spectators that were now his best friend, wanting to give him a cigar or a drink from their bottle. Joe turned all this down politely and then spotted O'Reilly over by the door. As he approached O'Reilly, put his hand into his trouser pants and pulled out a bundle of bills. He counted off five $10s and gave them to Joe and asked if he wanted to fight tomorrow night?

Joe took the five $10s and called KO over and gave him a $10 bill.

"Mr. Joe, just give me $1, I didn't take them blows, that was you Mr. Joe."

"KO, I was honoured to have a professional in my corner and I believe in paying professional fees for good support and work," with this Joe turned and headed through the door, "I'll let you know when I'm ready for another bout" called Joe over his shoulder as he headed back to his room at the YMCA.

Once he was out of sight Joe slowed down and allowed the pain to have an effect on how he walked back the four blocks to room.

As he entered the YMCA, he looked at the three flights of stairs to his room and wondered if he would ever make it to the third floor and his room.

He gritted his teeth, grabbed onto the railing and pulled himself stair by stair up to his floor. Once he made it to the third floor, he used the wall to hold himself up as he made it to his room.

Once in his room, Joe slowing and painfully lowered himself onto the bed. As he wriggled his body to find a position that hurt least, Joe realized he was exhausted.

When he woke up, 12 hours later, Joe was hungry and as he moved, he remembered he also hurt, but nowhere as much as last night. This morning, almost afternoon, he was sore all over but it was bearable.

Joe went down to the kitchen area and was greeted as a local hero. Everyone he met on the way down and in the common room seemed to know he had won his fight last night and eagerly extended their congratulations.

Cook offered him a special omelet as her way of showing her appreciation.

Joe slowly and carefully lowered himself in to his chair. A small crowd gathered around as he tried to have his breakfast.

Cook came into the room with orange juice, his omelet and toast and jam. She immediately cleared the room with her stern, in-control voice.

Once the room was just the two of them, she turned to Joe, "Well young man, you've certainly made a name for yourself rather quickly."

"Cookie, I just needed some quick cash, and boxing is something I know a little something about. But you know Cookie, I would not have been successful last night if it hadn't been for Rev. Brown and my Bible Study Group."

"What do you mean?" inquired Cookie.

"I told Rev. Brown about my fight and he used the story of David and Goliath as the scripture for the Bible Study group that evening. We spent time exploring how David was successful over a giant like Goliath and I used this information to develop my strategy for my fight last night. Like David, I had one chance to be successful and thank goodness it worked. Although I have to tell you that I sure know I was in a fight. Mahoney maybe didn't win, but I can assure you that I will remember the man for a number of days. I think every bone in my body was shaken up and bruised last night. But I have to tell you, it was all worth it for this breakfast. This is great! Thank You!"

Cookie was not used to complements and just shrugged them off.

'Awe, it's nothing. What are you going to do now, continue fighting?"

"Not if I can help it Cookie. I have a contract to start teaching at Central Public School tomorrow and have a meeting with the Superintendent at 3:00 pm today."

"Well I never, a teacher. You might need those boxing skills with the little ruffians you'll be teaching. Them is hard core street kids. The boss tries to get them into the programs, but he hasn't been very successful at this point. A few kids come to the gym for basketball but most of the kids just make fun of him."

"I'll see if I can't reinforce the YMCA's programs at the school, once I have been there a while," responded Joe and again he thanked Cookie for the special breakfast and made his way out of the building into the beautiful late summer day.

Chapter 6

Slate and Chalk

"Now about the midst of the feast Jesus went up into the temple, and taught."(KJV) John 7:14

At 3 pm, Joe entered Central Public School through the doors with the words "BOYS" chiseled in stone over the door.

Although the windows of the classrooms appeared large from the street and there were windows in the doors, the hallway was dark and dingy.

Joe headed down the hall to a door with a wooden sign "OFFICE". He opened the door and stepped into a small room with a large wooden desk. Behind it, seated on a wooden chair an older woman with her hair in a bun, her spectacles at the end of her nose, looked up over the spectacles and in a voice that suited her asked, "What can I do for you, Sir?"

"My name is Joseph Robins and I have an appointment with Superintendent Smythe."

"Of course Mr. Robins," she responded in a manner only school officials can really achieve. It made you feel you had done something wrong, even when you knew you hadn't.

"Superintendent Smythe is waiting for you in the Principal's Office. Just go out the door and turn right – down two rooms, you'll see the sign on the door."

The Principal's Office! He hadn't been in the school for five minutes and he was off to the Principal's Office!

Joe thanked the lady and headed out of the office, turned right and just as she said, he was in front of a door marked, "Principal's Office". He knocked and was invited in.

There were two men in the office. The man behind the desk was an over-weight, man in his forties, wearing a dark, wrinkled suit and a stained shirt. Both the shirt and suit looked like the buttons might pop at any moment.

The other man was small in stature, in his fifties, well groomed with an expensive wool suit with vest and a pocket watch in his right vest pocket held in place with a gold chain and watch fob. He had a neat salt and pepper beard and looked like a person in charge.

Joe turned to this latter person and inquired, "Superintendent Smythe?"

"Mr. Robins, how punctual, it is a pleasure to meet you. May I take this opportunity to introduce Mr. Gleeson, the school Principal here at Central Public School, and my Brother-in-Law."

Joe quickly took the measure of both men. Smythe impressed him. Gleeson looked like a disaster ready to happen.

Joe acknowledged the introductions and seated himself on the chair indicated by Superintendent Smythe.

Smythe went on to explain that the teaching position Joe was being hired for, was a grade 7/8 class. He explained that as the children got to the last two years of their Public School, they started to leave school, the girls to help out at home and the boys to find work to help pay the bills or more likely to pay for their pa's booze.

It was very obvious that Smythe didn't have a high regard for this school or the children that attended and he certainly didn't have any respect or empathy for the parents of the children.

Principal Gleeson, just sat there with his hands clasped across his protruding belly, as if he was holding it in from exploding and shook his head in agreement with his brother-in-laws comments. Joe wondered if he could speak for himself?

Smythe went on at length about the type of children, or kids, as Smythe referred to them

Joe would be teaching and he indicated he knew this was Joe's first teaching position, however, he was the only male teacher on staff and to hold discipline with these "kids", they needed a strong male. Did he feel he cold control a class of 25 "kids" ready to take on the world?

Joe assured him that he was ready and looked forward to the opportunity.

Gleeson spoke, for the first time in five minutes, "Mr. Robins, your class will be beside my office and I do not tolerate noise well. I expect you to have complete silence in your class at all times."

Joe was caught off guard by such a request but it didn't take him long to formulate a retort.

"Mr. Gleeson, my job is to teach these children and I believe that involved, happy children learn much better than fearful children. I'm sure that as Principal, you must be out of your office on a regular basis as you perform your most important role as leader and role model for the children of this school. I'm sure we will work out an agreeable compromise with respect to noise and learning."

Joe caught Mr. Smythe grinning out of the corner of his eye, as he watched his brother-in-law pump himself up even more with respect to the comments of Gleeson's leadership and role model roles. If only this was true, wished Smythe! His brother-in-law was a family disgrace and he had given him this position as a favour to his sister who he loved very much. Smythe had decided that Gleeson couldn't do any worse than the last Principal and if he actually improved scholastic levels at the school, who knows, maybe he could work his way towards a better school. However the latter, much as Smythe had anticipated, had not happened. Central was still the worst school in the system and Gleeson wasn't doing much, if anything to turn this around. Maybe this young Robins was just what the doctor ordered.

Smythe stood and Joe and Gleeson quickly followed his lead. He then went over to the door and opened it and invited Joe and Gleeson to follow him to Joe's classroom, which was as Gleeson had said, right next door.

As they entered the room, Joe observed the 5 straight rows of wooden desks and his mind flashed back to his one room school in Port Rowan and Mr. Snodgrove sitting at the front of the class, smiling at Joe and telling him he could do this.

Smythe handed Joe a piece of paper, which was his teaching contract, indicating that he was to be at school by 8 am and stay until 4 pm and teach grades 7 and 8 at Central Public School. He was an employee of the Detroit Board of Education and he would be paid $5 weekly, but he must finish the week to be paid. Further, he was not paid for any days he missed or for any extra assignments he might take on.

When Joe signed this contact, both Smythe and Gleeson shook his hand and left him in his classroom with a Teacher Lesson Book Gleeson gave him.

"I'll see you tomorrow at 8:00 am for the first day of classes," said Gleeson with a lack of enthusiasm. It was almost as if he was dreading it and he likely was.

Joe had been given no training, just a Teacher's Manual that had the lesson for the day and a few suggestions for books to read at different grade levels.

Joe left the school and went to the local library which was around the corner and became a member for 25 cents.

He was told by the lady behind the desk, who could have been a sister of the lady in the school office that the library would be closing in half an hour.

Joe quickly found the books he needed, signed out and headed off to his room at the YMCA to prepare for his first day of school.

It didn't take long for the children to test him. He quickly and effectively established discipline in his class, especially when the word was out that he was a professional boxer.

CHAPTER 7

Young Minds

*"But Jesus said, Suffer little children, and forbid them not, to come
unto me: for of such is the kingdom of heaven." (KJV)*
Matthew 19:14

With a start Joe woke up, freezing cold. He had kicked the blankets
off himself when he was hot with the fever. Now he was shaking with
chills.

He had been dreaming. How did he get from Detroit to this barren frozen
foothill of the Rockies?

He checked his pocket-watch, it was only 12:30 am. He was sure he'd
been asleep for at least 8 hours. How could he have dreamed so much in
such a short period of time?

They say that your life flashes before you just before you die. Was he going to die?

Well at least his life wasn't flashing by, it had taken three hours to get
this far.

He had another four hours before day break. If this storm didn't let up,
he didn't know if he could drag himself the remaining miles back to town.
He wasn't even sure how far that was!

The fire had died down and needed restocking. He slowly got himself up with a blanket still over his shoulder; shaking so hard it was hard to get his hands to grasp the piece of wood that needed to be placed in the fire.

The wind was still howling and the snow blowing in funnels around the fire.

Joe poured himself a cup of tea and added lots of sugar. It was hot warming his hands and his inners, all at the same time.

Joe got a couple of stones that had materialized as the fire burnt down and placed them against his back as he snuggled into his blankets. The heat from the stones was soothing and slowly Joe stopped shaking, but the sweating started again on his forehead.

He definitely was ill!

His eyelids were so heavy.

He was back at Central School.

It was the first day of class and as the children arrived, excited about having a new teacher, Joe quickly realized that this was not Port Rowan!

About two thirds of the class was made up of black children and most of the others had names he could hardly pronounce: Starvinsky, Goldstien, Mattuwich, Von Glauss.

The boys looked as surly and fed-up as one could imagine. For a couple of them, it was school or the prison. They looked like they might have made the wrong decision

Yes this was going to be a challenging year.

Joe wrote his name on the Slate with a squeaking chalk. It made a shudder run up and down his back and caused most of the girls to scream.

In a matter of seconds, Principal Gleeson came crashing through the door and demanded to know what was the trouble.

"Trouble?" Joe expressed with a whimsical response, "No trouble Principal Gleeson, we were just practicing our singing and I admit we have a little work to make it more harmonious."

Gleeson didn't know what to make of this young man. The children sat quiet, hands folded and with eyes that seemed ready to pop out of their heads.

"Remember Mr. Robins, I expect quiet at all times from this class." Gleeson stated with a look that implied, "you better follow my orders."

Joe looked back without causing his eyes to move from Gleeson's, "We shall do our best to accommodate you Sir, but as we discussed yesterday, I am here to help the children learn and where that will lead, or where that will end, or how loud that shall sound will depend upon the adventure we are about to jointly engage upon over the next few months. I know you wish us well in that adventure. Now children, I would like you to stand and say good morning to Principal Gleeson."

There was a rustle of feet and banging of desk tops as all the children stood and in unison responded, "Good Morning, Principal Gleeson." Then they all sat down and watched their Teacher. Something big was happening here and they weren't sure what it was, but they felt like Mr. Robins had just fought and won a battle for them. It was only five minutes into the new school year! This was going to be a really interesting year, if Mr. Robins stayed past the first week.

"Good morning children and remember, keep the noise down!" With that, Gleeson left the room knowing he had just been put in his place by this young upstart of a teacher. He better mind his Ps and Qs or he won't end the week!

Joe turned back to the class, "Thank you for getting up and saying good morning to Principal Gleeson. I'm sorry for the noise that piece of chalk made. I should have had it on more of a slant.

Does anyone know why it made that terrible noise?" a teaching moment Joe thought to himself.

One of the larger boys, Joe looked to find his name on his seating plan, "Jim", had put up his hand.

"Yes, Jim" Joe said

"Would it have anything to do with the point of the chalk Sir?"

"Why yes Jim, that is exactly what happened. The point is sharp and a small surface. It's difficult for me to keep it from flipping back and forth, causing the point to catch the slate and to vibrate causing the unpleasant noise we just experienced. That was a very good observation Jim."

Jim never received many compliments at school, and never any at home. He broke out in a grin that seemed to encompass his whole face.

This teacher was going to be OK as far as Jim was concerned and nobody better mess with him, including Principal Gleeson.

The Classroom

The class numbered more girls than boys, about three to one.

As Superintendent Smythe had said, the boys tended leave school when they reached grade 7 and 8 to help support their family.

Those that remained were young men who were good at school or had parents who had jobs.

Joe had decided to have a short test for everyone, which was on a short story he had written on the black board and asked them to write out the answers to the four questions about the story.

He also had put a sample of adding, subtracting, multiplying and dividing on the black board.

When he gave out the paper out for the class to do their work on there was a lot of talk back to him that he wasn't expecting.

Joe went to the front of the class and turned to face the group.

"All right!" Joe shouted and slammed a book down on his desk. The class became instantly quiet, "I'm not testing you, I am trying to find out where we should begin our learning journey this year.

Learning should be fun, but it is absolutely no fun if I develop a learning plan that is too hard for you. I want you to read the story on the blackboard and put the answer the questions on the paper I just gave you. If you're unable to answer a question I want you to put a question mark after the question number.

When you're finished I want you to copy the math questions that are on the black board on to your sheet and enter the answers. This should take you about 15 minutes. Please start now."

There was a rustle of paper and feet as the young people settled in and started to work on the assignment.

Joe sat at his desk and watched his students. He had a master seating plan and he jotted down comments about students he saw struggling to read the story. He observed students that were sounding out words, reading with their lips and one or two with an obvious blank look on their face unable to read the story at all.

Joe asked the students to make sure their names were on the papers and collected them.

Then to the surprise of the class he announced they were going on a field trip. He told them they would need a piece of paper and a pencil and their coats.

Before they left the classroom he assigned each person a partner and told the class that it was the responsibility of each of them to know were their partner was at all times. If he asked for a check and a person didn't know where their partner was – the field trip would be ended right there and they would return to their classroom.

Now Joe hadn't asked Mr. Gleeson about leaving the school and he decided that if this was going to work, the class would have to help him.

"Quiet!" Joe said as he stood before the closed door leading into the hall.

A unsettled quiet fell over the group.

"Listen up! Mr. Gleeson made it very clear that he didn't want to hear noise from this class. If you want to go on this field trip, it is imperative, that is, very important that no one talk as we leave the building. I want you to walk as quietly as possible. No dragging your shoes or shuffling along the floor.

Can we do this?"

There was a resounding "yes!"

Joe once again regained quiet then he opened the door and started the class out into the hall.

They were great! – not a noise as they went down the hall and out the of the building.

Once on the playground, Joe gathered the class around him and reminded them the importance of knowing where their partner was at all times.

He then informed them that they were going down the street to a Grocery Store and a Deli Store and he wanted the following information.

The cost of the following items:

Group one –   how much was bread at each location
Group two –   cost of sliced baloney
Group three –   cost of butter
Group four –   cost of apples
Group five –   cost of milk
Group six –   cost of lettuce
Group seven –   cost of mustard
Group eight -   cost of bananas
Group nine -   cost of smoked meat
Group ten -   cost of apple juice

Joe then divided the group in two having one go to the first store and the second group to the second store – once they had their information they were to change stores – but not until the other group had left the store.

He then divided each group into ten teams with each team responsible for finding the price of a specific food item as listed above.

When they were finished they were to gather under a large maple tree in the school yard.

Off they went and in about 15 minutes they all gathered back under the tree.

Joe did a quick check and they were all there! Thank goodness!

"What did you find out?" Joe asked

"Prices were different."

"The deli was higher."

"Not for meat."

And on and on the discussion flowed.

Joe then tried to pull this together by suggesting that stores that specialize in certain types of food, tend to have prices lower than a General Store. He also pointed out that it was important to compare before you buy – especially if money was in short supply. The class laughed at this comment.

Joe then set the class a project of developing a lunch for the whole class.

Group one was asked to figure out how many loaves of bread would be needed to make a sandwich for everyone and how much it would cost.

Each group was asked the same question.

By the time they were finished their math and decision process was challenged; (could you really get 10 slices out of one loaf of bread?) they didn't even realize they were doing a school assignment!

The class decided that baloney, with lettuce, mustard sandwich, a glass of milk and an apple was the cheapest lunch that could be shared by all for a cost of eight cents.

Therefore the cost of lunch for twenty was going to be $1.16

Joe gave each team the money needed to buy their ingredients and sent them back to the store to purchase their item at the best price they could negotiate.

When they all re-assembled, Joe led them back into the school with his warning about being quiet.

However, the children were excited about their project and weren't as quiet as they had been going out.

The last group of students were entering the classroom when Mr. Gleeson came bounding out of his office.

"Mr. Robins! What is all this noise and what is going on out here?"

"Ah, Mr. Gleeson, we were just outside for a few minutes to get some fresh air. I'm sorry we disturbed you from your important work. I must get back to the class right away or they will become unruly and we wouldn't want that would we?" with that Joe entered the classroom and closed the door behind him, leaving Gleeson gasping for a retort, looking like the buttons on his vest were going to pop at any moment.

Joe went to the front of the class and quickly had their attention.

He then asked a couple of the students to pull their desks together and clean them off so they would have a work area.

At breakfast, Joe had persuaded Cookie to loan him a bread knife (he told her he needed it for self protection from his school kids), and then he set them up in an assembly line, bread cutters, butter spreaders, mustard adders, lettuce appliers, meat stuffers, sandwich assemblers, sandwich cutters (more than one student offered their knife for this task!), apple polisher, and milk pourers.

After all the work was completed, Joe asked the class to bow their heads and he offered a short grace thanking God for the food and the class for their preparation. After that, they had their lunch and didn't realize that they had just had a math lesson and a reading lesson, plus a learning experience on how to work together.

It had been a very successful morning! Even if it meant that Joe had taught for the day for nothing, since the lunch had cost him more than one day's pay.

It was obvious from the way some of the kids were eating, that this was the best meal they had had for sometime. It was worth it!

How could he do this more often? He sure couldn't afford to work for nothing!

During lunch, Joe started talking with the children and asked how many had brought a lunch. About five indicated that they had something to eat.

Joe found out that one of the children's parents ran a Bakery and another had a Deli.

Joe realized that he couldn't ask each child to bring money in each day for lunch – many of the families just didn't have anything to offer and he wasn't going to embarrass any child or make coming to school uncomfortable.

He wondered if there was a product they could make and sell and use the money to buy the basics for making a lunch.

One of his students, Billy, indicated that his father worked at a hide curing plant.

All of sudden Joe had an idea he would follow-up that evening.

The rest of the day went well and the students worked hard on their assignments and left happy at 4:00 pm.

After supper, Joe wandered over to Billy's home, which was a flat on the third floor of a wooden walk-up, a fire trap waiting for a fire to happen.

Joe knocked on the door and could hear parents screaming at kids from all over the building and crying and fighting of children from behind the door his knuckles had just wrapped on.

The door was partly opened by a woman who looked fifty, but was likely only in her late twenties, with a baby hanging on her hip.

"Mrs. O'Mallory? Joe Robins, Billy's teacher, may I come in?"

"O my God, is Billy in trouble already? Billy, you come right here!" she screeched as she opened the door wider to allow Joe to enter.

The place was a disaster – dirty dishes on the table, the smell of cigarette smoke hung over the whole place. Clothes were everywhere and children were running around fighting each other.

Mrs. O'Mallory quickly knocked a pile of clothes off the wooden chair and offered it to Joe.

Joe refused with a shake of his head and asked if Mr. O'Mallory was home.

Just at that moment, a man came out of the one bedroom in the flat and stared at Joe. He had a tankard of beer in his hand and a cigarette hanging out of his mouth.

"What do you want?" he snarled at Joe.

Joe looked over and saw Billy staring at him with a worried look on his face.

"Hello Billy, glad to see you again." Then he turned to Mr. O'Mallory, "I'm your son's school teacher and I have a favour to ask of you." Joe could see a surprised and worried look pass over O'Mallory's face – he wasn't quite sure what to make of this person standing in his kitchen.

"Mr. O'Mallory, Billy tells me you work at the hide curing plant making leather. I was wondering if there were pieces of leather that couldn't be used in your process and if there is, what happens to it?"

This question completely caught O'Mallory off guard and he found himself liking this young man and answering the question. "Why yes, there are scraps not large mind you, and these are bundled up and thrown out at the end of the day."

"Would the scraps be as large as say 1 inch x 2inches?" Joe inquired.

"Oh at least that size – some even bigger." responded O'Mallory.

"Do you think I could get permission to retrieve these scraps at the end of day?" asked Joe.

"I don't see why not, they are garbage. But what do you want with them?" responded O'Mallory.

"I have a project in mind for the class and I don't have the money available to buy the supplies. Would it be too much of a burden to ask you to bring home a bundle and send it to school with Billy, if your employer agrees you can have the scraps?"

"I don't see this as a problem, I will ask tomorrow and if all is approved Billy can have the scraps to you in a couple of days." O'Mallory offered.

Joe thanked everyone and left feeling his plan was coming together.

In two days time, Billy arrived at school with a bundle of leather scraps and everyone was excited about why he had them and what they were going to be used for.

Joe looked over the leather and was very pleased with what he saw.

He called the class to attention and then started to explain his plan.

He would like to have a class lunch twice a week – but what did that cost? Immediately he received the answer, $1.16

How could they find a way to have $1.16 available twice a week?

The response came back from bringing money in (and as he had thought, he could see some heads dropping down and staring at their desks in shame), to stealing the money.

Joe indicated to the class that there were ways they could make this money as a class. This caused the class to become very quiet as they waited for the next shoe to drop.

Joe proposed that they make a product that could be sold at one of the stores or at the market on the weekend. The profit (the difference between the cost of making the product and the selling price) could be used to buy the supplies for their lunches.

Joe indicated that Billy's father had received permission from his employer at the hide factory to let the class have scraps of leather left over from making their product.

What could be made from leather?

The list included purses, change purses, whips, hats, chaps, belts, (but their scraps weren't large enough for most of these items).

Joe helped them focus to items that would be 1"X 2" – key fobs, link belts, book marks.

Now they were getting somewhere!

Joe then helped them to decide on one item they could mass produce, like the sandwiches they made. It was decided they would make a key fobs and they would etch an initial in each one to make it different from the others they had seen being sold. But how would they know which initial to put on – they couldn't add it at the point of sale – they wouldn't be there.

After a lengthy argument that Joe had to work back into a discussion they decided that they would have to produce the whole alphabet, but make more of certain letters than others and monitor their stock to produce the most purchased letter. For example, they might only need one or two "Q"s but they might need ten "B"s. They knew there were 26 letters in the alphabet, so they would need 26 key fobs, likely two full sets, to start and then add extra letters that they felt might sell.

Joe had each student in the class start a set of books with date, item, revenue, expenses and a balance column. He had them enter the date in the appropriate column, then in the item column leather and enter a "0" in the expense column. He told them that right now their supplies were free, but if later on they had to pay for their supplies, they would know where the cost should be entered.

Now Joe had them all set up an inventory and production sheet.

Like the cash flow journal, this had columns also.

There was the date, item, number made, number on consignment, number sold, Amount per Unit.

He then explained they had to known how many key fobs they had made. How many they had out in the stores? How many they had actually sold? And what they had received per unit for each fob sold?

Joe then had them develop a shipping slip, an invoice and a receipt.

After much discussion and a vote they decided to call their business:

"Central Leather Works".

Joe then had them open the pile of scrap leather and separate it into salvageable pieces and cut away the unusable pieces. Once again, it was not a problem getting knives, since nearly every boy in the class had a penknife in their possession. However, Joe soon realized that most of the knives were very dull and could be more of a danger than a help. He spent a few minutes showing the boys how to sharpen their knives on a whet stone he had found in the boiler room.

Joe asked one of the girls, Becky, who had demonstrated a gift in drawing during their "art classes" to design the key fob. He asked her to keep it rather simple.

Becky's design was a tear drop design with an inner line that encompassed the etched "letter".

Joe had her transfer the outside design over to six pieces of cardboard and had one of the boys cut these out. He then had Becky transfer the inner outline onto another six pieces of cardboard and again had these cut out.

The six outside designs were given to six girls and they were asked to trace these on as many pieces of leather as they could find that would fit the design; being creative and turning the designs around to obtain as much use of each piece of leather as possible.

One girl was assigned as "carrier" and it was her job to move the traced pieces of leather to one of the boys with a knife.

The boys were to cut out the design from the leather and another "carrier" would then collect them and move them over to students who would lay the "inner" cardboard design on the cut piece of leather and trace it with a pencil. The carrier would then move this over to two students that had a hammer and a block of wood and a nail that had the point filed off. The "fob" would be placed on the piece of wood and the student would proceed to hammer the nail into the leather hard enough to make an indentation, but not hard enough to go through the leather. The student would follow the penciled line until the whole design was complete. This soon became the bottle neck of the assembly and Joe had to find four more hammers and move the girls who were doing the first stage into doing this stage until they were caught up.

Becky got the job of drawing the "Letter" of the alphabet onto each "fob" and she was able to use calligraphy in designing her "Letter" giving an Old English appearance to the "Letter". Once again it was given back to a student to "set" the "Letter" with the use of a nail – and since hammers had become difficult to find, they used small rocks as hammers.

While all this was going on, Joe had another boy using his knife to cut long straight pieces of rawhide, about ½" in width from any scrap he could find. These where then cut into 6" pieces and were fed through a hole that was punched at the bottom of the "fob" and tied off – this is how the keys would be attached!

As you can imagine, with all the moving around and all the banging, Principal Gleeson made a number of appearances demanding that the noise be reduced.

Each time, Joe was able to fend him off by explaining the advantage of practical education and how positive the Superintendent would view the outcomes of his grade 8 class – this would really be a feather in his cap as principal, and each time Principal Gleeson reluctantly returned to his office hoping Joe was right!

The third day of their Central Leather Works project, a really severe wind and thunderstorm hit the area.

The storm subsided by the time school was about to dismiss and Joe asked Billy and Ben if they would mind staying on for a while and helping him with a project.

The boys quickly agreed and the three of them left the school grounds with Joe carrying a hand saw, he had found in the boiler room, that had seen better days.

They went about two streets over from the school and saw a large tree that had a number of limbs that had snapped off in the storm.

Joe asked Billy to go to the door of the house and ask permission from the owner to cut a couple of these limbs and take them back to the school.

Billy really didn't see the need to do this since the limbs were already down, but if this would make Mr. Robins happy, he would humour him.

An older lady answered the door and glared at Billy. "What is it!" she demanded.

Billy proceeded to ask, "M'am, we're from Central Public School and we're doing a project and need a few limbs to finish it. That's my teacher, Mr. Robins over there." He said pointing to Joe, "Can we please have a couple of the limbs that have blown down in the storm, M'am?" inquired Billy not quite sure how this old battleaxe would respond.

All of a sudden, the lady broke into a smile and said, "Why of course you can have as many limbs as you want young man. The more you take, the less I'll have to arrange to be cleaned up." She said and waved over to Joe.

Joe all of sudden recognized her as a member of his Congregation and waved back.

"All right boys," Joe said, "I didn't realize this was Miss Hector's house. She goes to my Church. I was just going to take a couple of branches but I think it would be a nice gesture if we cleaned up this mess for her. Are you game?"

There were a couple of groans, but they mumbled their consent.

When they had finished, Joe had his limb, six feet long – straight and about 4" in diameter, and number of smaller straight sticks about one inch in diameter and a foot long. The rest of the fallen tree was neatly piled up on the side of the yard. Joe and the boys hauled their wood back to the class and left it there for the next day.

The following day, while production was proceeding Joe, Billy and Ben retrieved their wood. Joe showed the boys how to drill holes into the six foot limb. Four holes at the bottom then 24 holes drilled into the limb in a spiral design starting three feet from the bottom right up to the top.

The four holes in the bottom allowed for four smaller limbs to be inserted to act as legs to hold the limb up straight. Smaller limbs were inserted into the 24 other holes. These had been drilled on a slight angle to allow the limbs to point up about ten degrees.

When done, Joe went over to the finished "key fobs" and began placing them on the tree in alphabetical order with "A" at the top and "Z" at the bottom. The class was thrilled to see how their work was shown off so professionally by this moveable display.

Joe asked for volunteers to work at the market on Saturday and had no trouble getting four girls who would be glad to volunteer. It was decided that two would work from 7:30 am to 12 pm and the other two would work from 12 pm to 5 pm. Joe agreed to meet the first shift at the market at 7:30 am with the display and make sure they had some petty cash to get them started.

On Friday Joe had the class open their Financial Journals to the page marked Inventory and Production Sheet.

He had the class put in the date, under item "Key Fobs", under Production Number 80 units, cost per unit 0, Consignment 80, selling price .05, number sold was left blank until Monday.

Saturday Morning Joe met Sally and Becky at the Market at 7:30 am – they were already there looking for him. Joe had attached a sign to the top of their display that read

"Central Leather Works,"
A project of the grade 8 students of Central Public School,

Key Fobs $.05 each

Sally and Becky really liked the sign and were ready to hawk their merchandise.

It was agreed that if they sold out of a "letter" they would take down the name of the individual and their address and give them the choice of picking it up next Saturday or having it delivered to them, if they lived in the neighborhood. They could pay upon delivery of the Key Fob.

Sally and Becky had a sheet that had all their product listed and columns to check off the items they sold. This would allow for a quick check of inventory against the sales and the cash they had taken in. On the bottom of the sheet Joe had marked that he had given them four one dollar bills and twenty, 5 cent pieces as petty cash. Joe had each girl sign that the petty cash was as he stated and date their signature.They were now ready to open sales.

Business was brisk and at 12 pm when Sally and Becky passed over their responsibility to Sadie and Helen they had sold about half of their stock and had taken three orders for "letters" that they had sold out.

Joe was there at 12 and congratulated the girls for their hard work and went through the training with the two new girls, Sadie and Helen.

At 5 pm Joe arrived to find Sadie and Helen sitting beside a nearly empty display. Except for "Q", "U" "X" and "Z", all the other key fobs had been sold and the girls had orders for 15 more, plus the three from the morning. They had orders for 18, plus they would have to restock their display. It was going to be a busy week ahead!

The class had made a double run of the alphabet, so there were 8 key fobs left making their sales 72 key fobs at .05 for a net profit of $3.60, plus advance sales of 18x.05 = $.90

The class was thrilled. They had enough money to host 2 lunches this week and they decided it would be on Tuesday and Thursday.

Joe continued with the **Central Leather Works** as his Math Class and over the course of the year the class made bookmarks, link belts, pocket watch pouches, change pouches and rawhide laces and enjoyed their lunches as a class.

Joe was extremely proud that at the end of the year, he had the same number of students as he had at the beginning of the year. He received a number of complements from parents as to how well their child had done in school and how eager they were to go to school every morning, even when they weren't feeling well. They felt they had to be at school or they would be letting their class down.

Principal Gleeson was his usual self and attempted to take credit for Joe's work with the class. However, it was obvious the students and their parents weren't going to allow that to happen and many of the parents made sure they spoke to Superintendent Smythe about the work Joe had done with their son or daughter.

Joe remembered the next two years with mixed emotions. There had been a constant battle between Principal Gleeson and himself. But, Joe usually won.

The children were great. Their home environments were something else.

Over the course of the two years Joe stayed, he coached a softball team that made it to the City finals, ending up third in year one and second in year two.

Most of his boy students ended up coming over to the YMCA and taking boxing training, or playing indoor organized sports. At Joe's insistence they attended special classes on the bible and some became involved in a choir that Joe started. The choir had girls as well as boys and all of the girls from Joe's class made sure they were available for Tuesday night rehearsals.

Where was Nellie when he really needed her?

However, he did remember Nellie's suggestion of having the choir hum the song before they started to sing it. Joe also borrowed the idea of explaining the song/hymn and telling about the composer. If he told them why the song was written, and a little bit about how the composer expected the song to be sung, when the choir quietly hummed the melody, with the feeling and expression, then finally added the lyrics, he was amazed at how wonderful the end product sounded.

Nellie was a genius and he missed her so very much! He did manage to get back to Port Rowan when the Archers' were scheduled to hold services. It was good to see the family and it was really good to see Albert and Nellie.

Joe had become very fond of Albert. He was like a brother to him. This put Will's nose out of joint a bit, so Joe made sure he spent extra time with Will, just the two of them. It might be fishing or taking the sailboat out for a run or just sitting on the front porch with Will catching Joe up on the local gossip or Joe telling about his class.

Joe also shared with Will, on a promise he'd never tell, his exploits as a Professional Boxer. He didn't tell Will that he'd already told Albert about these adventures. Let Will think he was the only one who knew. This secret really drew the brothers closer together.

Joe fought six more fights without loosing over the course of two years and earned $150 that helped him commute, by train, between Detroit and St. Thomas for those special weekends with Nellie.

Of course there were daily letters that kept her informed of his class activities and how much he missed her.

Joe wasn't really good at writing the romantic letter. He wrote as he would speak and kept his feelings still quite formal, since he never knew who might read his letters and he didn't want to get on the wrong side of Albert or particularly Rev. Archer.

Now, Nellie's letters, as well as keeping Joe informed of family and worship experiences, tended to express a more intimate response of her feelings. Joe would read those sections over and over again. He made sure he told Nellie how much he looked forward to her letters when they were together.

After two years, Joe knew that teaching wasn't what God had planned for him. He didn't want to be this far away from Nellie.

He gave his notice at Christmas to give the School Board time to find a replacement.

Superintendent Smythe made a number of visits to the school over the course of the last semester and tried to get Joe to change his mind. However, once Joe had made up his mind – it wasn't easy to change it. Joe stayed true to his decision.

On the last day of school, Joe almost changed his mind!

The parents from this year's and last year's graduating class came together to host a "Thank You Mr. Robins Party" at lunch and into the afternoon of his last day of school.

Almost all of his first class were back for this event, and in reality, Joe had kept in touch with many through boxing, sports, choir and Bible Study classes at the "Y". The parents who owned the Deli and Bakery had provided all the food and Principal Gleason and Superintendent Smythe were invited. It was a great party and Joe was so pleased that most of his former students had continued on with their schooling or had jobs that had a future, like apprenticing in carpentry, or working as an apprentice making barrels or at the forge. The parents from both classes couldn't say enough and even offered to pay him under the table if he would consider staying. Joe realized that he had had an effect on the young people and as he looked around, realized he had even brought the families together in a common goal. He was temped to stay, but then he thought of Nellie and his resolve to leave held fast.

If only he had known what was before them in the future. Detroit wouldn't have seemed so far away!

CHAPTER 8

The Adventure Begins

*"In the beginning was the Word, and the Word was with God,
and the Word was God."(KJV)*
John 1:1

It had been a whole hour since Joe last looked at his watch. The chills had stopped, thank goodness, but the wind and snow hadn't.

What would tomorrow hold?

Joe was thinking of Nel and how much he missed her. He remembered the last time he had seen her; she was standing on the platform of the railway station, waving as Joe's train pulled out of the station on its way to British Columbia.

She had been a vision of loveliness and a memory worth having for the next two years while he went to his mission field for the Methodist Church in the frontier of British Columbia in 1898.

Superintendent Rev. McCloud had met with the six candidates that were heading out west at Victoria College in mid September and assigned them their mission fields. A couple of guys were going to Manitoba – three to Alberta and Joe, to British Columbia.

Superintendent McCloud explained that they would be given $100 per year and a ticket to the station closest to their destination.

They would be expected to pick up some part time work to keep them from starving. Also, they could count on members of their congregations to help them out. However, Robins had no congregation, and in fact his responsibility was to open new churches in Rossland and other locations determined by his Supervisor, Rev. Johnston of Revelstoke.

"Where do I hold my services?" Joe inquired

"The same place Jesus did," responded McCloud, "wherever two or three are gathered in my name" or rather where the people are: in the lumber camps, by your tent, in the saloon if you feel it is appropriate."

The others broke out laughing at this, but Joe felt this might not be a bad idea if he could find away to make it work.

The Church had provided them with the cheapest tickets they could purchase. The passenger car they were assigned to was Spartan by any definition, with wooden slat benches and a wood stove at one end.

Joe went to the end of the car where the stove was located. It was warm today in Toronto, but he guessed that the evenings and nights would be cool if not cold as they headed up around Lake Superior and off onto the Prairies.

This was going to be home for him for the next 12 days, until he arrived at Revelstoke.

Joe had one valise with him and in it was: a pair of work pants, two work shirts, a Sunday white shirt with black vest, two pair of long underwear, and four pair of wool socks knitted for him by his Mother. Beside his shaving kit of straight razor, soap and brush he had packed a small box of tools for repairing pocket watches and a bottle of light oil, his Bible, the Pastor's Ritual Book, a Hymnal, his wooden flute, two blankets and two sheets. A pillow case and towel rounded out his traveling possessions. He wore his good suit and overcoat and had a woolen jacket stuck between the handles of the valise. He wasn't sure if he'd regret it, but he had slipped four books into the bottom of his bag. One was a book of poetry that Nellie had given him, a novel by Charles Dickens called "Scrooge", a book of sermons he had picked up at Victoria College and a book on the power of prayer that Rev. Archer had recommended plus his Methodist Black Book Manual and a Pastor's Service Book.

The trip was long and boring, but the scenery was incredible. Especially when they approached the Rockies and traveled over tracks that hung out over gorges that dropped 200 to 400 feet below them. He was amazed at the engineering techniques that kept the trains running through avalanche areas. They passed through long snow sheds that were built into the stone walls with roofs to deflect the snow over the train. These sheds were almost haunting as the train passed through and the smoke from the puffing stack had nowhere to go but hang inside the enclosed shed and seep into the passenger cars making breathing very difficult. It was miles after these sheds before the passenger car stopped smelling of smoke and that depended upon how cold it was outside and how long the passengers could last with the windows down.

Joe didn't know what to expect when the train chugged into Revelstoke, but since most of the stops prior to this had been pretty primitive, he was not surprise to see that Revelstoke had only a few wood frame buildings. A General Store, saloon, railway station, a Hudson Bay Outlet, an RCMP police station and two wooden churches with a wooden house sitting beside each church were all the permanent buildings he saw.

The first church he passed was an Anglican Church with stained glass windows facing the road, the wood painted white with a white picket fence around the church and the house, which obviously belonged with the church.

At the end of the street stood a large tent with a wooden cross planted beside it and a log cabin that was obviously the manse for the Methodist Church of Revelstoke.

Joe carted his bag up to the front door of the Manse and knocked. The door was swung opened by a big bear of a man with a long beard and a scowl on his face.

"What can I do for you young man?" asked the man.

"Rev. Johnston?" Joe ventured, "My name is Joseph Robins and I just arrived on the train from Toronto. I'm your probationary student for Rossland." Joe responded with an even voice.

"Well come in, come in young man. Don't just stand out there. I wasn't expecting you for another week. You made good time." A smile had replaced the scowl and Mr. Johnston had his hand out to take Joe's bag from him.

"Mary, come quickly," Mr. Johnston shouted over his shoulder, "Our student has arrived, just got off the train." With that, Mr. Johnston placed Joe's suitcase on the floor behind the door and put his huge arm around his shoulder and steered him into what Joe surmised must be the parlour, although it looked like it was also the study as he observed a desk before the window and a bookcase full of books against the far wall.

At that moment, a rather large, both in height and weight, woman appeared with a big smile on her face. She was as pleasant from the start as Rev. Johnson had been miserable on first contact.

"Welcome to Revelstoke! We are so glad you have arrived safely." gushed Mrs. Johnston.

"My dear, let me introduce you to Joseph Robins." Rev. Johnston explained. "He just got off the train and I'm sure he must be very tired after that trip."

"Come Mr. Robins, leave your bag there for now and come with me. I have just finished baking some cookies. They're still hot! I'm sure a cup of coffee and a few cookies will pick you right up."

Joe was taken back at how motherly this woman was.

"Rev. and Mrs. Johnston, please call me Joe. I'd love a cookie, although I don't drink coffee – but water or milk would be greatly appreciated." Joe responded.

With that Joe followed the bustling Mrs. Johnston across the room to a kitchen table that was Spartan by any person's definition. A wood burning iron stove, a wooden table and four chairs and a wooden set of shelves that had a piece of fabric over them for a curtain.

Joe sat down at the table and Mrs. Johnston was as good as her word. In an instant there were four oatmeal cookies with raisins, on a plate before him still steaming from having come right out of the oven in the old iron stove and a glass of cold milk.

Joe felt at home!

Rev. Johnston sat down across from him and Mrs. Johnston sat at the end of the table near the stove.

Joe bit into the cookie and it melted in his mouth. Mrs. Johnston must have used a pound of butter and he didn't know how much brown sugar to make cookies this good!

"These are great!" exclaimed Joe.

Mrs. Johnston just beamed and Joe knew he had made a life-long friend.

Joe spent a week with the Johnston's and conducted the Service of Worship on Sunday for Rev. Johnston while he and Mrs. Johnston took a few well deserved days off.

On his return, Rev. Johnson who was the Supervisor of three students in this area told Joe he was to proceed to Rossland by work train that went only as far as Rossland, where the tracks ended and begin establishing his Ministry.

Rev. Johnston made it quite clear that he wanted a Church building and a congregation functioning within a year. He indicated that he had received excellent reports from Sunday's Service and he had high expectations for Joe.

Rev. Johnston promised to come out in about three months and see what progress Joe was making. However, Rev. Johnston didn't know what God had in store for him when he said this.

CHAPTER 9

Rossland

*"And the hand of the Lord was with them: and a great number believed,
and turned unto the Lord." (KJV)*
Acts 11:21

The next day Joe started off early to catch the work train to Rossland, carrying his bag and a paper bag with a lunch and a dozen cookies, a gift from Mrs. Johnston!

Joe arrived in Rossland in the late afternoon. The work train stopped about every five miles to drop off trappers, supplies, and pick up wood.

As Joe stood on the platform at the Rossland Station he reflected that he thought Revelstoke had been primitive – welcome to the real west!

Rossland was comprised of four wooden buildings and several hundred large canvass tents.

The train station, bank, general store and saloon comprised the wooden structures. The street was a giant mud track that ran from the rail station to the end of town, which was about a mile, then a few fields and woods.

The saloon was the only two storey building in town and had a sign hanging off the veranda that said "Rooms for let – by the hour, day or month".

Joe remembered wondering why anyone would rent a room by the hour, until he entered the saloon and saw the bevy of painted women sitting around the tables. Joe had seen many women like these in Detroit, in fact a few of his children's mothers were plying their trade to make ends meet. However, none had looked quite as bizarre as this flock of felines. Most of them were well past their best years and trying to make themselves look younger by applying layers of rouge and lipstick. They looked almost like china dolls. They came in all shapes and bulges. One thing they all had were breasts that were abundant and doing their best to pop out of their low cut silk dresses.

It was 10 am when the train pulled in, September 15th, 1895 and the ladies were just starting to function after a night's activity. As the five passengers from the train wandered into the saloon, the "ladies" immediately got up and started to move towards the fresh "meat".

One "lady" expertly slipped her arm under Joe's arm and started to gently rub his biceps.

Joe carefully unwrapped himself, tipped his hat to the lady and enquired where he registered for a room.

"Hey handsome," she continued, "spend some time with me and I'll arrange a discount on your room You'll experience how close you can come to heaven without actually dying."

"I've already experienced that feeling," Joe responded, "when I met Jesus and I've come to help others experience that feeling. It sounds like we are in a competitive business. Your experience only lasts five minutes, mine lasts a lifetime."

The "lady" pulled away from him and snapped, "What are you, a 'Sky Pilot'?" she asked with utter disgust in her voice.

"If that means Missionary, then you are absolutely right. I'm a Pastor for the Methodist Church of Canada and I've been sent here to start a Church in Rossland." Joe explained.

"Hey Pastor, over here," called the bartender, "You'll have to forgive Lil', she ain't used to loosing customers to something she can't see." laughed the bar-keep.

He stuck out his hand and said, "My Name is Bradey, Bill Bradey, but people just call me Dutch." And he accepted Joe's hand and gave it a good squeeze with the shake. Joe gave back as good as he got. This impressed Dutch.

"Dutch? You don't appear to be Dutch." Said Joe.

"Nope" laughed Dutch, "Don't think anybody in my family ever came from Holland. However, somehow I got stuck with Dutch as a nickname. I don't mind what they call me, as long as they don't call me late for dinner." laughed the bar keep – it was obvious he had told this joke many times and appreciated having someone new to try it out on.

Joe observed that 'Dutch' hadn't missed many dinners. He was a big man with a peppery beard and a well established pot belly that shook when he laughed. His eyes twinkled with mischief and although he was plying a business that went against everything Joe stood for, he liked this man and hoped he would have an opportunity to get to know him.

As one of the requirements as a candidate for Ministry, Joe had to sign the 'pledge' to abstain from all alcoholic beverages and to campaign for stamping out alcoholic drinks in society. While fasting had caused Joe concern, signing the pledge had presented no problem. He had never consumed alcohol and never smoked and didn't feel he had missed anything of importance, so, didn't see why he would want to start later in life.

"Here" said Dutch as he slid over a hotel register, "sign here and I'll give you a room at the back."

As Joe signed he looked up with a query on his face and before he could ask, Dutch explained, "It's as far away from the main stair case as I can get you and it won't be quite as noisy as some of the rooms. This place gets pretty noisy at night."

Joe thanked him and started towards the staircase and his room, when Dutch called, "Hey Pastor, I'm sure you're as honest as they come, but it's my policy that everyone pays up front. That will be 25 cents a night."

Joe came back and smiled at Dutch, "I think that's a smart policy, how much to have food thrown in?"

"For you Pastor, I'll include three squares for that price, but liquor is extra!"

Joe took out a dollar twenty-five and gave it to Dutch, "Let's go for five days at this point and see what God has in store for me."

Joe then turned and headed back towards the stair case and climbed to the second floor.

It was a darkly lit corridor with rooms off each side and a water basin at one end under a window with no curtains, which really didn't matter since this window hadn't been cleaned since it was installed.

Joe proceeded down to the end of the hall and noted his room was #12. As he opened the door the smell that hit him was of stale smoke, body odor and booze. He had a rough wood framed bed, with a sagging mattress, a chair and a chest of drawers that had seen better days and a wooden table with a coal oil lamp on it.

The first thing he did was to go over to the window and force it open as far as he cold get it, which was about half way. He would have to take the window sash off to raise it the rest of the way – and this he did right away since he was going to need all the fresh air he could get in this room.

His room at the YMCA in Detroit was starting to look like a palace.

First thing Joe did was to go back out into the hall and bring the wash basin back to his room. The water was relatively clean. This was one of the advantages of washing up so early in the day.

Joe took his shirt off, which was filthy from being worn for twelve days, sponge bathed himself and put on one of his work shirts. He also changed into his work pants. Then he took his jacket and pants and shook them out the window. The dust just flew off them. He then hung them up on the peg that was driven into the back of the door.

Should he lay down for a while and catch up on some sleep, or go out and explore the town? He decided he was too keyed up to sleep so he would see what this community had to offer.

Maybe Dutch would know someone who would wash his shirt?

As he re entered the Saloon, Dutch called over, "Well Pastor, does the room meet your standards?'

Joe laughed and responded, "Dutch, it's the best room I've seen in Rossland. By the way, is there a place I could get a shirt washed?"

"Sure. There's a Chinaman down about four tents on this side of the road has a laundry business. Make sure he doesn't charge you more than 2 cents."

"Thanks," Joe called back as he went out the door to the wood stoop in front of the Saloon. He walked to the end of the stoop and down a few stairs to the mud. It was like goop and nearly sucked his shoes off as he took every step.

Joe found the Chinaman right where Dutch had said but wasn't quite sure how to knock on a tent door.

"Hello," Joe called out and the flap of the tent flipped back. The Chinaman was bowing and indicating that Joe should enter.

"I've got a shirt that needs washing and ironing, how much?"

"Two cents," responded the Chinaman with a singing accent.

"Sounds good! How long before it will be ready?"

"You back at sunset."

"Alright, I'll see you at sunset."

Joe looked around and saw a big iron pot, steaming away, and steel irons lined up in the fire.

"This for you," said the Chinaman and he gave Joe a piece of paper with pencil marks that looked like Chinese characters. "You give back when get shirt."

Joe nodded and headed out the door closing the flap behind him.

Joe headed over to the General Store and as he entered the man behind the counter lifted his head and called out, "Elsie, the new Pastor is here"

"How do you know I'm the new Pastor?" Joe asked in total shock.

"Name's Herman Schmidt, Pastor and this here is my wife and my store and we know everyone in this area. One of the girls from Dutch's was over a few minutes ago and told us about how Lil' tried to pick you up. Never laughed so hard in all my life! You have to know Lil' Pastor, she's got a good heart, but she certainly has a high opinion of herself and usually doesn't take no for an answer. Elsie and I really enjoyed how you responded to her and how she didn't know what to do."

"Well, I'm pleased to meet you Mr. and Mrs. Schmidt and I'm pleased I brought a little levity into your day. My name is Joseph Robins."

"Please Pastor Robins, just call me Herman, everyone around here does and this is Elsie."

"In that case Herman, call me Joe."

"Oh we couldn't Pastor, it wouldn't be respectful. May we call you Pastor Joe?"

"That will work just fine," responded Joe

While this conversation was going on, Elsie had gathered a number of the ladies that were in the store and brought them over to meet the new Pastor.

"This is Mrs. Green, her husband is the blacksmith and Mrs. MacIntosh, her husband runs the lumber mill and over here is Mrs. Tuck, her husband is off prospecting."

Joe doffed his hat, "Ladies it is a pleasure to make your acquaintance. Mrs. Green, I'll be over to see your husband about a horse and Mrs. MacIntosh,

I'll be over to see your husband about the possibility of work out in the lumber camp." Joe responded.

The ladies expressed their pleasure at meeting him and asked if he planned to hold a Church this Sunday, which was only two days away.

Joe didn't know what to respond, but decided there was no time like the present to start with God's work.

"Why of course ladies, if the weather holds, we'll have an outdoor service – is there a place where we won't be mired in the mud?" Joe asked

They all chuckled and then Mrs. MacIntosh responded that there was a nice pasture area at the end of the town with a large chestnut tree that would be lovely to sit under.

"This sounds like a plan. What does 11 am sound like for a service this Sunday?"

Everyone agreed this was a good time and then Mrs. MacIntosh asked, "Pastor Robins, would you do me the honour of joining our family for lunch after the Service?"

"Why I'd be very pleased to accept your invitation." Joe responded. This was great. He didn't have any idea as to the meals he'd get at Dutch's and this would at least give him one good meal for this week. But remember you would call me Pastor Joe.".

Not wanting to be outdone, Irene Green spoke up, "Pastor Joe, Herman and I would like to have you for Saturday dinner."

"Well Irene, I once again accept and since I arrived only a couple of hours ago, I can assure you my dance card is very open."

Everyone laughed at this response.

"Pastor Joe," said Mrs. Green, "I hate to see you with an open dance card, especially since you likely don't dance. My husband Jim and I would like to invite you to dinner on Sunday, if Mrs. MacIntosh doesn't have you stuffed. Maybe we could have a late dinner at around 8 pm?"

Again Joe responded with a slight bow. "I would be deeply honoured to accept."

Joe turned to the group. "It is obvious I'm going to have to get a job as soon as possible, or I'll become so large that my Preaching clothes won't fit me."

Mrs. MacIntosh spoke up, "Pastor, if you go over to the tent at the end of the town, it carries the family name, you'll find my husband there. I know he'll have something for you. He's always looking for good men."

"Why thank you Mrs. MacIntosh, I'll head off right now." With that, Joe thanked everyone for the warm welcome and the lunch and dinner invitations. He headed out the door and turned towards the end of town. He soon found himself before a tent with a sign indicating "MacIntosh Lumber Company". This time the flap was held back and he could see two men at desks working on accounts and a larger desk on the far side with a gentleman reading a document and making notes.

Joe guessed that the latter was Mr. MacIntosh the owner of the business and proceeded inside and stood in front of the desk.

"And what can I do for you young man?" enquired a stately gentleman in his mid fifties, likely 20 years older than his wife Joe whom had just left.

"Mr. MacIntosh I believe?" Joe started out, "I just met your wife at Schmidt's General Store and she suggested I come down to meet you and inquire if you have any positions open. My name is Joseph Robins and I'm the new Methodist Pastor, just arrived on the train this morning."

"Pleased to meet you Pastor, I'm Angus MacIntosh." MacIntosh had risen from his desk and extended his hand across it to invite Joe to shake. Once again, the shake was extremely firm and was obviously an attempt to measure the man. Joe didn't hesitate to squeeze back and certainly held his own.

"Pastor Robins, I'm afraid I don't have any office positions available. I try to keep my office staff lean and mean, which means that I can keep my overhead as low as possible. The margin of profit on lumber is extremely small."

Joe knew from his experience with Big Jake, that MacIntosh was blowing steam, in fact the margin of profit was extremely high, or MacIntosh was a poor businessman, and Joe didn't feel this was likely.

"I wasn't thinking of the office Mr. MacIntosh, but rather one of your lumber camps, one close enough to allow me to get back for Sunday Services and respond to emergencies in my congregation."

"My boy, do you have any idea how rough the work is out in a lumber camp?" MacIntosh exploded, "Why, you wouldn't last a day!"

"I think you underestimate me Mr. MacIntosh; I used to run a boat building yard prior to becoming a Pastor and have handled lumber from break of dawn to well into the night to meet my orders. Do you have a camp relatively nearby that needs a worker?"

MacIntosh looked Joe up and down. It reminded him of when O'Reilly had checked him out prior to signing him as a fighter.

"Well, I would never have guessed it." MacIntosh admitted, "I do have a camp about half day's ride from here. I'd have to send one of the lads there out to one of the other camps.

As it turns out, I have a request from one of the lads there to join a camp further north, where his brother is working. I think this could work for all of us. When could you start?"

"I just arrived in town today and have to buy a horse. I have also met a group of the ladies at the General Store, your wife being one, and have agreed to hold our first service of worship Sunday at 11 am – out in the meadow just beyond this tent. I would be more than willing to head out to the camp first thing on Monday morning. Is this agreeable to you Mr. MacIntosh?"

"Of course Pastor Robins." MacIntosh then went on "We pay our lumberjacks 25 cents a day and provide your meals. We don't allow drunkenness in camp, but I don't expect that would be a problem for you Pastor? To get your pay we expect that you can cut 25 trees a day, anything over 25 we pay 2 cents a tree. You have to put in a full day to get your pay. We expect you to be in your cut area by 7:30 am and you'll knock off at 5 pm.

Breakfast is served at 5:30 am, lunch will be brought to the site and you'll have 30 minutes to eat and have a smoke and dinner will be served at 7 pm – everyone takes a turn at helping to prepare or clean up dinner – you'll be fitted into the schedule. Any questions?"

"No, I think you've covered everything but if I think of anything I'll be sure to ask when I have lunch at your home after service on Sunday. Mrs. MacIntosh was so kind to invite me."

With that Joe reached over and extended his hand, this time he applied the pressure and MacIntosh had to do everything he could not to show how it hurt.

Joe nodded and turned back towards town, where he saw on his right a corral and a blacksmith forge over behind the row of tents.

Joe crossed over and headed towards the forge. The blacksmith, Mr. Green, was smeared with perspiration and ash from the forge and the sun danced off his biceps as he swung his hammer down on a horseshoe that was fitted around the anvil. The sparks flew from the red hot piece of iron as his hammering continued to shape the shoe into the well- known horseshoe shape.

As Joe approached, Mr. Green stopped hammering and moved the piece of iron from the anvil and stuck it into a pail of water that was sitting beside him. Steam hissed up around him causing a cloud of vapor that almost encompassed the man.

"You must be Pastor Robins?" Mr. Green said extending his hand for the compulsory shake. This shake was firm but didn't have the challenging attitude of MacIntosh.

"Word soon spreads," laughed Joe, "yes I'm Joseph Robins."

"My wife was down here almost before you had a chance to get to MacIntosh. Any luck with the job?"

"Yes, he signed me on for a camp that's about a half day's ride from here, start Monday."

"He didn't find you an office job?" Green inquired.

"No, said he couldn't afford to increase his overhead with more administration, but a lumberjack's position is just fine. Like I told MacIntosh, I used to run a boat building yard in Port Rowan, Ontario after my father died. Hard work doesn't scare me in fact I look forward to keeping in shape."

"Good for you," said Green, "Jim Green the name."

"I'm pleased to meet you Mr. Green."

"Just call me Jim, Pastor Robins."

"Tell you what Jim, people seem to want to use the Pastor and that's fine, but let's go with Pastor Joe. Now Jim, I need a few things and I don't have a lot of money available to spend." explained Joe.

"Well, you tell me what you need and I'll see if I can fit it into your budget."

"First I need a horse." requested Joe.

"Well, livestock is in high demand out here and carries a hefty price," explained Jim

"I have a black stallion I took in as part of a trade for a wagon and team of horses. This was not one of my better deals. This horse looks beautiful, but is a handful for anyone to ride. If you can ride him, I'll give him to you for $25 and I'll throw in the saddle and bridle which came with him. But I have to warn you, he is hard to ride."

"Saddle him up," Joe said with a confidence he didn't feel in his gut, "and we'll see if this lad from Port Rowan Ontario can ride a western horse."

Jim went over to the corral and got a rope from the post and proceeded to lasso the black beauty. He then led it over to the fence and put the bit into its mouth and the bridle on.

Joe noted that the horse didn't seem to like this and started to raise and lower his head and give it a shake. His right front hoof started to paw at the ground. He was not a happy horse.

"Jim, is there some other type of bridle that could be used that doesn't have a bit in it?" Joe asked.

"Yes, there is a nose bridle, but unless the horse has been trained with it, there is no way to make him stop. You need the bit to saw back on the mouth to bring the horse under control, especially a spirited stallion like this one." Jim responded.

"Do you have one?" inquired Joe

"No, but one can be made quite easily with a little rope."

"Could you make me one for this horse? What's his name by the way?" Joe asked.

"His name is Tar and I'd be glad to make you a slip bridle. I have to warn you that you could be riding back to Port Rowan before you can stop Tar or he'll flip you out of the saddle, one or the other." Jim warned.

"I hear you Jim, I just think Tar will respond better without a bit and I'd like to give it a try. I'll accept full responsibility." Joe stated with a tone of calm that he certainly wasn't feeling. This was a hunch and it could backfire on him badly.

Jim slipped off the bitted bridle and replaced it with a rope that encompassed Tar's nose, and went up over his ears.

Joe saw that Tar was far more relaxed with this bridle and didn't flinch when Jim placed the saddle blanket and saddle on his back. Jim tightened up the cinch and looking over to Joe to take his measure, then shortened the stirrups.

"Well, Pastor Joe, I think he's ready." Jim said with a lack of conviction.

A couple of men had wandered over to the corral fence to watch this newcomer ride Tar. Everyone knew that Tar was not an easy horse to ride and this could be worth a really good laugh. Joe nodded and climbed over the fence. He walked over to where Jim was holding Tar, moved around to the front and spent a few minutes petting the nose of the big horse.

One of the onlookers called over, "Hey Pastor, saying a payer?" and everyone laughed

128

"Yes I am," responded Jim and looked over to where the man had a sheepish smile on his face.

"I guess the time has come Tar," said Joe as he proceeded around to the side and placed his foot into the stirrup. Joe gabbed on to the saddle horn and started to pull himself up throwing his other leg over the rump of the horse and settling into the saddle.

Tar began to prance and drop his head. Joe pulled back on the makeshift bridle and much to his surprise and delight, Tar immediately lifted his head and settled down.

Like all children in small Ontario villages, Joe had grown up around horses. The Robins had owned a team and a least one riding horse since Joe could remember, but none were like this stallion. He was a beaut!

Joe applied a gentle kick to his flanks and Tar lifted his head, gave a snort and started off with a walk, moving into a trot at Joe's urging. Joe pulled back on the makeshift halter and Tar responded immediately. Almost too immediately as Joe wasn't expecting this instant response and was getting ready to really pull back on the bridle. He almost lost his balance, but his boxing training kicked in and he found his centre of gravity quickly, and repositioned himself in the saddle.

"Well, I'll be," exclaimed Jim, "this horse must have been trained with a nose halter. I would never have thought of changing the bridle. How did you ever know to suggest this?"

Joe just laughed, "I can assure you Jim, it was pure luck."

"I don't think so! One doesn't see a horse for the first time and make that sort of suggestion without some reason, what tipped you off?"

Joe looked down from Tar and patted Tar on his shining black neck, "Tar seemed relaxed until you started to put the bit into his mouth, then he became restless, pawing the earth and his ears went forward. We had a couple of mules at the Ship Yard back home and whenever their ears went forward, you could be guaranteed that they were going to kick. I guessed that Tar was giving the same signals. If I had been wrong, you would have been picking me up in pieces, just like you said. I was lucky and Tar has responded as I hoped.

Why don't you open the corral gate and I'll open him up and see if I can control him when he's really going?"

Jim went over to the gate, shaking his head in disbelief that a greenhorn from Ontario and a Pastor at that, could read a horse better than he could. Jim opened the gate, and Joe urged Tar into a trot, then a canter, then into a gallop. As Tar stretch himself out heading to the tree line just beyond the town, Joe felt like he was one with this black beauty. The wind whirled by his head and the horse's feet didn't seem to touch the ground. Joe could envision himself on the mythical horse Pegasus.

The time had come to see whether Tar was going to respond to the concept of stopping.

Joe started to pull back on the makeshift bridle, causing Tar's head to go down and pull back towards his chest. It didn't take much of a pull and Tar broke stride and started to slow up. Another tug and Tar was coming to a halt as compliant as one could ever ask.

Again, Joe leaned up over his neck and patted the horse on the neck, showing his appreciation for responding so quickly to the hand signals. Joe knew he had been lucky, but more importantly, he knew he had made a really good deal with Jim. He hoped he wouldn't change the terms now he knew how to control this beautiful animal. Tar was worth a couple of hundred at least and the saddle, although well worn, was worth $5 to $10.

Joe turned Tar around and rode her back to the corral in a gentle canter. As he approached there were shouts of: "Well done Pastor!", "Ride 'm cowboy!" and one or two, "I don't believe it!"

Joe smiled and swung off Tar. As he turned to Jim, he stuck out his hand, "Got yourself a deal Jim."

Jim shook his head, "To think, it took a greenhorn from Ontario to teach me about riding a horse Pastor Joe. You earned your bargain today!" With that, Jim took the reins and led Tar over to the corral, took off the saddle and saddle blanket. Then he grabbed a grooming brush and started to brush Tar down until his coat was gleaming. As he worked he continued talking with Joe.

"My wife tells me you're having your first service this Sunday. I'm looking forward to it. Where are you holding it Pastor?"

"We have agreed that if the weather is good, we'll hold it over there in the pasture, by the big chestnut." Joe responded pointing towards the pasture just beyond the corral.

"Jim, if I'm going to be working at the lumber camp, do you think I'll need a gun to ward off wild animals."

"Pastor Joe, you would be a walking invitation to bears and wolves if you don't have a gun."

"Where can I get a pistol, Jim?"

"You've come to the right place. I have a Smith and Wesson Model #2, Army Colt made in 1860, six shooter with a holster, I'll let you have it for $10."

"Jim, I'm sure that's a good price, but I can only afford $5.00." countered Joe.

"Pastor, you drive a hard bargain, but I'll take it," again Jim stuck his hand out for the bargain sealing shake.

Joe counted out $30.00 and handed it over to Jim.

"I hear you're coming over for dinner on Sunday after you have lunched with the MacIntoshs. Don't eat too much over at the MacIntoshs, Irene is a really fine cook. I know that she will have quite a spread for us.

When do you want to pick up Tar?"

"Jim, I need to stable him with you until I take off on Monday, what's the rate?"

"For you Pastor, 5 cents per day food included."

"What's the usual rate Jim?" Joe asked.

"Five cents a day, food included." Jim responded with a laugh.

Joe waved his goodbye and wandered back towards town. As he passed one tent, a squaw was sitting out front working on making clothing out of deer-hide. Joe stopped and looked at the leggings, moccasins, and shirts she had piled up for sale.

"You like?" she asked Joe.

"Yes, may I feel the softness of the hide?"

"Of course" she said and watched as Joe picked up a shirt that was almost white and was so soft that it felt like you could put your finger through the hide.

"For you?" she asked

"Maybe." Joe responded.

"The shirt you have is made for woman on her wedding day. You want this type of shirt." She picked up a heavier hide shirt that was a basic shirt with a design worked into the 4" button flap at the neck. The design was made of many coloured cotton threads.

Joe held it up to his chest and realized that it would fit just fine. He picked out a pair of pants and tried on a couple of pair of moccasins before he found a pair that were comfortable.

"How much?" Joe inquired.

"Five dollars for shirt, same for pants and four dollars for moccasins, total fourteen dollars." She replied.

"I don't think so," said Joe "I could buy a horse for that much." He said with disgust and started to turn away hoping this action would make her realize that he wasn't going to pay these prices. It was a gamble because he really did like the workmanship that this lady had put into her merchandise.

"Wait! I can do better," she said, "You take all three for $10."

"No!" Joe responded, "I take all three for $6."

"Done!" the Indian woman stuck out her hand to make a deal. Joe shook hands with her and dug into his trouser pant's pocket and counted off six dollars. While doing this he noted his cash reserves were starting to get low. He would have to start finding sources of cash until he started to get paid for his work in the Lumber Camp.

Joe collected his goods and continued back to his room over the top of the Saloon.

On his way to his room through the saloon, Joe stopped and asked Dutch if he could put a poster up by the door.

"Advertising a Church Service, Pastor?" Dutch asked.

"No, but that's a good idea Dutch, maybe I should put two posters up, would that be ok?" Joe responded.

"Of course Pastor, but remember most of these guys can't read." Said Dutch.

"Thanks for the reminder Dutch," and with that Joe went up to his room.

Once in his room he put his purchases on his bed and went over to his valise and took out two pieces of paper and put them on the table. On the first one he drew a cross then a map of how to get to the meadow from the saloon and finally a watch with its hands pointed at 11 am. He had to print Sunday and drew a small picture of a church beside the words.

On the second piece of paper he drew the picture of a pocket watch, then below it a picture of the watch open with its gears showing and printed the words – clean and fix 25 cents, and his room number 12. He went downstairs and posted the two notices.

Immediately one of the patrons came over and looked at the poster that showed the pocket watch, pulled his watch out of his pants pocket and asked Joe if he could get it running on time. Joe looked at the watch and noted the second hand was still moving but the watch was about an hour behind the current time. This watch just needed cleaning and a little adjustment.

"I think I can get this timepiece in good working order in about an hour." Joe said and then he realized he hadn't thought through how he was going to identify people's watches from each other and ensure that the right watch got back to the right person. Joe then remembered the ticket he had in his pocket from the Chinaman.

Joe proceeded to take a piece of paper from a little note book he carried in his shirt pocket and wrote the number 001 on it twice and asked the man his fist name and wrote that down below the top number. He then folded the page in half tore the page in half and gave the man the bottom half with just the number 001.

"When you come back give me this piece of paper and I'll be sure you get your watch." Joe explained.

With that Joe went back up to his room and sat down at his desk and proceeded to pry the back off the watch with his jackknife. As expected the workings were filthy. He proceeded to take out gears and place them in the oil he had put in a small can lid. Joe checked the jewel in which the main wheel fits and found it to be in good shape. He then reassembled the gears and wheels and adjusted the mechanism that controls the speed of the fly wheel and put a very small amount of grease around the back, where the back lid snaps on to the back like a gasket. Joe snapped the back in place, then polished the watch, cleaned the lens and rewound the watch. This had taken about 10 minutes and had earned him 25 cents. A few more watches and he would be ok until he got to the lumber camp.

In fact the demand for repair to watches was almost more than Joe could handle.

Over the next two days he repaired about 100 watches. Three he wasn't able to repair because of problems with gears or worn jewels. He went back to these three customers and explained the problem and offered to pay them 25 cents to buy the broken watches. They of course wanted to know, if they weren't working, why would he want to buy them?

"There are good working parts in each of these watches that I can use to repair someone else's watch and I believe you should be paid for these parts." Joe explained. In all three cases the customer was more than pleased to receive something for a broken item and sold Joe the watches. This seventy-five cent expense soon paid for itself as he worked on the twenty-five watches he repaired over the next two days.

It was time to start working on his sermon for Sunday. Joe sat and looked at the blank page before him and picked up his pen and dipped it into the ink well that was sitting on the table.

He always liked Psalm 23 and the pastoral nature of the Psalm. It was too often relegated to funerals. Joe felt strongly that this was a Psalm with a message for the living and he would use this as his text for his first sermon. He opened his well-thumbed Bible to the middle, which brought him to the book of Psalms. Then he leafed over to Psalm 23 and began to read.

Psalm 23:1-6
"The LORD [is] my shepherd; I shall not want.
He maketh me to lie down in green pastures: he leadeth me beside the still waters.
He restoreth my soul: he leadeth me in the paths of righteousness for his name's sake.
Yea, though I walk through the valley of the shadow of death, I will fear no evil: for thou [art] with me; thy rod and thy staff they comfort me.
Thou preparest a table before me in the presence of mine enemies: thou anointest my head with oil; my cup runneth over.
Surely goodness and mercy shall follow me all the days of my life: and I will dwell in the house of the LORD for ever." (KJV)

Joe had learned that even though you thought you knew scripture well, it was important to read it once to get it in rhythm and into your mind, then you read it again to absorb the feel of the scripture, then you read it at least once more and allow yourself to reflect on the meaning and implications and how it might be used in the situation. After finishing the third read Joe felt the words starting to form in his mind. Joe proceeded to jot down these key words:

"Shepherd", "maketh", "Leadeth", "Restoreth", "comfort me", "preparest", "runneth over", "goodness and mercy"

Then on a new page he wrote a sermon that drew upon the role of the Shepherd who looks after his flock – The Shepherd in this case was God and we are the flock of sheep. The Shepherd will protect his sheep, ensure that that they have what they need with green pastures and cool water. God will protect us when we are in danger. If we believe in God we will have everlasting life.

Then he moved to Mark 6:34 and read the following:

> *"And Jesus, when he came out, saw many people, and was moved with compassion toward them, because they were as sheep not having a shepherd: and he began to teach them many things."(KJV)*

And a later reference to Jesus as a Shepherd, Mark 14:27

> *"And Jesus saith unto them, All ye shall be offended because of me this night: for it is written, I will smite the shepherd, and the sheep shall be scattered."(KJV)*

How to tie these into Psalm 23 he wondered? Then he decided that he could make reference to the Shepherd of Psalm 23 as the Father and the Shepherd of Mark as the Son – and like the Son, Joe had been sent to begin to teach.

Then Joe wondered whether he should have an altar call at his first service and thought Luke 15 would go well with this idea:

> *Luke 15:4-7*
> *"What man of you, having an hundred sheep, if he loose one of them, doth not leave the ninety and nine in the wilderness, and go after that which is lost, until he find it? And when he hath found [it], he layeth [it] on his shoulders, rejoicing. And when he cometh home, he calleth together [his] friends and neighbours, saying unto them, Rejoice with me; for I have found my sheep which was lost. I say unto you, that likewise joy shall be in heaven over one sinner that repenteth, more than over ninety and nine just persons, which need no repentance."(KJV)*

After a lengthy review of Mark 14:27 Joe decided not to include this in his first sermon, since he had no desire to suggest to them that they may find themselves disbanding when he left. It was his job to find elders to assume a leadership role while the charge was without trained leadership. He had to instill in the people of Rossland that God was with them at all times, not just when a Pastor was available to lead worship. No, he would not include any possible negative themes in his sermons. He had a message of comfort (from Psalm 23), and hope and building for the future (Mark 6:34). He was ready to start his mission work!

As for an Altar Call, Joe felt that this might be too much at the first service and decided he would introduce it at the next service using the Luke parable to tie it into this Sunday's sermon.

Joe then took out his wooden flute and practiced a couple of hymns he felt the people of Rossland would remember from their days back East.

After dinner, Joe went to his room feeling like he had accomplished much in his first 24 hours. He had a place to stay and eat his meals, he had a job, a gun, a horse and his first Church Service scheduled for Sunday and finally his sermon started. What more could he ask for? Oh, his shirt!

With that Joe jumped up off his bed and headed down to the Chinaman's Tent and found him sitting outside waiting. He had Joe's shirt in a package. He asked for his piece of paper and his two cents and then gave Joe his shirt with a bow and encouraged him to come back again.

Joe headed back to his room and had to move through a Saloon that was starting to fill up for an evening of activity. The "girls" made sure they recognized him and encouraged him to stay around for some "Fun". Joe thanked them and headed upstairs laughing. Ready to settle at last! 'What more could he wish for after one day?' he asked himself again.

Sleep!

Dutch had said the saloon got noisy after dinner, but the din that echoed up through the floorboards was incredible. He would just get off to sleep and there would be a fight or a chair flipping over and around 2 pm the sound of a gun going off. Hopefully the floorboards were thick enough to absorb any stray bullets that might fly into the ceiling of the room below him. It will be nice to get out to the lumber camp and get some sleep!

Morning came quickly and Joe was not feeling very refreshed. He wandered downstairs and stopped for some breakfast, porridge with brown sugar and dark bread.

Dutch had the nerve to ask him how he had slept!

"Sleep! With all the noise down here, you have to be kidding," responded Joe with a level of disbelief in his voice that Dutch would even ask the question.

"I know it gets loud down here, but I put you as far away as I could from the noise." Dutch insisted.

Joe just shook his head and headed out the door to the General Store.

"I need some bullets," Joe said as he showed his pistol to Herman.

"I have just the ammunition for that gun," Herman in his best sales voice responded, "one box or two?"

"How much a box?" inquired Joe.

"Fifteen cents a box or two for twenty-five cents."

"I'll take two."

Joe took the boxes and headed out of town and walked about a couple of miles down the logging road until he was sure he was out of hearing distance of the town. He then went over to a tree and tacked a paper target he had created by using different sized circles – using his watch, for the centre circle, a bean can for the next circle and a plate for the outer circle. He then counted off 100 steps and turned, looked around to make sure that no one was in the area, then cocked his revolver and brought it down for sighting and squeezed the trigger. The bullet exploded from the gun barrel and the recoil of the gun itself threw the barrel back up towards his face.

Joe walked over to the target and checked. He had just grazed the outside edge of the right side of the paper, another inch and he would have missed the sheet entirely. This was terrible. Joe was a fair marksman with a rifle. How could his aim be so poor with a revolver?

Back at his firing mark, Joe analyzed what had happened. He had brought the revolver down to a position for aiming. When he fired his rifle he always brought the stock of the gun up to the position of firing, aimed and pulled the trigger, the recoil was back and up.

Why did he think he had to bring the gun down to the aiming position? Just because this was the convention of how to shoot a pistol didn't make it right. If he followed this logic, he should box right handed, yet he had been successful as a left handed boxer. Why not bring the revolver up to the aiming position with his arm out straight, with just a slight bend in the elbow to allow the recoil to continue the upward movement smoothly after he fired. He practiced this movement a number of times, slowing at the aiming position and then letting his forearm continue in an upward flow. This felt comfortable and allowed him to get the sight by the chamber and the nose of the barrel lined up. Once he felt comfortable with this movement, he would try again and see if the sights were lined up or if he had to make adjustments to his aim.

Joe positioned his feet with his left foot forward and his right foot in a position to allow him to be comfortably balanced, allowing his left arm to be square to the target when extended. The time had come to try again.

Joe positioned his feet, looked squarely at the target with his left eye, cocked the gun and brought it up with his left arm extended, quickly lined up the sights and squeezed the trigger. Once again as the bullet exploded from the barrel, the gun continued up with its recoil and Joe squinted towards the target. He was going to have to walk over to the target and examine it up close. As he walked towards the target his ears were ringing from the sound of the explosion.

Just off dead centre, the paper was torn where it hadn't been before. He was about an inch to the right of dead centre. The sights were obviously well aligned. The slight off centre was not the sight. It was human error - not feeling totally comfortable with the new firing arm. A few more shots and he should be able to put the shots dead centre, like he could with his rifle.

Joe continued to practice for the next two hours and used up a box of 100 shells. At the end of this time, Joe was feeling comfortable with his new side arm and knew that if he continued to practice each day he would be as accomplished a shooter as any around. However, he wasn't sure he could afford to expense more than a couple hundred shells without affecting his budget.

He would practice for the next day and take a couple hundred shells with him to the Camp.

On Saturday, Joe arranged for Jim Green and a couple of his pals to meet him in the Pasture where the church service was to be held. Joe wanted to install a tent-like canopy that would be run off the east of the big chestnut tree. This would allow worship in any weather. They dug holes for four 14' poles set them in their holes and stabilized them with guy ropes. Then they dug four more holes on each side of the centre poles – lined up with them and inserted eight 8 foot poles.

Then they ran ropes from the top of the centre poles, one pole to the top of the next. Over these ropes they hoisted canvas and that they lashed together with rope to make it large enough to stretch to the outside poles. These were tied off and the poles reinforced with guy ropes to hold the make-shift worship tent in place.

Finally they cut sections of a log about two feet in length and strung planks on top of these stumps to act as seats.

Jim brought an old wagon he was working on over to the front of the "tent" and backed it into place. This gave Joe a stage to work from. Joe arranged for two rows of benches to be placed to the right of the stage looking out towards the other rows of benches.

If he could find members, these would be for his "Choir".

It took the whole day to accomplish this and at the end of he day Joe offered to pay his help for the day. To a man they turned down the offer – much to Joe's appreciation, since money was still tight – even with the money from his watch repair.

These were good lads and Joe had gotten to know them well over the course of the day. Jim of course was a blacksmith. Allen and James were the sons of Herman Schmidt and they were 15 and 17 respectively. Both boys were strapping young men and eager to work. Larry was one of the "cowboys" that had been near the corral the day that Joe had bought Tar and was impressed with this Sky Pilot and his apparent lack of fear. It was hard to tell his age, but Joe guessed he was in his late twenty's. He was a drifter and went where there was work.

Finally there was Bill Tuck, the husband of Ellen Tuck whom he had met in the General Store on his first day. Bill looked like a mountain man with his barrel chest and beard that hadn't been trimmed in months. He had arrived home from prospecting the day after Joe had met his wife. He had been in the mountains for three months and indicated that he had had a bit of success. Prospectors tended to either understate their situation or they bragged so much you knew they were lying through their teeth, Joe soon learned. In this case, Bill was understating his success, since he didn't want anyone following him out when he returned to his claim in a few weeks.

Joe soon realized that it was Ellen that had sent her husband over to help out, but as it turned out, Bill and Jim were close friends and had a great deal of respect for each other. In fact, Bill often helped Jim out at the forge when he was home and Jim had extra work.

This group of men worked well together and enjoyed ribbing each other as they worked. Thankfully the pasture wasn't as rocky as most of the surrounding area and most of the poles went in quite easily.

However, Allen and James hit a spot for the last centre pole that had a number of large rocks that needed to be wedged out. Well, the language that started to come from this area was something to behold. Joe called over to the two lads and suggested that they remember that this was going to be a sacred place of worship – maybe they should find more appropriate ways of expressing their frustration. Both young men looked at each other and broke out laughing, then turned to Joe and James said, "Sorry Pastor, but I'm sure God has heard these words before." he said with a snicker in his voice.

"You know James, I'm sure He has, but one of the reasons He has sent me out here is to see if we can't find other ways to express our frustration that doesn't profane His name or embarrass those around you.

It looks like you guys have hit a potential gold mine there by the size of the rocks you're working out of that hole. Maybe we should have our resident prospector take a look. What do you say Bill?"

"I'll be right over there Pastor!" called Bill as he left Jim to finish their hole.

On his way over Bill pulled an iron pry bar off the wagon that Jim had brought as a stage and showed the lads how to wedge the pry bar under the stone and use it as a lever to work the rock loose. In no time they had the rock out of the hole and were able to finish their work.

"I'm afraid there is no gold here Pastor," Bill called out, "Sorry to say, I'm afraid you'll have to depend upon the service offering tomorrow, so it better be a good sermon!"

With that they all had a good laugh at Joe and he assured them he would have them all eating from the trough by the time the service was over.

Once the tent was up and the seats and stage were in place it was mid afternoon and they all headed off to do their own chores before sunset.

Joe couldn't thank them enough!

Sunday came and as Joe got out of bed he looked out his filthy window and could determine that the sun was out. It was going to be a great day for a service.

He dressed in his Sunday clothes and headed down to the saloon for a bite to eat before starting off to the tent.

It was around 8 am and the ladies were just starting to stir from their rooms. They sure gave Joe a hard time about his duds and he told them come to the service. They laughed at him and told him the ladies of the town wouldn't appreciate their attendance. Joe told them that God didn't mind who came to worship Him. They were more than welcome.

Joe had a bowl of porridge and a piece of stale brown bread for breakfast then headed down to the tent. It was about 9 am when he arrived and there were already a group of boys hanging around. Joe called them over. They shuffled their way over, not sure what to expect.

"Hi, I'm Pastor Robins," Joe told them, "and I'm glad to see so many eager beavers this morning. How would you like to go on a scavenger hunt?" Joe asked.

"What's a scavenger hunt?" asked the oldest boy, who would have been around 12.

"What's your name?" asked Joe.

"Jake!" the boy responded defiantly.

"Well Jake, I believe that God has created the world and all that is in it and a scavenger hunt helps us appreciate what God has made. I will give you a list of things I want you to find and you can either do them as a team, or you can do them as individuals It can be a race."

"Let's do them as individuals." said the smallest boy in the group, who was likely around eight.

"What's your name?" asked Joe

"They call me Shorty," he responded.

"I bet they do," laughed Joe, "but one day you're going to shoot up and likely be taller then most of these chaps you're with. What does your Mother call you?"

"I don't think you would like to hear that name Pastor, but my real name is Richard." He responded.

"What about you guys?" Joe asked, "do you want to do your own hunt or do it as a team?"

"As a team," the other two shouted.

"Well, we seem to have a difference of opinion." Joe said, "What are your names?"

"I'm Mike and he's my brother Jack." responded a boy of about 10 as he pointed to his younger brother who was about 8.

"Tell you what Shorty, let's try the first scavenger hunt as a team and next week, if you want, you can have an individual scavenger hunt. How does that sound?" Joe asked.

The boys all nodded their heads in the affirmative and Joe went on to explain that this scavenger hunt had to be done in and around the pasture and the stream that ran beside the pasture. The boys agreed to these ground rules.

"Alright, here is the list of items I want you to find. I'll give you 15 minutes. Any one of you have a watch?" Joe inquired. The Boys all shook their head no.

"Then I'll loan Jake my watch and when the big hand of the watch is here, time is up and I want you to bring back all the things you found. If you get done early, come back and we'll mark the time you took and use it as the record to beat next time.

Now, I'm going to tell each of you four different things and you have to remember what they are for the team. Are you ready?" Once again the boys shook their heads yes.

"Jake, your list is a broken bird's egg,. a chestnut, a red pebble, a yellow flower.

Shorty, your list is a burr, a piece of garnet, a maple leaf, a cattail.

Mike, your list is an oak leaf, a red flower, a grey pebble, a milkweed pod

Jack, your list is, a bird's feather, a leaf from a poplar tree, a frog, a dandelion.

Off you go." Joe shouted.

With that the boys were off arguing which item they should find first. Joe was fascinated to watch Shorty take control of the group and suggested they all head off for their four items and meet back at the wagon as soon as they had collected them.

144

When the boys arrived back in ten minutes, Jake gave Joe back his watch.

Joe checked over the material the boys had brought back and listened to their stories about how they had found the items. The boys bubbled with enthusiasm as they explained how items were found.

Joe asked the boys whether they could sing?

"Gee, Pastor, I'm not sure?" said Shorty, "We of course whistle and hum, but we have never been asked to sing before."

"Tell you what," explained Joe, "Let me play you a tune on my flute. Then I'll play it again and see if you can hum along with me?"

Joe played "Jesus loves me, this I know".

He played it again and the boys hummed along then he played it one more time and the boys hummed it again.

Then Joe taught the boys the words:

> "Jesus loves me, this I know
> For the Bible tells me so,
> Little ones to him belong,
> They are weak but he is strong.
>
> Chorus
> Yes, Jesus loves me!
> Yes, Jesus loves me!
> Yes, Jesus loves me! The Bible tells me so."*

Joe was really pleased with how well the boys sang the hymn. He then had them work on the Chorus. He explained to the boys that they needed to shout out musical note.

The boys loved this challenge and made the "Yes" ring across the meadow. They laughed so hard they could hardly sing the next three words.

---

* Words: Anna Barlett (1821-1910) Music: William Batchelder Bradbury (1816-1868)

"Very good!" Joe said, "This is a happy song, but not so happy that you breakout laughing and can't sing the most important words of the song. What are these words?" Joe asked.

Jake responded, "Jesus loves me!" in a voice that was almost a shout.

"Right!" Joe assured him, "and it should be sung like you really mean it. Do you think He does?" asked Joe.

"I don't really know much about this Jesus." Said Shorty.

"Well, we are going to have to make sure you hear about Jesus and how He loves you. After you've learned about Him, I hope you'll learn to trust and love Him like I do." Joe stated.

"Let's try the hymn one more time and add the emphasis like we just tried."

Joe explained he would play the first line, then he would go back and start the hymn from the beginning at which point the boys would begin to sing.

Joe started to play his flute and when it was time for the boys to come in, he nodded his head and the voices of the boys sounded like a choir of angels as they sang the verse, then with great enthusiasm they sang the Chorus, staying together with the loud "Yes", and made the "Jesus loves me!" sound forceful, yet melodic.

Joe couldn't have been more pleased!

He then asked if the boys would be willing to sit in the front pews facing the congregation and be his choir. He promised the boys that he would call on them early in the Service. If they didn't want to stay after they had sung their hymn through twice they could go.

The boys gathered together and had a little conference and then Shorty turned back to Joe and said, "Pastor, we'll be your Choir, but we might leave after we sing – depends how we feel." With that he spit on his right hand and stuck it out for a bargain shake.

Joe pretended to spit on his hand and made the deal making shake.

It was 10:30 am and people were starting to gather either under the chestnut tree or under the canvas awning Joe and the crew had put up yesterday. Joe moved out into the congregation and shook hands and either introduced himself or reintroduced himself.

When he came upon Herman, Elsie Schmidt and the boys, Joe made sure he told the parents what excellent workers Allen and James were and how much he appreciated their help yesterday.

When the MacIntosh family arrived, Joe made sure to thank Angus for the job and turned to Jane MacIntosh and bowed, "I look forward to joining you for lunch after worship today." Joe said to Jane.

"We look forward to having you Pastor Joe. Angus has agreed to wait until you're ready to go and he'll bring you out to the homestead." Jane explained.

Joe turned to Angus, nodded his head and said, "Angus, I appreciate the offer, but if you give me instruction, I'm sure I can find my way out to your home."

"Nonsense, it's all been arranged. The Schmidt Family will be joining us and Herman has offered to take Jane home.

We are really looking forward to the service today Pastor." Angus said with emphasis.

"Thank you so much. I hope I live up to your expectations, Boss!" Joe said in a laughing manner.

At that moment, Irene and Jim Green arrived.

"Pastor Joe, don't forget you're coming for dinner." Irene reminded Joe.

"Of course not!" Joe replied, "But since I'm having lunch out at the MacIntosh's, would you mind if it was around 8:00 pm?"

"I was going to make the same suggestion Pastor Joe.

Our cabin is right behind Jim's shop – over there." she pointed to the blacksmith shop at the end of the meadow.

"We live the closest to the service of worship, yet somehow, we seem to be near the last to arrive. Sorry!" There was a feeling of frustration in Irene's voice.

"It was my fault," Jim explained, "I didn't get my chores finished on time. I've got a sick horse that needed pampering to get her to eat. Just took more time than I allotted."

Joe looked at Jim and extended his hand, "Can't thank you enough for all you did yesterday to help get everything ready. It sounds like you should have been with that horse instead of here digging holes. Thank you Jim! Both jobs are God's work in action." With that Joe nodded to the Greens and started towards the wagon that Jim had put in place to act as a stage.

As he passed the boys, he stopped for a second and thanked them again for being his choir! They were a bit embarrassed as they noticed everyone looking at them and in some cases snickering that Joe had these ruffians sitting at the front of the church. Joe rubbed Shorty's hair and proceeded to the wagon and climbed on. The hum in the meadow began to subside and Joe began to speak.

His Call to Worship was taken from Psalm 100

In a clear voice that echoed out over the meadow Joe proclaimed:

> *"Make a joyful noise unto the LORD, all ye lands. Serve the LORD with gladness: come before his presence with singing. Know ye that the LORD he [is] God: [it is] he [that] hath made us, and not we ourselves; [we are] his people, and the sheep of his pasture. Enter into his gates with thanksgiving, [and] into his courts with praise: be thankful unto him, [and] bless his name."*[1]

Then Joe looked over the congregation, there were about forty people, mostly families that had gathered for worship today.

Joe had a flashback to his days in Port Rowan – the day he stood before the Congregation at his Father's funeral and then of his Sunday afternoon

---

[1]   Psalm 100 verses 1-4 King James Version of the Holy Bible

services that he conducted for a couple of years as a teen at the school house in Clear Creek, a small community about 9 miles west of Port Rowan along the Lakeshore Road. Joe used to attend his own Church at 11 am and when Rev. McPherson was finished – usually about 12:30, depending on how the spirit was moving him that Sunday, Joe would hitch up the buggy and head off to Clear Creek for a 4 pm Service.

The faith community at Clear Creek, would have moved the wooden desks back beside the wall and placed the chairs in rows facing the Teacher's Desk.

Joe had built a small lectern that could be placed on the desk that had a cross carved in the front of it and was slanted, with a lip at the bottom to hold his Bible and notes. Joe had built this in the ship yard and left it at the school house.

There were usually 15 to 20 in attendance on any given Sunday and after worship they would stay and have a pot luck dinner together, which Joe really enjoyed if Ma didn't want him home for dinner. This had been a new Ministry that had grown over the two years Joe conducted worship. However, once Nellie came into the picture, he made it clear that if Rev. Archer was conducting a worship service in Port Rowan, he wasn't available for Clear Creek and he would arrange for one of the lay people to conduct worship that Sunday.

Here he was again, starting a new Ministry in God's frontier.

As he looked back towards town, he saw the mud street, the Saloon, the Railway Station and a scattering of dirty, once white, canvass tents of all shapes and forms that made up Rossland with a few log cabins around the edge and thought, "Be with me Lord as I do your work."

Joe took in all this in a matter of seconds.

Then Joe said, "Let us pray." And Joe began to pray in a voice that reached the far end of the awning area, "Lord, be with your people today as we start on a new journey together. Bless this community of Rossland and the people who have braved many obstacles to make it a reality.

Father, we thank you for giving us a beautiful day to hold our first service of worship. We take this as a good sign of the things to come.

Father, we thank you for the opportunity to come together as a worshipping community. We ask your blessing on those that haven't found their way to us yet. Help them realize that life is only worth living if we believe in you.

These things we ask in Jesus' name. Amen"

Joe continued, "My friends, I had the opportunity to meet some new young friends before the service of worship today and they were kind enough to bring some of God's precious gifts to us today. We have wild flowers, pebbles, feathers, sticks, and stones.

Let me introduce you to my new friends, Jake, Richard, who most of you know as Shorty, Mike and his brother James, a good biblical name.

These young men have agreed to be the first Choir for Rossland Methodist Church and I am very pleased to introduce you to them as they sing, 'Jesus Loves Me'. Let me just get my flute."

With that Joe indicated he wanted the boys to stand and he played the introduction to the hymn and as they had practiced, he nodded his head toward them as a signal to start on his first note.

The boys sang better than they had in practice. Their voices swirled out over the congregation and you could see the people smile. As they listened attentively to the "First Choir of Rossland Methodist Church" sing their hearts out. The boys really gave the chorus a work out and hit the "Yes" with meaning and made their pause before they went into "Jesus loves me…"

They might look like a group of ruffians, and most times they might act like it, but today at this specific moments, they were as close to angels as they could attain, without actually being dead!

As one, the congregation rose and applauded the boys and Joe at the end of the hymn. Joe put up his hand in a stop motion and said, "Thank you for your generous outpouring of support, but this is a worship service not a performance, we are offering our talents to God, and we do so with humility and no expectation of recognition from our fellow members of the congregation. However, if you like or don't like something someone has said, sung, played during this worship, I encourage you to speak with them after the service of worship and share your thoughts with them."

Once Joe had established the parameters of his expectation of worship, he continued on by reading the scripture for the day.

He took his Bible in his left hand and began to read from Psalm 23,

> *"The LORD [is] my shepherd; I shall not want. He maketh me to lie down in green pastures: he leadeth me beside the still waters. He restoreth my soul: he leadeth me in the paths of righteousness for his name's sake. Yea, though I walk through the valley of the shadow of death, I will fear no evil: for thou [art] with me; thy rod and thy staff they comfort me. Thou preparest a table before me in the presence of mine enemies: thou anointest my head with oil; my cup runneth over. Surely goodness and mercy shall follow me all the days of my life: and I will dwell in the house of the LORD for ever."[2]*

As he read this well-known Psalm, he saw people reading from their family Bibles or reciting the words from memory.

He knew he had picked the right Psalm and he had the congregation with him. It felt good and his confidence grew in the Spirit.

Then he offered the New Testament Lesson Mark 6: 30 – 34.

Joe explained that today's scripture occurred just after Jesus' Disciples had informed Him of the beheading of His cousin John the Baptist and that John's Disciples had come to Jesus.

> *"And the apostles gathered themselves together unto Jesus, and told him all things, both what they had done, and what they had taught. And he said unto them, Come ye yourselves apart into a desert place, and rest a while: for there were many coming and going, and they had no leisure so much as to eat. And they departed into a desert place by ship privately. And the people saw them departing, and many knew*

---

[2]   Psalm 23:1-6 King James Version of the Holy Bible

him, and ran afoot thither out of all cities, and outwent them, and came together unto him. And Jesus, when he came out, saw much people, and was moved with compassion toward them, because they were as sheep not having a shepherd: and he began to teach them many things."[3]

After reading this scripture, Joe asked the young people to come forward, including the Choir and asked that they sit on the first bench or on the grass in front of the wagon.

Joe then sat himself on the edge of the wagon with his legs hanging over the side.

He looked up at the Congregation and said, "Excuse me a few minutes while I spend time with these young disciples of God." Then he turned his gaze upon the 10 young people that gathered in front of him.

"I would like to share with you a story today that I hope will be like a parable. Do you know what a parable is?" There was no answer and Joe watched as he lost eye contact with most of the group. He laughed and said, "Don't worry, today you're going to learn a new word, 'Parable', a parable is a story told that has a second meaning attached to it, or usually has a lesson to be learned. Jesus used Parables all the time when he was teaching His disciples.

See if you can figure out what this parable is saying, what's the hidden meaning?

'Once upon a time there was a grandfather bull frog that just sat on a lily pad all day long. He was very old and very wise, but the young frogs used to swim all around him, jump on his lily pad, jump off, swim to shore and go on land and all the time they were hunting for food. They sought a tasty fly', with this all the kids made 'ugh' noises and Joe laughed and continued on, 'remember, frogs like flies like you like apple pie. Now the more the young frogs bounced and jumped around the fewer flies they seemed to catch. But our Grandfather Bull Frog, just sat on his lily pad as still as still can be, and every once in awhile, his tongue would lash out and he

---

[3]   Mark 6 30-34 King James Version of the Holy Bible

would catch a big juicy fly. Over the hours of the day, Grandfather Bull Frog caught almost twice as many flies as our young frogs and never left his lily pad. Do you know why he was so successful?' asked Joe

Shorty shot his hand up and Joe acknowledged him, "There were two reasons Pastor Robins, first by sitting in one spot he blended in with the Lily pad and the flies didn't realize he was a frog and second, he was older and wiser and had learned how to hunt flies over the years." responded Shorty.

"Right you are, Shorty!" exclaimed Joe. "I couldn't have said it better!"

Shorty beamed with this compliment.

"Now the parable section of this story is, you can scurry and look for the meaning of life, but if you go to your Bible, which is always there for you – you can find the answers you're looking for. It's tried and true – just waiting for you!" Joe said. Then he asked the children to join him in a prayer by repeating after him. "Dear Lord – when we feel confused – help us to remember - that if we read our Bible – we can find the answers to our questions. Amen" and Joe sent the children back to their parents. To the choir he said in a quiet voice, "good chance to leave if you wish." The boys looked at each other and Shorty said, "Think we'll stay Pastor." And they proceeded to take their places in their pews facing the congregation and rocking their feet back and forth.

Joe picked up his wooden flute and played:

> "O Lamb of God that takes away the sins of the world, have mercy upon us:
> O Lamb of God that takes away the sins of the world, have mercy upon us:
> O Lamb of God that takes away the sins of the world, grant us Thy peace."[4]

After playing it through once, Joe taught the congregation the words and had them sing it four times as he played the flute.

---

[4]   Angus Del J. Merrecke 1523-1583
      "O Lamb of God…"

The Boys Choir caught on right away and was a great help in helping the congregation keep the beat and the tune.

Upon completion of this hymn, Joe approached the congregation to make an offering and indicated that whatever was given would go into a building fund for the new Church in Rossland.

Joe asked the boys to take small wooden boxes that Joe had scrounged from Dutch that used to hold cigars and had them move through the congregation while Joe played Henry Purcell's tune that originally had the words of Poet Laureate John Dryden's words that were part of a song from the Opera 'King Arthur' and expounded upon the Goddess Venus. This song was written in the seventeenth century. However, Charles Wesley had decided that this music was too good to be wasted upon a pagan goddess and re-wrote the words to praise Jesus and it became the much loved hymn "Love Divine, all loves excelling..."[5]

As Joe looked out into the congregation he could see the smiles on peoples faces as he played and he knew that the offering would be a good one. He had learned this from observing Rev. Archer when he was in Port Rowan when he had Nellie and Albert sing and play together – if they caught the right mood of the congregation the offering was always higher than those night when people were down.

Once the offering was brought forward Joe prayed over it: *"Lord we give you all that we have, for all we are is thine alone. Lord, please bless this offering and the hands that have made it possible. May this offering be a new beginning for the congregation for Rossland as they start towards the establishment of their first Church building. Amen."*

Joe then started his sermon which was based on the concept of God as the Great Shepherd and we are His flock. Then moving on to Jesus as the Shepherd and once again we are His flock and finally the importance of the flock to stay together for protection and how the Shepherd will go looking for the lost sheep to ensure His whole flock is safe.

---

[5]   Music Henry Purcell 1659 - 1605, Arrangement Rowland Hugh Pritchard 1811-1887 Words, Charles Wesley, 1707 - 1788

Joe stressed that the time had come for the "Flock" in Rossland to start worshiping together on a weekly basis and to start studying the Bible in small groups as they worked towards the establishment of the first Methodist Church structure in Rossland.

Joe felt he was into the delivery, the words and the examples were flowing nicely and only one or two of the men had drifted off to sleep. This really was no surprise. From his experiences at Clear Creek, he knew that when men who worked six days a week outside in the fields are asked to sit still for half and hour to an hour their eyes just shut naturally. It was no exception at this service.

Upon summing up and saying his Amen, he led the congregation in one more hymn. It was one they all knew by heart, "Amazing Grace". Before he played it he did what Nellie had suggested and explained to the congregation the story behind the hymn.

"John Newton had been an orphan at six," Joe explained, "and had gone to sea at eleven. As a teenager he was press ganged into the navy. He was a rebel and had been flogged for desertion. Then he had become involved in the slave trade and had almost died of starvation when he lived in Sierra Leone.

At the age of twenty-three in 1748, Newton was on a slaver cargo ship that got caught in a severe storm. He found himself fighting for his life against the elements of nature. Exhausted from working the pumps and frozen from the water that was splashing over the gunnels of the ship, he called out to God to save him, and was amazed when the weather broke and he found himself saved from certain death.

Newton's life took many twists and turns, renouncing the slave trade and at the age of thirty- nine Newton became a Minister in he Christian Church and led the fight against Slavery.

Out of his experiences of the storm and his conversion to Christianity John Newton wrote the much loved "Amazing Grace."

Joe explained he would play the first verse then when he repeated it he would like the congregation to join him.

As Joe played the first time, he could see people were thinking about the story he had told about Newton and when they joined in and sang the hymn, they sang with a feeling that resonated deep within their souls.

It was a beautiful, sacred way to end their service of worship together.

Upon completion of the Hymn, Joe pronounced the Benediction "*The grace of our Lord Jesus Christ, and the love of God, and the fellowship of the Holy Spirit, be with you all evermore. Amen*" Joe said with his arms raised to heaven as he blessed his sheep.

As people started to leave the Worship Area, they stopped and thanked Joe for a wonderful first service and pledged their support to be back next week. Plus many of the men indicated that once Joe had land and was ready to build, to let them know and they would be more than willing to help build the Church.

The parents of the Boys Choir came over to Joe and told them how proud they were to have their sons involved in the service and how surprised they were that their children could sing so well. As far as they were concerned, Joe was a miracle worker!

Joe assured them that the boys had been a treasure to work with and real gentlemen. This the parents found hard to believe, but Joe assured them they had. By this time the boys had joined their parents and had heard the glowing comments of Pastor Robins. These lads hadn't received many complements in their short lives. In fact, they spent most of their time trying to explain their way out of trouble. This was a new experience for them and they kind of liked the attention and the praise.

When Joe asked them if they would be back next Sunday at 10 for Sunday school and choir practice, he received a resounding "Yes!" from all of them. They were now in tow of their parents and heading away from Worship.

Joe took a quick look around and picked up a bit of garbage, then turned back to where Angus MacIntosh was waiting beside his rig.

As Joe swung up onto the seat of the buckboard, Angus, who had already seated himself and was holding the horses still by tightly holding back on the reins, said, "Well my boy, that was some service! I can't get over how you turned those ruffians into a choir of angels. I've chased those kids away from my office daily over the last year. They are always in trouble. I just couldn't believe you could get them to settle down long enough to learn a song and then to sit through the whole service without causing problems. You have a real talent young man. Have you ever thought of being a teacher?"

By now the horses had their head and were trotting down the rut that led out of town towards the forest about a quarter mile ahead.

"Well Mr. MacIntosh, I just finished two years as a teacher in the downtown area of Detroit, across the border in the USA." Joe explained, "But God had other plans for me, and here I am."

"And we are mighty fortunate to have you, I think." exclaimed Angus McPherson.

The rest of the ride was taken up with McPherson pointing out areas of interest, types of trees in the area and soon they were pulling up to a clearing that sat on a ridge that had a beautiful panoramic view of the area, even capturing a waterfall about a quarter mile away as the bird flies. It was an awesome view!

Joe observed a large log cabin compared to most he had seen with a wide wrap-around porch that had rocking chairs and a table and chairs set up for lunch Joe was pleased they were going to eat out where they could admire the view and enjoy the wonderful weather they were experiencing that day.

Already sitting around the table were the Schmidt boys and Herman. Elsie and Jane were busy bringing the food outdoors and placing it on the table.

McPherson turned to Joe once they had dismounted from the buckboard and said, "There's a wash stand at the side of the cabin if you feel like washing up. I'll just stable the horses and join you."

Joe wandered over to the wash basin that was sitting on a wooden shelf attached to the side of the wall and waved to those by the table as he wandered by them. He was just finishing when McPherson hurried up and started to scrub up. "Have to hurry," he said, "Jane doesn't like her food to get cold. However, if you're going to eat outside it's bound to get cold, don't you think?" he said with a laugh.

Both men walked around to the front of the house and up the three stairs to porch. The discussion that had been happening as they arrived and McPherson stated how pleased he was to have Pastor Joe and the Schmidt Family as their guests for lunch.

Joe was asked to say grace.

Joe soon found that if you're really hungry, which he was, grace tended to be short. He offered a thank you for those who prepared the food, to God for allowing them to share the food and to their host for inviting them to his table. Amen, let's eat!

As the food was being passed around, Joe received compliments from everyone, which he received humbly and was able to move the conversation off himself and towards the future of a new Church in Rossland.

"Where do you think we might obtain land for a new Church?" inquired Joe to those around the table.

"Why I have land that I would make available," responded MacIntosh, "but none of it is close enough to town to make it very attractive for a Church site."

"If I were you, I'd make some inquiries from Jim Green, he owns the pasture that we held the service on today. It's all part of the parcel that he bought when he established his Blacksmith Shop" offered Elsie.

"As you know, I have been invited to dinner with the Green's tonight. I'll bring up the subject and see what sort of response I might get. However, how I'm going to eat any more today after this lovely lunch, I just don't know? Thank you Jane for your very gracious hospitality!" with that Joe lifted his glass of apple cider and saluted Jane MacIntosh and everyone joined in.

"Tell you what Pastor, you get yourself a lot and I'll give you the lumber to build your Church." MacIntosh said.

"And I'll donate the hardware necessary to put the lumber together." offered Schmidt, not wanting to be out done by his friend.

"We'll help build it Pastor." said Allen, "won't we James?"

"You can count on us Pastor Joe!" exclaimed James.

"My goodness, with all these offers, we nearly have the Church built. Now if God will help us with the next step, maybe we can arrange the land before the day is over." Joe stated with a feeling of confidence that this was certainly a God driven project.

After lunch, the men walked over toward the corral, while the ladies cleaned up and Schmidt and MacIntosh lit up a cigar after offering one to Joe, which Joe most graciously turned down. Both Allen and James indicated they would be quite willing to take Pastor Joe's cigar for him, but Herman quickly stamped out that offer.

The discussion turned towards Joe's first encounter with the lumber camp tomorrow.

"As I indicated when I signed you on Pastor, work at the Camp is pretty rugged." MacIntosh stated again.

"I understand the situation Mr. MacIntosh, but as I mentioned during my interview, my Father died when I was a young teenager and I had take over my Father's Boat Yard and finish off three ships due within a few months of my Father's death. My younger brother and myself worked before school and long into the night to get those ships finished on time. I don't mean to downgrade the hardships that face me or the amount of work you expect out of your employees, but I'll be surprised if it comes close to the pressure Will and I were under for those few months." Joe explained.

There was quiet for a few moments with all there absorbed with what Joe had just shared. For the brothers, there was an air of hero worship that came over them. Schmidt and MacIntosh just nodded and appeared to have accepted Joe as an equal in a man's world.

After the cigars were smoked, the men joined the women on the porch for lemonade and coffee.

"Pastor, I really like the 23rd Psalm and was really pleased you used it in your first Service," said Elsie, "but you know, I'm not sure I understand all the symbolism that is part of that much beloved scripture."

"I'll tell you what," Joe responded, "you promise to come to worship next week and I'll base my message on the symbolism of Psalm 23."

"Well that's an easy promise to keep, since I wouldn't have missed next Sunday's worship for anything." exclaimed Elsie.

"You have a deal!" Joe committed. "As much as I have enjoyed my time with you all, I think I had better be getting back to Town and getting ready for my next engagement."

"I'll go out and hitch up the horse." MacIntosh offered.

"That won't be necessary Angus, it's time for us to be leaving and we'll be glad to take Pastor Joe back to town with us." looking at his family, Herman asked, "are you folks ready?"

There was general consent that it was time to go and the boys went out to hitch up the carriage and brought it up to the front of the house with Allen driving. He quickly hopped down and moved to the seat in the back of the carriage facing backward and was joined by James. Herman helped Elsie into the back in the front facing seat and Joe was assisted in beside her. Herman then climbed up into the driver's seat.

They all waved good bye to the MacIntoshs and shouted their thanks as the two matching black horses jolted the carriage forward and they were off at a good trot.

Herman drew up in front of the Saloon and Joe climbed down and extended a hand to shake to Herman as a way to thank him for his hospitality. It was agreed that Joe would see them early the next morning to get his equipment before he headed out to the camp.

Joe wandered into the Saloon and was surrounded by a bevy of buxom blonds, with the odd redhead thrown in, as they asked about the service and kidded Joe about offering a Sunday Special that would make him a real man.

Joe laughed good naturedly with the ladies and encouraged them to attend next week's service, at which, Lil, still smarting from Joe's earlier retort to her on his first day in Rossland, responded, "Why Sky Pilot, your Service is at 11 o'clock, by that time we are just getting up and helping to wake our men up after a night of heaven."

"I'm sure it was heaven for them, but you must wonder if hell could be any worse and I'm sure you'd like to remember the days when you attended Church and felt that glow that doesn't come from man, but from God."

"God doesn't pay a dollar a lay, Pastor!" Lil shout back.

"You're right Lil, God only offers you eternal life." Joe responded and with that he headed up to his room to the laughs and shouts of those around him.

It was already 4 pm and Joe was stuffed. He decided he would change into his casual clothes and go for a walk to attempt to work up an appetite. Joe slipped on his buckskins and headed down the backstairs so he wouldn't have to have another round with his special "friends" in the saloon.

He slipped out the backdoor and just about fell over a man who was lying in the alley. Joe bent over to see if the man was alright and quickly realized that he was passed out from too much drink. He reeked of alcohol and his own vomit. Joe rolled him over to get him out of his vomit and realized that he was going to have to sleep it off. It wasn't cold out here, he'd be alright and Joe would check on him when he came back.

Joe headed down the lane and turned right at the corner of main street. He walked at a good pace and started towards the train station, then turned again to the right and walked parallel to the tracks. On his right side were rows of white tents, which was home to most of the inhabitants of Rossland. They weren't pitched in any order that made sense. One would have thought that someone would have marked out the streets on a grid and that the tents would have been pitched in a nice straight order. Instead, tents were pitched wherever the owner felt like pitching them, causing an impossible number of alleys and switches if one were to attempt to wander from point "a" to point "b" though the tents.

For that reason, Joe had decided to walk around the outside of the town and not try to maneuver through the forest of scattered tents. Someday, someone was going to have to attempt to make some sense out of this mess.

As the sun was starting to set the weather was starting to get colder and Joe was able to see his breath as he walked along. He was very surprised at how warm the buckskins kept him as he walked along.

It took about an hour to walk the perimeter of the Town and Joe was starting to come to the alley that led to the back door of the Saloon. As he turned down the alley he was surprise to see that the drunk was no longer curled up by the back door.

As Joe entered the Saloon by the back door he tripped over a figure sitting against the wall cursing at him for disturbing his space. Joe caught his balance and knew from the smell in the hallway, he had just re-met his friend from outside.

"If I give you five cents for a coffee, will you promise to spend it on a coffee?" Joe asked the man.

"Sure buddy." came the slurred response.

Joe gave him the five cents and watched him use the wall to steady himself as he made his way towards the saloon proper.

Joe was positive that his five cents wasn't going towards a coffee, but rather was a grubstake towards the 15 cents for a shot of whisky. However, one had to have faith!

Joe continued up stairs, changed back into his Sunday clothes and felt much better for his constitutional. In fact, it was hard to believe he had worked up an appetite. He then wandered back downstairs, stood at the end of the bar and chatted with Dutch for a few minutes before going to the Green's.

"I heard you had a good service, Pastor." Dutch opened up the conversation.

"How did you hear that Dutch?" asked Joe.

"Oh, a couple of the lads had taken their wives to the Service and then came over for a 'chat' before heading home for dinner," explained Dutch.

Joe laughed, "Obviously I didn't have a great impact on them if they headed over here right after." Joe said.

"Oh come on now Pastor, Rome wasn't built in a day. I thought you must have done something right if you were able to get those kids to sing like angels. I tell you, this story has gone around the Town like forest fire. The kids have been in so much trouble over the last year that most business owners would welcome buying them a one way ticket to Vancouver." Dutch shared his frustration with them.

"They're good kids," Joe said, "they're just bored, Instead of shooing them off, why don't the merchants come up with some jobs they could do and pay them a little for the work."

"What do you have in mind?" Dutch asked, not quite sure he wanted to hear the answer.

"I'm not really sure," Joe said, "but what about sweeping the wooden sidewalks a couple of times a day, or, how about cleaning up the horse manure out on the street, or filling in the ruts in the street with dry sand, or maybe washing windows. Now there is something I'd pay for, the window in my room hasn't been cleaned since this building was first built."

"Well you know, Pastor, you might have something there. I'll talk it over with Herman and some of the other merchants. You just might have an idea that would work! Do you think those little ruffians would stay at a job until it was finished?"

"Yes" Joe said, "I'm sure they would, if they were paid for their work and if they were recognized for the effort they put into it. I think the praise is more important than the money for these lads. However, I'm not saying they shouldn't be paid an honest amount for their work."

With this, Joe left the saloon and started to walk down the street towards the Blacksmith Shop. When he arrived he noted a log cabin behind the shop he hadn't noted on his earlier visit. It was nestled into a clearing at the edge of the woods. As Joe walked around the path beside the shop he was struck how perfectly the cabin fitted into the clearing and what a nice view it had off the west side of the cabin towards a valley with a small stream flowing through. Nice again, there was a porch that wrapped around the front and two sides of the cabin. However, unlike this afternoon, it was far too cool to sit out for dinner tonight. Joe noted that smoke was curling up from the chimney built on the outside of the east side of the cabin.

As Joe approached the steps up to the veranda, he could smell the food that was being cooked on his behalf and he found it hard to believe that he could be hungry again after the meal he had only a few hours ago. But he was!

Joe knocked on the door and within seconds it was whisked open by Jim.

"Pastor, right on time! I hope you brought your appetite with you! As I told you, Irene has been cooking up a storm ever since we got back from the service today."

"Hello Jim. I could smell the most wonderful cooking smells as I arrived at your home and now that I'm inside they smell even better. I'm sorry Irene that you've gone to all this trouble. I would have been content with leftovers." Joe explained, "however, I do appreciate the time and effort you have put into this dinner."

"Pastor, please sit down over here," Irene said as she pointed out a rocking chair by the fireplace, "Dinner will be about ready in about fifteen minutes."

Joe ambled over to the rocking chair and sat down as instructed and Jim joined him in the other rocking chair that was positioned on the other side of the fireplace hearth.

"Well, how did lunch go at the MacIntosh's?" asked Jim

"Extremely well," responded Joe, " Angus had invited the Schmidts to join us and we were able to sit out on their veranda and enjoy a lovely lunch. I'm amazed that I can even think of eating again. However, I went out for a constitutional upon arriving back to town and found that I've worked up quite an appetite. I'm quite sure I can do justice to your dinner tonight."

Joe went on to explain, "I was thrilled to learn that MacIntosh has offered the wood for a new church and Schmidt has offered all the hardware. I believe God has a plan and it's coming together."

"Where do you plan to build this Church?" Jim asked

"I'm not sure Jim, it needs to be near town and highly visible. I want it to be a meeting place as well as a worship space. I can even see it being used as a school when not in use as a church. I have no idea what land is available around the edge of the town." Joe explained, hoping Jim might jump in at this point, but it was Irene that spoke up.

"Pastor, Jim and I were really impressed with the Service today. It brought back so many memories for me of my upbringing in Orangeville Ontario. I felt like a bit of Ontario had at last found its way to Rossland. I really like what you did with the boys. That Choir was very special and meant a lot to those boys, and to us.

Jim and I had a long talk while the dinner was cooking, and we would like to offer an acre of our land, right were you held the service today. We would be honoured to have the Church and the manse built on that site if you think it would suit your needs?"

"Irene, Jim, I can't tell you how happy this makes me. I can't think of a better place in all of Rossland for the Church. God is moving this project much faster than I could have dreamed. Your gift is the corner stone that makes it possible. May God bless you both! Yes, I know the Church would be honoured to accept your gift. We will have to form a Board of Trustees to assume control of the property and the buildings on behalf of the Methodist Church of Canada. Jim I hope you will consider being a Trustee, and I was thinking of asking Angus and Herman to get us started. Would you agree to this idea?"

"Pastor, I would be honoured to accept and I think the other two gentlemen you have named would make excellent Trustees for Rossland Methodist Church." Jim responded all grins.

"I think dinner is ready," called Irene,

"Pastor Joe, will you say the blessing?" Irene asked as the three of them assembled around the wooden table that was laden with food.

"I would be honoured." Joe responded, "*Dear Lord bless Jim and Irene for their very gracious offer of land to build Your Church, bless the fellowship that we are experiencing around this table. We give thanks for the hands that have made this feast and we ask that we be mindful of those that are without and that you bless the nourishment of this food to our strength as we plan ahead for the future. To you may we give all honour and Glory! Amen!*"

"Amen!" came the voices of Irene and Jim in unison.

When they sat down and Joe looked at the spread before him he was overcome by the work that Irene had put into the dinner. Here was a roast of venison that was glazed with a cranberry sauce, roasted potatoes, carrots glazed in maple syrup, peas that floated in butter, fresh baked buns, and a turnip dish that had apples and nuts in it. It was a feast fit for a King!

Joe and the Greens had a very pleasant dinner and finished off the meal with a fresh apple pie and some of the best cheddar cheese he had ever tasted.

What an evening!

What a day!

In the morning, Joe was up early and went down to the Blacksmith Shop, where Jim had Tar saddled and ready to hit the trail. Joe again thanked Jim for dinner and his most generous offer of land for the Church.

Joe swung up into the saddle and headed off to Schmidt's General Store to pick up his supplies for the week.

Once again, Herman had everything ready and Joe was able to run a tab for his supplies until he was paid after his first week.

Joe was able to share with Herman and Elsie the good news that Jim and Irene were willing to deed one acre of land to build the Church.

They all agreed this was definitely God's plan for Rossland and they were as excited about everything as Joe.

Chapter 10

"The Scrapping Sky Pilot"

"And he took his staff in his hand, and chose him five smooth stones out of the brook, and put them in a shepherd's bag which he had, even in a scrip; and his sling [was] in his hand: and he drew near to the Philistine." (KJV)
1 Samuel 17:40

Once Joe had his saddlebags tied off, he once again swung up into his saddle and headed Tar out of town towards the lumber camp, which according to MacIntosh was about a half day's ride into the woods.

Joe's first impression as he left "civilization" was how dense the forest was off the trail and how little light actually broke through the roof of vegetation that arched over the trail. Even Tar seemed to be uncomfortable with his surroundings and gave a few neighs, and head drops to express his dissatisfaction with his surroundings. Joe leaned over Tar's neck and gently stroked his ripping muscles and spoke gently to him until he settled down and proceeded along the track to the lumber camp.

Joe arrived at the camp in the mid afternoon. It was an uneventful ride and in fact it gave Joe much needed time to think through what had happened yesterday and what he needed to do for next week's Service.

Joe had been so tired that when he left the Green's about nine o'clock that he had gone right home to his room and fell asleep immediately. In fact, he was so tired, he didn't even hear the noise from the Saloon downstairs and it wasn't until the sun broke through the soiled window that Joe stirred and remembered he had to get up early and head off to the lumber camp to start his new job.

Now he had arrived to the looks and sneers of the men that were in camp. There were only 3 men in camp, since most of the men were out at their cutting station.

A burley red-bearded man walked towards him as he dismounted Tar and said, "I'm Frenchy, the camp Supervisor. You must be Robins? Boss told me to expect you today. You can put your horse over there in the corral," he said as he pointed to the split rail corral.

Joe swung down and extended his hand to Frenchy, "Thanks Frenchy," Joe said, "Where should I store my gear?" Joe asked as he walked over to the corral and took off his saddlebag, saddle and saddle blanket and swung them over one of the rails of the fence and walked Tar into the corral. Then he tied Tar and wiped him down with a towel before he took off the rope halter and let him roam the corral with the other horses.

Frenchy pointed over to a large tent on the far side of the camp, "You can bunk in the main bunk tent," Frenchy said, "You'll find there's an empty cot there – used to belong to the person you're replacing. He left this morning to one of our other camps to be with his brother. He was a good man. I hope you'll be able to keep up his production numbers."

"I'll try my best," Joe replied and started to walk towards the tent. As he approached it, he met another large man coming out the flaps in a hurry, nearly knocking Joe over.

"Watch where you're going Sky Pilot!" the man shouted at Joe.

It was obvious word of his arrival had not only been shared with the camp, but his profession had also been shared.

"Hey Al, knock it off!" yelled Frenchy from across the camp.

"I'll knock it off alright!" shouted Al in Joe's face, "You caused my best friend to leave the camp today Sky Pilot!" he said as he pushed Joe back with a sharp jab at the right shoulder.

168

Joe lost his balance and dropped his gear on the ground.

It didn't take Joe long to regain his balance, especially after all those years of boxing.

Out of nowhere, Big Al threw a right hook right at Joe's head. Joe easily side-stepped the blow and in the process caused Big Al to go off balance. Joe gave him a shove in the back as Big Al's haymaker caused him to swing right by Joe, and crash to the ground on his face.

The words that came out of Big Al's mouth would have caused any Mother to get the soap out!

Big Al gathered himself up and started to come back at Joe. By this time, Frenchy had run across the Camp and was trying to get himself between Joe and Big Al. Frenchy was thrown out of the way by Big Al for his trouble.

Joe was in his boxing position now and feeling quite comfortable about handling this monster of a man.

Joe realized that this man's anger wasn't really aimed at him but rather at the person that had left him behind and Joe was an easy target to release his anger.

"Better stand back Frenchy, it would appear that this gentleman and I need to clear the air before either of us is going to be able to work together." Joe stated.

"There won't be enough of you left to send back to base camp when I get through with you Sky Pilot! I hope that God of yours is ready to receive a visitor."

"I can assure you Sir, that my God is always ready to welcome a visitor, but I'm afraid the closest I will get to Him today is in prayer." Joe responded.

"Well start praying Sky Pilot!" shouted Big Al as he ran at Joe with both fists swinging wildly.

Once again, Joe stepped back and let Big Al swing right by him. This time as Big Al was loosing his balance, Joe hit him just under the ribs with a powerful right jab that nearly knocked the wind out of Big Al and really hurt.

This made Big Al madder than before and once he had sucked in some air he was right back at Joe like a wild bull, then he pulled up and took a fighting position and started to jab at Joe with one or two of these jabs hitting home and really hurting. Joe knew that he had to put Big Al down quickly! He had about six inches difference in his jab and Joe had to find a way under the jabs to get a good "left handed" hook aimed at Big Al's chin or temple.

Joe danced around, much to Big Al's disgust and derogatory comments about his blood line, telling Joe to stand still and fight like a man.

Now Big Al had more respect for Joe's jab after receiving that shot in the rib cage. If he could time his right hand with this guys weaving and dancing, he could knock his head off.

Joe dropped his left guard and appeared to give Big Al a free shot at his head. Big Al pulled back his right hand to deliver the knock-out blow and in doing so, dropped his left guard. Before Big Al could bring his right hand forward, Joe's left hand shot out in an upper cut hook that caught Big Al on the point of the chin and shot his head straight back. His eyes glazed over, his arms went limp and he folded to the ground as if he was attempting to re enter the womb.

Frenchy stood there for a minute with his mouth wide open, "Oh, my gosh! I've never seen Big Al beat in the five years I've known him. He has hurt a lot of men over that time. He's a great worker, but he has a terrible temper!"

With that Frenchy turned to Joe, "Are you alright?"

"Fine," Joe said "How is… 'Big Al', did you call him?"

"Yeah, he's in the next bunk to yours. It looks like he is starting to come around. I'll get some water to throw on him." Frenchy went over to the horse trough, grabbed a bucket filled it half full of water, proceeded over to Big Al and dumped it over him. With that, Big Al sat up, spluttering and gasping for air.

"What are you trying to do Frenchy, drown me?" yelled Big Al

Big Al slowly started to get to his feet and found himself falling over to his left, needing Frenchy to hold him steady will he shook his head to clear the cobwebs.

"What happened?" asked Big Al still shaking his head.

While all this was happening, Joe had picked up his belongings and proceeded into the tent that housed eight cots, four on one side and four on the other. Joe spotted a cot at the far end of the tent that didn't have gear on it, or around it, and headed off to put his belongings on the cot.

As he placed his blanket on the cot he looked up to see Big Al and Frenchy enter the tent.

Joe immediately positioned to defend himself if necessary. However, Big Al, still rubbing his jaw with his left hand extended the right for a shake.

"Never been beat before," Big Al said in a voice that was filled with awe, "I'll never live down that I was bested by a Sky Pilot! What did you hit me with, a horseshoe?" Big Al inquired.

"Just caught you with a lucky hook," replied Joe as he took Big Al's hand and gave a shake equal to the one that Al was giving. "Robins is the name, Joe Robins. People in Rossland have decided to call me Pastor Joe, but let's keep it simple – just call me Joe and don't call me late for dinner." Joe said laughingly.

"Pastor, I'm pleased to meet you and I'm sorry I took a shot at you." Al said, "I'm afraid I was in a bad mood because my buddy Harry decided to change camps to be with his brother. I can understand his desire to be with his brother, but I don't have many close friends and I was feeling bad. I'm afraid I took out my frustration on you. However, I'm the one who learned a lesson today. That was one good hook! I've never met a Scrapping Sky Pilot before and I look forward to getting to know you Pastor."

"Thanks Al for sharing what was bothering you. I'm sure my Superintendent for the Methodist Church will not share your enthusiasm for my fighting ability. You know, the Lord said turn the other cheek, but I'm afraid if I had turned my other cheek to you, I would have ended up on the other side of the camp.

I also should tell you, I boxed professional in Detroit Michigan, for two years to supplement my income when I was teaching in downtown Detroit.

Al, although I can never replace your buddy, if you give me a chance I would like to be a friend."

"Pastor, are you going to tell everyone about this fight?" Al beseeched.

"He likely won't Al, but you can bet your bottom dollar, I will," exclaimed Frenchy, "this is the best story that's happened in this camp in years."

Once Joe had settled in he and Big Al had walked the camp. Al had shown him the double headed axes, the bucksaws and the two man saws.

At the far end of the camp was large platform that was built over a large pit with belts that were attached to a huge blade and ran out to a wheel. This wheel had another belt that was attached to a wooden gear that was connected to a pole. The pole had a place to hitch a horse or a mule that walked in a circle that made the belts turn, which made the blade on the platform turn and cut the logs into planks.

As they returned to the cook tent, the other men were coming in at the end of their day of cutting and ready for dinner. Al made the introductions all around.

Joe was convinced that he'd never remember the names. Since most of them were nicknames, it even made it harder. There was Big Tim, Curly Jim (except he didn't have any hair), Lazy McQueen, Stubby Pete (in this case it did make some sense, since most of the fingers on his left hand were sheered off at the first knuckle), Yukon MacPhee, and finally, Spud Brown, the cook.

As they sat down for dinner, Spud Brown turned to Joe and said, "Pastor this meal deserves a grace!"

There was rumble of complaints about waiting for food and a few comments about the quality of Spuds cooking, but Joe decided he had been given an opening and he would take it! He stood up and said, "Spud, I think you're right and I'm sure this is a feast to be blessed. 'Dear Lord, please watch over these men of the forest, keep them safe we beseech thee. Lord bless this meal that we are to partake and bless the hands that prepared it. All this we ask in Jesus' name Amen!' Now, let's see if Spud's cooking tonight lives up to our expectations."

Platters of roasted chicken, bowls of beans, boiled potatoes and fresh cooked sourdough bread were passed around for each to help themselves. It was a fine meal with a cornmeal cake with maple syrup dripping over the top of each piece for desert and coffee and tea and for Joe water.

It didn't take long for the story of Joe and Big Al to be told by Frenchy and Spud.

Big Al sat there with his eyes fixed upon the ground while his camp mates shot rude comments at him. It was not often that the others could best Big Al or had the courage to make these comments.

Joe could see that the comments were starting to go beyond of fun and were starting to hurt. He quickly jumped in. "I have to tell you that Big Al got a couple of quick shots in that I thought would break my shoulder," Joe said, "and if it weren't for a lucky shot, I would likely be sitting in one of those branches over there," Joe continued as he pointed to a big pine tree that was at the far end of the camp, "all Big Al had to do was catch me with one of his punches and the story would have been very different."

"He didn't, Sky Pilot, and that's what makes this story so great. We all have seen Big Al fight and most of us have been at the end of that punch you were talking about," Frenchy said, "but you, you danced, you weaved, and all of a sudden you snaked a left hook that knocked Big Al right out. It was a wonder to see!"

"I have to tell you," Big Al added, "I've never lost a fight in my life and to loose it to a Scrapping Sky Pilot really hurts, but not as much as that hook! Pastor Joe tells me that he fought professionally in Detroit a few years ago. I suggest you respect this man."

Big Al turned to Frenchy, "Now that Harry is gone, we need to reassign teams and I would like to request that Pastor Joe becomes my partner."

Frenchy looked around the table and inquired, "Is everyone else satisfied with his work partner?" All the heads nodded in the affirmative. "Alright, Big Al and Pastor Joe will team up tomorrow and will cut in section B. Curly and Big Tim, you have section A to clean up. Stubby and Lazy, you'll open up section C and Yukon and I will run the mill."

There was a nodding of heads around the table and Lazy got up and walked over to the tent and returned with a guitar and started to tune it. With that, Joe excused himself from the table and went back to the tent and pulled his wooden flute out of his saddlebag and came back to the table.

The men were very pleased to see Joe become involved in their evening activity. Joe didn't know all the songs that Lazy did, but he knew many and was able to join in and provide the melody with Lazy chording. At the end the men asked Joe to play something on his own and he immediately started into Amazing Grace.

When he was finished there was dead silence for a moment or two as memories of family, home and friends, flooded the thoughts of those around the table.

"What a great way to end a good meal! Stubby, Lazy, Pastor Joe, thank you!" With that Frenchy got up and headed for his tent. Being the Supervisor, Frenchy had a tent of his own.

Some of the men started a card game and Joe excused himself and headed for his tent and an early sleep, for he knew that before the crack of dawn he would be at this table again for breakfast and his first day of being a lumberjack.

Joe crawled under his blanket and thought to himself, this cot is quite comfortable.

Clang! Clang! Clang!

Joe shot out of the bed as if shot from a cannon. The others around him moaned and groaned as they slowly pulled themselves off their cots. It was still pitch black.

"What time is it?" asked Joe

"About 4:30," answered Big Al, "breakfast will be at 5 and we'll be heading out about 5:30. We want to be at our cutting area as the sun rises and use as much of the daylight as we can."

Joe grabbed his shaving kit and his towel and soap and headed to the creek that ran past the camp. He needed to stop by the fire that Stumpy had going to grab a stick that he could use as a torch to see were he was going and to assist with his shaving.

About half way between the camp and the creek, Joe headed into the forest and relieved his natural urges, using leaves to wipe himself.

Once he had completed his toiletry, Joe had forgotten how cold running water could be up in this area, he headed back to his tent, put on his buckskins and a pair of black farming shoes that he bought prior to coming west. These were high cuts. Went up over the ankles and covered the Achilles tendon. As it would turn out, a wise investment for $2.00, which at the time seemed like a lot of money.

Breakfast was pancakes, bacon, coffee, tea and lots of Maple Syrup. Joe ate well and had a very weak tea to drink.

Before heading out with Big Al, Joe went back to the stream and filled a canteen with cold water to take along with him.

Five-thirty on the dot, Big Al and Joe were heading out of camp both carrying a two edged axe, a bucksaw each holding the end of a two man saw, with Big Al in the lead.

They walked for about forty minutes into dense forest following a trail that Joe realized had been blazed by tying red ribbons around branches of tress. Big Al always kept these marked trees to his left as he wound his way to the cutting area.

When Big Al slowed up and came to a stop, Joe could see that the tree in front of Big Al didn't just have the branch marked with ribbon, but had a piece of ribbon wrapped around the trunk and a "B" carved into the bark.

The sun was just rising as Big Al said, 'We're here. Our job is to cut as many trees as we can going in this direction," as Big Al pointed to the north. "The first part of the cut will be tricky as we cut trees so they fall without getting caught in the surrounding trees. Once we have a little clearing it becomes easy, we just continue cutting in a circle and let the trees drop into the clearing. We'll have to stop every five trees and trim off the branches and pile them or we'll end up with a mess to work around."

Big Al moved over to a big pine and said to Joe, "First we decide where this tree is going to fall. I suggest along this line," he said pointing at a small break in the trees, "the weight of the tree should allow it to fall through this hole."

"How are we going to make sure it falls were you want it to, and not were it wants to go?' asked Joe.

" We notch the tree like so," Big Al took his axe and at waist height he put a "V" notch into the tree on the side he wanted the tree to drop, "then you and I get on this side of the tree and we're going to cut this tree down by alternating our swings down and up. The rhythm is what makes this work Pastor. It's like being on a chain gang. I'll start with a downward swing, and I want you to swing upwards, then get your axe out of there and be ready to swing down, while I swing up. Ready to try?"

"Sure!" answered Joe.

Big Al's axe came down with a crunch and a piece of wood separated from the tree trunk.

Joe swung up and caused the piece of wood to fly out of the "V", but his axe was stuck in the tree and it took a second or two to get it out. By that time Big Al's second blow was hitting the tree and jamming Joe's axe. It took a minute or two to get both axes freed.

"You need to go in on more of an angle and let the axe do the work. It's important not to get your axe struck or you'll throw the whole rhythm out of whack. Let's try again." Big Al encouraged.

Joe swung his axe on a downward plane and quickly had it released and ready for a swing upward. After about twenty blows in tandem, Joe started to hear the tree crack as it started to get ready to follow.

"Timber!" yelled Big Al and made sure Joe was well back of the tree in case it kicked to the left or the right. But in fact, it fell right along the line Big Al had chosen and thundered to the ground between the trees on either side.

Gradually, Big Al and Joe chopped the trees on either side until they had six trees dropped. Then Big Al instructed Joe to start trimming trees on the left, move into the centre tree and pile the branches by the marked tree. This was time consuming and sticky work, since the sap ran off on his gloves as his grabbed the branches to haul them out to the dump site. It took them about an hour and half to do their first six trees.

"It should move a little faster now that we have a falling clearing," said Big Al

Just then Joe heard the sound of a horse coming through the clearing.

It was Lazy, driving a big draft horse. "I see my timing is perfect as always," he said to Big Al.

"You should have been here about half an hour ago." Declared Big Al in a disgusted voice, "that way we would have had a place to put our third tree. Now we have a mess for you to clean-up. You better start moving those trees past the marker, cause we're about to fell five more."

"Bitch, bitch, bitch," Lazy replied as he fastened the clamp onto the first tree and started the big horse pulling it up the trail. Soon he was back and hitching the second tree to the rig and off they went. Within fifteen minutes he had the are cleared and Big Al was calling Joe back to the next tree they were going to drop.

An hour later they had their next five trees dropped and trimmed Joe's hands were starting to blister.

As they took a break and waited for Lazy to arrive to move out the next set of logs, Joe took off his gloves and ran some water over the blisters.

Big Al came over and looked at Joe's hands. He took out a bar of home-made soap and told Joe to wash his hands in it.

As Joe started to wash his hands, the soap made the sores sting like no tomorrow.

"Are you trying to get back at me?" Joe inquired to Big Al.

"Of course not! A little soap shouldn't hurt a lumberjack like you." Big Al laughed, "You soap those cuts each break and by tomorrow or the next day, you'll have developed calluses that won't hurt when you swing the axe."

It was a long sore day for Joe, but he stuck at it and held his end up quite well. Big Al and he cut twenty-eight trees in a new cut and this was close to the camp record of thirty-one. But, oh, did his hands ever sting and the washing sure made them sting even more. By the end of day, the palms of his hands were so raw, they were numb and bleeding.

When they got back to camp, Frenchy dressed his hands with bandages after he had covered them with a salve made of bear grease and other ingredients guaranteed to stop the aching and help the healing.

At dinner, Joe gave a very short grace, ate quickly and quietly and headed straight to his bed aching in every muscle in his body. He hadn't been this sore after a fight in Detroit.

Tonight, as tired as he was, it took a few minutes to find a position that didn't hurt before he nodded off to sleep. Every time he rolled over or moved his eyes shot open with pain. It wasn't a restful night, but when he did fall asleep, he slept soundly until the Clang, Clang, Clang.

This time he didn't jump out of bed, but slowly rolled into a position that allowed him to sit up and swing his legs over the side of the cot without too much pain. Instead of heading down to the creek to wash up, Joe went into the woods and responded to natures call and then came back to camp were he slowly went through some exercises to loosen up his muscles and make walking bearable.

Joe was the brunt of the breakfast jokes today and he took them good naturedly. Why shouldn't he, he deserved them.

Joe might hurt in many spots, but his appetite hadn't been affected by a hard day's work. In fact, he was as hungry as he could remember for his breakfast today. Joe had a plate full of pancakes, some corn bread, a couple of eggs and a bunch of bacon. When he was done, he didn't know if filling himself so full was a good idea, but he did feel satisfied.

It was Joe's turn to help with the dishes and once done he headed off to the creek to fill his canteen and then join Big Al to their cutting spot.

Today, they just had their axes, since they had left their saws at the site.

Once again, they were at the site in about forty minutes and had started dropping their first tree as the sun broke through the trees into the clearing.

Joe had his hands wrapped as if he were going to fight, with gauze bandages under his work gloves. This provided some protection for his palms, but made it more difficult to grip his axe. By noon he had discarded this layer of protection and proceeded with the soap washes and gritting his teeth. By late afternoon his hands were numb again, but they had dropped thirty trees. Their cutting clearing was getting bigger and their pile of branches even bigger.

It was time to head back to camp.

Joe didn't seem to ache as badly today and in fact he could feel the skin starting to heal over his palms.

As they got back into camp, Joe went down to the creek and did the toiletry he had skipped in the morning. Frenchy redressed his hands with his special salve and gauze bandages.

As Joe said the blessing he could smell the dinner that was ready to be served by Stubby and could hear his stomach rolling. As soon as Joe was done, Stubby was there with a venison roast, corn bread, beans (there were beans at every meal), and a pot full of potatoes, (where he got these potatoes was a mystery, since they cost a fortune at the general store. But, Stubby seemed to have his own resources with respect to vegetables, (much to the men's delight!). Once again, Joe did justice to the food placed in front of him and was feeling well enough to join in with the sing song after dinner adding his wooden flute to carry the melody to songs like "Com'n around the mountain" and "Daisy, Daisy", a new song that was made popular just before he headed out west by Harry Darce, written in 1892.

Joe taught the group this great new song, known to only a few.

There is a flower within my heart,
Daisy, Daisy!
Planted one day by a glancing dart,
Planted by Daisy Bell!
Whether she loves me or loves me not,
Sometimes it's hard to tell;
Yet I am longing to share the lot
Of beautiful Daisy Bell!

Chorus:
Daisy Daisy,
Give me your answer do!
I'm half crazy,
All for the love of you!
It won't be a stylish marriage,
I can't afford a carriage,
But you'll look sweet on the seat
Of a bicycle built for two !

We will go "tandem" as man and wife,
Daisy, Daisy!
Ped'ling away down the road of life,
I and my Daisy Bell!
When the road's dark we can despise
P'liceman and lamps as well;
There are bright lights in the dazzling eyes
Of beautiful Daisy Bell!
Chorus:

I will stand by you in "wheel" or woe,
Daisy, Daisy!
You'll be the bell(e) which I'll ring, you know!
Sweet little Daisy Bell!
You'll take the lead in each trip we take,
Then if I don't do well;
I will permit you to use the brake,
My beautiful Daisy Bell!!!
Chorus:

The lads stumbled on the verses, but bellowed out the chorus like they were in a saloon hall!

By the end of the week, the lads knew the whole song by heart and requested it every night as their second last song.

Their last song request was always for Joe to play 'Amazing Grace'. Lazy would play a haunting chord backup to this hymn on his guitar. It never seemed to loose its power.

Saturday after lunch, Joe would head out for Rossland riding Tar.

Joe arrived just in time for dinner at the saloon, but was very pleased to see he had an offer for dinner at MacIntosh's for 8 pm.

He went up to his room, which Dutch had made sure was available Saturday and Sunday night, got the wash basin from under the window in the hall and brought it back to his room without stirring it up too much. Most of the dirt from others had settled to the bottom. Joe was able to get relatively clean water from the top to wet his wash cloth and using the soap that Big Al had given him to toughen his palms. He proceeded to wash his face, neck and hands and ran a comb through his uncooperative hair. He had a definite hat ring, causing his hair to stick out over his ears and try as he may, he couldn't seem to get his hair to lay flat. He would just have to accept the fact that until he could arrange for a bath and a proper hair washing, he was destined to have wings.

It was approaching 7:30 pm and Joe went down the stairs that lead through the dance hall and out to the street.

The ladies immediately acknowledged his presence and tried their best to embarrass him. Joe took their ribbing in good stride, then Joe noted that Lil wasn't in the group. Joe turned to one of the girls and said, "A little early for Lil to be tied up isn't it?"

"Pastor, in our line of business it's never too early, but actually, Lil is in her room coughing real bad and seems to be sick." Said one of the girls Joe knew as Beth.

Joe knew that to stop and see Lil at this point would make him late to the MacIntosh's and turned to the girl and said, "Tell Lil I'll stop by and see her when I get back. Ask the Doc to come over and see her right away."

"Lil hasn't got money for the Doc," Beth responded.

"Tell the Doc, I'm paying. Now off you go!"

With that Beth ran out of the saloon and headed up the street for Doc Butler's tent. Joe headed out and climbed aboard Tar.

Joe turned Tar's head slowly towards the road leading out of town and towards the MacIntosh holdings.

It was about 8:15 when Joe tied Tar up to the hitching post outside of the MacIntosh home.

Angus and Jane were on the porch waiting for him. Joe immediately apologized for his tardiness and indicated that someone was sick at the salon and he needed to spend a few minutes with them arranging for Doctor Butler to see them. The MacIntosh's didn't inquire who was sick, thank goodness, but accepted Joe's apology on face value and invited him in for dinner.

A roaring fire was crackling in the fireplace and the room had the smell of good food ready for the offering.

Joe was asked to say the blessing and he made sure to ask for blessings upon the MacIntosh Family. He gave thanks for the preparation of the food and asked that it be blessed to their needs.

The MacIntosh's had invited the Greens to join them for dinner.

"How's Tar doing?" asked Jim.

"Couldn't be better," responded Joe, "I just have to remember to be gentle with her when I'm giving her directions through the reins. She responds well and she has enjoyed her time in the corral at the camp. I got a good buy there Jim, thank you!"

"Well, I still can't believe a greenhorn from the east solved that horse's problem. She sure had me fooled." Jim said with laugh and a shake of his head.

"Joe, I hear good things about your first week, especially the run-in with Big Al on your arrival." MacIntosh said.

"Tell us about your meeting with Big Al!" begged Jim, "We all know big Al and his temper!"

"Oh. It was just a misunderstanding. Big Al was missing his buddy Harry and was in a bad mood when I arrived. We settled it and are working as a cutting team now. Big Al has become a close friend." Joe explained.

"I don't believe even you could win over Big Al when he's in a foul mood." stated Jim and all around the table nodded their heads except Angus MacIntosh, who knew the whole story.

"It seems that Pastor Joe would like to leave this story in the camp, but I have to tell you that there is a biblical reference you might like to check – the story of David and Goliath, only this time it wasn't a pebble that did the damage, but a left hook to the jaw the knocked Big Al to the ground according to my sources.

Pastor Joe has a new nickname at the camp, 'The Scrapping Sky Pilot'." MacIntosh said with a deep belly laugh.

"Please" Joe pleaded, "Let's not let this story get out of hand. Big Al and I have become close friends. I can assure you he certainly handled himself well when we experienced our initial encounter.

Further, I wouldn't like Superintendent Johnson to hear me called 'The Scrapping Sky Pilot'. I'm sure it won't stand me well when I go before the Board for approval of my ordination.

Let's move on to more interesting topics. Can you tell me how last week's service was received?" inquired Joe, hoping to deflect the stories of the Camp as soon as possible. But, alas, there was no way he was getting out of it that easily.

"Pastor," asked Jane, "Angus tells me that not only did you best Big Al, but that you told the Camp that you had been a professional boxer. Is that really true?"

"Mrs. MacIntosh, the dinner is delicious, but it seems the old cliché, 'what happens in camp, stays in camp,' doesn't really apply," Joe responded, "yes, before I was accepted as a candidate for the Methodist Church of Canada, I taught grade eight in downtown Detroit. I couldn't survive on the salary they paid, so I supplemented my salary as a professional fighter and had a record of 8 and 0. I quit while I was ahead. But enough about me, are we set for tomorrow's service?" inquired Joe.

Irene could see that Pastor Joe was becoming very uncomfortable with all this attention being centered on him, even though she was fascinated that this seeming meek and mild spectacled young man could beat a brute like Big Al, had a past that included working with some of the toughest kids around and had been a professional boxer.

"Yes, Pastor Joe, we have let everyone know that a service will be conducted on the Green at 11 am tomorrow. Anyone that wishes to sing in your choir should meet at 10:15 for rehearsal. The boys, wanted to know if you would be at the Green around 9, like last week?" Irene updated him.

"I hope you told them I would be." answered Joe with an expression of concern in his voice.

"I told them to be there at that time. I felt likely you would be there by then or shortly after. That seemed to please them. You have some real fans there Pastor," responded Irene.

"They are a great group of kids and I'm so pleased they agreed to sing last week. Hopefully the hymn I've picked for them this week will be as easy for them to learn. They're smart kids and eager to please," said Joe.

Jim jumped in at this point and said, "They have really been trying to help out around the town. The older ones have been working part time for Herman and the younger ones have been sweeping the sidewalks and helping to fill in some of the ruts in the streets, as best they can and have received a small token from the town for their work. It's been a miracle to watch the transformation from hoodlums to saints."

"I doubt they're saints," Joe said with a laugh, "but they are good kids that want to feel needed and respected. Isn't that what we all want?" asked Joe.

There was a general nodding of heads around the table.

"Well Mrs. MacIntosh, I can't thank you enough for such a lovely dinner and arranging for such pleasant dinner guests, but I need to get back to my room and finish my service for tomorrow. I hope you will forgive me for eating and running." With that Joe rose and wished all a goodnight, mounted Tar and headed back to the saloon.

When he arrived, he called Dutch over for a minute and asked what Doc had said about Lil.

"She has a bad case of pneumonia," relayed Dutch, "Doc has given her something for her cough and to bring the fever down, but he said he wasn't sure whether Lil was going to get better from this bout, it was pretty advanced."

Joe nodded and thanked Dutch for the information and asked if there was someone who could accompany him while he visited Lil.

"This is a saloon Pastor, you didn't need any company to visit a girl in a room." Dutch retorted.

"Dutch, it's not Lil's reputation I'm concerned about – but mine! Now can Beth please join me for a few minutes?"

"Sorry Pastor, I wasn't thinking. Of course Beth can join you – she has been going up and seeing Lil about every hour."

Joe went over to Beth and asked her if she would join him as he went up to see Lil?

"Of course Pastor!" responded Beth

When Beth and Lil entered the dark dingy room that was lit by an oil lamp, Joe could see that Lil was in bad shape. With her make-up off and the rouge removed from her lips she showed her real age, which would have been pushing 50 Joe guessed. Her colour was grey and she was coughing continually and spitting up phlegm into a cloth she used to cover her mouth. Her eyes were watery and she had her arms wrapped around her chest to help with the wracking pain that the coughing caused.

Beth immediately informed Lil that Pastor Joe was there to visit her. She took a towel that had dropped to the floor, went over top a wash basin that had been brought into the room, wrung the towel out and replaced it on Lil's forehead.

Joe sat beside Lil and took one of her hands and squeezed it gently.

"Lil, I would like to say a prayer if you would allow me?" Joe asked

Lil croaked between coughs, "Pastor, thank you for sending the Doc! Pray to your heart's content. Don't think I've ever had a man in my room who wanted to pray with me? Usually it's play with me." Lil said laughingly which brought on another bout of coughing.

Joe spent a few minutes praying with Lil, asking God to easy her pain, grant His blessings upon her, and to give her the strength to face the days ahead.

Lil had tears on her cheeks as Joe readied to leave, but the coughing had subsided and she was in a quiet sleep.

Beth tiptoed out of the room with him and once in the hall, turned to face him and planted a kiss on his cheek. "You are the nicest man I've ever met. I bet you have someone waiting for you when you return south?"

"Why thank you Beth, that's kind of you to say. Yes I have my Nellie waiting for my return and I hope we can marry shortly after." Joe explained.

Beth nodded her head and said, "I've found all the good ones are taken."

Joe smiled and patted her hand, "Beth, I'm sure you'll find your man before long, I just have one of those feelings."

Joe returned to his room and sat down at his little table after having lit his oil lamp. He looked at his sermon notes that he had worked on during the week and put them aside feeling they were in good enough shape. He then took a fresh piece of paper and addressed it to Nellie.

It had been a week since he had written her and it would be months before she received this letter, but he felt he just had to share with her his feelings and his adventures over the last week.

His heart ached, he missed her so much. Maybe he should pack all this in and go back home to his Nel! Who could blame him? He was homesick, lonesome and he missed his girl. He remembered how she stood at the side of the tracks as the train pulled out, waving until the smoke of the engine blocked her from view and they had started around their first turn, loosing sight of the station completely. She had looked so petite, almost like a child, yet Joe knew that she was no child.

Oh to feel her in his arms once more!

'Stop this Joe' said a voice in his head. 'This is the Devil talking to you! Obviously you are winning doing God's work and temptation has entered your mind to take you away from your responsibilities!'

Joe looked back at the blank piece of paper and his pen started scratching upon the clean page and soon he had told Nel about his first service, his first week at the Lumber Camp (minus his encounter with Big Al) but about making friends with Big Al and his dinners with members of the community. He shared with her his thrill of having a commitment for land for the new church and wood to build it. He told her about the "boys" and how they had moved from hoodlums to "saints". Finally he shared with her his prayer session with Lil and his prediction that before he returned next week, he would be called back to conduct her funeral. His first! Of course he spent the last couple of paragraphs explaining to her the battle he had just gone through to give up and return to her loving arms and how much he missed her. He added a post script asking to be remembered to her parents and family, especially Albert. When he was finished the letter he was emotionally spent, yet he felt cleansed and ready for tomorrow.

Joe's sleep was interrupted a couple of times during the night as he heard Lil in what seemed like a never ending fit of coughing. Joe went to her at around four am and found Beth and a couple of the girls with Lil.

Joe suggested that they put a couple of extra pillows behind Lil's shoulders to keep the phlegm from dripping back into her throat and made sure they were giving Lil the medicine the Doc had left.

The sun broke through the filthy window panes causing Joe to rise and prepare himself for the day ahead.

Before going down for breakfast, he stopped off and spent a few minutes with Lil and Beth.

Once again, by 9:00 am Joe was down at the "Green" and was adjusting the tension on the lines and the canvass after a week of no one looking after them. However, Joe suspected that Jim Green likely had kept an eye on things for him.

As Joe started to walk back towards the wagon, "stage", he spotted the "boys" coming up from the creek bed with their fishing lines.

"Any luck?" Joe asked

"No, not even a bit." responded Shorty.

"Maybe the fish know it's Sunday." Joe replied

"What difference does that make?" asked Jake

"You boys do know that God made heaven and earth in six days and told man that he should rest on the seventh, which means no work." Joe responded

"But fishin' ain't work, it's fun!" called back little Mike.

"Well gosh, now you've got me trapped in a theological dilemma." Joe shot back.

"What's that mean Pastor?" inquired Shorty.

"'Theological' means discussing things that are in the Bible, and 'dilemma' means hard to make a decision. In other words, you have presented a good argument for fishing on Sunday Mike, but as I understand God's direction to us through the stories of the Bible, I think fishing would be considered work. It would certainly be considered work in the time of Jesus. Many of the men that came to support Jesus, or as we call them, His disciples, were fishermen by trade. There were twelve disciples." And Joe opened his bible and read from Luke 6:13-16:

> 'And when it was day, he called [unto him] his disciples: and of them he chose twelve, whom also he named apostles; Simon, (whom he also named Peter,) and Andrew his brother, James and John, Philip and Bartholomew, Matthew and Thomas, James the [son] of Alphaeus, and Simon called Zelotes, and Judas [the brother] of James, and Judas Iscariot, which also was the traitor.'(KJV)

"Of these we know for sure that Simon Peter, Andrew, James and John had been fishermen, and likely a number of the others."

Joe opened the bible again and read from Mark:

> Mark 1:16-20

'Now as he walked by the sea of Galilee, he saw Simon and Andrew his brother casting a net into the sea: for they were fishers. And Jesus said unto them, Come ye after me, and I will make you to become fishers of men. And straightway they forsook their nets, and followed him. And when he had gone a little further thence, he saw James the [son] of Zebedee, and John his brother, who also were in the ship mending their nets. And straightway he called them: and they left their father Zebedee in the ship with the hired servants, and went after him.'(KJV)

"Wow!" said Jack, Mike's little brother, "imagine, they had fishermen back in Jesus day!" he said with wonder in his voice.

"Of course they did!" said Shorty, "man has been fishing since the time of Adam and Eve."

"Who is Adam and Eve?" asked Mike.

"I think we'll talk about Adam and Eve next Sunday Mike, if that's ok with you? I would like to teach you a new song if you're willing?"

The boys all nodded their consent and thought back to how they were received after last Sunday's Service. It was nice to be recognized and appreciated!

"By the way guys, I have heard that you have all been very busy over the last week. I've heard some very positive comments about your involvement in the town. Well done!"

"How did you hear that pastor, you've been at the lumber camp all week?" asked Shorty.

"Shorty, Pastor's hear all." Joe responded and left it at that. Let the boys wonder how he received his information. Maybe they would realize that they were being watched, not just by God, but by him and hopefully this would keep them out of trouble for at least another week.

"Now how about singing the first two verses of, Jesus loves me this I know," Joe asked and he boys all nodded their heads showing their support.

Now, as Nellie had taught him, he took a few minutes to talk about this hymn. He told the boys that the lady who had written this hymn, Anna Warner had been the daughter of a very wealthy lawyer. Her father had lost most of his money by making bad business decisions and he and his family had retired from New York to a quiet community near West Point. To help with the family finances, Anna and her Sister taught Bible Studies at West Point and Anne wrote a number of Hymns. This one, Jesus loves me this I know," was written at the request of her Sister, Susan, for a Sunday School Teacher who had asked her for a hymn to be sung to a dying boy in her Sunday School Class.

"The words are beautiful and so full of meaning. There are four verses and a chorus, do you think you can remember them from last week?" Joe asked.

"Let's try Pastor!" said Jake

Joe had them hum the melody a couple of times and then they sang the hymn:

> 'Jesus loves me this I know,
> For the Bible tells me so;
> Little ones to Him belong,
> They are weak but He is strong.
> Chorus:
> Yes, Jesus loves me!
> The Bible tells me so.
> Jesus loves me, He who died
> Heaven's gate to open wide;
> He will wash away my sin,
> Let His little child come in.
> Jesus loves me, loves me still,
> Though I'm very weak and ill;
> From His shining throne on high
> Comes to watch me where I lie.
> Jesus loves me, He will stay
> Close beside me all the way:
> If I love Him, when I die
> He will take me home on high.

The boys had the first two verses down pat as their rehearsal time wrapped up.

"Pastor, I can read," said Shorty, "Not good, but I can read a little. If you give me the words, we can try to learn another verse before the service. We know you are going to be busy between now and the start of the service – leave it with us. We'll let you know how much we know before we start singing."

Joe handed over his Hymnal to Shorty and showed him that Jesus Loves me was number 623.

Shorty was right, Joe was needed in many areas all at the same time!

Joe met with a number of the women of the congregation who had indicated that they would be willing to be his 'Choir'. Some of them could even sing!

Once again, Joe followed Nellie's recipe for success, or at least for the prevention of disaster. Joe decided that they would sing "Breathe on me, Breath of God".

> *Breathe on me, breath of God,*
> *Fill me with life anew,*
> *That I may love what Thou dost love,*
> *And do what Thou wouldst do.*
> *Breathe on me, breath of God,*
> *Until my heart is pure,*
> *Until with Thee I will one will,*
> *To do and to endure.*
> *Breathe on me, breath of God,*
> *Blend all my soul with Thine,*
> *Until this earthly part of me*
> *Glows with Thy fire divine.*
> *Breathe on me, breath of God,*
> *So shall I never die,*
> *But live with Thee the perfect life*
> *Of Thine eternity*

Joe explained that this was a relatively new hymn that had been written by theologian, Rev. Edwin Hatch who had come from England to teach in Toronto.

He played the melody on his wooden flute and had the women hum along with him. Like always there where one or two who were trying to out "hum" their colleagues.

"Ladies," Joe addressed them, "this hymn is a prayer and needs to be sung quietly and reverently. It is important that your voices blend together as one. Altos, let me hear your part please?" Joe listened carefully as he conducted with his flute as a baton.

"Lovely! Now Sopranos let your voices be one." and once again Joe conducted and had to use his one hand as a signal to help one or two overpowering voices to blend with the group.

"Now, let's put these two sections together." Said Joe as he lifted his flute to his lips and started to play the melody again. This time the ladies sounded like a choir!

Joe had written out six copies of the hymn when he was in his tent out in the camp, before heading off to bed on Friday night. He gave a copy of the words to the ladies and had them sing them with the flute accompaniment.

He asked the Sopranos to let their voices become louder in the second line, like they were speaking directly to God, which he reminded the ladies they were!

"You are pleading with him, let the feeling of this request fill the air, but, don't overdo it! It's a sensitive balance between volume and melody – it's melody we are searching for here. Now again ladies." and Joe started with a short lead-in with the flute and nodded his head that he wanted the Choir to come in on the next note.

They did it!

It sounded great! When they were finished he complimented them on how quickly they had picked up this hymn that they were going to do as an anthem and how great it sounded. He beseeched them to do it just like that during the service and he thanked them for coming early and practicing.

They all left at that point and went to sit with their families, beaming as they headed back into the congregation.

The time had come to start the service.

Joe welcomed all to the service of worship today. He indicated that he had a couple of announcements he wished to share before the service actually started. He thanked Jim and Irene Green for donating the land they were sitting on for a new Church. He also thanked Jane and Irene MacIntosh for donating the lumber for the new Church. And finally he thanked Elsie and Herman Schmidt for donating the hardware that would be needed for the construction.

Joe then indicated that he would be putting forward Jim, Angus and Herman as Trustees for Rossland Methodist Church and that he would be willing to accept other nominations during the week and he would hold a vote prior to the service next week.

Joe then indicated he would like to hold a pot luck luncheon after next week's service and ask by a show of hands if this was acceptable to those in attendance. There was a flurry of hands up and Joe declared that the first Pot-Luck Lunch of Rossland Methodist Church would be held after service next Sunday.

Joe then moved into the Call to Worship and opened with a short prayer thanking God for the Spirit that was moving through the community of Rossland, recognizing again the gifts of the Greens, MacIntoshs and Schmidts and thanking God for giving them two choirs, a Youth Choir and an adult Female Choir – "voices like angels," he said.

He then asked the congregation to rise and join him in singing Amazing Grace. Not having hymn books or the time to write out a number of copies of any hymn he wanted to use, he had to rely on hymns that most knew by heart. It was apparent from last week this was a favourite.

Before Joe read his scripture, he indicated to the congregation that he had had a request to deliver his sermon this week on the meaning of the words in the 23rd Psalm. There was a good turn out this week, nearly 100 people including children

Therefore he was going to repeat some of the readings from last week, starting with the 23rd Psalm then he went onto John 10:1-6

> "Verily, verily, I say unto you, He that entereth not by the door into the sheepfold, but climbeth up some other way, the same is a thief and a robber. But he that entereth in by the door is the shepherd of the sheep. To him the porter openeth; and the sheep hear his voice: and he calleth his own sheep by name, and leadeth them out. And when he putteth forth his own sheep, he goeth before them, and the sheep follow him: for they know his voice. And a stranger will they not follow, but will flee from him: for they know not the voice of strangers. This parable spake Jesus unto them: but they understood not what things they were which he spake unto them.'(KJV)

Then Joe asked the Youth Choir to come forward to sing. The boys had assumed their seats in the front row looking out over the congregation and worked their way up onto the stage to stand beside Joe.

"We know it all!" whispered Shorty in a stage whisper that could be heard at the back of the gathering. There was a little laughing from the congregation, then they sat back to listen as Shorty stepped forward and spoke in a loud well enunciated voice; "Pastor Joe has asked us to sing a hymn today that was written by a lady who lived in America near West Point. She was asked to write a hymn for a Sunday School Teacher that had a little boy who was dying. We think it's a beautiful hymn and we hope we can do it justice." With that the other boys gathered around as Shorty held the sheet of words and nodded to Joe that they were ready.

Joe played the intro that they had agreed upon and nodded his head for them to commence.

Shorty was right! They had learned it all and they sang it with feeling and understanding, especially the verse that said:

> "Jesus loves me, loves me still,
> Through I'm very weak and ill;
> From His shining throne on high
> Comes to watch me where I lie."

There was a gasp from the Congregation as they heard the real meaning of these words for the first time and their thoughts went to the child that "where I lie." but realized that the words were more like "where I die."

After the boys were finished, there was complete silence, then a chorus of "Amen!" – "Praise God!" – these weren't expressions that were usually heard in a Methodist Church – but the congregation felt they had to recognize the hymn sung by the Youth Choir – as it had brought many in the group either close to or actually to tears.

Joe put down his flute and walked over to the boys and in a very low voice said, "Thank you – may God bless your gift to us today." And the boys proceeded back to their seats.

Joe decided right then and there that at every service he did in the future, there was going to be a time set aside to talk with the Youth using a parable style story if possible. Next Sunday he would ensure that he had a story ready for the young people.

Joe then turned to the congregation and started his sermon by opening with a short prayer where he prayed that the words of his mouth and the mediations in all their hearts were acceptable to God.

"My dear brothers and sisters in Christ,

"Some think that this Psalm, the 23rd Psalm has two parts – the first under the figure of shepherd, the 2nd turning to the figure of a banquet with the host and the guest.

But in fact, it's **all** a simple shepherd's Psalm.

See how it runs through the sound of a Shepherd's life from first word to last.

"The Lord is my Shepherd, I shall not want." There is the opening strain of its music; in that chord is sounded the keynote which is never lost till the plaintive melody dies away at the Shepherd's end. All that follows is that thought put into varying light.

"He maketh me lie down in green pastures" – <u>nourishment</u> and <u>rest.</u>

"He leadeth me beside he still waters" – <u>refreshment</u> – you think here of quietly flowing streams and another picture of rest. But streams are few in a Shepherd's country and the shepherd does not rely on them. To the shepherd, "still waters" are wells and cisterns – not for rest, but to bring up water to quench the herd's thirst.

The varied needs of the sheep and the many sided care that the shepherd are pictured 'consummated skill' use of short sentences and phrases.

Each is distinct and adds something too precious to be merged and lost.

"He restoreth my soul" Soul means the life or one's self and the Hebrew's writings.

There are private fields, gardens and vineyards and shepherd's country – issue of sheep straying into these fortified areas and being caught.

So, "He restores my soul," means the shepherd brings back and rescues my life from forbidden and fatal places (private lands).

"Restores me when wandering." Is the way it is put in one of our hymns:

"He leadeth me in paths of righteousness for His names sake." It is hard for the shepherd to choose the right path for the sheep, one leads to a precipice, another to where sheep can't find their way back – the shepherd always goes ahead and leads them along the right path, proud of his good name as a shepherd.

Some paths that are right paths still lead through places that have deadly perils – "yea, though I walk thro the valley of the shadow of death," is the way the Psalmist touches this fact in a Shepherd's life.

"Thy rod and thy staff" the shepherds carry a weapon for defense and one for guidance and stability.

You should see the sheep cuddled near the shepherd to understand the wording – "They comfort me".

The shepherd calls and the answering patter of feet as the sheep hurry to him, are fit sounds to be chosen out of the noisy world to show what comfort God gives to souls that heed His voice.

Now we come to where some think the figure of the shepherd is dropped and the banquet is added – but this would cause the final climax of the shepherd's care.

"Thou preparest a table before me in the presence of my enemies." Ah, to think that the Shepherd's highest skill and heroism should be lost from view as the Psalmist begins to sing of it – image of an indoor banquet.

There is no higher task of the shepherd to go from time to time to study places and examine the grass and find good safe feeding places for his sheep. All his skills and great heroism is often called for. There are many poisonous plants and grasses and shepherds must find and remove them before the herd can be moved. One shepherd lost 300 sheep by a mistake in location.

Further there are snake holes and the snakes bite the noses of the sheep if they aren't killed or driven way before the flock arrives. The shepherd must burn the fat of hogs at the holes to drive out the snakes. Further, around the feeding grounds there are jackals, wolves, hyenas, and tigers in holes and caves in the hillside. The bravery and skill of the Shepherd are at the highest point is closing up these dens with stone or slaying the wild beasts with a long bladed knife. Of nothing do the shepherds boast more proudly than of their achievements in the past of their care of flocks.

And now do you not see the shepherd figure in that quaint life.

Psalm 23:5
Thou preparest a table before me in the presence of mine enemies: thou anointest my head with oil; my cup runneth over.(KJV)

Do you not see that God's care of man out in the wild is a grander thought than that of seating him at an indoor banquet table.

But, what about anointing the head with oil and the cup running over?

Ah, there begins the beautiful picture at the end of the day.

The Psalmist has sung of the whole round – day's wandering – all the needs of the sheep – all the care of the shepherd. Now the Psalmist closes with the last scene of the day.

At the door – sheepfold, the shepherd stands and the 'rodding' or counting takes place as the sheep pass.

The Shepherd stands turning his body to let the sheep pass; he is the door, as Christ said of Himself.

With His rod He holds back sheep while He inspects them one by one as they pass into the fold. He has cedar tar – he anoints a knee bruised on the rock or a scratch from the thorns and here comes one that is not bruised but is simply worn and exhausted. He bathes his face and head with refreshing olive oil and takes a large two-handled cup – dips it brimming full from the vessel of water provided for that purpose – he lets the weary sheep drink.

There is nothing finer when the Psalmist shares this.

God's care is not for the wounded only, but for the worn and weary.

"I will dwell in the house of the Lord forever." – sheep are safely in the fold – resting safely, ready for the next day – shepherd has protected them, watched over them and now able to rest in the knowledge that all is well.

We are the sheep – God is the Shepherd and God will look out for us if we obey His direction, follow His lead, and rest in the knowledge that He has watched over us every day.

Amen." (*Actual sermon notes of J.U. Robins*)

Joe then asked the Adult Choir to come forward and he had the ladies hum the prelude to the hymn as he played it with his flute. Then with a nod of his head they broke into song: "Breathe on me, Breath of God, Fill me with life anew..." and the Choir allowed their voices to blend beautifully and the Sopranos let their voices lift on "Fill me with life anew...". Joe was thrilled! Nellie would have been so proud of him. How he wished Nellie was there to hear "his" Choir! Then he reminded himself that it wasn't "his" choir – it was God's Choir – and he had better learn to be humble – for false pride leads to disaster. Thankfully, there was no disaster this time, only the voices of a group of ladies singing in harmony to the glory of God.

As Joe looked out, he could see the families of the Choir beaming with satisfaction for the quality of music that was being shared this morning – and proud their Mother, Wife, Girl Friend, Sister was one of the Choir.

As the service came to conclusion, Joe felt that everything had gone well. He also felt that he needed to work more on his sermon next week and to make it more "Jesus oriented" – he would draw on the Gospel of John, which was Joe's favourite Gospel. Joe liked the writing style and the imagery that the writer of John used to explore the divinity of Jesus.

The sermon today was ok, and he was able to respond to the desire of one of his parishioners. However, it was a history lesson, not an evangelical sermon that this community needs.

Next week he would fix it!

Joe was once again invited for lunch and dinner and the day flew by into the early evening and he was on his way back to his room over the saloon.

Dutch called Joe over as he arrived in the tap room, "Pastor, Lil isn't doing well. I had to call Doc back late this afternoon and he gave her some poppy juice to help her sleep and stop the cough, but he indicated he felt she only had a few days. If she dies while you're up at the camp, do you want to be notified?"

"Of course," Joe responded, "I will speak with Angus MacIntosh before I head up in the morning and let him know that I might have to leave the camp for a day to perform a funeral."

"Pastor, are you willing to do a funeral for a saloon hall lady?" Dutch inquired.

"Yes!" Joe was emphatic in his response, "Jesus didn't spend his time with the good citizens of his time, but with those that were considered outcasts, tax collectors, widows, gentiles and women of ill repute. If Jesus feels these people were worth his personal attention, he felt he had a responsibility to ensure that Lil had an appropriate funeral."

Joe went upstairs ad looked in on Lil and noted she was asleep as Dutch had indicated, but he also noted that her breathing was very laboured and she had a very distinct rasp in her chest as she breathed in and out.

When Joe entered his room he went over to his wooden table and sat down and wrote his letter to Nel. He told her about the choirs and how the "boys" had been accepted by the community. He went on to describe the condition of Lil and his decision to make himself available to conduct a Christian funeral service, when she died.

Of course he wrote a number of paragraphs about his love for her, how much he missed her, and how close he had come to packing everything in and returning to her open arms and reassuring smile.

When he was done, he opened his bible and read a section of John that he thought he might use next week. John 1:1-14

> *In the beginning was the Word, and the Word was with God, and the Word was God. The same was in the beginning with God. All things were made by him; and without him was not any thing made that was made. In him was life; and the life was the light of men. And the light shineth in darkness; and the darkness comprehended it not. There was a man sent from God, whose name [was] John. The same came for a witness, to bear witness of the Light, that all [men] through him might believe. He was not that Light, but [was sent] to bear witness of that Light. [That] was the true Light, which lighteth every man that cometh into the world. He was in the world, and the world was made by him, and the world knew him not. He came unto his own, and his own received him not. But as many as received him, to them gave he power to become the sons of God, [even] to them that believe on his name: Which were born, not of blood, nor of the will of the flesh, nor of the will of man, but of God. And the Word was made flesh, and dwelt among us, (and we beheld his glory, the glory as of the only begotten of the Father,) full of grace and truth.(KJV)*

Joe loved the symbolism of "light" and felt he would preach about "In him was life; and the life was the light of men." John 1:4 (KJV). He felt he could do justice to this and draw it to the new beginning of the Rossland Congregation. It would be a lively and a meaningful sermon. Maybe he should consider an altar call at this service. He would have to explain what an "Altar Call" was since many of those in attendance hadn't attended a service before. He would explain, that if they felt they had they had come to know Jesus through this service and were willing to accept Him as their Saviour, they were to come forward and kneel before the "Altar". Joe would place his hand upon their head and pray that this commitment to Jesus would change their life.

Joe turned out his oil light, climbed into bed and was asleep in no time.

As the sun broke through the filthy window in his room, Joe rolled out of bed and quickly washed in the ice water that was in the hall, and dressed in his "work cloths" buckskins and boots. He quietly stopped off to see Lil, who was still asleep but breathing with a rasp that made each breath sound as if it were the last.

Joe grabbed some stale bread from the bar and started out to the stable to saddle Tar.

Once he was in the saddle, Joe rode down to MacIntosh's tent and left a note explaining he might have to come back during the week to perform a funeral. It wasn't a request, but rather a statement of fact.

Joe rode Tar hard to make it back by mid morning to camp. As they rode into camp, Joe saw that everyone was out at the cutting areas, except for Spud, who was peeling potatoes by the fire pit and putting them into a big cast iron pot of boiling water.

Joe rode over to the corral and waved to Spud as he swung down off Tar. All of a sudden Tar reared up just as Joe was swinging off the saddle, almost causing him to fall. He gained his balance and realized that he was standing beside a rattle snake that had moved out into the sun beside a rock to sun itself. Joe heard the rattles make that dreaded sound before the snake was to strike and he jumped back, letting go of Tar's reins. Just then the rattler shot its head out and bit at Joe. In the process of jumping back, Joe had raised his right leg enough that the rattler's poison-giving teeth struck his work boots just below the top and thankfully didn't break the skin.

Joe didn't know he could move so fast. He had gone for his gun at the same time he had jumped back and had it cocked and fired all in one motion and put three bullets into the rattler almost as fast as it had attacked.

Tar had taken off across the camp and the other horses were all neighing and causing a fuss in the corral.

Joe couldn't believe how fast Spud was able to get up from his squatting position and race towards Tar waving his hands and forcing him into the large tent they used for sleeping. Once cornered, Spud quietly moved forward talking continuously to Tar and trying to qualm him down. Once within range, he grabbed hold of Tar's reins and start patting his neck and leading him back towards the corral.

Joe in the meantime had removed the snake from the corral area by using a stick.

"Thanks Spud!" Joe said as he took the reins from Spud and continued to lead Tar to the corral. He took Tar's saddle off and rubbed him down before letting him into the corral to graze.

"Are you alright, Pastor?" inquired Spud, "Did that snake get you?"

"No" answered Joe, "I was lucky. It just bite the top of my boot. I'll have to wash the venom off before it rubs on my skin."

Spud brought over a cloth he had been using having dipped it into the boiling water before giving it to Joe. Joe washed off his boot and threw the cloth into the fire.

"Well, that was an exciting welcome back to camp." Joe said.

"Pastor, every time you come to this camp you seem to be involved in some excitement. Last week it was your introduction to Big Al and this week a rattler. I can't wait to see what happens next week. We likely won't be able to get the guys out to the cutting zones until after you arrive for fear of missing something."

Joe laughed and headed over to his tent and put away his gear. He then joined Spud and helped carry out the lunch to the cutting crews along with his axe.

When he arrived at his cutting area, he was greeted by Big Al showing him the number of trees he had dropped without his help and kidding him that their production would likely drop off now that the Sky Pilot had arrived.

Spud rang the lunch gong, which was made of wrought iron formed by Blacksmith Jim into a large triangle hanging loose by a rawhide strip and wrung by a short straight rod. This gong was used to wake the camp up, in case of emergencies and to call everyone to meals. In this case it was being used to let everyone know that lunch was available at Big Al and Sky Pilot Joe's cutting site.

Once the gang had gathered and everyone had food and a drink, Spud started into telling them about Joe's experience with the rattler.

The actual event had been exciting enough, but the way Spud told the story you would have thought it was David and Goliath, all over again. Spud, like many cooks, was a first rate story teller and had the gang hanging on very word.

Joe just sat there and ate his lunch nearly choking when Spud told the gang that Joe had pulled his gun out of his holster so fast that before the snake could strike again, Joe had shot it through the eye with one shot, blowing the head right off. He failed to mention that Joe had fired three times before he was able to kill the rattler.

Of course, Spud spent a considerable amount of time expounding on how he had corralled Tar and calmed him down.

Joe felt he should support Spud at his point and indicated that Spud had been a life saver with respect to catching Tar. If he hadn't caught him before he left camp, Tar would likely have not stopped running much before the Manitoba border.

Once lunch and the entertainment was over, they all headed back to their cutting area's. Joe made sure that he cut as hard and fast as he could to ensure that their team met their quota, plus.

It was on Wednesday that a rider came into camp with a message for Joe.

Lil had died Tuesday night in her sleep.

Joe started to ready himself for the ride back and was surprised to see everyone preparing to head back to camp.

"What's going on?" Joe asked Big Al.

"I can assure you Pastor, that we all knew Lil intimately and want to pay our respects. Also, we are all very interested how you will perform a funeral service for a prostitute."

So, Joe had quite a group as he rode back into town. He really had wanted to use the time to think about his eulogy and he hadn't realized that the funeral of a lady like Lil would have such interest. He had thought he would likely be by himself, just with the girls Lil had lived with and likely Dutch. But the response of the guys at the camp made him realize this was going to be a large funeral. He just hoped that Dutch would control the drinking prior to the funeral!

As they rode along, Joe found himself trying to think of a scripture and a theme he could use for this funeral.

His first, since he had helped with his Father's back in Port Rowan.

He had his "Pastoral Pocket Ritual" book that had been issued by the Board of Home Missions prior to leaving Hamilton.

All of sudden the right verse came to him and he was able to think through how he was going to perform this funeral and respect Lil in the process.

When they arrived in Rossland and entered the Saloon, Joe saw that Lil was laid out in a wooden casket at the end of the bar, bedecked in one of her favourite red dresses. Her hair was carefully made up and was held in place with a jeweled clasp.

It was obvious that the bar had opened early and that those in attendance had been drinking quite heavily toasting Lil's passage into paradise.

The saloon was very crowded and noisy as everyone was sharing stories about Lil and the ladies that had worked with Lil all sat around her, like princesses in the court of the queen. They were all decked out in their best, but they had attempted to tone down their colours to black, blue or white to show their respect of their friend and colleague.

Beth was taking it very hard Joe could see. He went over to her and drew up a chair and held her hand for a few minutes without saying a word.

Then he bowed his head and said, "Father, accept our sister Lil into your Heavenly Kingdom. I ask your blessings upon her all her close friends gathered here, especially I ask a blessing upon Beth, who sat with her, held her and nursed her in her time of greatest need and upon Doc who did everything to make Lil's passing as comfortable as possible. Amen" Joe then lifted his head and looked into the hurting eyes of Beth.

"Pastor, thank you!" Beth whispered with anguish and sincerity.

Joe then rose and turned to Dutch. "Is the room available?" he asked.

"Sure Pastor! We thought we would hold the funeral at Boot Hill at 12 pm, if that is ok with you?" Dutch leaned over closer to Joe and whispered, " Lil is starting to smell, if you know what I mean?"

Joe nodded and indicated that 12 would be fine. That gave him about an hour to clean-up and put his service together.

"Dutch, could you see if you could control the drinking for the next hour. I don't want a bunch of drunks at the service if I can help it."

"I'll try," Dutch said, "but I can't promise and I don't want a fight breaking out in here until we can get Lil buried."

Joe nodded again and started up to his room. He stopped and took the basin of water carefully into his room trying not to disturb the dirt at the bottom. Then he peeled off his buckskin shirt and took his face cloth and washed the trail dust off his chest, neck, face and then soaped up and washed his hands and arms. Joe toweled off and put his Sunday clothes on. Then he sat down at the table and began to write a few notes.

When he was done, he proceeded downstairs and noted that the lid for the coffin had been nailed on and people were gathering around the door, ready to process up to 'Boot Hill", which was the graveyard for the community of Rossland. It had been created on a flat area at the end of town, but one had to walk up quite a step hill to reach "Boot Hill". The path to the grave yard was still muddy and slippery.

Joe asked for Pall Bearers and eight men stepped forward – four on each side and they lifted the casket up onto their shoulders. Joe should have realized that these men were in no condition to be carrying the casket, but he had already started out of the saloon and was playing his flute as they started to process up the street and veered off to the right, up the path towards "Boot Hill". It was here that Joe realized he should have insisted the bar to be closed down. One of the lead Pall Bearers, lost his footing on the slippery mud and let go of the front end. All the others were too drunk to quickly make the necessary adjustment, and the casket fell heavily on the ground with the men lying around it laughing their heads off. The lid of the coffin separated from the sides and slid off to the ground.

Much to Joe's surprise, Lil was naked! The beautiful red dress was gone, so were the stockings and the shoes.

Joe immediately grabbed the lid and quickly shifted it back on to the coffin and asked that someone get a hammer. In a matter of minutes, Joe had a pistol handed to him and he turned it to use the butt to re-nail the lid of the coffin.

Joe then chose men from his camp, whom he knew hadn't had the time to get really drunk and again started the procession to the cemetery.

At least a hole had been dug and 2x4s were strung across the 6' hole to allow the coffin to rest on. Two shorter 2x4s were laying perpendicular to the walls of the grave. This would allow the coffin to rest on them when lowered by ropes then the ropes could be pulled out before the dirt was shoveled onto the coffin.

Joe stood at the front of the grave and looked back to the nearly 50 people who had gathered around the grave and down the side of the hill. Most were men, the ladies from the Saloon and a few women from the Town, like Irene Green, and Elsie Schmidt who were there as much to support their Pastor as to say good bye to Lil.

"What are you goin' to say about her Pastor?' called a drunk from half way down the hill who was having difficulty standing straight – Joe wasn't sure if it was the booze or the hill that was causing him some difficulty. A couple of his buddies were holding him up and "shushing" him in a very loud stage whisper.

Joe looked at him. Looked at the crowd that had joined them at the side of the grave and waited for the muttering and talking to settle down.

"Friends, we are gathered here to bid far well to Lillian Graham of Port Perry Ontario, known to most of you as Lily of Dutch's Place.

Listen to the words of the Gospel as heard in the Gospel of John: 8:1-12

> *Jesus went unto the mount of Olives.*
> *And early in the morning he came again into the temple, and all the*
>   *people came unto him; and he sat down, and taught them.*
> *And the scribes and Pharisees brought unto him a woman taken in*
>   *adultery; and when they had set her in the midst,*
> *They say unto him, Master, this woman was taken in adultery, in*
>   *the very act.*
> *Now Moses in the law commanded us, that such should be stoned:*
>   *but what sayest thou?*
> *This they said, tempting him, that they might have to accuse him.*
> *But Jesus stooped down, and with [his] finger wrote on the ground,*
>   *[as though he heard them not].*
>
> *So when they continued asking him, he lifted up himself, and said*
> *unto them, He that is without sin among you, let him first cast a stone*
> *at her. And again he stooped down, and wrote on the ground.*
> *And they which heard [it], being convicted by [their own] conscience,*
> *went out one by one, beginning at the eldest, [even] unto the last: and*
> *Jesus was left alone, and the woman standing in the midst.*
>
> *When Jesus had lifted up himself, and saw none but the woman, he*
> *said unto her, Woman, where are those thine accusers? hath no man*
> *condemned thee?*
>
> *She said, No man, Lord. And Jesus said unto her, Neither do I*
> *condemn thee: go, and sin no more.*

Then spake Jesus again unto them, saying, I am the light of the world: he that followeth me shall not walk in darkness, but shall have the light of life.(KJV) John 8:1-12

Listen to these words again from chapter 8: verse 8 "...and said unto them, *He that is without sin among you, let him first cast a stone at her."*

I say to you, who among you is without sin?" and Joe stood there for at least 30 seconds looking out over the gathered throng and noted that as his eyes fell upon theirs, they immediately looked down to the ground. They couldn't or didn't want to keep eye contact with Joe.

Then Joe opened his "Pastor's Pocket Ritual" Book and began to read selected verses that he had marked while in his room before going downstairs to lead the procession.

From Isaiah we here these words, Isaiah 40:11

> *He shall feed his flock like a shepherd: he shall gather the lambs with his arms, and carry [them] in his bosom..."(KJV)*

And the Psalmist:

> *Psalm 103:13-14*
> *Like as a father pitieth [his] children, [so] the LORD pitieth them that fear him. For he knoweth our frame; he remembereth that we [are] dust.(KJV)*

And Samuel:

> *1 Samuel 20:3*
> *..., and [as] thy soul liveth, [there is] but a step between me and death.(KJV)*

And finally:

> *Psalm 116:15*
> *Precious in the sight of the LORD [is] the death of his saints. (KJV)"*

The Joe turned away from the gathering and looked directly at the coffin

> *John 11:25-29*
> *Jesus said unto her, I am the resurrection, and the life: he that be-*
> *   lieveth in me, though he were dead, yet shall he live:*
> *And whosoever liveth and believeth in me shall never die. Believest*
> *   thou this?*
> *She saith unto him, Yea, Lord: I believe that thou art the Christ, the*
> *   Son of God, which should come into the world.*
> *And when she had so said, she went her way, and called Mary her*
> *   sister secretly, saying, The Master is come, and calleth for thee.*
> *As soon as she heard [that], she arose quickly, and came unto him.*
> *   (KJV)"*

Joe turned back to the gathering and reminded them again: "…and said unto them, He that is without sin among you, let him first cast a stone at her."

"My friends and friends of our dear Sister, Lily Graham, we have come to pay our last respects to this gracious lady, who has been taken from us at far too young an age. I have not been here long, but I have been here long enough to know the love and support that Lil had from her friends at Dutch's. People like Beth that sat beside her bed, day in and a day out, listening to the rasp of death that had taken hold in Lil's body. Friends like this don't just appear, they are fostered over a long period. I also know how hard Doc worked to first help Lil overcome her infection, then to make her last hours comfortable as she slipped into the ever-loving arms of Jesus.

You all know this is a hard life out on the frontier, especial for women. Yet Lil never lost her dignity or her humour and by the turnout today – I would say that Lil would be very appreciative that so many remembered her with fond memories.

Rossland is a long way from Port Perry Ontario – the climate's different and the terrain is certainly different. We are even in a different time zone. But one thing is constant, no matter where we are in this world, we are all under the protection of our God and Maker. He made us and He is waiting to accept us back when our time on this earth is finished.

May the Grace of our Lord Jesus Christ embrace our Sister and accept her into the Company of Saints who have gone before us.

Now is the time to say goodbye to the earthly body of our Sister Lillian Graham

Let us Pray:

O GOD, our Father, Who holdeth all good things in Thy sake keeping, we pray for our sister who has completed her earthly span. Bless her and guide her, and help her to learn quickly the way of spiritual progress, so that she may indeed be one of Thy devoted servants. Amen.

Now we will proceed into the Committal Service:

Seeing now that our sister has been set free from the physical body to enter into a new life with a spiritual body stronger and better than the flesh, we commit her spirit into God's hands. We give thanks to God for the gift of her earthly life; for the promise of a sure resurrection, and a happy reunion in the Life to come. Glorious is the Life of the Spirit, and glorious is the thought that each stage of life faithfully lived is a step nearer to that Heavenly Home promised by God."

Joe stooped and picked up some of the dirt that was beside the grave and started to let it fall between his fingers onto the casket as he concluded the service with the following prayer,

"UNTO Almighty God we commend the soul of our sister departed, and we commit her body to the ground; earth to earth, ashes to ashes, dust to dust; in sure and certain hope of the Resurrection unto eternal life, through our Lord Jesus Christ, at whose coming in glorious majesty to judge the world, the earth and the sea shall give up their dead; and the corruptible bodies of those who sleep in him shall be changed, and made like unto his own glorious body; according to the mighty working whereby he is able to subdue all things unto himself. Amen."

With this Joe closed his book and bowed to the grave. The Pallbearers came forward and lifted the ropes lifting the wooden coffin enough to pull out the cross boards that were holding the coffin up and lowered her, not too gracefully, but at least didn't drop her again to the bottom of the grave.

Then at Joe's nod, those on the left let go of the rope and those on the right pulled the ropes free and up out of the grave. As each person left they took a shovel and put one or two shovel full of earth back into the grave on top of the wooden lid. The Caretaker would fill the rest in after the people left.

They all headed down to Dutch's where Dutch announced the bar was open and he would cover one round of drinks in memory of Lil. The party was on and Lil was soon forgotten by most.

Not, however, by Beth or Joe!

Joe saddled his horse and started out to the camp. He recognized there would be no sleep if he stayed in town.

It was the overall impression by everyone that the Sky Pilot had done Lil good and had seen her off in a fine way.

For the next two months everything seemed to follow a regular routine – cutting wood five and half days a week and holding Sunday Services in Rossland.

Joe felt things were developing well and he was confident that they would be building a Church by spring.

Then God had a new calling for him.

As fall started to close in, Joe noted a stranger coming up to the lane from the train station as the Sunday Service was coming to a conclusion. Joe noted that this lad was able to join in the last hymn without the words and had a really fine Baritone voice.

As people were leaving, the stranger came up and extended his hand, "Brother Joseph, I'm Bill Yoke, your replacement."

"Replacement!" Joe exclaimed, "Heck, I just got here and now you say I'm going to be reassigned already?"

Bill went on to tell Joe that the Johnston's had to leave Revelstoke because of a death in the family, one of their sons back east. Superintendent Rev. McCloud from Winnipeg had heard reports about how Joe had established a thriving mission Church in Rossland and had decided to reassign him to Revelstoke to over see the building of the first Church there. Rev. Johnston had done a great job starting a mission Church and had been busy supervising students all across the area, he just hadn't had the time to see to the actual construction of a Church in Revelstoke. The Methodist Church North-West Conference wanted to see a building up by the winter.

Joe went over to Angus MacIntosh and asked if he could impose upon him and his family to host Bill and himself and invite the Greens and Schmidts for the afternoon to meet with Bill and help with the transfer of responsibility from Joe to Bill. Angus was shocked to hear of the reassignment, he had developed a real liking for this young man, and a respect for him as a lumberman also.

Angus, of course, invited all identified by Joe to their home and extended an invitation for dinner. The Schmidts and Greens offered to bring food along for a pot-luck dinner.

When they had all gathered and were sitting on the veranda, one of the last days that would be warm enough for such a gathering, Joe introduced Bill Yoke to the group and explained that he had been reassigned to Revelstoke to fill in for Rev. Johnston, while he and his wife headed back east to attend the funeral of their son.

Everyone, of course, knew Rev. Johnston and his wife and were deeply moved to think that they had lost one of their sons.

Joe suggested they spend a moment in prayer:

"Dear Lord, please be with Rev. Johnston and his dear wife as they travel great distances with aching hearts. May they find Your Grace encompasses them and gives them the strength to face this time of sorrow and loss. Lord, this couple has done a great job in your vineyard growing the faith and bringing Your word to those who are anxious to hear the Gospel. Give them the strength to take up Your cause in

the near future. These things we ask in the name of Jesus Christ, Our Lord and Master. Amen"

Joe did his best to bring Bill up to speed with respect to the work that had been accomplished in establishing a Church and the roles those in attendance played in achieving this goal.

Over dinner Joe expressed to Bill his desire to continue, if he could, with supporting his "boys". Bill immediately agreed to make this one of his first priorities and also agreed to take Tar off his hands, since he wouldn't be needed in Revelstoke.

The MacIntosh's offered to put Bill up until he was established and Joe headed off to Rossland and his last night at Dutch's Place!

When Joe arrived back in Rossland he immediately headed off to find the "boys". They were over at Shorty's place playing in the sand beside the tent. Joe pulled up a log and sat down. The boys immediately stopped their play and knew something was wrong.

"Didn't we do good today Pastor?" asked Jake.

"You did great guys! I had a lot of people tell me how much they enjoy your singing and how they look forward to it every Sunday. Promise me you won't give this up." Joe responded.

All the boys nodded their heads in the affirmative.

"Boys, I've been called back to Revelstoke to replace Rev. and Mrs. Johnston who have had to go back East to attend the burial of one of their sons. I've good news for you, a friend of mine, Pastor Bill Yoke has arrived and he will be taking my spot here in Rossland. I've told him about you guys and how wonderfully you sing and how you've been coming early for Sunday School to learn a new song each week. He is really looking forward to meeting you tomorrow and I know you'll give him the same support you gave me!"

The look of shock and disappointment registered with Joe immediately. He had to get the boys to support Bill.

"I've only told the Schmidt's, Green's and MacIntosh's about this move and then I came right over to you guys. I didn't want you to hear it by rumour – you're too important to the survival of this Church not to hear it first hand. To tell you the truth, Pastor Bill is rather new at this Pastor thing and is going to need all the help you can give him. I can count on you can't I?" Joe asked, knowing he had them and was pleased to see them acknowledge their shared responsibility to assist Bill.

Joe stood and offered his hand to each young man and had a few parting words for each. Then he headed down to Dutch's Place and started his packing. Thank goodness he only had a few things to pack! He wanted to get to bed and be ready for the early train out of Rossland, which usually left at around 6:30 am – depending what shape the engineer was in from the previous night's carousing at the Saloon or at a poker game.

Joe was downstairs by 5:30 am and Dutch had porridge ready for him.

"Heard you were heading out this morning Pastor. You're going to be missed!" said Dutch.

"It doesn't take long for news to travel in this town." Joe laughed, "thank you for getting up early Dutch, a bowl of porridge would go down good right about now!

I also want to thank you for your hospitality while I was in Rossland, it was very much appreciated and I hope you'll extend the same to my replacement, Pastor Bill Yoke. Bill is staying out at MacIntosh's for a day or two, but I'm sure will be seeking lodging here in the future."

After breakfast, Joe went for a quick walk around the town and came back to Dutch's for his bags. He then headed down to the "train station", which was a deck built beside the tracks just in front of a switch that allowed the train to do a loop and return facing Revelstoke.

To his surprise there was a crowd down by the station. This was very unusual, since the early train seldom had riders, usually just logs to be pulled back to Revelstoke. The passengers usually sat in the Caboose with the brakeman.

As Joe approached he soon recognized that almost all the "Ladies" from Dutch's, the Schmidt's, Green's, MacIntosh's and many of those that attended the Sunday Services, including the "boys" were there to bid him farewell.

As Joe shook hands with those in attendance and gave hugs to the "Ladies", much to the delight and comments of all present, Joe climbed aboard the Caboose, stood on the little platform at the back and waved until he was out of sight of the assembly. He had tears in his eyes. Must be the smoke from the engine!

Joe went inside and sat down with the Brakeman, Chuck Gross and struck up a conversation about Rossland and Revelstoke that filled in most of the trip. When Chuck went to look after "train stuff" Joe went out onto the platform and sat on the step and watched as the scenery flashed by and thought, this is definitely "God's Country!" Magnificent streams and crystal clear lakes, hills and mountains off in the distance, trees everywhere and the odd meadow to break up the forest, no wonder an outdoors person would think this is paradise.

CHAPTER II

Revelstoke
How firm a foundation

*"And we know that all things work together for good to them that love God,
to them who are the called according to [his] purpose." (KJV)*
Romans 8:28

When Joe got off the train and said goodbye to Chuck, he at least knew where he was going, after having stayed with Rev. and Mrs. Johnston, prior to Joe's assignment to Rossland.

Joe walked up the wooden sidewalk towards the Manse of the Presbyterian Church. As he opened the door of the log cabin, he felt the difference in the building from his last visit at once. There was no welcoming smell of home cooking, or warm welcome from Rev. Johnston with his arm ready to put around his shoulder.

As Joe looked around he saw the books in the study and the desk were now gone and with them the feeling of the wisdom and knowledge that was contained in those bookshelves.

When Joe was here earlier he had been intrigued that the bookshelves were assembled by piling wooden boxes on top of each other. The wooden cover layered between each box. When it was time to pack, all one had to do was take the top box down, turn it so the open shelf allowing access to the spine of the books was placed face up and place the cover over the open space and hammer nails into the cover to hold it in place. In a matter of minutes the books would be ready for shipping. Joe planned to use this technique when he was ordained and on his first charge. It was obvious that Rev. Johnston had already prepared his books for shipment.

But now, his first job was to start a fire in the fireplace and in the big cast iron stove that Mrs. Johnston had used to ply him with home made bread and goodies. Joe realized his use of the stove would be far more Spartan to say the least.

Joe took his bags up to the room he had used before and decided it would do just fine – it would sure be quieter then Dutch's Place!

As Joe was unpacking, he heard a knock at the door. He went downstairs and opened the door and was pleasantly surprised to see some of the congregation that he had met when he had preached for Rev. Johnston standing outside his door carrying baskets of food and baking.

"We heard from Chuck that you had arrived," Mrs. Beth Sparrow, the wife of the General Store owner, Jim Sparrow said, "and we brought you a few things to help you get settled."

"Why thank you, Mrs. Sparrow isn't it?" Joe responded.

"I'm surprised you remember, Pastor Joe!" Mrs. Sparrow exclaimed.

"Of course," said Joe, "and this is Eve, your daughter, isn't it?"

"Yes Pastor Joe," responded Eve.

"I don't know if you remember me or not Pastor Joe," said the second woman standing at the door,

"My name is Ellen O'Rourke and this is my son Colin."

"Of course I do Mrs. O'Rourke! Your husband Murphy is the blacksmith for Revelstoke if I remember. But please, come in. I'm afraid I haven't had much chance to do anything but get the fire place and stove lit.

Colin, would you mind bringing in a few logs for me while I put these kind gifts of your Mother's away?" Joe asked.

218

"Pastor, I'll give Colin a hand." offered Eve.

"Thank you Eve, that would be very much appreciated." Joe responded.

Once the food had been put away and Joe had put some water on to boil he invited the ladies and Eve and Colin to sit at the kitchen table while he made some tea and cut into a loaf of Ellen's fresh bread

"Well, you'll have to bring me up to date on what is happening here in Revelstoke." Joe said.

Before they could answer, Colin jumped in and asked, "Is it true you knocked out Big Al from MacIntosh's lumber camp when you first met him?"

"My goodness, how stories travel up here," Joe laughed and found it hard to answer without making it seem more than it really was and having the church members report him to the Superintendent before he even had an opportunity to start his work in Revelstoke.

"It's true that Big Al and I had a disagreement when I first arrived in camp. He blamed me for one of his chums wanting to leave for another camp. I was fortunate and we quickly settled our disagreement and became good friends before I left Rossland. I really thank Big Al for all he did to teach me the lumber jack business. The man has a wealth of knowledge and was a really good worker and good pal." Joe responded hoping that would put an end to this topic, but Colin wasn't going to let him off this easy.

"Pastor, I heard tell that they called you the Scrapping Sky Pilot, is that right?"

"Colin, you stop pestering the Pastor, you hear me?" his Mother issued the warning.

"It's ok, Mrs. O'Rourke, it seems my fame – or lack of it has preceded me – yes Colin, that was my nickname in Rossland – I'm sure they decided I was David in David and Goliath – but I hope I'm remembered for other things as well as my boxing background."

"We have heard nothing but positive feedback from Rossland, Pastor Joe and I apologize for Colin's forward questions." Ellen offered

"Thank you for your kind words. Now you were about to tell me what was happening here in Revelstoke." This time Joe was able to deflect the conversation from himself to the ladies and wasted no time in bringing Joe up on all the gossip, good and bad, that was circulating the church circuit.

When they left about 40 minutes later, Joe realized he had his work cut out for him if he was to get a Church built over the fall and early winter.

Rev. Johnston was well loved by the congregation but had been absent much of his time supervising his students and conducting the sacraments in congregations throughout the region.

The people of Revelstoke realized they had to share their Pastor but had found it hard to develop a cohesive congregation with guest speakers every other Sunday.

The Anglican Church had a rector that was stationed in Revelstoke for two years and had developed a good congregation. Many Methodists had moved over to this Church for the stability it offered. Yes Joe had his work cut out for him. Also Ellen had mentioned that the property that the Church had an option to build on would run out within the month. The congregation didn't have the $250.00 needed to buy the land.

Rev. Johnston was a good supervisor and missionary, but he didn't like fund raising or administrative issues.

Joe realized that if he were to get this church built he was going to need land and therefore $250.00 mighty soon!

As Joe was cleaning up after his visitors, he saw a stack of mail on the corner of the counter and decided to go through it to see what needed to be forwarded to the Johnston's and what was related to Church business.

To his surprise he found four letters addressed to him. They should have been forwarded to him by Rev. Johnson, but had been put aside, much like the need for money for the building lot.

One letter was from his Mother and brought him up to date on the happenings in Port Rowan. Who had died, who had married, that Will had made a decision to follow his brother into Ministry and that the Archer's had been there last Sunday (which would have been about a month ago) for dinner, but Joe already knew this from the many letters he had received from Nel. However, there hadn't been a letter for over a week and he was getting concerned that something had happened to her. However, picking up the three remaining letters addressed to him, he realized that nothing had happened, just his mail had been detoured until his arrival in Revelstoke.

Joe went over to a big rocker by the fireplace and sat down to read and reread the letters from his Nel. They were full of family adventures as they continued on their circuit every week to a new location to offer worship. Nel would describe in detail the challenges with her music and her "choirs" and how Albert had been teasing her that Joe would find an eligible young woman out in the wilds and never return to the East and the welcoming arms of his sister!

Nel would draw pictures in the corner of each sheet of paper of a flower or landscape and tell Joe about art classes she was taking at the Hamilton Art Gallery when they were home for a few days. Then came the part of the letter that Joe would read over and over again when she described her love for him and how much she missed him. He missed her so much!

After indulging in "Joe" time, Joe realized he had to do the rounds and make some contacts as quickly as possible and then there was his sermon to start on and arrange for his Thursday night choir practice.

Since a Church was already established, they had developed certain traditional routines, like choir practice at the manse on Thursday night at 7 pm.

Joe headed to the downtown and the General Store and upon entering it was met by Jim Sparrow, Beth's husband, who looked much like his name. He was a little man in his late thirties, starting to bald and with a sharp pointed nose and a set of bifocals perched on his nose. His bushy neatly trimmed moustache seemed to demonstrate his ability to grow hair, however, not on the top of his head. He looked the perfect image of the shopkeeper, with his clean white full apron and a broom in his hand as he attempted to sweep the floor of the never ending mud and dirt that each customer brought from the bog that was affectionately referred to as the Main Street.

Jim stopped his sweeping and lifted his head to look at what he hoped was a prospective customer. Joe stuck his hand out and announced, "Mr. Sparrow, Joe Robins, I'm replacing Rev. Johnston for the interim."

"Pleased to meet you Pastor," Jim said as he extended his hand and shook with a surprising good grip, "I've heard tell about you. Beat Big Al in a fight I heard?"

"My goodness," responded Joe, "I'm afraid my fighting ability has far outweighed my Preaching abilities. I can assure you, when I left Rossland, Big Al and I were the best of friends."

"I'm sure you were Pastor. You've made quite a name for yourself in far more than your boxing skills. I hear that you conducted the Lil's service and did a splendid job. Well done Pastor, I hear the boys were ready to give you a hard time, but you soon had them eating out of your hand. They had a great respect for you in Rossland and in the lumber camp and were very sad to hear you had left. I can't think of any other Pastor that had a gathering at the station to say goodbye. I think we are very lucky to have you here Pastor and I look forward to working with you to get the Church built." Jim enthusiastically proclaimed.

"How did you hear about the people at the station? I only arrived this morning. Oh, Chuck has been around hasn't he?" Joe inquired

"Yes, Chuck the engineer and fireman all come in here upon arrival with their list of supplies for me to get ready for their return run and have a cup of coffee. While the ladies were visiting you, I was getting a firsthand report from the train crew and I must say they had nothing but positive things to say," responded Jim. "I understand from the boys that you like to be called Pastor Joe. Please just call me Jim."

"Well Jim, thank you for the greeting and the vote of confidence," replied Joe.

Just at that moment two more men came into the room accompanied by two young boys of around ten, one Joe identified as Colin O'Rouke. He was quickly introduced to Colin's father, Murphy O'Rouke, the Blacksmith in town and to Nick Black, the owner of the Saloon. The other young man turned out to be Jim's youngest son Ned, who was also ten.

"I was over at Murphy's when I saw you enter the General Store," said Nick, "Colin, who was playing with Ned, told us you were the new Pastor. So, I asked Murphy if he had the time to meet you and here we are! Welcome Pastor, your reputation precedes you."

"Thank you Nick," Joe said clasping Nick's hand in a shake, then Murphy's and Ned's and Colin's again, "Let's not let this reputation tarnish the work I want to accomplish here in Revelstoke."

"I can assure you Pastor, anything I hear was positive and any man that can take Big Al in a fair fight has my respect," responded Murray with Nick bobbing his head up and down emphatically and the boys standing with their mouths open in awe of this new Pastor.

"Gentlemen, let's remember that our Lord told us to turn the other cheek. I must admit I was afraid if I turned my other cheek I would be back in Rossland without the luxury of riding Tar, my horse. That man had a punch to shake the cobwebs out of any man's head. I'm sure our Lord would have had a way of persuading Big Al to stop fighting, but I found it necessary, for self preservation, to have a quick round with Big Al. May I also say that we left the best of friends and he trained me well in working in the camp.

Now enough of Rossland, I would like to spend a couple of minutes talking about the Methodist Church here in Revelstoke and our need to come up with $250 in the next 20 days. Any ideas?"

"I can tell you we don't have enough members with the resources needed to raise that type of capital in 20 days," declared Jim and both men shook their heads in agreement.

"Then we are going to have to raise the money." Joe stated as a matter of fact.

"How?" asked Nick, "There are so many restrictions placed on fund raising in the church, according to Rev. Johnston. I suggested we have a raffle, but as I understand it, that's gambling and not acceptable?"

"You're right Nick, the Church doesn't sanction gambling – but your idea of a raffle has given me an idea. Do you carry meat or poultry Jim?"

"No, I can't keep the product cold enough and don't sell enough in one day to warrant having meat or fowl in the store. However, Fred Cartwright is a butcher and has an Ice House, maybe he can be of help? However, he's an Anglican. What do you have in mind?"

"Cartwright you say? I don't suppose you know if he came from the Port Rowan area of Ontario do you?" inquired Joe.

"Why yes, his family was from Simcoe, which I think is close to Port Rowan isn't it?" replied Jim.

"Yes it is, right next door actually, and our County Seat. I think he might be related to the butcher in Port Rowan, Jack Cartwright. Mr. Cartwright was also our Sheriff.

Listen, let me have a talk with this Fred Cartwright and if I can make the deal I want, I'll let you in on my idea. Tell me where his shop is and I'll be back before you finish your coffee," Joe said.

"Fred's butchery is across the street and down two stores. Here I'll show you," and with that, Jim walked Joe to the door and pointed to a clapboard store with a large warehouse attached to the back. Joe should have realized this was a butcher shop and a cold house – it looked a lot like the one in Port Rowan.

Joe made his way across the road, nearly loosing his Mukluks in the mud and clay that passed as the road through town.

Once across the street, Joe proceeded into the Butcher shop and was taken back to see a young version of Jack Cartwright behind the counter serving a couple of ladies.

Joe waited until the ladies left the store then walked over to the counter as Fred turned to Joe and offered to serve him.

"Mr. Cartwright, my name is Joe Robins and I'm the new Pastor replacing Rev. Johnston at the Methodist Church," Joe stuck out his hand and firmly shook Fred's, "I believe we have connections back East. I come from Port Rowan and our butcher's name was Sheriff Cartwright. By looking at you I'm sure you must be related."

"Well I'll be!" exclaimed Fred, "sure enough, Jack Cartwright is my Uncle. Imagine meeting someone from Port Rowan way out here. When did you arrive?" inquired Fred.

"I came in May and was assigned to Rossland and then just last week was reassigned to Revelstoke to fill in for the Johnston's," responded Joe.

"Are you the Scrapping Sky Pilot I've heard tell about that bested Big Al?" asked Fred.

"I don't think I'm ever going to live that handle down or the events around Big Al, but let me stress that when I left Rossland, Big Al and I were the best of friends."

"Pastor Joe, I sure have heard of you and am pleased to make your acquaintance, how may I help you?" asked Fred.

"Well Fred, you don't mind me calling you Fred do you?" inquired Joe and Fred nodded his consent, "I've been told you and your family attend the Anglican Church, looks like we let one get away from us," Joe said laughingly, "we have a problem over at the Methodist Church with respect to the land, we need to build our building on this fall and winter. We have to come up with $250 in twenty days."

"Pastor Joe, I can only give a little," Fred responded a little embarrassed, "the store is just starting to pay its way and I don't have much extra."

"Wow Fred!" Joe exclaimed, "that's very generous of you to offer anything, but that is not why I'm here." Joe went on to explain, "I would like you to sponsor a Turkey Shoot. I need two big Toms and a smaller bird for the junior shoot and I need them at cost. Would that be possible?"

Fred was so relieved he would have agreed to almost anything, "I can give you two Toms weighing in at around 30lbs each for $5 each and I'll throw in a 20 lb bird for the junior shoot. I think this is a great idea! To my knowledge we have never had a Turkey shoot in Revelstoke."

"Fred your price is great! This will really help out the Church fund. I'll make sure that your business gets the advertising as our sponsor. Thank you!" and Joe reach his hand over the counter and they shook on the deal.

"Fred, can we pay you for the birds on the day of the draw?" asked Joe aware that funds were tight.

"Of course!" responded Fred, "If I can't trust a fellow Port Rowan person, who happens to be a Pastor, who can I trust? The day of the shoot-off will be fine. By the way, since I'm a sponsor, does that mean I can't shoot for my own bird?"

"That's a good question Fred," responded Joe, "I really hadn't thought through the rules but since this isn't a lottery but rather a public show of skill, I don't think it matters if you participate, as long as you buy your ticket. In fact, I think I'll join in.

I'll need a couple of judges that people will perceive as honest and will respect their decision if it comes down to judging two shots that are close. Any suggestions?"

"I don't think Father Harris will be entering. I'm not aware that he even owns a gun. Also, Miss Tyler the School Teacher would be another that people would respect." Fred offered.

"Excellent suggestions, Fred, thank you!"

With that resolved Joe left the premises of Fred Cartwright and headed back to the General Store. There were Nick and Murphy just finishing their coffee and the boys sipping on what smelled like apple juice.

"We were just about to get back to work Pastor, but we really were curious about what you had up your sleeve as a fund raiser that could raise that type of money." said Nick on behalf of everyone.

"We are not far from Thanksgiving and I've just negotiated with Fred for a couple of Tom Turkeys for a turkey shoot and a smaller turkey for a junior shoot." explained Joe. He could see from their faces they were excited about the idea.

"What a great idea!" exclaimed Murphy, "I don't know why any of us didn't think about it, but we didn't! You've been in town for only a day and have already come up with an idea that could save our property. You're a God send Pastor!"

"I hope God sent me, that's true, but this will only be successful if people will sell the entry tickets. I think we should make 200 tickets for the rifle shoot and 200 tickets for the pistol shoot and," Joe looked at the boys, "would 100 tickets for the youth shoot be enough?" he asked.

Both Ned and Colin agreed they felt that 100 tickets would be more than enough. They couldn't think of 100 kids in the area.

"What do you plan to charge for the tickets?" asked Ned

"Good question," responded Joe, "do you think we could sell all 400 tickets if we charged fifty cents each and how about ten cents for the youth tickets?"

"I think that's doable." Murphy said, "When do we want to hold it and who should we have as judges?"

"Since we need the money immediately, I suggest we hold it a week from Saturday. Once word gets around, it won't take long to find out how many are interested and willing to buy tickets. As far as judges, I asked Fred and I would be interested in your feedback. He suggested Father Harris and Miss Tyler. He didn't believe that either of them would want to enter and would be willing to help us out. Thoughts?"

"I think that's a great suggestion, Pastor. What about yourself?" responded Nick

"I would like to buy my ticket and enter. Do you think that will cause any problems?" asked Joe.

"Of course not Pastor. It's skill that's going to decide the winner and the more tickets we sell the better. I didn't realize that you shoot as well as fight, pastor?" laughed Murphy.

"You couldn't grow up in our area of Ontario and not learn to hunt. One of our main staples in the fall was the geese we shot migrating over Lake Erie. Yes, I'm not a bad shot and I've learned to shoot a pistol since I arrived. I'm likely totally out of my league in this company, but I do enjoy a good challenge." Joe stated with conviction. "We need to get this project started immediately if we are going to be ready in two weeks."

"Pastor, I can gather some of our brothers and sisters and friends and make the tickets for you," offered Colin.

"That would be great," said Joe, "and I'm sure no one would trick us, but when they're finished and numbered, bring them over to the Manse and I'll initial each one to prevent someone making their own.

"I'll provide you with the paper to make the tickets – keep them small and make sure you mark them for which event and as the Pastor has said, number them," offered Jim who had been leaning on his counter and silent through most of this planning. As he watched the interaction of those present and the excitement grow, he thought to himself 'we have the right man at the right time!'.

"I'll speak to Jean about organizing the ladies to bake pies to sell at the event and putting together a lunch, which people could pay for," offered Murphy

"I know Beth will help out and I'll make the flour available to the ladies. All they have to do is let me know they are baking for the Turkey Shoot." Jim offered.

"Jim, that is very generous of you! Thank You! I can't believe it's going together so well. I'll go down and visit Father Harris and Miss Tyler and see if they will assist us.

"By the way, where should we have the competition?" Joe inquired.

"I think on the property where we want to build the Church. We have permission to use it for Sunday Services. There's the tent there where we could set up the lunch and if we started the rifle shoot at 10 am, junior shoot at 11 am pistol shoot at 12 pm and lunch at 1 pm we could have it all over and cleaned up by 3 pm." Jim suggested. It was soundly accepted by them all.

"Thank you Gentlemen, it has been a very productive morning for me, I hope your businesses haven't suffered too much by your absence." Joe shook hands all around and headed off to solicit the help of Father Harris.

As Joe walked up to the white picket fence surrounding the Anglican Manse he noted a small white haired man working in the garden raking leaves.

"Father Harris" Joe called out. The man looked up and smiled.

"Pastor Robins I believe, I was going to come over and visit you once you got settled in but somehow got started on this job," as he held up his rake, "and couldn't seem to stop unless I finished another section, then another and so on. Poor excuse I know, but I do have a very compulsive nature that has gotten me into trouble more than once," responded the gentle white haired man as he set aside his rake and came over and gave Joe a sincere hand shake and invited him into the manse for a cup of tea.

Joe followed Father Harris into the house and soon discovered that Father Harris lived on his own. The house had the air of a male who lived alone in the home. Books spread on tables, dishes not done in the wash bin, a sweater hanging on the back of a chair and the smell of a pipe in the air. The house wasn't dirty, just untidy and well lived in. Joe felt quite at home in this house. More so than the sterile manse he was now living in since Mrs. Johnston wasn't there to make it feel like home.

Father indicated that Joe should sit on a chair at the table and he went over to the stove where there was a kettle boiling away and poured water into a Brown Betty Tea pot, just like the one his Mother had at home.

"Always keep the water boiling," said Father Harris, "helps put a little humidity into the air and tea making quick. With my English background, tea is next to God!"

Joe watched as Father carefully measured out the tea from a canister and placed it in a metal tea ball and then dipped it into the pot with the same reverence that Joe was sure he used when he was administrating the Eucharist to his congregation.

"Father, I've come on a mission seeking help." Joe explained.

"Pastor, you've just arrived, how could you need help so quickly?" responded Father Harris.

"First of all, Father, please call me Joe, and second, when I arrived I was informed that the property which had been under option to buy the church building, was coming due at the end of the month. I have organized a Turkey Shoot as a way to raise the necessary capital to buy our land and I need your assistance to act as one of the judges for the competition," explained Joe.

"Well Joe, you have been busy, and please call me Brian. I would be pleased to act as a judge if you tell me where and what I'm to do. You said one of the judges, you of course would be one but who are the others?" asked Father.

"Thank you for offering to call you by your Christian name, but I would feel more comfortable if I called you Father, do you mind?" Joe asked and Father nodded his head in agreement. "Now that you've agreed, I plan to ask Miss Tyler. I won't be a judge, I have decided to enter the competition which we are planning to hold a week this Saturday from 10 am to 1 pm and follow with a lunch. We would be honoured if you would be our guest."

"That will work well with my schedule, Joe, and I would be pleased to stay for lunch. Since my wife passed away nearly three years ago, I seek as many meal invitations as I can. Saves cooking!" responded Father.

Joe was right, this was a male home. It still had the touches of his wife in the parlour with the lace table cloth and fine dishes and nick knacks scattered around.

"Father, as you know I'm staying on my own also, however, not for the reason you are. I am sorry to hear of the passing of your wife. I can't fathom the loss you must feel. I know how I long for my Nellie back in Port Rowan, Ontario, but I have the prospect of seeing her within the next year and receiving her letters. Why don't we agree to get together, if our schedules allow every Monday night for dinner. I enjoy cooking and would welcome the opportunity to talk with someone with your vast experience in the Pastorate. I'm so new, I'm going to make many mistakes and so brash I fear I'm going to make many political enemies within the Church. It would be so good to have a chance to talk and share. Would you be agreeable?" Joe asked in sincerity.

"Joe, I would be honoured to join you this Monday and accept your invitation. Thank you for your words of sympathy, but you know you are wrong about a couple of things. I don't get letters from Millie, but she does still talk with me all the time and I do look forward to seeing her once again in the future."

Joe was embarrassed at how he had handled his earlier statement, "Father, I didn't mean to imply you wouldn't see your wife again, of course you will."

Father laughed, got up and brought over the pot of tea. He offered Joe sugar and milk, both of which Joe turned down. However, Father put two spoonfuls of sugar and milk into his cup before he poured the tea.

"Joe, Joe, relax. Of course I realize that you were aware of my beliefs and didn't mean to suggest that I didn't believe in heaven. I am interested in hearing about this young lady of yours. Nellie, did you say? Has she any idea of the life style she is looking at if you two decide to marry? Not that it's any of my business," asked Father.

"Nellie is wonderful," expressed Joe full of enthusiasm to talk about his 'girl' to someone who would understand and not repeat the conversation as village gossip, "she is the daughter of Rev. Archer, who is a circuit rider for the British Methodist Church out of Hamilton Ontario. Nellie plays the pump organ and leads Rev. Archer's choirs at his services and along with her brother Albert sings duets that make the hair on the back of your neck bristle. She is the most beautiful woman in the world and has promised to wait for me until I finish my mission field work and obtain my degree at Victoria College. I am so lucky and I do miss her so much!" Joe exclaimed nearly all in one breath.

"You are a very fortunate man, Joe, to have some one waiting for you who understands the role of a Minister's wife. It was a very hard transition for Millie who had grown up in a large family and whose father was a baker. She found it very hard to be on display all the time, to say the right things to the right people and not to gossip. One of the main sports in a large merchant family is to gossip and of course that just can't happen in a Rector's home. Unfortunately we experienced a couple of situations that caused us to move charges before Millie realized the importance of keeping information inside the Rectory walls. But oh my, I did love that wild lass," exclaimed Father.

"Father, I'm sorry to have to rush off, but I do have to confirm that Miss Tyler will agree to be a judge so I can make this announcement. I do look forward to our dinner on Monday and continuing this conversation," with that, Joe got up and shook Father's hand and was surprised that his grip was so strong for an older smaller man.

Joe went directly up to the school house and was lucky to find Miss Tyler at her desk marking her students test work.

As Joe looked around he thought of his classroom back in Detroit and realized he was a world away. This was the traditional one room school house. Two rows of smaller desks and then three rows of regular sized desks with a large teacher's desk at the front and the proverbial slate board across the front of the classroom. There was an iron stove just to the right of the door that would be used to heat the room during winter and a pile of wood stacked neatly beside it, ready for the soon-to-come onslaught of unrelenting winter.

Miss Tyler lifted her head, startled that the door would open on a Saturday and interrupt her private time. She saw a young man sanding in the light of the door that washed into the schoolroom making it hard to make out his face.

"May I help you?" asked Miss Tyler in the unsure voice of one not quite sure she appreciated this interruption or of her own personal safety.

"I'm sorry to startle you," Joe said, "and I'm sorry to interrupt your work. My name is Joe Robins. I'm the new Pastor for the Methodist Church replacing Rev. Johnston." Joe could see Miss Tyler relax when she knew who was in her classroom and a smile break across her face as she got up and came forward to greet Joe with an extended hand. This hand shake was firm for a woman, but still very lady-like.

"I'm pleased to meet you Pastor. I had heard you were arriving but hadn't realized that you were here already. We will miss Rev. and Mrs. Johnston but we look forward to your ministry here in Revelstoke," offered Miss Tyler.

Joe was impressed at how lovely Miss Tyler looked in her blouse and skirt with her long red hair tied back into a pony tail, rather than having it up in a bun , a style that was popular with ladies with longer hair. Joe noted she had green eyes that sparkled with mischief when she talked and he was surprised she was still a "Miss" in a land of eligible bachelors. She was about Nellie's age.

"I use to teach in Detroit prior to being called to the church and I know that Saturday's prep was essential to a good week with my grade eight class. I promise not to take too much of your time.

Miss Tyler by the way you spoke a moment ago I take it you might have been in Rev. Johnston's congregation?" Joe asked

"Yes, I was honored to attend his services and missed him dearly when he was called to support his mission churches. Not to say that those that substituted weren't good – by the way, didn't you take a service back a few months ago?"

"Yes, when I first arrived in Revelstoke, prior to my assignment to Rossland, I conducted one service for Rev. Johnston. You have a good memory – but I agree, I would not be at Rev. Johnston's level." Joe replied.

"I should have remembered earlier that that was you. You did very well, and I was quite impressed. However, tales of your success in Rossland proceeded you and I'm afraid overshadowed your involvement here in Revelstoke. You have become quite the folk legend, Pastor," offered Miss Tyler, "but please call me Mary."

"Thank you Mary, please feel free to call me Joe," responded Joe.

"I think Pastor suites you better if you don't mind?" Mary answered

"Of course Mary, but I'd better get to why I'm here. Since you're a member of the Congregation, you're likely aware that the property we have to build our Church Building needs to be purchased by the end of the month and we are substantially short on cash to purchase it.

As a fund raiser, I have suggested a Turkey Shoot and hope to sell enough tickets to be able meet our commitment.

I have asked Father Harris to be a judge and he has accepted I was hoping you would consider being a judge. Oh, I forgot to tell you we are planning to hold this next Saturday from 10 am to 1pm and then hold a luncheon.

There would be a pistol shoot, a rifle shoot and a shoot for the younger people.

Could I convince you to accept this challenge," asked Joe.

"Of course I would be happy to help out. What does a judge do?" inquired Mary.

"After each round of shooting, and depending on our numbers, we will have two to ten shooters at the shooting line. The judges will review all targets and decide who was closest to the centre. The winner in each round will enter a second round and maybe a third round, depending again on numbers until we have a final winner" explained Joe

"I think I can handle that challenge, with Father Harris's assistance" responded Mary, "I was just boiling some water for tea, could I interest you Pastor Joe?"

"Why yes, that would be lovely," offered Joe, "this classroom brings back lots of memories, some good and some bad."

"I think once you've been a teacher, you are always a teacher. In many ways, the work you are doing with the Church is a teaching role if ever there was one! I can't think of anything more demanding or at times frustrating than trying to explain to a group of adults the teachings of Jesus in a language and with examples they can understand.

Why in every congregation you will have people who are well read to those that might not be able to read at all. Further, you will have people who are just learning about Jesus to those that read their Bibles everyday and think they know all there is to know about Jesus and God.

At least with the children I know their learning level and can adjust my teaching lessons to take them the next step. How do you prepare yourself for so many levels?" Mary asked as she poured the tea into two china teacups she had magically produced from the bottom drawer of her desk and set them on the corner of her desk where she had drawn up a chair for Joe to sit on while she sat herself behind her large "Teacher's" desk. She then pulled out a bowl of sugar, two spoons and apologized she didn't have any milk.

"Not a problem," Joe said, "I take my tea clear and with no sugar thank you.

How does one aim their message at all ages and levels of literacy? You have certainly hit the nail on the head. It is the challenge of any Preacher! It's a challenge I'm still learning as my career is in its very early stages. So far I have decided that I can't take for granted that people have a detailed understanding of the scripture and have decided that it's a good refresher course for even those who feel they have a good working knowledge of the scripture. I try to use examples that people can relate to. Like Jesus, I try to use everyday experiences and explain that the parables Jesus used were familiar experiences to his audiences.

As I look out over the worshiping congregation, I can soon tell if I am talking above their heads. People start to fidget and look around or fall asleep when they can't understand or if you haven't got them engaged. I think this is why many of the famous evangelists tend to shout and yell a lot, they want to make sure they keep people awake and excited by what they are saying. This isn't my style. I guess I'm more of an orator and story teller.

If I feel I'm loosing the congregation, I'll try telling a story they can relate to, or even stop – sing a hymn and start again, but this time at a different level.

I'm sorry! I didn't mean to bore you with that answer. You are just very easy to talk with and I don't have very many people who I can consider as a colleague. As one teacher to another, I find this opportunity very comfortable and this tea excellent.

Tell me something about you! What's a pretty young lady like you doing so far west in this pioneer town teaching school? I'm sure you had many opportunities to teach back East." Joe inquired noting that Mary had adjusted herself into a comfortable position and seemed pleased that Joe had accepted her as an equal and a colleague. However, this personal question seemed to bother her and Joe could see her eyes becoming misty.

"I came out here about two years ago to meet my fiancé and accept this teaching position. Jeff was a young lawyer and had established a new practice here. But when I arrived I found out that he had caught gold fever and headed off to Vancouver to catch a boat to the Klondike. He left me a note and told me he would be back within two years, rich beyond our wildest dreams. By the time he got to Vancouver it was early fall and the steamer he booked on got stranded in the ice at the Port of St. Michael's and like so many on the paddle steamer, he was ill prepared for the harsh frigid weather that was about to set in. There was not enough food in St. Michael's to handle the influx of boats that had been on their way to the Klondike. Each of these boats had been well over-subscribed – if built for two-hundred, they were carrying four-hundred in improvised wooden bunks built to the ceiling in the inner of the ship. Most people brought all sorts of mining equipment, shovels, picks, pans, even lumber to build slews, but not nearly enough food to last the winter.

Jeff joined a throng of gold hungry greenhorns attempting to enter the Klondike across the mountains and through a very narrow path that was lined with animals of every sort and humans carrying packs that would break the backs of most animals. There were dead animals all along the path and in some areas the path narrowed to a ledge that hung out over the side of the mountain. If a storm hit, no one could seem to get their footing and there was no place to hide to wait out the storm. You had to proceed, one step at a time.

I received a letter from a person that befriended Jeff that said they were working their way together towards the gold field. He indicated graphically the events I shared with you and that Jeff had lost his footing and fallen over the side of the path to his death some 1500 feet below." At this point, Mary could not hold back the tears.

"I'm sorry for your loss," Joe said as he leaned forward and held her hand for a moment, "your loss is like so many I've heard since I arrived. A number of the lads I worked with at the lumber camp took off to find their fortune against the advice of many of us. Angus MacIntosh, the owner of the lumber camp told me that getting employees to work in the lumber camps was getting to be harder and harder as more men have taken off to the gold fields. I think for most it's going to turn out to be fool's gold and hopefully they will return, not end up like your fiancé.

You're a very brave woman to have remained on to teach after receiving this terrible news. I'm sure the children appreciate your dedication to them."

Mary wiped her eyes and apologized for her crying spell.

"Mary, if you can't express your feelings to your Pastor in confidence, whom can you trust and turn to in times of sorrow or conflict?. I appreciate that you were so willing to share with me and once again it shows the need for colleagues to have a true confidant. I look forward to our chats in the future. Any feedback you can give me on my Worship Services will be greatly appreciated," Joe said with meaning.

Joe realized that he needed to establish his lack of availability quickly so a friendship could be established based upon the right expectations.

"I also have a fiancé," Joe explained, "Nellie is the daughter of a Circuit Riding Evangelist in the Hamilton Area of Ontario. Nellie and her brother Albert are part of the Worship Team. Albert sings and reads scripture and Nellie plays the pump organ and leads a new choir every service. She has really become an expert at putting choirs together on short notice and has taught me a couple of tricks that I have used successfully, to this point. Although, I must admit playing a wooden flute does present some challenges Nellie doesn't have leading a choir.

She has a very strong and lovely voice and helps keep the choir on tune. I have to rely on my flute and hope it's in tune when I'm playing it.

Nel and I plan to be married once I complete my mission field and my studies at Victoria College at the University of Toronto.

It seems a long way off, four years, but we are both still young and have a full lifetime ahead of us. At least, when I get back to Toronto, we should be able to see each other on the weekends."

"I think Nellie is a very fortunate young lady and I look forward to meeting her in the future when I get back East." Mary responded with sincerity. She appreciated that Joe had been up front with her about his status.

She would respect it and looked forward to a close "friendship" with this young Pastor.

"I better be going and see how my tickets are coming along," Joe said.

"Who do you have making them?" asked Mary

"Why the Sparrow and O'Rourke children," answered Joe.

"They are all very good students, but check their spelling – it has never been a strong suit for either family." with a laugh Mary replied, remembering some of he assignments she had gotten back. If she marked for spelling, rather than content, they would have been in a negative position!

When Joe got back to the Manse, Colin and Ned were waiting outside with a box full of tickets. There were three bundles each tied with string.

"Hi guys, done already?" Joe asked.

"Yes Pastor, got one bundle for the pistol shoot, one for the rifles and one for the youth shoot." Ned said.

Joe looked at the tickets carefully after what Mary had said:

Turky Shoot
Saturday, Sept. 17th, 1898
10 am
Methodist Church Fund Raiser
Lunch available for $.50
Ticket for Rifle Shoot $.50   #1

Joe thanked the boys for organizing this project and for all their hard work, took the box from the boys and went into the Manse and sat down at his desk and proceeded to insert an "e" in Turkey on the front of each ticket and initial the back with *JUR*.

This took most of the afternoon and when he was done he went back over to the General Store and asked Jim Sparrow about distributing the tickets. Jim took a bunch and suggested that Joe should go over to see Nick Black at the saloon.

Joe had no hesitation about entering the saloon after his experience in Rossland. However, as he walked through the door the conversation dropped off to a whisper as everyone stared at the new Pastor walking over to the bar to talk to Jim.

"I seem to have put a damper on the party Jim. Sorry about that!" Joe said.

"Alright everyone, listen up, this is Pastor Joe Robins who is taking over from Rev. Johnston –

most of you have heard about him – he's called the Scrapping Sky Pilot – you know, the one that knocked Big Al out in Rossland." Nick shouted to the gathering and there was a big "oh" when they heard this young man had knocked out Big Al.

"Folks, go back to having a good time, just remember you Methodists, Church is at 11 am tomorrow and I expect you to be there – you hear!" Joe said with a laugh in his voice.

In a moment the noise of the saloon had risen to its normal hum.

"Nick, I have some of the tickets here for the Turkey Shoot. Jim has taken some. Do you think your kids could look after the Youth Tickets and do you think you can get rid of the adult tickets that are left?"

"Sure Pastor, leave it with me. I should have all my tickets sold by tonight and I'm sure the kids will get the Youth Tickets sold at school on Monday."

Jim thanked Nick and started out of the Saloon back to the manse for dinner. As he reached the door of the saloon, he heard Nick announcing the Turkey Shoot. There was nearly a stampede to the bar to buy tickets. There would be no trouble selling out, Joe soon realized.

Joe had spoken to the Sparrow and O'Rouke children about meeting him at 10 am prior to the service of Worship on Sunday to put together a youth choir and to invite their friends along.

Right at 10 am the children and young adults arrived, there must have been 20 of them.

Joe went through his usual approach with the youth. He explained the hymn he was going to ask them to sing. Then he had them hum the melody while he played the flute and finally had the children sing the words while he played the flute. He decided to reuse "Jesus Loves Me" since it was simple and easy to learn.

Two of the older youth had already developed baritone voices and a number of the young ladies were able to sing alto. Joe struggled with whether he should attempt to have them sing harmony but decided that for a first appearance, he would stick with unison.

By the time he was finished with the youth it was 10:45 and he proceeded out into the congregation meeting people and introducing himself. There was a good turnout and Joe recognized a number of the lads from the saloon sitting there with their wives. He made sure to thank them for attending and winked at a couple of them who were looking a bit uncomfortable about what he might say in front of their spouse. As he moved on, he noted a sense of relief come over their faces and he smiled to himself. It was obvious their spouses thought they were somewhere other than the saloon on Saturday afternoon.

At 11 am sharp, Joe proceeded to the lectern and in a firm voice that carried well to the back of the tent he proceeded to open the service with the Call To Worship. He invited the Youth Choir to come forward and sing "Jesus Loves Me". As they had practiced, Joe did a short introduction on the wooden flute and nodded to the choir to begin. Even Joe was taken back at how beautifully their voices blended and how strong their voices were in singing this favourite children's hymn.

When the Youth had resumed their seats with their families, Joe told a children's story about Noah and the covenant of the Rainbow. Every child was listening intently as he told the story and he noted most adults seemed to be right into the story.

After the story, he led the congregation in a hymn, "This is my Father's World", which he played on his flute and then led them in prayer. After the prayer he led them again in a hymn of celebration, "Holy, Holy, Holy, Lord God Almighty", and then read from the Old Testament, Psalm 93, the Gospel of John 1:1-14 and from 1st Corinthians 3:9-16

Joe's sermon was based upon 1st Corinthians 3:9-16

> *For we are labourers together with God: ye are God's husbandry, [ye are] God's building. According to the grace of God which is given unto me, as a wise master builder, I have laid the foundation, and another buildeth thereon. But let every man take heed how he buildeth thereupon. For other foundation can no man lay than that is laid, which is Jesus Christ. Now if any man build upon this foundation gold, silver, precious stones, wood, hay, stubble; Every man's work shall be made manifest: for the day shall declare it, because it shall be revealed by fire; and the fire shall try every man's work of what sort it is. If any man's work abide which he hath built thereupon, he shall receive a reward. If any man's work shall be burned, he shall suffer loss: but he himself shall be saved; yet so as by fire. Know ye not that ye are the temple of God, and [that] the Spirit of God dwelleth in you?(KJV)*

Joe spoke to the congregation about the fact that they were the Temple of God and that they had a responsibility to build a Church on this site based

upon their belief in Jesus Christ as their Lord and Saviour.

He told them about the need to come up with $250 by the end of the month and the plan to have a Turkey Shoot to raise the funds necessary. Once they owned the land they would proceed to build their Church over the winter – and that their commitment was one more step in their own personal salvation. The Spirit of God dwells within you. Everything is possible with the power of God on your side.

Joe felt he had the congregation with him. He saw heads nodding their agreement and support. He wondered if he should have an "Altar Call" but decided he would introduce that next Sunday. Better to let them get to know him and his preaching style and hopefully next week there would be individuals captured by the spirit willing to come forward and confess their witness to Jesus.

Joe received an offering and closed off with a final hymn, "Glory be to the Father".

The service had run hour and fifteen minutes but he didn't feel people were fidgeting at the end. He was convinced he had them!

As he greeted people as they left the tent he received much positive feedback and commitments to help with the Turkey Shoot or to help with the build when the time came for that to happen.

Yes, Revelstoke was ready for a Methodist Church – Praise be to God!

Joe was invited to the Sparrow's for Sunday dinner and had a very enjoyable evening. He was surprised to learn that Jim had sold all his tickets and he thought all of Nick's were sold also. The kids indicated that most of the Youth Tickets had been sold and they were sure they would be sold out by Monday night.

Beth indicated that she had spoken to a number of the ladies after the Worship Service and the lunch was organized. A number of them were baking extra bread, cookies and pies for sale.

Joe felt good that everything was going together so well.

During the next week Joe looked into the small details related to the event. After school, he had some of the older boys bind bundles of hay and move the bundles of hay into twenty separate backstops, ten at 150 feet (for the rifle shoot) and ten at 75 feet (for the youth and pistol shoot).

He arranged for a number of planks from the wood mill to be dropped off and these he put on saw horses to act as tables and positioned sawed off logs under other planks to act as seats for the lunch under the tent. He then placed a number of planks on sawhorses to place the food on and covered these with white bed sheets, since he didn't have any table cloths big enough.

He asked Mary Tyler if the children would make targets. He provided her with three different sized plates to trace on paper and a small circle painted red to be pasted in the center of each target as the "bulls eye". Joe showed Mary how to set up the making of the targets in an assembly line – much like he had done in Detroit.

The first person used their ruler to place lines from one corner to the opposite corner, making an "x" that identified the center of the paper.

The second person measured down 3inchesfrom the top on both sides of the paper and drew a straight line. Then measured 5 inches and drew another straight line across the paper.

The third person measured in 1 inch on both sides and drew lines the length of the paper and then measured in 3 inches and did the same.

The fourth person took the lined paper and placed their large plate on the outside lines with charcoal and drew a line around the plate and handed it to the person behind them.

The fifth person took the smaller plate, positioned it within the inner lines and drew a circle around it and passed it to the person behind them.

The sixth and last person pasted the red circle in the middle and put the target aside to dry.

With five rows of six participating, the project went well. Even the little ones were able to participate. Joe had them sitting at the back of each row and gluing the "Bulls Eye" in place. They took great pride in placing it dead centre.

The class made five hundred targets in a little over two hours and had fun in participating in this novel "Art" class.

The week flew by as Joe handled many logistical issues.

However, Joe did spend a really enjoyable evening with Father Harris on Monday night and prepared a very tasty venison stew that Cook had taught him while at the lumber camp.

Joe had purchased a nice roast of venison from Fred Cartwright on Monday morning and cut it up into small cubes and had purchased potatoes, carrots and onions from Jim's General Store and had placed them in a large cast iron cooking pot with water, covered and put it on the stove about 10 am. He brought it to a boil and then put it on simmer for most of the day. Joe had found garlic buds and bay leaves in the pantry along with salt and pepper and some dried thyme. He added these to the stew about half way through. Around 4 pm Joe added two cups of cream to the stew and one cup of flour and stirred it until he had a smooth thickened gravy. Also in the afternoon Joe had made some biscuit dough and the batter was placed in the stew to cook and rise.

Father Harris arrived with a bottle of red wine, which Joe accepted graciously proceed poured him a glass and took a glass of water for himself.

"I'm sorry," Father Harris said, "I never thought you didn't drink wine."

"It's alright," Joe said, "when I received my call to the Methodist Church for Ordination, I had to sign a pledge card to never partake of alcohol."

Joe then went on to tell Father Harris about the fiasco he had created when he refused to acknowledge the oath to abide by regular fasting.

By the time Joe was finished he had Father Harris almost lying on the floor with laughter. This young man was going to be a gem to have around and nobody was going to stand in his way. Father Harris thought to himself, 'I hope he becomes ordained. He will be a breath of fresh air in the Methodist Church. They sure need the doors swung open to let in that fresh air.' He was aware that the Anglican

Denomination was in need of major changes – some of the Bishops must have been direct decedents of Archbishop Thomas Moore, considering their lack of movement in responding to the need to make changes that reflected modern society and the needs of the parishioners. However, he was reflecting on Joe and in him he saw a man that was going to make things happen – here in Revelstoke and in the Methodist Church wherever he was called.

Father Harris couldn't remember a more tasty meal or better company since he had arrived in Revelstoke. It was too bad that Joe couldn't share the bottle of wine with him, but he was quite accustomed to finishing a bottle off on his own on a daily basis – sometimes even two!

The Turkey Shoot

Saturday arrived, a fall morning with a light breeze and SUN! Joe was down to the field by 7:30 am and already people were there working away.

Beth was organizing the ladies to have coffee and tea available when everything started at 10 am and of course muffins, hot out of the oven! Joe had to have a couple of these just to make sure they were up to the Methodist Church's standard! They melted in his mouth and the molasses he poured on the second just added to the flavour of the bran and raisin muffins. Everything was working well.

Joe had organized a couple of the ladies to look after the registration and a couple of men who didn't wish to participate in the shoot had volunteered to man the "line" and keep the contestants moving through. There were, after all, 200 people shooting in the adult rifle and pistol competitions and as promised, all 100 Youth tickets had been sold.

When Joe registered he was given number 150 and went to the area were the contestants were assembling. Joe had his pistol on his hip, but he had to borrow a rifle from Jim Sparrow, since Joe had left his rifle back East, in Port Rowan.

Joe had bought a box of shells for the rifle, an 1890 model Winchester that was the first slide-action rifle that Winchester produced. The gun was actually designed by John and Mathew Browning. It was chambered for a new shell, the Rimfire. In fact, the Rimfire (WRF) cartridge was developed specifically for the Model 1890.

Joe had found time during the week to go out into the woods a couple of miles from town and practice with the rifle. It wasn't as comfortable as his own and he soon found that even with the sight adjusted it shot slightly to the left.

After a couple of hours of practice, Joe had decided that he would not embarrass himself, but didn't feel as comfortable with the rifle as he did with his pistol.

Joe had arranged for Mary and Father Harris to have chairs under a tree about 50 yards parallel to the targets, the ten stacks of hay that were 100 yards away from the shooting line. On each stack of hay a target had been secured at eye height, held in place by four sticks pushed through the four corners of each target and into the hay stack.

The first ten shooters approached the line and on the signal of the starter, Nick Black. The roar of the guns was deafening.

Once the line had been cleared, Mary and Father Harris walked the line and where necessary measured the distance from the centre to the bullet hole and then stuck a red flag on top of the winning shot's hay stack.

Jean Black recorded the name of the winner and they were told to report back to the line after all twenty flights had shot.

This process continued until flight 15, when Joe came forward to the line. There had been a great amount of kidding prior to his flight and people had drifted back and forth from the refreshment area and saloon. When Joe appeared at the line the crowd was as large as it had been all day.

Joe took a fair amount of ribbing about God helping him out and steering his bullet.

Joe stood beside nine other men of different ages, shapes and sizes. The one thing they all had in common was their desire to win this round of shooting.

Joe took a bit of grass and threw it up in front of him and watched it blow gently to the left. As he thought, there was a slight cross wind from his right and he would have to aim a hair off centre to the right to compensate for the breeze.

Nick gave the men the command to ready, and they all brought up their rifles and sighted their guns on the target. Then there was the command to aim, and Joe took in a deep breath and held his rifle steady by having his right hand out the stock and his elbow tight in against his ribs, the butt tight against his left shoulder and his left finger wrapped gently around the trigger, with his left eye shut and his right eye looking through the "v" at the start of the barrel and the sight notch at the end of the barrel lined up between the "v" and just off centre of the red dot to the right.

"FIRE!" and ten guns went off like an explosion of dynamite.

"Clear the range!" yelled Nick and all ten men cleared their rifles, put on their safety locks and moved back from the firing line. Then, when Nick was sure the firing line was clear, he lifted a green flag that notified Father Harris and Mary that it was clear to review the targets.

It didn't take long for Mary to place a red flag on top of the bale of hay that was Joe's.

There was a round of applause and Mary's voice called back, "dead centre!"

There had been few dead centre calls announced until this round.

Joe was given the number 15 and told to return to the firing line after the first round of shooting had ended.

The process of completing the next five sets of shooters took place over the next half hour and a horn was blown to reassemble the finalists.

One to ten went to the line first and prepared to shoot. Nick gave the command and the echoing sound shattered the surrounding area.

In this group was Constable Greg Riley from the North West Mounted Police and to no one's surprise Mary raised the red flag over his target and a lumberjack, Pierre, from one of the camps was designated as second.

Then came Joe's group. This time there wasn't the same joking about Joe's ability. People were really interested to see if the last time was a fluke or was this Sky Pilot for real?

Nick gave the command and once again the rifles discharged as one with a tremendous deafening noise.

Father Harris and Mary walked the line and inspected each target and once again the red flag was hoisted over Joe's target to the delight of the crowd who broke into applause and shouts of encouragement.

"Just off centre," called out Mary.

The second place marksman was from the Town. He worked over at the stable and was noted as an expert hunter and tracker called Rawhide.

Nick called the four finalists to the line.

"You have one shot left, there will be a first, second and third place finisher designated by our judges. It

is obvious you are all excellent marksmen to reach this level. Good luck and let the best shot win."

Before Nick could give the command to get ready, Mary held up the red flag and asked Nick to clear the line. Prior to the final round, Mary had met with Father Harris.

"Father, the Pastor and the Constable are very close to center on their targets, I suggest we use one target for the last round, examine it after each shot. I think we should draw a diagonal line from each corner in charcoal. This will create an "x" and will ensure we know the exact centre of the page. We'll make it dark enough that the shooters will be able to see it. That way if we have to measure, we'll be measuring from the same centre spot." Mary explained.

"That is an excellent idea Mary, I was getting concerned about how we would determine first and second, likely third will stand on its own, but if it doesn't we can use the same procedure to determine that position." Father agreed with Mary.

Mary then took one of the targets, made the adjustments and then walked back up to the firing line. She explained what she was proposing to the four shooters and Nick.

All agreed with her suggestion.

Mary had four straws of different lengths in her hand and had each shooter draw one. The long one went to the lumberjack, Pierre, the next shorter one to Rawhide from the stable and the next one to Joe and finally, Constable Riley got the short straw.

Mary went back to her position and raised the red flag to indicate she and Father were ready.

The first shooter, Pierre, readied himself and waited for permission to fire. Nick checked the range then told the shooter to fire when ready.

Crack!

Mary and Father went over and checked the target.

"Pierre, you are about one inch off centre to the left," yelled Mary and the crowed applauded loudly.

The second shooter came to the line and waited for Mary to raise the red flag indicating that they were safe and to fire when ready.

Crack!

Mary and Father proceeded back to scrutinize the target.

"Rawhide, you are about a half inch from centre on the right side." Mary yelled back to the Line.

Once again the audience showed their appreciation with a loud round of applause and a few cheers. Nick once again checked the Range and waited for Mary to indicate they were in a safe position and then asked Joe to assume his position on the Line.

"Fire when ready" Nick instructed.

Prior to assuming his firing position, Joe checked the wind again with a few blades of grass, lifting them high in his fingers and letting them drop to the ground. He noted the wind was stronger than during his first shot. He would have to make a minor adjustment to his aim. Joe assumed his firing position, stabilized the rifle with his one elbow tucked into his side and sighted the rifle towards the target. He could see the 'bulls eye' and the "x" and he moved his rifle a bit more than last time to the right and gently squeezed the trigger.

Crack!

Joe stepped back from the line and awaited his results.

Mary and Father took a little longer reviewing this shot then Mary turned to the Line and yelled, " 'Bulls eye', just to the right and snuggling up to the "x" cross points."

Joe knew he had sited a hair too far to the right and left an opening for Constable Riley.

The crowd went wild and Joe received slaps on the back and hand shakes all around.

He graciously accepted these, but quickly held up his hand and asked for silence to allow Constable Riley an opportunity to prepare himself for the final shot.

Constable Riley acknowledged the sportsmanship being shown by Joe and looked to Nick for permission to approach the line.

Nick checked down the range and saw Mary raise her red flag indicating that they were clear of the target.

Constable Riley carefully took aim at the target. His rifle looked like it was part of his body and moved smoothly and confidently into the firing position. Without hesitation, Constable Riley squeezed the trigger and lowered his rifle to await the results.

Father and Mary went to the target for the last time for this round of shooting and without hesitation Mary turned and yelled, "Dead center, cut the "x" at the cross points. Constable Riley is our winner!"

The crowd went wild. Never had they seen such shooting as these four men had shown today.

Joe went over to Constable Riley and extended his hand. "Nice shooting Constable. I tried my best, but I couldn't beat a shot like that!"

Constable Riley accepted the handshake and indicated he had never been up against a better shooter than Joe and asked if he had entered into the Pistol Shoot also?

"Why yes," Joe responded, "I think I feel a little more comfortable with my pistol than I do with the rifle. I look forward the competing with you in the next round."

Mary led the Big Tom Turkey out on a rope and presented it to Constable Riley. Joe made sure that everyone knew that this Bird came from Cartwright's Butcher Shop.

Joe received a small smoked ham, which Fred had also donated and Rawhide received a box of shells donated by Sparrow's General Store.

Once this event was over, the youth event took place using the same system. Danny O'Rourke came first with Ned Sparrow second and Colin O'Rourke third.

The final event was the pistol shoot and in the final round it was Constable Riley, Rawhide a new shooter who only participated in the pistol shoot, Gary White from the Railway Security and Joe.

Straws were issued to the four and this time Rawhide drew the long one, Gary the second longest, then Constable Riley and finally Joe.

Rawhide shot first and was marked one inch from centre.

Next Gary White shot and was a half inch from centre.

Constable Riley looked as comfortable with his pistol as he had with his rifle. It was obvious this was a man who was used to using firearms!

"Dead Centre, slight to the right," yelled Mary to the delight of the crowd.

Finally Joe approached the line and with his left handed stance and his unusual aiming process looked like he would be doing well if he hit the target.

Crack!

The recoil of the shot carried the pistol up towards his shoulder.

The crowd was hushed and sure he could do no better that second, but that would be well done in their minds.

"Dead Centre, Mary yelled, "crossing the "x" intercepting lines, Pastor Joe wins!"

The crowd went crazy and this time it was Constable Riley who came forward and extended his hand. "Never thought I'd be bested by a Sky Pilot in a pistol shoot," said Constable, "I'll never live this down back at the barracks when word of this gets back to Vancouver!"

Joe accepted the congratulations of the Constable and turned to receive his Tom Turkey from Mary.

Joe held up his hand to quiet down the crowd and said, "As you know, this is a fundraiser for the Methodist Church here in Revelstoke. I wish to thank all who helped organize this event, a special thank you to all those bought tickets to participate. I would like to also recognize our judges, Miss Tyler and my dear friend, Father Harris, and to our sponsors, Fred Cartwright from Cartwright's Butcher, Jim Sparrow from Sparrow's General Store, the ticket makers, from the Sparrow and O'Rourke family, the children from the school who made the targets and finally to the ladies from our Church who have prepared a delicious lunch for you for only one dollar.

Before we proceed to the table, allow me to say grace.

> *Dear Lord, thank you for giving us a beautiful fall day for this event. Thank you for allowing us to have fun as a community and for friendships renewed and new friends made.*

> *Now Lord, Bless this food which has been made with loving hands, bless it to our use, may we be aware of those in need, and may we act as your agents in helping them. Amen.*

Let's eat!"

With that people started to line up at the table that Joe had set up for the food. A table that was overflowing with casseroles, breads, muffins and roasts of venison and chickens cooked in many different ways. At the end of the tables was a table of pies and cakes.

It was obvious the Methodists knew how to host a party! After everyone was sitting down and enjoying their food, Joe stood up and called for the group's attention.

"Ladies and Gentlemen, boys and girls, as you know this is a fund raiser for the Methodist Church and if the ladies of the Church are willing, I'm willing to donate 'Tom the Turkey' to the ladies, if they will host a fund raising dinner for the Church before Thanksgiving?

Ladies, do I have your approval?" Joe asked.

Beth stood up and asked the ladies, "Who is willing to help host this Thanksgiving dinner?"

Hands shot up all over the gathering.

"Pastor Joe," Beth said, "looks like you have a deal!" A round of applause developed spontaneously. Beth looked around the group and said, "Two weeks from tonight, 5 pm – right here – how does that work for everyone?" again there was nodding of heads and consent appeared to be unanimous. "Pastor, thank you for your generosity and after seeing how you shoot, and the stories about how you fight, I think you can count on a good attendance at Church tomorrow! I don't think anyone here wants to cross you Pastor."

There was laughter and another round of applause as Joe resumed his meal with Mary, Father Harris and Constable Riley.

The Turkey Shoot had turned out to be a great success financially, but more importantly, it had turned out to be a great community builder. People were enjoying themselves and having an opportunity to meet their neighbours.

One of the men, Pierre from the lumber camp, came up to Joe and said, "Pastor, do Methodists, allow dancing?"

"Pierre, I don't know whether or not Methodists approve of dancing, but I see you have a fiddle in that left had of yours. If you are as good with that fiddle as you are with your rifle, I'm not going to argue with you! Go ahead Pierre and crank it up and let's see what complaints we get.

In fact Pierre, I'm going to pull my flute out and see if I can't pick up a couple of the tunes you're playing." Having given consent for music, Joe excused himself and wandered over to the Manse, picked up his flute and headed back to the stage area where Pierre had begun fiddling a reel. Joe was able to recognize a few tunes he knew and joined in with Pierre. Out of nowhere another person arrived with a laundry tub, a broom handle and a long rawhide strip, which he tied off to the handle of the upside down steel laundry tub. The broom handle which had a notch cut into one end, was placed into the rim of the tub, and the rawhide slipped through the hole in the top of the broom handle.

Then Tubby, as he was called, placed one foot on the rim of the tub to stabilize it and began to pluck the rawhide. As he moved the broom handle back and forth, Tubby was able to achieve different bass notes. He had an ear that allowed him to pick up the tune and provide harmony that any Contra-Bass player would have been proud of.

Soon they had two guitars chording along with Pierre and Tubby on the 'gut bass' and Joe playing the odd melody that he was able to remember.

As people finished their dessert, coffee and tea, they moved out onto the grass and began to join in jigs and even some square dancing, thanks to Jim Sparrow agreeing to come forward as a "Caller". For the next two hours people partied.

There was still food left and around five o'clock, Joe invited people to head back to the food table, have their dinner and stay for some more music and dancing afterwards.

The party went on until 8 pm.

By 9 pm the area had been cleaned up and reset for Church the next day. Joe was thanking the helpers and heading off to the Manse. Father Harris was walking along with Joe.

"Father, I think there is a couple of drinks left in the bottle of wine you brought on Monday, do you want to stop off for a nightcap before you head back to the rectory?"

"Thank you Joe, I would really enjoy relaxing in quiet for a few minutes and if it doesn't bother you, a glass of wine would cap off a wonderful day." Father Harris replied as he followed Joe into the comfort of the manse.

"You must be very satisfied with your accomplishments today" Father Harris inquired as he sat himself in front of the fireplace that Joe was starting to light.

"Yes, today exceeded my expectations! Especially how everyone came together to make it work so smoothly," Joe said as he watched the fire leap to life and spark and crack as the dry wood caught the flames from the kindling. "I owe a deep debt to both you and Mary for your diligent work today. I have to say, it added a level of creditability to the whole procedure.

Thank you very much. It is too bad Mary couldn't join us, but she had promised to visit one of student's families for the evening." Both men sat back and enjoyed the warmth that was radiating from the fire.

Reality

Joe realized that the warmth he felt was only in his dream. In fact, his fire had died down and he was shaking even more than before.

The wind hadn't died down overnight but was still whipping the snow in funnels through the camp and he was sure those wolves he had heard earlier were getting closer.

He had to get more wood and that meant leaving the warmth of his blanket. He would have to search farther out from the campsite since he had scrounged most of the loose or reachable wood from around the grove. He would have to be careful not to loose sight of the fire or he could end up wandering around in the snow. Lost, and frozen to death.

Joe remembered he had a coil of rope in his equipment and sought it out.

He went to the edge of the grove and checked that he could still see the fire. Yes, although when the wind blew in the right direction it was obscured from vision for a short while. Joe proceeded to tie the rope to a bush and wrapped the other end around his waist and tied it off. He then proceeded to his left and ploughed through the snow trying to find trees and bushes with their limbs close enough to the ground to break or cut off with his hatchet, drag them back to his base tree and start a pile. Joe didn't have the stamina to last long at this task but was able to gather enough branches to last till dawn, which he guessed was still a couple of hours away.

Back at the base tree he gathered his fuel and hauled it back to the fire pit, chopped it up into manageable pieces and fed the fire until he had a roaring blaze once again.

Joe moved his blanket and the boughs he was laying on as close to the fire as he could stand, for the heat being cast off was intense, but Joe knew this wouldn't last long with the wind whipping the flames. He better enjoy the warmth while he could and hopefully his fever would leave with the coming of dawn.

Joe drank a little water that he reclaimed from melting the snow in his metal cup. He needed water to replace the sweat that was pouring out of him from the fever. He snuggled back into his blankets and before he was aware of it was back into dreamland, reliving the last few months. Is this what Heaven is like, reliving, over and over again the events that happened on earth? Surely there was more to it...

Chapter 12

Revelstoke – Revisited
A Builder of God's Kingdom

"And I say also unto thee, that thou art Peter, and upon this rock I will build
my church; and the gates of hell shall not prevail against it." (KJV)
Matthew 16:18

Sunday morning after the Turkey Shoot came early to Joe. Father Harris had only stayed for an hour, but had managed to finish the bottle of wine , headed off to complete his sermon and to bed in preparation for Sunday.

Joe likewise, headed into the study and did a quick count of the moneys raised at the Turkey Shoot. All 200 rifle and 200 pistol tickets had been sold and the kids had sold all 50 youth tickets. That was 400 times 50 cents, equaling $200.00 and another $5.00 from the Youth tickets for a total of $205.00.

Beth had told him the ladies had raised $150.00 from the lunch and refreshments and they had received another $100.00 from donations that had been put into a chamber pot.

It would appear that they had raised over $400.00 with the event and they still had the turkey dinner to look forward to!

Yes this was a good day! Thank You Lord!

Joe was up at the crack of dawn and worked his sermon notes over while he prepared and ate his porridge.

He went down to the Church tent by 8:30 and took a quick walk around in the daylight to ensure that last night's party clutter wasn't evident for those that would soon be arriving for Worship.

Joe straightened a few rows of benches and picked up the odd piece of garbage that had been missed in cleanup yesterday. Yes, he was ready to worship his Lord!

This week he would teach the children the following hymn:

> "The wise may bring their learning, the rich may bring their wealth,
> And some may bring their greatness, and some bring strength and
>   health;
> We, too, would bring our treasures to offer to the King;
> We have no wealth or learning; what shall we children bring?
> We'll bring Him hearts that love Him; we'll bring Him thankful
>   praise,
> And young souls meekly striving to walk in holy ways;
> And these shall be the treasures we offer to the King,
> And these are gifts that even the poorest child may bring.
> We'll bring the little duties we have to do each day;
> We'll try our best to please Him, at home, at school, at play;
> And better are these treasures to offer to our King,
> Than richest gifts without them—yet these a child may bring."[6]

When he met with the children he had them hum the melody while he played it on the flute. Then he worked at having the children learn the first verse. Once they had it memorized, he went on to the second verse. Joe knew there wouldn't be time to learn the third verse. He would add it next week.

By the time the rehearsal was completed, Joe felt good about how the young people sounded.

---

[6] *Words*: Anonymous, in the *Book of Praise for Children*, 1881.
Music: Christmas Morn, Edward J. Hopkins (1818-1901)

He then went on to meet with the "Choir". There were 15 women of all ages and shapes and sizes ready to rehearse, sitting on their benches in the front of the Church.

Joe indicated to them that they were going to sing, "The Church's One Foundation," written by Rev. Samuel Stone

Verse 1

The Church's one foundation
Is Jesus Christ her Lord,
She is His new creation
By water and the Word.
From heaven He came and sought her
To be His holy bride;
With His own blood He bought her
And for her life He died.

Verse 2

She is from every nation,
Yet one o'er all the earth;
Her charter of salvation,
One Lord, one faith, one birth;
One holy Name she blesses,
Partakes one holy food,
And to one hope she presses,
With every grace endued.

Verse 3

The Church shall never perish!
Her dear Lord to defend,
To guide, sustain, and cherish,
Is with her to the end:
Though there be those who hate her,
And false sons in her pale,
Against both foe or traitor
She ever shall prevail.

Verse 4

Though with a scornful wonder
Men see her sore oppressed,
By schisms rent asunder,
By heresies distressed:
Yet saints their watch are keeping,
Their cry goes up, "How long?"
And soon the night of weeping
Shall be the morn of song!

Verse 5

'Mid toil and tribulation,
And tumult of her war,
She waits the consummation
Of peace forevermore;
Till, with the vision glorious,
Her longing eyes are blest,
And the great Church victorious
Shall be the Church at rest.

Verse 6

Yet she on earth hath union
With God the Three in One,
And mystic sweet communion
With those whose rest is won,
With all her sons and daughters
Who, by the Master's hand
Led through the deathly waters,
Repose in Eden land.

Verse 7

O happy ones and holy!
Lord, give us grace that we

Like them, the meek and lowly,
On high may dwell with Thee:
There, past the border mountains,
Where in sweet vales the Bride
With Thee by living fountains
Forever shall abide![7]

As he usually did, Joe explained this was a relatively new hymn written by Rev. Samuel Stone, curate of St. Paul's Church in England.

Once again he had the Ladies hum the melody and made sure they stayed true to their notes.

Joe had written out five copies of the hymn and made five groups of three, making sure he kept the sopranos and altos in the same groups if possible. Where he had an odd number, he ensured he had his best singers in both octaves in this group.

He went over the words of the first verse with the group reading it as a poem, then he had them sing it and did the same with each of the seven verses.

By the time he was finished with the Ladies a number of the congregation had assembled on the benches. Joe noted it was already 10:45 am.

Joe went around, greeted folks, thanked them for their contributions yesterday and welcomed them to worship today. Joe took a fair bit of ribbing and received many congratulations for his shooting exploits of the day before.

Joe was very pleased to see Constable Greg Riley in attendance at worship and went out of his way to welcome Greg and made sure he felt comfortable with the people around him.

---

[7]   *Words:* Samuel J. Stone, *Lyra Fidelium; Twelve Hymns of the Twelve Articles of the Apostle's Creed* (London: Messrs. Parker and Co., 1866).
Music: Aurelia, Samuel S. Weley, in a *Selection of Psalms and Hymns*, by C. Kemble, 1864

It was nearly 11 am and Joe started to the front of the Worship Tent and stopped at the bottom of the stairs before proceeding up to the "pulpit" which was an orange crate that had been elevated by positioning it on a log stump. It worked well since it had a wood divider as a shelf for his hymnal and bible. Joe stood still and bowed his head and prayed to himself, "Lord, be with me today. May the words of my mouth and the meditation in my heart be acceptable to you, my Lord and King." Joe then proceeded up the three steps to the platform in front of his Congregation.

"Good Morning!" Joe greeted the congregation and received a resounding, "Good Morning!" from the congregation.

"Before we start our Worship Service this morning, I would like to report on our event yesterday.

My calculations suggest that we raised $455 with our Turkey Shoot, excellent lunch, dinner and donations yesterday."

The congregation broke out in applause, then fell silent, remembering they were "in church".

Joe laughed and said, "I'm sure God is applauding right along with you. You all have reason to celebrate today!

You worked hard yesterday in the name of the Lord, and you can see the results of your labour in His vineyard.

Congratulations to all of you for your hard work!

It would appear we have enough funds to meet our payment on this property and a start towards the cost of construction of our new Church Building. We also have the funds yet to be realized from our Thanksgiving 'Tom the Turkey Dinner' to be held in two weeks time, thanks to the kind offer of the women of this Church!"

Joe invited the Youth Choir to come forward to open worship and they did themselves proud and set the atmosphere for the Call to Worship.

Joe felt the Spirit move through him and the service went well.

Near the end of the service Joe decided the Spirit was in the group and he should have an Altar Call. Joe explained to the congregation what he was about to do and invited anyone who felt the Spirit of Lord flowing through them, anyone who was ready to proclaim Christ their Lord to come forward and kneel before the platform.

Joe picked up his flute and began to play one of the hymns they had sung during the service. A number of the Adult Choir stood and began to hum the melody along with the flute. As he played he saw one person stand and come forward and soon there were about ten individuals kneeling before the platform. Joe carefully moved down the steps while he continued to play and stood in front of them. When he stopped playing he was pleased to hear that the Adult Choir continued to hum the melody of the hymn and he proceeded to place his hand on the head of each person who had come forward to profess Jesus as their Lord and Saviour. He prayed over them and with them in the moment of joy.

When the service was over and Joe was greeting people as they were leaving, a man Joe hadn't yet met came forward and introduced himself as George Farrow. He was the owner of the property the Church wished to purchase.

"Pastor," Mr. Farrow said, "I was deeply moved by your Worship Service and can't believe the success of your fund raising program yesterday. I am sorry I didn't have an opportunity to share in the day."

"Mr. Farrow, I look forward to meeting with you tomorrow and hopefully we can arrange for the transfer of this property to the Methodist Church of Canada." Joe replied.

"I also look forward to meeting with you. Would ten tomorrow morning be an agreeable time?"

"Yes, that would work with my schedule just fine," responded Joe, knowing that he had nothing scheduled for tomorrow. "Would you like to meet at our manse?"

"That would be fine with me," responded Mr. Farrow. "Do you think we should have a lawyer present?"

"I'm not sure there is a lawyer in Revelstoke at this point, but I'll arrange for someone who has responsibility for land transfers to be present if they are available. Otherwise we can do what we can and arrange for the documents to be sent to Vancouver for finalization." Joe offered.

Both men shook hands and Mr. Farrow proceeded towards town.

Joe quickly connected with Jim Sparrow and Murphy O'Rouke and explained what had transpired. Jim indicated that he could make himself available tomorrow and Murphy also agreed to be there.

Joe was correct, since Mary's fiancé had left for the gold rush, Revelstoke didn't have a lawyer, but Abe at the Post Office was also the Land Registry Officer for Revelstoke. Jim would see if he was available to attend tomorrow's meeting.

It was agreed that they would meet at 9:45 and Joe would have the coffee on when they arrived.

Next morning, Joe was up early, as usual, and did a quick dusting and swept the manse out, started the fire and had his breakfast, making a fresh pot of coffee and boiling some water for anyone who would like tea.

Between 9:15 and 9:45 Jim, Murphy and Abe Swartz, the Postmaster and Land Registry Officer all arrived and helped themselves to a cup of coffee.

While they were waiting, Abe filled Joe in about the name of Revelstoke. Prior to 1886, the majority of the area around was owned by a Mr. Farrow. He had been the town site developer had ended up in a legal battle with the Canadian Pacific Railway (CPR) and had lost. The CPR had then asked the Post Office to legally rename the town to Revelstoke to honour the first Lord Revelstoke, Sir Edward Baring from England who had provided enough shares from the Baring Bank to complete the transcontinental railway. Abe wondered if the Mr. Farrow who was coming to meet them was the same Farrow.

Just then there was a knock at the door and Joe invited Mr. Farrow into the manse and introduced him to those in attendance.

As it turned out, Mr. Farrow was the eldest son of the founder of Revelstoke. His father had died a few years ago.

"I have to tell you," Mr. Farrow said, "I was very impressed with the number that were in attendance at the service yesterday and couldn't believe that you had raised so much in a one day event. Whose idea was it to hold a turkey shoot?"

"That idea came from Pastor Joe." responded Jim, "The Pastor enlisted the children at the school to make the targets. I couldn't believe that he was able to get my children to make the tickets. Ladies of the congregation brought food for the lunch. It was a great day!"

Mr. Farrow turned to Joe and said, "I'm sure it was! I hear tell that your beat the local Northwest Mounted Police Officer in the pistol shoot for first place. I wouldn't expect a man of God to be proficient in fire arms."

"I grew up in farm country in Ontario and we learned to hunt at a very early age. Actually my Father was a ship builder in Port Rowan on Lake Erie. We went goose and duck hunting every spring and fall during the migrations since I was old enough to hold a gun," Joe responded.

"Well gentlemen, my family has asked me to come today to resolve the issue of the property with respect to the Methodist Church," Mr. Farrow stated, "as you know, our family had a major disagreement with the Railway over who owned what and after a legal battle a settlement was reached. My Father decided to move on. He spent a good part of his life establishing what we still refer to as the Town of Farrow. However, we still own land around Revelstoke and this is part of our holdings. We do have clear title and I'm instructed by my Mother that if I felt there was a viable chance for a church to be built on the land to make it available to the Church for," and here there was a pause and all in the room looked concerned and leaned forward to hear the amount, concerned it was going to be more than they had originally negotiated with Mr. Farrow senior, "one dollar!" said Mr. Farrow.

The room erupted with shouts of glee from the three men of the Church and even Abe showed his pleasure by slapping Mr. Farrow on the back.

"What a gift!" Joe exclaimed, "now our funds can be applied to the actual construction of the Church. We should be able to get enough done to ensure we have it enclosed before the really cold weather hits. This will allow us to work on the inside during the winter and be ready for an official opening in the spring, although, I think we should be able to worship in the sanctuary by Christmas.

"Mr. Farrow, please extend to your Mother and to your whole family our sincere appreciation for this precious gift.

Abe, how do we proceed with this land transfer?" Joe asked.

"I've brought the necessary documents completed, except for the amount, which I will now fill in as $1.00 Canadian," said Mr. Farrow.

"I will take these documents after Jim and Murphy sign as Trustees for the Church and register them in the Land Office. I've brought along my stamps so I can stamp Mr. Farrow's copy for his records, along with a registration number and will return your copy to Pastor Joe once all the filing is complete at the Office. You should have it by close today. Gentlemen shake hands to bind the deal! You've just made one of the best deals in Revelstoke's history!"

Jim and Murphy invited Mr. Farrow and Abe over to Nick's for a "wee" drink before Mr. Farrow headed back to Vancouver by the noon train.

Joe was of course invited, but graciously turned down the invitation by indicating he had a commitment with Father Harris. He didn't point out that that commitment wasn't until 4 pm but he knew the others would enjoy themselves much better without an abstaining Pastor sitting with them in the Saloon.

Joe did ask Jim if he had a horse he could borrow for the day and Jim told him to ask Rawhide, who was looking after things for him while he was at this meeting, to saddle up the black stallion that was in the corral.

After everyone left, Joe went down to the stable and met Rawhide as he was grooming a mare that had just come in for stabling. Joe explained his conversation with Jim. Rawhide pointed out the black and asked Joe if he needed help getting him ready.

"I don't think so, Rawhide," Joe said, "the saddle and bridle are in the barn?"

Rawhide offered to get the saddle blanket, saddle and bridle and placed them on the top rail of the fence. Joe proceeded to enter the corral and walked towards the black stallion. People weren't very original with names of horses somehow. "Blackie" was the name of this beautiful animal. Blackie was a good foot taller than Tar had been but obviously had been broken for awhile and was used to different riders. He didn't shy away as Joe approached, looked him in the eyes, then submissively lowered his head and gave a neigh and a shake of his head and nuzzled up to Joe's shoulder. Joe was able to slip the bridle, which unlike Tar, was a mouth bit into Blackie's mouth without any trouble and adjusted the bridle straps to secure it to his neck, leaving the reins hanging to be used to lead the horse over to the fence where Joe hitched him. He then smoothed the saddle blanket over his back, positioned the saddle and pulled on the cinch straps. Joe noted that Blackie had taken in a gulp of air just before he fastened the cinch straps and inflated his stomach. Tar used to do this, so Joe gave Blackie a good swat on the side and when he had expelled the extra air, Joe quickly re-tightened the cinch straps to ensure the saddle was secure.

Joe slipped the reins loose from the rail and threw them over Blackie's head and mounted him.

He was a beautiful horse. Joe was surprised that Jim would use such a beauty for hiring out and expressed this to Rawhide.

"Well Pastor," Rawhide said, "this here is Jim's own horse and he don't usually let strangers ride him but obviously you aren't no stranger anymore." Rawhide said as he spat a glob of tobacco to the ground. Joe was always fascinated how accomplished tobacco chewers could spit a wad and not end up with it all over their face.

Joe swung Blackie out onto the road that led out of town and kicked Blackie into a canter and settled back to enjoy the good weather, which he knew wasn't going to last long before the snow would start cover the town with a blanket of white, ensuring that green wouldn't be seen again for another six months.

Joe had received direction from Father Harris to a local logging camp that was about five miles out of town. It was owned by Angus MacIntosh's brother, Kyle MacIntosh.

As Joe rode into the camp he was amazed by how much one camp looked like another. However, in this case the Headquarters for the operation was in the camp, rather than in town like in Rossland.

There were the large bunk tents and the cook tent and over on the far side of the site there was the HQ tent with a scurry of people hustling in and out and a bear of a voice barking instructions with a few "choice" words thrown in.

Joe swung down off Blackie and hitched him to one of the poles at the corral. Then he walked over towards the HQ tent and was met by what Joe assumed to be the cook. He was an oriental man of good size with a once white apron tied around his waist.

"No jobs!" he said in a sing song dialect that Joe had often heard from his friend in Rossland who ran the laundry.

"That's alright," Joe said, "I want to see Mr. MacIntosh," and started to head to the HQ tent. The oriental gentleman crossed his arms and stepped in front of Joe, blocking his way to the tent.

Before Joe had decided what he was going to do, and with a quick flashback to his first appearance at a MacIntosh Logging Camp and Big Al, a big man who looked like a younger version of Angus MacIntosh appeared out of the HQ tent.

"Sing, back off!" the voice barked and the oriental gentleman stepped aside with a look of regret on his face.

"What can I do for you lad?" barked MacIntosh.

"I bring greetings from your brother in Rossland," Joe said, "let me introduce myself, I'm Joe Robins, Pastor of the Methodist Church of Revelstoke and recently Pastor of the Methodist Church in Rossland. I had the good fortune to work for your brother for awhile."

Joe extended his hand and it was swallowed up by a bear of a hand that nearly made him sink to the ground when he squeezed. There was no way that Joe was going to let MacIntosh know the pain he was feeling and squeezed back the best he could.

"Kyle MacIntosh," he said, "you are the Scrapping Sky Pilot that took Big Al when you first arrived in camp I was told."

MacIntosh turned to the oriental man and said, "Sing, I think I just saved your life." MacIntosh laughed and explained to Sing how Joe had knocked out Big Al, who was a legend in the area.

"I also heard that you beat Constable Greg Riley in a pistol shoot on Saturday. You are becoming quite a legend in the area, Pastor." MacIntosh proclaimed.

"Hardly," Joe said. "Do you think we might have a few words about the church I'm commissioned to build in Revelstoke?" Joe inquired.

"Of course, come into the tent." MacIntosh invited and held back the flap.

Inside were three desks and a couple of chairs. Sitting at two of the desks were a man and a women who MacIntosh introduced as his wife Betty and his Supervisor, Roy Gallant. Kyle MacIntosh went on to fill them in on who Joe was and what he had accomplished. Betty indicated that she had heard Angus and Jane talk glowingly about what Joe had accomplished.

"Is this confidential?" asked MacIntosh.

"Not as far as I'm concerned," said Joe, "I want to fill you in on what has transpired over the last couple of days in Revelstoke with respect to the new Church we wish to build."

Joe then told them about the Turkey Shoot and how they were aiming to raise money to purchase their land and how Farrow had offered the property today for $1.00. This meant that the congregation could start building before the snow fell. Joe was hoping they could be enclosed before it became too cold to work out doors.

"This brings me to why I'm here," Joe said, "I need studding and dressed planks for our Church, plus cross beams and cedar shakes and I need them at a price that God will smile at."

MacIntosh threw back his head and laughed. "My brother was right, you do drive a hard bargain and are a good salesman for God."

For the next hour they sat and sketched, figured and counted quantities of planks, cross pieces, beams, and calculated the number of cedar shakes that would be necessary to roof the Church.

When they were done MacIntosh had calculated the cost of wood at $1,000.00 delivered on site.

Joe said, "I can give you $400.00 now and you'll have to take a note for $600.00 at .25% interest for the rest to be paid off within 12 months of delivery."

MacIntosh responded, "If you have volunteers come out here to run the rip saw and load and deliver the lumber, I'll reduce the remaining $600.00 to $400.00 and take a note for 12 months at no interest."

Joe stuck out his hand, ready for MacIntosh's grip this time, and shook to make a deal.

Joe figured that the money from the Thanksgiving Dinner could be used to purchase the nails, hinges and windows for the Church.

Joe turned down the traditional drink that seals a deal by explaining his signing the temperance oath but would enjoy those present to have a drink on him and he laid down two dollars. MacIntosh poured out three drinks and a glass of water for Joe and handed back his two dollars with thanks. They sat and drank together to celebrate a deal well done.

Joe realized he had his work cut out for him to recruit enough men to cut, load and deliver the lumber before the winter closed the road. However, he was always excited about a challenge and was convinced that God wanted this Church up and operational before Christmas.

When Joe arrived back in town and returned Blackie to the Smithy, he thanked Murphy for the loan of Blackie and indicated how much he enjoyed riding him that afternoon. He then went on to explain the deal he had made with Kyle MacIntosh.

Murphy couldn't believe that Joe had been able to strike such a good deal with Kyle MacIntosh. He was known as a hardnosed businessman that didn't give away anything when it came to business.

"It's hard to turn God down," Joe said, "and I found Mr. MacIntosh an honourable man to deal with, but I am concerned that I have committed our men to a major commitment to get the lumber onto the site. Do you think we can accomplish this?" Joe asked.

"Pastor, relax," Murphy said, "I can assure you that we will have work crews that will be more than glad to help out. We should be able to mill and haul the lumber on two consecutive Saturdays. I'll put the word out and we'll get a crew ready to go this Saturday and next Saturday. We can end the day on the second Saturday with the turkey dinner to celebrate our success."

Murphy turned to Rawhide, "Go down to the saloon and then over to Sparrow's General Store and see how many volunteers you can get for a work crew this Saturday at MacIntosh's Logging Camp on the Rossland Road. When you're done head out to some of the homesteads and spread the word. Pastor Joe has put the call out."

With that, Rawhide headed out to spread the word and Joe, after thanking Murphy again for all his help, headed back to the Manse for his weekly meal with Father Harris. Tonight, they were having leftovers from Saturday's meals. Easy to warm up and great to eat!

Tuesday morning Joe went down to Sparrow's General Store and ran into Murphy and Nick having a coffee with Jim around the wood stove in the General Store.

"Pastor!" exclaimed Murphy, "I was just about to head up to your place to let you know that we have a crew of forty volunteers that will be at MacIntosh's Camp by 8 am on Saturday. This will include ten wagons with good hauling teams and a couple of teams that we can use on site to haul logs to the rip saw."

"I can't believe it!" said Joe, 'How did you get so many volunteers so quickly?"

"Pastor, you have quite a reputation and once they heard that Pastor Joe had put the call out, they were committed. I think we'll have closer to 60 for the second Saturday. Some of the guys had commitments already for this Saturday, but wanted to help out and committed for the following Saturday."

Joe bowed his head and prayed, "Lord, thank you for people like Jim, Murphy, Rawhide and Nick. I think we can fulfill your expectations of us Lord. Amen!"

Joe and the men spent the next half hour deciding how they would use the volunteers. With Joe's experience of working in a Logging Camp prior to coming to Revelstoke, he was able to suggest how best the men could be used and the locals were able to suggest which men who had volunteered would be best at which job Joe had described.

Jim kept notes of the meeting on the back of a piece of cardboard he had ripped off a case of lettuce.

Joe then asked Jim about the nails and Murphy about the hinges that would be needed. Both offered prices that were basically at cost or below. In the case of the hinges, Murphy offered to make them for the cost of the steel and he would donate the time it took to make them.

Joe then asked the three if anyone in town had a business repairing watches. He was told that to their knowledge no one did.

Joe then informed the group, that if that was the case, he planned to open up a repair shop at the manse to help cover his expense and purchased black paint from Joe to make a sign.

When Joe got back to the manse, he found a piece of wood and painted a sign that said, 'Watches Repaired - 25 Cents'

Before the end of day, Joe had 15 watches on his kitchen table needing repair. He used the same system he had used in Detroit and gave each person a piece of paper with a number on it. He had created 25 small boxes each with a number on it. Each box held the watch and he had given the corresponding number to its owner. This way, he could work on a watch and even if it was in parts, he had all the parts together in one place.

Joe spent two hours every day working on repairing watches and in most cases was able to clean and reset a watch in 20 minutes. Watches that needed a lot of work, Joe held over to the evening and filled in his evenings doing these repairs.

From this manse based business Joe was able to generate about $20 per week, much needed to cover his food expenses.

Joe had gone back out to the MacIntosh Camp and told Kyle that he had a commitment for 40 volunteers for this Saturday and nearly 60 for next.

Joe explained how he wanted to use the volunteers and how many logs he was going to need in the camp.

Kyle was amazed at the detail of the work schedule that Joe had created, but was secretly skeptical of the numbers.

It was agreed that Joe would be onsite at 7 am on Saturday to prepare for the day's work.

Joe had made arrangements for Blackie to be available to him on Saturday. Murphy would drive a team out with a wagon to be able to haul lumber to the Church site.

At 5 am, Joe was at the stable, had saddled Blackie and was on the road by 5:30 am. Joe arrived at the logging camp just before 7 am and could smell the aroma of bacon coking and coffee in the air as he arrived and tied Blackie up at the corral.

Sing came over with a big smile and bowed with his arms crossed across his chest, "Boss said have breakfast ready for everyone. You like?" he said gesturing his arm towards the tables that sat on saw horses with benches on each side.

"Sing," Joe said, "this is so kind of you. I would be honoured to share your breakfast," as Joe bowed his head towards Sing and wandered over to the fire to pick up a plate on which Sing piled hotcakes, bacon and poured maple syrup. He offered Joe a coffee but Joe declined and went over to the water bucket and filled a cup of cold water to take to the table along with his food. Joe bowed his head, said grace, dived in to one of the best breakfasts he could remember.

He was just starting to eat when a number of the men arrived and all were welcomed by Sing and offered breakfast. Before long there were over fifty men sitting at the table and sharing in a fellowship that is hard to define. Part of it was expectation of the day ahead. Part of the mystery of the moment was the sharing of food and the telling of tales, as only men can when the mood is right.

Kyle MacIntosh arrived around 8 am and was shocked to see the numbers that had turned out.

At 8:15, Joe stood on the bench and got the attention of those around the table. He suggested they start with prayer and there was an uneasy stir around the table but Joe jumped right in.

> *"Lord, be with this group of men today. Guide their measuring, ease their burden and protect their fingers and feet.*
>
> *We thank you for the fellowship of the table, and we look forward to doing your work as we work together to build your Church. Amen"*

As Joe looked up, he saw smiles on the faces of the men. Many of these men a moment ago were fidgeting about having to pray. It was obvious these men hadn't been used to this type of prayer and appreciated the practicality and brevity.

Joe then explained what Jim, Murphy and he had designed for the day and the work assignments they had put together. He thanked them for coming and suggested they work in teams drawing logs to the pit.

With that, everyone headed off to their assigned tasks.

Joe had scheduled himself with Rawhide to run the saw and Kyle MacIntosh climbed up on the cutting platform to help them.

Joe had the list that Kyle, Betty and Roy had created and it was decided they would start with cutting beams, since these would be needed first to create a bottom frame and provide cross pieces on which to lay the floor.

The saw was started up by having a horse led around the gear assembly that started the pulleys all to run and the blade to turn. It was obvious that MacIntosh had had the blade sharpened prior to the work beginning. As the log was drawn along the cutting chute, the blade sheered off a piece of wood that created a flat side on the log that was 12" in diameter. Once this was cut, the log was brought back and the flat side was placed on the deck of the cutting chute and another 12" slice was cut out. This happened twice more until they had a 12" x 12" beam ready for transport to Revelstoke. This was loaded onto one of the wagons. The wagons could hold four beams and a horse could just draw this weight. Thank goodness the road was dry and not too rutted.

The first wagon was on its way by 9 am and the day proceeded well!

Sing prepared an excellent lunch for everyone!

However, the men didn't spend much time over their meal and were back at their tasks within 30 minutes.

MacIntosh laughed, "I wish my crews were this committed." Kyle said.

'It's the spirit of the Lord," Joe piped in.

By end of day, all the beams and studding had been delivered to the site. A very successful day!

The following weekend there were over 70 men at the Camp by 8 am and the planking and the cedar shakes were cut and transported to the Church Site. Everyone gathered for the Turkey Dinner that had been prepared by the ladies.

Once again the guitar, fiddles and gut string base broke out at the end of dinner. This time, Joe didn't get his flute, but just sat back and enjoyed the evening with Father Harris and Mary.

It was agreed by all that they would come together for two more Saturdays and frame the Church and see if they could get it shingled before the snow made working outside impossible.

The following weekend was Thanksgiving but during the week volunteers had appeared and staked out the Church's foundation and sunk piles that went beyond the frost line and were used to secure the exterior perimeter beams. Digging at this time of the year was a real chore but Joe worked along with whoever turned up to help out and by the weekend the outline of the Church building was established.

Over the course of the next week the first real snowfall began and the ground was covered with 10" of snow. Joe and the volunteers spent a day shoveling out the property around the Church and the inside of what would soon become the sanctuary.

With the freshly cut lumber, they were able to frame the building, plank the sides and roof. Because the roof was so slippery, the men tied themselves off, with ropes from the peak of the roof. Then they were able to shingle the roof with cedar shakes. This was a cold and slow job, but once accomplished the workers felt they had beaten the elements and could finish off enclosing the building.

Joe had ordered glass from Vancouver which arrived by train the week after Thanksgiving and he had arranged for one of the volunteer carpenters to build windows to fit the openings that the framers had left. Each window had panes for glass that would be 12" x 12" with some of the panes he ordered being blue, yellow and red coloured glass.

By November 15th, with the frigid cold of winter well established, Joe was pleased with the work that had been accomplished with the Church. They had brought in the wooden benches from under the tent and placed them on the floor to give temporary seating until proper pews could be built over the winter. A Pot Belly stove had been installed and two cords of wood had been chopped and stacked by the young people as their contribution to the project. Every morning, Joe would go over to the Church and start a fire in the stove, in case any of the volunteers happened to show up to work on the pews, the stage area or other parts of the interior of the Church. Joe wanted them to feel warm and at home the minute they stepped through one of the two big carved doors that greeted a visitor to the Church. Murphy had to design special hinges to carry the weight of the doors and had created special latches that went through a cover plate with a design of bunches of grapes. There were small square windows in each door where Joe had placed some of the red glass he'd ordered. When there was sun, it poured through in the morning casting the most fantastic image on the centre aisle of the Church Sanctuary.

One of Joe's carpenters had designed two doves in flight that he positioned in place with dowelling from top to bottom and from each side. The sun passing over these doves cast an awesome shadow on the floor. It was almost haunting to see it on a sunny day. As luck would have it, the shadows were at their best around 11 am, depending on the season and the sun's position in the sky. In November, there was little sun to see!

Joe held Christmas Eve and Christmas Day Services with a children's pageant, a fresh cut Christmas tree lit with candles on Christmas Eve and singing which was made much easier by one of the congregation donating a spinet and offering to play it at services.

However, Joe's fondest memory was when at the end of the service he invited Hank, who had brought out his guitar at their earlier fund raisers, to lead them in Silent Night.

Joe explained that the first singing of this carol was performed at the Church of St. Nicholas in Oberndorf, Austria on December 24th, 1818. Joe went on to explain that Father Josef Mohr had composed the words and had asked Franz Xavier Gruber to compose a tune for the words that would be played on a guitar. Legend had it, that the organ at the Church of St. Nicholas had broken just before the Christmas Eve service and

Father Mohr didn't want to disappoint his congregation with the lack of music, so led them with his guitar and sang this song at the end of the service as his gift to them.

With that introduction, Hank played the haunting opening strains of Silent Night and the congregation joined in with such emotion that it caused Joe to tear up. It was beautiful – a fit gift for a Saviour!

Revelstoke Methodist Church had come of age! It had a junior and an adult Choir that met Thursday Evenings, a Youth Group, a Women's Missionary Society, a Women's Auxiliary and a Methodist Men's Group, plus a Wednesday night Adult Bible Class.

Joe found his Monday dinners with Father Harris a special time that allowed him to share community information, to discuss theological issues that troubled him and most importantly they shared information in confidence.

Father Harris looked forward to the opportunity to share time with a colleague, enjoyed the enthusiasm of a young evangelist and looked forward to a good wholesome home-cooked meal shared with a good companion.

Everything seemed to fall into routine and Joe felt very satisfied.

In March, Joe received a special letter from Nellie indicating that Albert had been sent to Lamont

Alberta to help establish a Mission Hospital and that the family was coming out in August to visit him and bring out supplies they had collected in the Hamilton area. Was there any chance that Joe could get a few days off and come visit?

Joe realized that a few days wouldn't allow him get to Lamont and back. However, he would ask his Supervisor for a few weeks and see what he said.

Joe wrote to Superintendent Rev. McCloud and explained that his fiancée was going to Lamont to visit her brother who was establishing a Mission Hospital and asked for approval to have the last three weeks of August off. Joe explained that he would organize local lay leadership to cover the Sundays.

By return mail Joe was granted the time off, but in this letter he was congratulated in establishing the Church in Revelstoke and informed that an Ordained Minister would be arriving the first of August to take over the charge. Once Joe had his holiday he would be reassigned to Sandon where he would supply for a month while the Minister there and his wife had a holiday.

Joe received this information with mixed emotions. He was thrilled and couldn't wait to see Nellie again. Yet he felt a feeling of despair about leaving Revelstoke. This was his "baby". He had taken the congregation from a Sunday worship community to a Church Community with their own church home.

Joe had to remind himself that he wasn't ordained and the gift this new Minster was receiving was a gift he would be able to accept once he finished his studies. He was a Missionary not a Congregational Minister. His role was to develop a new church and turn it over to a protective shepherd. It was time to move on!

Joe spent the next few months preparing the people of his congregation for their new Minister.

CHAPTER 13

A Heart Filled Break

"And now abideth faith, hope, charity, these three; but
the greatest of these [is] charity." (KJV)
1 Corinthians 13:13

When Joe was packed and ready to head off to the train station for the 11 am train out of Revelstoke, he was amazed to see the people that had turned up at the station to say their good byes. Joe was overwhelmed by the expression of affection and did his best to greet as many people as possible and get on the train before he found himself crying.

Joe stood on the steps of the train and waved as his train headed out. A new adventure was soon to start for this young man.

Joe settled down on his hard wooden seat and began to think about seeing Nellie again. It took two days to get to Edmonton, where Joe hired a horse and buggy and headed off to Lamont, which was another two-day drive over some very rough roads. On the fifth day, after leaving Revelstoke, Joe arrived in the Town of Lamont. Like Revelstoke, it was basically a tent village with the usual Saloon and General Store as established buildings.

Joe stopped at the General Store and asked for directions to the new Hospital Mission. He was instructed to drive through town and on his left he would find the tents that housed the new Mission Hospital. Of course there were the usual questions as to why he would be seeking this place out? One can't be the source of all knowledge in a community if one doesn't seek knowledge. The storekeeper did an excellent job of trying to collect as much information as possible. At this point, Joe would only confirm he had business with those that ran the facility and wished the storekeeper well.

When Joe drew up in front of the "Hospital", which was a large tent flying a white flag with a red cross on it, Joe saw at once that the Archer's were indeed in residence. Joe recognized Rev. Archer as he came out of the tent flap to see who had arrived and he called out, "Joe has arrived!" In seconds Albert and his Mother were outside shaking his hands and offering their well wishes. But where was Nellie?

Albert laughed in that infectious baritone of his and said, "As glad as you appear to see us, I think there is someone else you would rather be greeting after this long journey. If you proceed over to that stand of trees by the creek, you will find my sister, busy with her paints and canvass capturing the true west as only she can."

Joe bowed towards Rev. and Mrs. Archer, nodded to Albert and asked if they would excuse him while he went to tell Nellie of his arrival.

Of course they all encouraged him. Albert even offered to look after the horse and buggy and move his stuff into his tent.

Joe proceeded to the grove of trees by a small creek and observed Nellie, busily painting the scene before her. She had a lot of oil paint on her smock, hands and the odd streak across her brow where she had obviously wiped away a fly or mosquito.

She looked utterly beautiful as the sun shone on her and cast a glow around her head as if she were an angel and to Joe she was. At that moment Joe stepped on a branch that snapped and caused Nellie to turn quickly. With a gasp she dropped her brush and was running to him and grasped him in a hug that just about took the wind out of him. How could such a small thing have so much strength? At that moment she looked up into his eyes and their lips met fiercely to start, then with gentle kisses all over his face and back to a long passionate kiss on the lips. It felt like she was trying to get into his body. This was all grand, but very inappropriate. What if one of the Archers came to see why they were delayed? How could he explain this breach of proper etiquette?

Nellie must have felt him stiffen, in more than one place and separating herself, grabbed his hand and started to talk as if everything had to be said in the first minute.

"Why didn't you tell me you were coming this morning? Look at me, I'm a mess. Oh how I've missed you. Have you missed me? What was your trip like? How long can you stay? Do you know when you're coming back East? Does my Mother and Father know you're here yet? What do you think of my painting? It is so beautiful out here. I'm sorry I was so forward just a minute ago, but I missed you so much, not that this is an excuse for my behavior, I hope you won't think badly of me? I dreamed so much of what our meeting would be like when you arrived and I had laid out a special outfit, just for you, and here you find me in my painting clothes. This is terrible!"

"Nel, Nel, relax! Yes I have missed you very much over the last months and I can't think of a better greeting. It is the kind of greeting I have dreamed of, but thought would never be possible with your parents with you. This has been very special, but we must make sure that we act appropriately around your folks, and Albert too.

I can't think of a better outfit to see you in than your painting clothes, you look so mischievous and impish. It is an image that will stay with me for the rest of our lives together.

Come, I'll help you pack up. We must get back to the others. Albert is a gem and offered to look after my horse and rig while I came here to greet you. But we best not tarry too long or your Father will be down here with a shot gun."

Nellie laughed with an air that she hadn't felt since Joe had left. She did note he hadn't answered how long he would be with her. "You didn't tell me how long you will be with us?" she inquired.

"I have about a week before I must head back and off to a new Mission Filed, a place called Sandon, where I'm to fill in for the Minister there for a month while he and his wife go on a holiday."

Nellie felt her chest restrict when she realized he would be leaving soon, then threw her head back and said, "Well my love, we are going to make as much of this week as we can!" and with that she gathered up her canvass and chair, while Joe carried her paints and easel and they headed back to the Hospital.

Nellie was right! It was a splendid week with the two of them always together, much to the concern of Rev. and Mrs. Archer but with the blessing of Albert.

Over one of the dinners, Albert told Joe he would be entering Medicine at the University of Toronto in two years, and wondered if Joe would be interested in sharing a flat to help keep their costs down. This seemed like an excellent suggestion since they would both be at University at the same time. A deal was struck that would be a lifetime friendship and support for both men.

A week seemed like an eternity when Joe dreamed about it back in Revelstoke, but it flew by far too fast.

Joe and Nel would take the buggy out in the morning to sightsee and for Nel to do some painting, then they would have a picnic lunch and be back for the afternoon clinic that Albert ran. Both Joe and Nel would help out. In the evening, Rev. Archer would hold open air services, if the weather allowed, or under a tent if the weather was inclement.

Joe was asked to preach at two of these services and would play his flute to accompany Nel on the mandolin she played, since there wasn't a pump organ or spinet in Lamont except at the saloon hall.

The days that he was scheduled to preach, Joe would have to spend the morning working on his sermon while Nel painted. He felt real pressure preaching with his future father-in-law sitting beside him listening to each illustration and nodding his approval over every biblical quotation or reference.

After the second service was completed, Joe told Nel that he would never be afraid to speak to any group again, since he had passed the test of preaching before Rev. Archer with flying colours .

"Nel, it is like you painting for Michelangelo and having him look over your work and make suggestions and give his approval." Joe stated.

For the first time, Nel appreciated the pressure that Joe had felt during those two sermons for to her, they were good sermons and she had heard her Father tell Albert what a fine job Joe had done. She now realized the anxiety that Joe had been experiencing and assured him that her father was impressed with his preaching and she apologized for not sharing this information with him after his first sermon.

Joe was very much accepted as a member of the Archer family and over meals they would share information about his family and express their gratitude at how Charlotte Robins welcomed them when they preached in Port Rowan. They told Joe that Will had made the decision to follow his big brother and become a Minster and Margaret was growing into a fine young lady. His Mother was doing well and appreciated the support that Joe sent and was seeming to manage from the money that was put aside for her from the sale of the Boat Yard. As Joe knew, the house was paid for and she grew most of her own vegetables in a garden at the back of the house and kept the crop in a root cellar under the house for use during the winter.

Joe felt better about being so far away when he knew that the Archer's were keeping tabs on his Mother for him. It felt good to receive a family update first hand rather than through letters. Although his Mother wrote once a week the letters were stilted and lacked personal information it seemed – yet there was very little he wasn't aware of from the information his Mother had shared and what was told by the Archers. Only, now it seemed real.

Joe and Nellie were hardly apart for the week, strolling hand and hand everywhere and finding time to be by themselves to capture for a few minutes the excitement of the first meeting by the creek. Joe didn't have a lot of experience with the art of making love, except what he had read from books and observed at the Saloons, but he soon learned that the "art" came rather naturally to a couple that was very much in love. He quickly learned that Nellie went almost crazy when he nibbled her left ear, not so much the right, cradling her in between his legs when they sat beside the creek and wrapping his arms around her and holding her just under her breasts gave him the most secure feeling he had ever experienced and made him a desire more than any man should endure!

Ah, but far too soon the time had come for Joe to head off for his next assignment.

Early on Saturday morning, he was out to the corral and had hitched the chestnut to the buckboard that he had rented from the stables in Edmonton and came in for a quick breakfast before heading out.

Nellie and her Mother had a spread laid out that was fit for a King.

After breakfast Joe made the rounds and said goodbye to everyone, thanked them for their hospitality and made arrangements to meet Albert in Toronto after his mission field was completed. He had another eight months before he was to be allowed to enter University in September 1901.

The family stayed behind to clean up to allow Nellie and Joe to go out to the buckboard to say their goodbyes in private. Just as well they did, since Joe had already decided that he was going to give Nellie a good bye appropriate to their "hello" even if Rev. Archer was beside them.

Joe climbed up on the buckboard and headed the chestnut down the rutted lane towards Edmonton, turning every few minutes to see Nellie, standing there waving until he reached a point where he only thought he saw her.

On his way back to Edmonton and on the train ride back into British Columbia Joe lived the last week over and over again in his head. The dreams he and Nellie had made about how they would work together in their own Church. How she would play the organ/piano and lead the choir. How he would establish a boys group and she would run a girls group. They had every minute planned. He just had to finish his mission assignment and graduate from University as an Ordained Minster in the Methodist Church. How were they going to wait four years to get married? Joe decided it was time to get back to reality and live one day at a time. From Edmonton Joe took a train to Calgary and from there to Sandon.

Unlike Revelstoke and Rossland, Sandon was a boom town. It was known as the Monte Carlo of North America. It lay in the Selkirk Mountain Range and was famed for its rich deposits of silver-lead ore. Eli Carpenter and Jack Seaton had made the discovery in 1891 and like the gold rush to the Klondike, Sandon had become a destination for men from all over the world.

With the sudden discovery of great wealth came the vultures preying upon it. In no time Sandon had 29 hotels to handle all those who came to find their fortune, three breweries and of course one of the largest "woman of the night" districts found west of Toronto. Besides these "necessities of man" Sandon also had theatres and an opera house, a soft drink company, a cigar factory, three sawmills, two newspapers, a schoolhouse, a hospital and even a curling rink and a bowling alley. Finally as a counter-balance to all these influences from the outside, Sandon had three churches to do God's work.

CHAPTER 14

Sandon

An Oriental Experience - Mission to the World

*"There are, it may be, so many kinds of voices in the world,
and none of them [is] without signification." (KJV)*
1Corinthians 14:10

Sandon had a population of 5,000 when Joe got off the train to make it 5,001. Joe asked the Station Master where he could find the Methodist Church.

"Don't get asked that much," said the Station Master, "Usually the first question is, where is the silver or where is the saloon. Well Mister, see that white church at the end of the road on the other side of town, well that's the Anglican Church. The Methodist Church is a block to your right. Painted yellow. Can't miss it."

"Thank you," Joe said and leaned down to pick up his knapsack and his travel trunk. He lifted his travel trunk up on to his left shoulder, swung his knapsack to hang from his other shoulder and started off down the road towards the Anglican Church.

The wooden sidewalk was busy with people and it was difficult to walk straight without hitting people. It would appear that no one was used to moving aside for someone carrying a load. What should have been a very simple walk up the street turned into a very frustrating few minutes but once he was by the saloons and hotels the number of people on the sidewalk quickly thinned out. By the time he came to the end of the sidewalk, a few hundred yards from the Anglican Church, Joe was on his own. When he came to the corner and made the turn around the Anglican Parish Rectory, he saw immediately what the Station Master had meant. Standing like a huge canary, stood the frame structure of the Methodist Church with a Cross on its roof, also painted yellow. Someone must have gotten a real deal on yellow paint or the person that selected it was colour-blind!

Next to the Church was a small frame building that was also painted yellow and had a sign in front of it that stated it was the Methodist Manse, as if one couldn't guess by the colour!

Joe approached the front door of the Manse, lowered his trunk and knapsack to the ground and stretched to get the aches out of his shoulders. That was one trip he was glad was over.

Joe proceeded to knock at the door and was greeted by a middle-aged woman. Joe introduced himself and there was a gasp of excitement as the woman came forward and hugged him and kissed him on the cheek. Then remembering her position and manners, stepped back and introduced herself as Heddie Greer the wife of the Minister of Sandon's Methodist Church, the Rev. Malcolm Greer.

She invited Joe to come in and helped carry his knapsack as he carried his trunk in. She showed him to a bedroom on the second floor that had a window that faced out onto the street.

Heddie explained that Rev. Greer was conducting the funeral of a prospector who had fallen from a cliff and had been brought in by his partner yesterday. Heddie had emphasized the word "fallen" when she explained Rev. Greer's absence. Joe had no trouble grasping the innuendo in her voice. The funeral was being held at Boot Hill, which was at the other end and just outside of town. He would be home in about an hour explained Heddie.

She invited Joe to sit down in the parlour while she put some tea on. Joe had learned how to nurse his tea to appear as if he as drinking, yet only take small sips. He really didn't like tea very much, even though his Mother used to serve it at every meal. Joe would rather drink cold water.

Over the next 40 minutes Joe learned that Heddie disliked Sandon with a passion. She had seen herself as the wife of a Minister in a small Eastern Ontario community, where she would be the leading socialite. Instead, upon graduation, the Settlement Board of the Methodist Church had appointed Rev. Greer to this hellhole in the middle of nowhere. The only thing that had any importance was who struck silver where?

Heddie made it very clear, now that Joe was here, the Greers would be heading off for a holiday within days. Tomorrow, if Heddie was able to convince her husband! It was apparent from what she said that Heddie had been packed for a few days hoping Joe would appear, even though they had been told officially he wouldn't arrive until next Monday.

At that point the door opened and a small frail man entered the room and stopped to stare at Joe.

Joe stood and Heddie quickly introduced her husband to Joe and Joe felt he was shaking a cold fish when they shook hands. Joe had to quickly back off on his grip in case of hurting his colleague. Joe assumed his seat while Malcolm slipped out of his black "preacher coat" of Albert tails and dusted it off before hanging it up on a peg behind the door.

"Wasn't expecting you for a couple of days," Malcolm stated, " although I must say, Heddie sure felt you would be here earlier."

"So Heddie mentioned," said Joe, "sounds like Heddie is ready to hit the road on your holiday."

"Holiday…" there was a pause in Malcolm's speech, "yes, we are very much in need of a break. Heddie finds it hard out here away from family and all. We are looking forward to a change."

"I'm ready to start just as soon as you wish," stated Joe.

"Would you be willing to start tomorrow? It will give you a few days to get to know the community before Sunday service and it would give me time to get ready to leave," asked Malcolm.

"Tomorrow it is!" stated Joe and accepted some more of Heddie's terrible tea. How could anyone not know how to make tea?

If Joe felt the tea was bad, he was in for a great surprise with respect to dinner. Once again, Joe didn't know that someone could ruin a pork chop and potatoes with such skill. The pork chop needed an axe to cut it and the potatoes had been allowed to boil dry.

Joe had been wary of what dinner might be like when he smelled something burning while he was in his room unpacking. He had hurried out of his room and called Heddie, who was busy putting the washing out on the line, to tell her something was burning. In the meantime, Joe had pulled the potato pot off the stove and poured some water into it and opened the door to let the smoke out.

Heddie came running in and was all flustered about the state of the kitchen but seemed to have everything under control when Joe went back up to his room, where he opened his window to help get the burnt smell out of his room.

When Heddie announced dinner, Malcolm gave a long grace thanking God for his relief, and Heddie for preparing their dinner. After the first bite of the food in front of him, Joe added another request to God, help me eat this dinner without being sick.

Malcolm talked about his congregation and indicated that he had taken over the charge about a year ago, right out of University. When he arrived, the Missionary Student had formed a small congregation and had built the Church and Manse. However, Malcolm found Sandon a hell hole full of sin and sinners and very little support for the local church. The congregation had shrunk from the original congregation and he found it to be quite transient as people left for prospecting or heading home after not finding the riches they thought they might find. Joe asked what groups were functioning and Malcolm indicated that he only performed Sunday worship, weddings and funerals. There was no interest in weekly groups.

Joe thought back to Revelstoke and what he had left for the new Minster and hoped that the person that was given Revelstoke would continue with the development of the congregation he had left with so much love and hope. He hoped Revelstoke wouldn't receive a looser like Malcolm!

When Joe woke up the next day, he was surprised to find that he had slept until 8 am. He must have been really tired from his trip yesterday for he never slept in this late.

When he went downstairs there was a note on the kitchen table that said the Greers had caught the 8 am train to Vancouver and would be back in a month.

Well, that didn't take long! When Malcolm had asked him if he was willing to start the next day, he must have already decided he was leaving in the morning. When Joe looked around the house he noted that it had been striped of all personal belongings, except for his books, and Joe began to wonder to himself if he would see Malcolm and Heddie in a month. In fact Joe was right on! Before the month was over he received a telegraph from Malcolm asking him to pack up his books and send them to an address in Vancouver. There was no other information with this request. Joe did as he was asked and sent the books COD to the address in Vancouver.

On his first day as interim Minister of the Methodist Church in Sandon, Joe headed off to the main general store. He had been informed by Malcolm the owners and operators were members of his church.

Joe entered the General Store, with a sign, that indicated that Pat Burns was the Proprietor. He was greeted by what appeared to be a traditional store clerk with his white apron and his striped shirt held up by arm garters and the ever present smile of a good salesperson. The man was in his forties, balding, but with a physique that suggested he was used to hard work. Behind the counter was a woman of about the same age, tall and thin with a very sharp featured face, hair up in a tight bun, as if it were pulling her already tall body straight up. She too had a professional smile pasted on her face when a potential customer approached.

Joe doffed his cap and introduced himself to the man, but was careful to ensure he captured the woman's eye while he made his introduction.

"I'm Joe Robins, the newly assigned Pastor while the Greers take a short holiday."

"Short holiday my eye!" declared Mrs. Elsie Burns, "I saw all the baggage they had with them. I think they had more than when they arrived! I don't think we'll be seeing them again!" the smile had gone off Elsie's face and a sneer of disgust had replaced it as she responded to Joe.

"I don't know about that," Joe stated, "I only know that I have been assigned here for a month, then I need to move off to Nelson River. I do need your help to get things started while the Greers are away. I'm told there isn't a Youth Group here at Sandon and I would like to start an Epworth League for teenagers. Can you help me identify a few young people who might be interested? How I can contact them?"

"Why our daughter is fifteen and she has many friends in town. I had heard that this organization is just for boys, are you planning to include girls?"

"You're right, the first group that was started in Cleveland was started by a group of young men, but most groups that start today are co-ed. I would plan for this to be a group of young men and women.

Do you think your daughter would be interested?" Joe asked.

"I'm sure Beth would be very interested if the group is to be co-ed. She is at the stage where boys are of great interest to her and her group. It would be nice to know there was a Christian group with Christian values where they could gather and have fun, but not get into trouble, if you know what I mean?" Elsie said.

"Yes, I do know what you mean and I can assure you the values you expect will be part of the group structure. I'll be looking for leaders to help chaperone. However, I have to tell you, and you know this was well as I do, we can watch, we can lead by example, but if a couple wants to explore on their own, they will find a way to do it. You know this as well as I do! All we can do is provide a healthy environment where friendships can develop with certain expectations placed upon the participants." Joe responded.

"Of course we do Pastor, and we will be more than willing to help out as much as we can. We are, however, rather tied to the business. I have a Meat Market in Nelson. It was my first business when we arrived out west, and another General Store in Rossland. We have made Sandon our main centre since it has become the centre of development over the last few years.

By the way Pastor, were you ever in Rossland?"

"Yes it was my first Mission field when I arrived about a year ago." Joe offered.

"Of course, you're the Scrapping Sky Pilot! Pastor Robins! I should have realized. Why I heard stories of your exploits both in Rossland and again in Revelstoke. Beat Big Al in a fight in one of Angus MacIntosh's Lumber Camps and then out-shot Constable Riley of the North West Mounted Police in a pistol competition. Pastor, you're a legend in these hills." Pat told all around.

By this time, shoppers had stopped their shopping and were gathering around the stranger. There was a murmur of recognition of the stories.

"By any chance do any of these legends mention the fact that I conduct a great worship service or that I'm one of the greatest preachers in the West?" Joe asked.

Pat laughed and responded, "Yes Pastor, your reputation as a preacher and a hard working Pastor also follows you around, but I have to tell you, that doesn't excite us as much as the story about Big Al or a pistol competition. In fact, I hear you conducted the burial service of a Prostitute and were able to put the hecklers' in their place. Well done Pastor! Just then, a whistle was heard blasting three times, repeated three times, then repeated again.

Everyone in the store gasped and Pat yelled: "To the train station! There's an emergency!"

Everyone dashed out of the Store and Joe noted that Elsie and Pat didn't even take time to lock the building. They all ran down to the station as the train came to a puffing, hissing stop. People started to the flatbed car that was loaded with people who were yelling for help or moaning in pain.

The Train Man jumped off the flatbed car and announced there had been an avalanche onto the tracks they were working on. Eight men were seriously hurt and four were dead. People helped lift those that were hurt down and carried them up to the tent that flew a red cross. The Town's undertaker arrived and began to remove two white men that had been killed and place them into his wagon. He started to climb up onto his seat when Joe yelled to him.

"What about these two people?"

"They're Chinks!" he responded, "Let their people look after them!"

"Whoa there, friend," Joe said, "they're just as dead as the two you have in the wagon. I suggest you come back here and pick them up also!"

"I'm not touching any Chinaman!" said the Undertaker.

"My name is Pastor Robins of the Methodist Church. Now unless you have enough business without Methodists using your service, I suggest you experience what it's like to touch a Chinaman and help me place them in the back of your wagon." Joe exclaimed emphatically.

Not sure what to do, the Undertaker sat for a moment pondering his options. Quite honestly, he could do quite well without the Methodists, however, he would hate to have this new person affect his relationship with the Catholics and Anglicans. There was a new Undertaker in town who would be only too ready to move in on his business. The tall gentleman, dressed in black tails with a top hat, slowly climbed down without saying a word and proceeded to move over to the flatbed car and waited until a couple of people on the flatbed dragged the dead people over to the edge. Joe grabbed the first person under his armpits and the Undertaker grabbed his feet and they carried the body over to the wagon and then went back and got the second body and also placed it on the wagon. The Undertaker then covered all four bodies with blankets and proceeded back to his driving seat. He turned and looked a Joe, "Who is going to pay the carting fees for these two?" he asked.

"How much are you charging the two white men?" asked Joe.

"They'll be charged 25 cents and it will be added to the funeral cost which will be $5.00." the Undertaker said.

"Then I'll pay the 25 cents for these two individuals and we'll see what the family or friends wish to do about burial." Joe stated and started to walk back towards the hospital tent. It was like the one that he had seen in Lamont only a few days ago.

As he approached the opening, a small man came scurrying out with Pat at his side.

"This is Dr. Gomm," Pat said, "Dr. Gomm, this is our new Pastor, Joe Robins."

Joe nodded his head, noting that Dr. Gomm had blood on his hands and was moving towards a tub of water.

"Doctor, how can I be of assistance?" Joe asked.

"Ever been in a hospital Pastor?" asked Dr. Gomm

"I left my future brother-in-law in Lamont Alberta just a couple of days ago. He was establishing a mission hospital," said Joe, "not sure how much use I can be, but blood won't bother me."

"Good to have you available Pastor," Dr Gomm responded, "grab a pail of water and follow me."

Joe grabbed his pail of water and followed Pat and the Doctor back into the tent. The eight men occupied all the available beds in the Hospital. Dr Gomm instructed Joe to wash up the wounds of three of the men who had superficial wounds and bandage them as best he could. He indicated that he had to operate on the other five men. Once Joe was finished he asked if he could join him in the next tent to help with the surgery.

Joe proceeded to clean up his "patients" and ensure there were no other wounds that should be addressed. He then proceeded into the "operating" tent and found the Doctor busy preparing one of the patients for surgery.

Dr. Gomm asked Joe to talk with the patient, a man who would have been about 50, bald, with a crushed leg that was going to have to be amputated at the knee, if the Doctor was lucky. This would give a good stump to which an artificial wooden leg could be attached.

Joe proceeded to talk to the patient whom he learned was called Luke in a calm and reassuring voice,. As Joe talked with Luke he explained he was going to put a mask over Luke's nose and pour some ether on it and Luke would go to sleep. The Doctor would see to his leg. Joe then administered the ether to Luke and asked him to count back from a hundred. Luke reached 95 and was out cold.

Doctor Gomm asked Joe to hold the leg while he proceeded to amputate it. It was barbaric but quick and soon Joe was holding a human leg in his hand. What to do with it?

"Put it in the wooden box behind you," stated Dr. Gomm, "we'll burn all the extra parts after we get finished."

It took over three hours to finish the work on all five men. Dr. Gomm saved their legs or arms by resetting the bones, stitching the gashes closed and placing splints on the broken areas to ensure the patient didn't move the bone before it set. An arm and another leg had to be amputated, to save the lives of those who had been trapped in the falling rock. Building this railway was a very dangerous business!

Upon completion and after washing up, Dr. Gomm introduced himself to Joe. "I'm Bill Gomm, local

Doctor," Gomm said, and extended his hand to Joe, "and I have to tell you, I couldn't have done that work in there today with out your assistance, Pastor."

Joe accepted the extended hand and shook with a firm grip, "Thank you Doctor, I'm glad I could help out."

"Please call me Bill. There are very few in this town who could have stomached the work, or been as fine an assistant as you were today Pastor." Bill stated with surety.

"And please call me Joe," Joe responded and immediately knew he was going to like this man of science. He reminded Joe very much of Albert, the same self-assurance, quiet personality, yet a person who seemed to fill the space around him with confidence. Yet, unlike Albert, there wasn't the same warmth and compassion. Dr. Gomm had a cold personality, one that had seen far too much grief over the last few years and seemed to have a hurt within him that needed resolving.

Joe excused himself after agreeing to meet Bill at his home for dinner and headed down the street towards what appeared to be the Undertaker's, marked by the wooden coffins stacked up in front of the building.

There was a group of Orientals standing around the front of the Undertaker's and there was a heated, and because of the sing-song nature of their language, confused argument underway.

"What's going on?" Joe demanded.

The Orientals stopped their cries of protest and turned and bowed to Joe.

"These slant eyes want a Christian burial for the dead Chinks!" exploded the Undertaker.

"Sir, what is your name?" Joe asked.

"Joshua Strickland, Pastor," responded the Undertaker.

Joe turned to the bowing Orientals and asked, "Why are you asking for a Christian burial for these men? Did they become Christians?"

An Oriental man who was quite a bit taller than the others, thin as a rail and wearing a floppy hat and boasting the famous "pig tail" of the Chinese workers, stepped forward and addressed Joe, "Pastor," and he bowed to Joe as he addressed him, "thank you for helping our friends have dignity in their death. We all heard how you stepped in and made arrangements for them to be brought here.

Yes Pastor, many of us have become Christians since we came to this land. All three of those that died had professed their faith at a revival meeting about a year ago and although we weren't allowed in any of the Churches here, we did attend the traveling Tent Ministries that came regularly to the area."

"What is your name?" Joe asked. By this time a fair sized crowd had formed around the group, interested to see what was happening and how it would turn out.

"Sung Wong," responded Sung and he bowed again towards Joe.

"Brother Sung," there was a gasp from the community that had gathered. The Pastor had used a formal greeting to an Oriental, "if you and your friends have accepted Jesus Christ as your Lord and Saviour, let me tell you that you are welcomed in the Methodist Church to worship at any time. I will personally conduct the funerals of your friends. I further assure you that Mr. Strickland will be pleased to handle the arrangements, won't you Mr. Strickland?" Joe said with a withering stare at the Undertaker.

The crowd was now very angry and started throwing insults at Joe and the group of Orientals that were gathered round the Undertaker.

"Who is going to pay for these funerals?" demanded Strickland, not sure that the groups of rabble gathered around him could come up with enough money for three burials.

"Why I don't know Mr. Strickland?" Joe responded, "What would the cost be?"

"Five dollars each!" declared Strickland with a voice that was like a sneer and definitely meant to be a put down to the young whipper-snapper Pastor.

"I'm not sure my Brothers here have that sort of money?" Joe responded looking to Sung for feed back and seeing a look of shock in Sung's eyes, Joe continued on, "however, I see the Sheriff over there at the back of the crowd, Sheriff, how much does the town pay for a funeral when there are no relatives to assume the cost?"

"Joshua knows that he gets $1.00." shouted the Sheriff.

"I see, Mr. Strickland you are trying to make a substantial profit on to the death of these men." Joe stated.

Now the crowd was starting to turn their mumbling towards Strickland for although they didn't like Orientals, they hated cheats and gougers even more.

Before it could get ugly Joe stuck his hand into his pocket and produced some money. "Here is $3.75," Joe declared, "Three dollars for the funerals and twenty-five cents for each person to be brought here on your wagon." Joe then turned to Sung, "Would you agree to a funeral at 4 pm today?" asked Joe.

"Would you conduct the funeral pastor?" inquired Sung.

"I would be honoured," responded Joe and turning to Strickland, "will this work for you Mr. Strickland?"

"Of course Pastor." Strickland said in a low and professional undertaker voice, knowing he had to save face with the crowd if he was going to continue to work in this community. He had his furniture business to think of also.

The crowd proceeded to disperse and Joe agreed to meet with Sung and the others from his group after lunch to assist in preparing his remarks for the funeral.

Joe proceeded to the closest Hotel. He entered the restaurant of the establishment, sat down and ordered a sandwich. As he ate the sandwich he thought to himself the price of this sandwich was almost a week's salary, he must be nuts to have ordered this! At that moment, Pat Burns came in and spotted Joe. Pat headed to Joe's table.

"May I sit down and join you, Pastor Joe?" Pat asked.

"Yes Pat, I could use some friendly company right now, however, I'm not sure your reputation is going to be enhanced by having lunch with me." Joe stated.

Pat laughed and sat down at the table with Joe, "Well Pastor, you haven't been in town long and you are likely better known than Rev. Greer ever was."

"I'm not sure that is a positive comment, Pat?" Joe questioned.

"It would appear that while I was running my business, you were opening the doors of our Church to all Orientals. Some of the Session members are quite concerned."

"Yes, I can imagine they would be," responded Joe, "however, since I saw you this morning, I have had to argue with Mr. Strickland, the Undertaker to handle three dead Orientals with respect and transport them to his establishment, assist Dr. Gomm in caring for the superficial wounds of five survivors and then assist with the amputation of one arm and two legs. I ended the morning by having another argument with Strickland about arrangements for burial of the three deceased Orientals – in public no less! It turns out that these men were converted Christians and not accepted by any Church in town, but rather had to wait for a circuit rider evangelical preacher to come monthly to worship. Pat, that is not acceptable! The Methodist Church sends missionaries to China, Africa and India to preach the word of God and convert the masses to Christianity. Right here in Sandon we have converted Christians – with no Christian home to accept them. You tell our Session Members that Jesus didn't preach to the converted! He went to the prostitutes, the poor and the Gentiles, which in the time of Jesus, were like the Orientals to the Jews and the tax collectors, one of the most hated professions at the time of Jesus and welcomed them all into His fellowship. If that was good enough for Jesus, then I can assure you, welcoming the Orientals of Sandon to our Church is an invitation that we must extend if we are to call ourselves Christians!"

Pat sat there accepting Joe's lecture with good grace and smiled as Joe wound up his mini sermon, "Well your nickname really suits you Pastor. The Scrapping Sky Pilot! I don't think there is a member of Session that will want to take you on with respect to your position on the Orientals."

Joe leaned back in his chair as his lunch arrived and said to Pat, "I'm sorry to dump on the messenger, it has been a really busy morning and not one I had planned, I can assure you. Even ordering a sandwich in a place like this is something I would not normally do. In fact, I hope it's a good sandwich, because it's costing me a week's salary!"

"I know you'll enjoy the ham, since this establishment only serves my meat, and Pastor Joe, don't worry about the cost, you're my guest today for lunch." Pat extended the invitation.

"Pat, I didn't mean to cry poor. I'll cover my own lunch. You don't need to buy my lunch!" Joe exclaimed, embarrassed that he had put Pat into a situation that he had to offer to pay for Joe's lunch.

"Pastor, you came in here and ordered your lunch knowing you would have to cover the cost. I invited myself to your table and I would like to offer to buy your lunch as a welcome to Sandon gesture. This is not a handout, but a business lunch, plus since I am a supplier of this Hotel, I do get a special rate! Please accept my offer in the spirit it was made," Pat said.

"Pat, you are the voice of reason and I'm looking forward to working with you over the next couple of weeks, until Pastor Greer returns."

"Pastor, from what I hear from the station master, it would appear that Rev. and Mrs. Greer seemed to have everything they owned with them when they boarded the train this morning. Do you think they are coming back in a month?" Pat asked.

"I don't know Pat. The manse does look pretty bare, except for his books, but I can assure you that the Conference will ensure you have a qualified Pastor assigned to you as soon as possible, if they don't return.

All I do know is I have another assignment to go to at the end of the month, but I'll do all I can to assure you have supply in place before I leave," Joe explained.

The two men had a very enjoyable lunch and Pat filled Joe in on the members of Session and those that had leadership roles within the Church. He also explained that he had started as a Butcher with a store in Nelson. He had followed the construction of the CPR across the West and supplied the work crews with beef. Once the railway had reached Nelson he decided to settle down in 1893. Then he had heard about the Silver strike in Sandon and decided that he would open a General Store with an emphasis on meat and also stores in Three Rivers and Kalso and had just opened his fourth store in Rossland.

Joe indicated that he was scheduled to set up missions in Golden, Three Rivers, New Denver, Silverton, and Clark Camp.

Pat indicated that most of these communities were like Rossland and Sandon, nonexistent about five years ago, but because of logging and Silver and Gold finds, they had become boom towns and were over-populated with people who had arrived without proper equipment to last the winter. Unless they struck a find immediately, many would starve over the winter time. Pat indicated there was definitely a need for the Church in these areas and wished Joe well in his mission commitment.

After lunch, Joe met with Sung and a number of the Chinamen who lived in a tent area behind the railway station. Joe learned that all three men were married and were working to raise enough money to have their families join them in this new country of opportunity. It was the hope of all around him that they could make enough money to have their families join them and that they could get land and start a farm.

Joe thanked them for meeting with him and agreed to meet them at 4:00 pm at the cemetery, or 'Boot Hill' as it was referred to in nearly all the small towns he had visited since he arrived.

At 3:30 Joe proceeded to the cemetery arriving about ten to four. There was already a number of people gathered around the grave sites. Three holes were dug side by side with three coffins sitting on boards spanning the grave holes.

Joe was interested to note that many of the people present were fellow Chinamen who had worked with these people. However, there were a number of townspeople who were here out of curiosity and also a representative of the CPR.

Joe conducted his usual burial service, reading from Psalm 23 and a statement made by Paul about the resurrection and life everlasting. Joe spent a few minutes talking about each person and their desire to make a new life for themselves and their family. Joe went on to talk about how these men had found Christianity in the new world and how he was pleased to assure them of life after death because of this new faith.

Just as Joe was completing the service, there was an explosion that sounded like gun fire! Joe, immediately went for his revolver and remembered he had left it at the manse. Then all of a sudden he realized what he was experiencing. Firecrackers! Joe had heard stories that when an Oriental is buried his family and friends would light firecrackers to scare off evil spirits as the earth was being placed over the caskets. Several of the individual's friends had brought firecrackers to the grave site to ensure their friend would sleep peacefully, without being disturbed by evil spirits. These men might have converted to Christ, but it was obvious that many of their friends still celebrated old traditions and faiths.

Joe had been so startled by the sudden noise of the firecrackers that he had to catch his balance, so he wouldn't follow the deceased into the hole that the casket had been lowered into.

In future, if he ever had to bury any more Orientals, he would steady himself for the firecrackers and not show his surprise, like he had today! As it turned out, Joe had a number of other funerals of Orientals to perform before he finished his mission assignment. The railway seemed to have very little respect for human life, especially if the life was that of a Chinaman!

Joe was running short of cash, having had to pay the funeral costs of the three Oriental gentlemen, Again he placed his sign for fixing watches and within two days he had 30 watches to repair. He was able to repair 28 at fifty cents a piece. It took Joe three days to get all the repairs completed.

The rest of Joe's time in Sandon was without any major controversy, except for the first Sunday he preached he noted four Orientals sitting in the back row looking very nervous. Joe made a point to go down to them before he mounted the steps to the pulpit to visit with them and welcome them to the Methodist Church of Sandon. There was a murmur in the congregation and Joe decided right there and then to put aside the sermon he had written for this Sunday and preached on the lecture he had given Pat Burns in the restaurant earlier in the week about Jesus approach to people and His expectation that we treat all people as we would like to be treated. The Rossland Rule of life!

> Mark 12:31
> And the second [is] like, [namely] this, Thou shalt love thy neighbour as thyself. There is none other commandment greater than these. (KJV)

This became his text for the Sunday service and when the service was over Joe was pleased to see many of his parishioners go over to the Orientals that were in attendance and welcome them.

Joe communicated with his Supervisor by telegraph that he was concerned that the Greers didn't appear to be coming back and was sent a telegraph indicating that he was right, they had resigned and that the Church was sending a newly ordained Minister to the charge and would be there the Sunday after Joe was scheduled to leave.

Joe was ordered to proceed to Slocan City and Clark Camp and establish a mission in the logging camps in the area. Clark Camp was just inside the US border and about five miles straight down mule path mountain trail. Joe would conduct an 11 o'clock service at Slocan City and then proceed down the trail to Clark Camp and hold a 4 pm service there. Because the trail was so steep and dangerous, Joe would sleep over at Clark Camp and trudge back up the mountain to start the next week back at Slocan City, late Monday morning.

The memory of that back-breaking, exhausting climb back up the mountain made Joe suddenly waken!

CHAPTER 15

The End Is Near

*"When Jesus therefore had received the vinegar, he said, It is finished,
and he bowed his head, and gave up the ghost."* (KJV)
John 19:30

The dawn was breaking and his fire was nearly out. His limbs felt like lead, yet if he didn't get the fire going again, he would be dead in a few hours.

Joe pushed himself up from the bedroll and crawled over to the small pile of firewood he had stacked earlier in the night. He fed the fire and slowly saw it catch and the flames start to crackle and spark as the wind caught them and brought them back to life.

Joe put the pot back on the fire to warm up the water and the piece of mukluk that he had boiled last night. Maybe there was still a little goodness he could get out of it!

Joe drew the blanket around him as he sat as close to the fire as he could and sipped his warmed 'broth' while he pondered how he was going to make it to town. He reckoned he was still a good five miles away. It was downhill thank goodness!

He thought back to the last part of his dream and the climb uphill from Clark Camp to Slocan City. If he had that to face, Joe decided he would have just curled up and let death take him, but Joe had never given up without a fight and so far he had never lost a fight. Once he had finished his drink he would pack up his belongings and head off downhill towards the town.

Joe was conscious of being watched. He looked over his left shoulder and saw the outline of a couple of wolves against the mist of snow that continued to blow and swirl. He wondered about getting his pistol out and shooting them but decided that his fingers would likely freeze to the trigger before he even got a shot off. He might need the bullets later on when he was in the open and they decided he was worth the risk for dinner.

The weather was a bit better than last night Joe decided. Although the winds still blew, he felt it wasn't as strong as it had been prior to making camp and the snow continued to fall, but the flakes were big gentle flakes, not the stinging almost hail-like sleet of yesterday.

It took Joe all of his concentration to pack his gear and re-strap his snow shoes. His chills continued and made working with his fingers almost impossible, but with determination, Joe was able to get ready to head off.

Once again, he concentrated on putting one foot in front of the next. Don't get the snowshoes crossed! If I fall I'll never get back up! Joe had taken a large branch that he hadn't used for firewood and now used it as a staff to steady himself. Also if he needed to set up another camp, it would give him instant wood to start a fire.

Without stopping, Joe plunged ahead over the next four hours seeing nothing but a screen of white in front of him and using his compass as his only life saving path to civilization.

Every so often, Joe would see the wolves move in to check him out and as long as he had the strength to shout and wave his staff, they would quickly run off into the protection of the white curtain that surrounded Joe.

Joe realized he had very little left and if he didn't soon see the town he would be dinner for the wolves.

Just then, the snow let up and Joe could see the outline of the town in front of him. It was likely about a half mile away. He put on a final spurt. He continued to put one shoe in front of the other for another fifteen minutes and then he remembered nothing. Everything went black and he was drifting in a dream-like state.

He could see his Mother at the dinner table surrounded by Will, Margaret and the Archers with his beloved Nellie looking at his Mother with tears in her eyes.

"I have just had the strangest shiver run up my back" said Charlotte Robins as she looked at Nellie, "I know something is awful wrong with Joe. He is sick and near death! Oh, God please protect my dear boy!"

"I just had a feeling much like you described, also!" said Nellie, "Father please pray for Joe's safe return!"

And as the image faded from Joe's vision he saw Rev. Archer praying and the family and the Archers all holding hands around the kitchen table in Port Rowan.

Joe groaned and tried to turn over. He ached in every muscle in his body and his hands and feet felt like someone was sticking pins into them. If this was heaven, he had been selling the wrong product over the last couple of years!

As he opened his eyes, he saw a man with a red beard and a couple of the ladies of the night huddled around him putting something hot against his sides and feet. He realized that they were placing hot stones around him and that was why he wasn't able to roll over. These stones were holding the blankets in place and were providing him with warmth that he thought he would never experience again.

"Where am I?" squeaked Joe in a whisper.

"You're in the loft of the saloon at Silverton," responded the man as he looked down at Joe, "we thought you were a goner! You sure fooled us. Big Jack saw you coming down the trail about four days ago in the midst of one of the worst storms in history. Then he didn't see you anymore. We got one of the dog teams out and went up to where he last saw you. There was a pack of about 10 wolves moving in on this brown lump that was fast becoming another mound of snow. In fact, if it hadn't been the wolves starting to tear at your pack, we would have likely missed you in the storm."

"Did you say ten wolves? I only saw two as I was trudging along. Thank goodness this Big Jack saw me. I sure would like to thank him," Joe said.

"I'm afraid that's not possible, he headed out as soon as the storm lifted yesterday to his stake. By the way, my name is Jed Newcomb. I own this

saloon and these are a couple of my girls, Bess and Lucy. They have been nursing you for the last four days."

Joe was starting to feel stronger and able to keep his eyes open. He hunched himself into a sitting position and introduced himself, "I'm Joe Robins, Pastor Joe Robins and I'm very thankful for the care you have shown me."

"We've heard of you," said Bess, "you're the one that buried Lily over at Rossland. They call you the Scrapping Sky Pilot."

"You're the one that beat the Northwest Mounted Police Officer in the Turkey shoot aren't you?" inquired Lucy.

"My, how rumours fly up here in the North! Yes to all the questions," Joe declared.

Then Joe turned and asked Jed, "How much do I owe you for looking after me all this time?"

"Pastor, for the room, nothing, the girls looked after you and by the sounds of it they aren't about to charge. For them any man in a room is money in their pockets. For the soup they force fed you, nothing. But, the ½ bottle of whisky we poured down you when you first arrived to thaw you out – that will be $1.00!" Jed responded.

Oh my, thought Joe, I've broken my pledge! I wonder if it counts that I don't remember receiving the alcohol? I wonder if this will go against me when I apply to University for my theological training? Surely I can't be held responsible for the actions of others when I'm not awake?

It took Joe another week of lying in before he had the strength to get out of bed and start to think about what was going to happen next. He still had the chills come on without warning and wasn't sure if he could head back into the wilderness for another three months.

Joe had notified his Supervisor when he was strong enough to compose a telegraph and sent it the nearest station for transmission to Edmonton.

Within a week he received a reply indicating that he was being replaced and that he should make arrangements to head home and recuperate before entering Victoria College in the fall.

Flash forward in time to 1964....

With a sudden start, J.U. Robins sat up and realized that he had fallen asleep again.

Darn it!

He would have to rewind the tape and try to find the spot where he had finished before his little sleep. With his arthritic hands, that definitely showed his 85 years of life experience, he found turning the dials on the reel to reel tape recorder a real task. His grandson had asked him to put his life experiences on tape and he had just finished with his mission experiences before starting university.

As he sat back in his big chair, in the home that he and Nellie had shared for over fifty years before she had been called to her Maker about 10 years ago, the sun washed over him as he looked out the porch windows onto Lake Ontario. Wellington had been one of his charges when it was still a Methodist Church, before Union in 1925. He loved the shoreline here and had bought four lots on the lake for a cottage, which he and Nellie had turned into a permanent home prior to his retirement in the early 40's.

It was the house that Joe built. He had started with a one room cottage with an add on kitchen. He had bought the floor from an old dance hall that had burnt down and all that remained was the floor. Cut it in sections and brought it by horse and wagon to his lot. He added a living room, sunroom and a small "master" bedroom on the main floor. He later added a second story, which was basicly an open loft. Years later they had added an enclosed porch that wasn't heated on the water side of the house. The heat of the sun made it a lovely place to sit in the afternoon and watch the sun sparkle off the tips of the waves.

As the Rev. J.U. Robins prepared the tape recorder for the next session tomorrow, he thought of how much more he had to tell.

There was the story of Albert and himself stealing a body from the morgue so Albert would have a cadaver to work on during his medical training and the chase by the Toronto Constabulary with their new friend hung over their shoulders.

There was the politics of a Methodist Church for newly Ordained Ministers and their placement and advancement within the Church.

Of course he would have to relay the story of how he was the first to 'broadcast' his sermons while in Bowmanville by having the local telephone company operator open all the party lines on her switchboard and having a telephone installed on the pulpit.

Then of course there were the meetings held at Mutual Street Arena in Toronto in June of 1925 when the United Church of Canada was formed. He was a representative of the Bowmanville Methodist Church and Chair of its Conference. It still irked him that the Methodist and Congregationalist had come into Union as nearly full denominations, but those pesky Presbyterians had had local votes and only half of their denomination had joined at the time of Union.

Yes, there was still lots to tell, but it was for another day!

Mrs. Fritz, his housekeeper and good friend had arrived from her home two doors away to make supper. If he was lucky, he had another hour to doze before she would call him to the table and once he had his food on the table, she would return to her own home and prepare her daughter's dinner. Mrs. Fritz was a gift from God!! If it wasn't for her he wouldn't have been able to continue to live on his own. She had been there through Nellie's illness and helped him care for her up to the time they had gone to their daughter Dorothy's home in Scarborough. Dorothy had gone through nursing and was married with two boys. It was on of these grandsons that had asked for the tape to be made. Marjorie, his eldest daughter had never married and had ended up in Winnipeg as a professor of Social

Work had bought this tape recorder. His grandson had shown him how it worked. He would be surprised at how many blank spots were on the tape from falling asleep!

When he returned from Scarborough, Nellie returned in a hearse and Joe followed her with his daughter's family back to Wellington where once again, Mrs. Fritz had stepped in to provide food and fellowship and assure his daughters she would look after him. This she had faithfully done!

"Now, what story would he record tomorrow?" Joe mused.

"The sun is so warm, so different from those early days in British Columbia..."

Shalom

Stoney Creek Bridge, Selkirk BC
298 Feet high – a typical railway bridge

Picture taken from the tracks looking up Main Street in
Revelstoke at the beginning of the 20th century.

Rev. J. U. Robins in buckskins, holding his Smith and
Wesson Army Colt Model #2, manufactured in 1860

James Robins master ship builder, father of J. U. Robins

The Archer Family
Back row: Rev. Joseph Archer, Mrs. Martha (Hardy) Archer
Front row: L to R, Rev. W.R. (Willie) Archer, Nellie
Archer, Maie Archer, Dr. A. E. (Albert) Archer

The Robins home in Port Rowan, Ontario with
Margaret, Charlotte, and James Robins on the porch

A revival meeting held at a work camp in British Columbia.

Probationary Yearbook 1903 Cover

yet his sterling character and personal magnetism have given him a prestige in college circles that will, now that he is leaving us, be felt wherever his lot may be cast.

Those who know Mr. Robins best respect him most. No one doubts his ability either as a preacher or as an administrator. We predict for him eminent success in the Master's vineyard.

REV. J. U. ROBINS.

Rev. J. U. Robins was born in Port Rowan, Ont., in the year eighteen hundred and seventy-four. While he was still a youth, he attended the High School there and prepared himself for the teaching profession, which vocation he followed for two years. Believing he was called to the work of the ministry, he entered the Hamilton Conference in 1895, and in July of the same year went to British Columbia. His work among the miners in the Kootenays was arduous, but Bro. Robins was indefatigable and knew not what discouragement was. If we who live in more settled parts knew of his trials, his struggles in the midst of innumerable difficulties, his dangers which stood thick on every hand, we would think our effort recreation rather than labor. The building of the first church in Rossland and the establishment of six missions was the visible result of three years' work in that district. Zeal led to an overtaxing of the body which resulted in nervous prostration. The hero of many a conflict was compelled to spend a year in Muskoka with a view to recuperation. Then he labored for two years on the Neepawa District, Manitoba, where he was very successful in building up the charges under his care. The last two years were spent in Victoria University, Toronto, pursuing the course in theology.

REV. J. U. ROBINS, '03.

38

Graduates in Theology 1903 – Rev. J. U. Robins with article

LaVergne, TN USA
30 December 2009

168609LV00001B/22/P

9 781449 044022